WAR COMES TO ALL

ARION

D.H. WEBB

Ark House Press
arkhousepress.com

Cataloguing in Publication Data:
Title: The Chronicles of the Corriian Wars: Arion (Book Two)
ISBN: 9780645594744 (pbk)
Subjects: Fiction; Fantasy;

Design by initiateagency.com

CONTENTS

FOREWORD

*S*ome readers of Beckwood Brae have commented on the differences between our world and the world of which the countries of Herelstrom, Corrii, Arion and Bernadia form a part.

It seems helpful to note that it is a different world. There are many differences and many similarities. It is a younger world than our own and simpler in many ways. The lifestyles of the people of the Southern End are less complex than our own, and in some ways comparable to the lives of people in our own world many thousands of years ago. Obviously, some things are very different, however. This world is unique in many respects; the trees in Herelstrom are larger, the coffee is different from our coffee and the goroths (called, 'wulves' in older Herelstrom) are larger and more terrible than our timber wolves. As you will see the Corlions somewhat resemble much larger versions of cave lions that once lived in our world. There are also creatures in this world that have long disappeared from our world, if ever they existed at all.

Some may ask if there are other worlds. I would answer that the very question limites the God who made our universe. We now know something of the vastness of our own cosmos. Who is to say that God stopped at creating this universe?

All stories of fiction that men write are just creations of their imagination. I have simply chosen a different world for the location of this story. There are always new frontiers; this world is just one that you explore with your imagination.

Those who read this story will discover that from the world of Herelstrom, you can gain entry into another greater world still. It is the same with our world. This is the greatest adventure of all.

PROLOGUE

The Spy

*B*enton moved cautiously through the forest keeping to the shadows. He had memorized the way through the forest to the underground river. He had the map Corianasta had shown him clearly in his mind, but it wasn't so easy among the great trees. The sun was hidden, and the forest made one disorientated.

"If only I was a real forester, not just dressed like one," he thought. He had gleaned much information and guessed more. He guessed that there were people living in the trees. Just who or what they were he was not sure. Perhaps they were like the tree-dwelling people that inhabited the forests northeast of Lake Corrimeer. These had proven hard to find and harder still to deal with, so the forest dwellers here were likely to be of the same kind.

He was taking a huge risk, but if it came off it would mean rapid promotion in the intelligence bureau. He had put his agile mind to how a simple forester from Egleton had done the impossible: obviously he had help – probably the tree-people. And they had probably used the river under the mountains.

He had worked among the many itinerant laborers on the building of the new castle at the river mouth. He had worked out its design and thought through its weaknesses with his military eye. He had even gotten, or appeared to have gotten, drunk with an old mason who seemed to have been working on some secret project.

Benton had acquired a green tunic and a large leather strap which he slung over his shoulder, not really forester's gear but enough to look the part. He hoped that if he was seen by the tree-people it may give them pause – thinking that he was *the* forester they may not shoot. He had interviewed the survivors of the battle of Cair Neren. The dog-soldiers had spoken of long wooden arrows with hardened points that pierced leather armor as if it were an ordinary woollen tunic.

He knew there were two risks: that he would be shot and if he managed to evade any enemies and find the underground river, and that there was no boat that he could steal to make his way up the underground river. Even then he didn't know if his strength was up to the long row that would be required.

As he crept from tree to tree, shadow to shadow, he rehearsed the spell of invisibility in his mind that they had taught him before he set out on the spying mission. It didn't really hide you from sight but caused others not to see you. Gaining this competence had cost him dearly. He winced as he remembered the encounter with the jungari; the agony of mind; the inquisition of the spirit, but he had passed the test; he had the power. There was a tiny doubt in some deep recess of his mind that the cost was too high, but he ignored it. He knew what he wanted. If he gained the position of power and influence that he sought, the benefits would be very worthwhile.

Benton remembered a girl in Dorantira, his home in the northern foothills. She had long dark curls, peaches and cream complexion, a trim, curvy figure, and the bright happy smile of a girl that has been raised in a happy home. He had paid court to her to no avail. She had married the son of one of the other ancient houses. If he got back to Corriamar with the information he had discovered, he would probably receive promotion to master of intelligence; he would wield terrible power. Priscilla's husband could be made to *disappear*. Then he would take her a concubine – not as a wife and she would have no choice.

Thoughts of vengeance and lust played through his mind as he moved warily through the great orkya trees. He stopped in a small grove and spoke the words of the spell.

The spy seemed to merge into the grey shadows of the trees. Four Driadora warriors in the trees above failed to see him as he slipped through their realm like a silent shadow. There were also other things with him that the guards could not see. All they knew was a momentary sense of cold malevolence, a fleeting dark shadow that passed quickly like a single cloud on a sunny day that briefly takes the warmth out of the sun. None of them thought much about it.

Benton stopped at a small grove of trees. It was really just four trees growing close together over some unseen water source. There were dry leaves on the ground, and it offered a place of concealment to rest. He was weary. He opened a pouch of food and ate a few sparing morsels. As he ate, he noticed a piece of black beeswax lying in the leaf litter. It looked as though it may have been there some time.

"Wax from a piece of cheese," he said under his breath. He looked closer; swept aside the leaves, there were some ashes from a small fire.

"Someone must have used this as a camp once." Perhaps it meant something and perhaps it didn't. Benton would add it all to the information that his brilliant mind was catalogueing. Cheese from the nearby villages: that meant that people had come here from the valley. Maybe it was his charge, 'the nutter' Beckman and Sanders had called him. Cute description! It implied he was one with the nuts he collected – not too smart; barely clever enough to outsmart a nut. Benton caught himself. The Egleton apprentices he had worked alongside were aggrieved and envious. Only a fool made the mistake of misjudging an opponent. He would not do so. Obviously, the forester had something about him. It wasn't just luck that brought down the Empress. In truth, Benton did not know how he did it. The only plausible explanation was that Norrimae Jung had help. The archgrimulf, Scriei believed it was the great enemy of the Jungari; could this be? Benton's mind rebelled, 'God!' he sneered, he had never stopped them before. But the thought would not go away. He wondered if God was really involved in the world in any meaningful way. Benton wondered if he was making himself God's enemy.

Almost as soon as the thought entered his head, a new thought replaced it. He thought about Priscilla: at his mercy; eager to please him and make up for past transgressions. He let his mind play with the thoughts; create new images of her, compliant; and afraid of him. The other uncomfortable thoughts disappeared.

He drank some of the water he carried and ate some of the bread and dried fruit. His musings about Priscilla were interrupted by a new awareness. He heard faint voices. The sounds came from below him.

Benton froze. He quickly re-packed his bag and checked in his boot for the knife he kept hidden there. The knife was a spy's weapon: curved slightly forward and razor sharp – a throat cutting weapon. The scabbard was made into the leather of his boot so cunningly that no-one by looking would be able to tell that the weapon was there.

Benton slung the bag over his shoulder, did up the strap across his chest so that it wouldn't impede him in any way. The forester's gear was suited to climbing; a good choice as it turned out. He spoke the secret words and faded again into the grey- green shadows.

Benton moved silently out of the cover of the orkya trees and crept along among the roots. He was following the voices. They were not loud, and the sound was somewhat muted. It was coming from an opening in the ground. He got as close as he could without breaking cover. He looked into the opening. It was dark and the filtered, afternoon sunlight did nothing to illuminate what was below, but this was certainly what he sought – the entrance to the underground river.

He couldn't hear the voices now. Maybe whoever was watching the entrance had gone. He trusted to the spell of invisibility and climbed down into the hole. The cavern opened out to the south, and he could hear the water below. By climbing down the steepest part, he could remain concealed from anyone watching the cavern. It took some time; feeling along the moss-covered walls for holds. When he reached the bottom there was a sort of underground beach with gravelly sand and driftwood piled randomly by the river in times of flood. There were also a couple of boats of different kinds – but alas, no oars or paddles. Benton stayed close to the rock walls of the cavern and edged away from the dim light of the entrance. There was still some light. He noticed the phosphorescence given off by the plants that grew on the limestone walls. At the other side of the small beach, he came to another wall. It seemed to be made of wood: the living roots of the great trees that grew above he thought. He wondered at the sheer might of trees that had such roots. No wonder his emperor craved these forests – what ships could be built from such trees? He pressed against the wood and noticed that it had a hollow feel. He felt along the wooden wall in front of him until his hand passed right through the wood, 'invisible door,' he thought, 'I wonder who placed it here?' With his heart beating like a drum, he stepped through the secret door into a passage inside the roots of the tree. There was a strange green light coming from the passageway ahead. He heard the voices again. They were coming from the direction of the light, so he went in the other direction. He could see his shadow moving ahead of him. The spell was not working. The usual comfort it afforded was gone, left behind in the cavern.

He thought of going back but it was as dangerous as going on. His boldness had always served him well in the past; he would trust to luck and go on. In only a short time he came to a place where there was a T intersection. One tunnel went down and the other steadily up. He chose the downward sloping tunnel and came to a small room filled with all kinds of foodstuffs and equipment. As his eyes adjusted to the dim light, he took in the contents of the storeroom for such it obviously was.

Benton debated poisoning some of the food. It might slow pursuit. It would also increase suspicion. If these people, whoever they were, realised some of their people had been poisoned, they would also be doubly indignant. It was a risk. He opened some of the containers and inspected the contents. One had nuts: big grey nuts, the like of which he had never seen; another had dried fruit; another flour of some kind. The flour would be the easiest to poison. Benton carried a small wax sealed wooden vial. Its contents would kill anyone who ate the flour, slowly and painfully over a couple of days. Benton had no thought for the victims, the only thought was: would it help him get away. He searched the room and finally found what he sought: short oars. That settled it. He would take the boat. He went to the door and listened. There were the voices again. He had to be quick. He broke the seal, and sprinkled the contents over the flour; took the oars and retraced his steps.

He could hear the voices coming down the tunnel toward him. He made for the hidden door as fast and as silently as he could, his hands passed through the tunnel wall and he stepped out of the tunnel just as the Driadora came around the corner.

Benton crawled away across the sand in the dark of the cavern. Stones and driftwood bruised his knees. He slid in behind a pile of flotsam left by the underground river in flood and lay still with his heart beating for more than an hour. He guessed at the time it would have taken to prepare and consume a meal; then he crawled out of his hiding place, pushed the small boat into the water and began to row, down the dim tunnel following the river under the mountains. He was some way from the guard post when he fancied, he heard calls and groans. He smiled to himself and rowed faster. He had to put as much distance between himself and pursuit as possible. Some hours later he slumped over the oars, exhausted. He had all but broken the oar blades several times running into the walls of the cavern or jutting rocks. Once he had run up on a sharp rock and smashed a hole in the bow. He had taken off his shirt and plugged the hole but had to stop far too often and bail out the water that seeped through his makeshift patch. He had to depend on the commotion caused by the poisoning. Perhaps the boat would not be quickly missed, and the tree-people would be busy trying to aid the sick guards. The poison had the same effects as a bad gastric illness. The hope was that they would think it was some kind of plague. Others might even avoid them for fear of catching it and he would get clean away. The guards were doomed, whatever they did; Benton knew there would be no recovery.

As he slumped over the oars catching his breath Benton hoped that the rain and snow would hold off and he would be able to get out of the low cave where the river joined Lake Corrimeer on the other side of the mountains. The other prospect was not a good one: trapped at the end of the river, unable to get out; unable to go back.

By then the tree-people would have worked out what had happened and returning down the river was not a good prospect. Benton faced the real possibility of starving to death in the dark.

1

New Castle

*N*orrimae Jung, king's forester walked down the main street of New Castle. Jungnuts were the ancient name for orkya nuts before the more modern name from the north came to be used in Egleton. His trade was a junger: a nutter. The old village of Egleton had been re-named New Castle by popular usage. The work on the castle overlooking the entrance to the River Erne was well under way. The keep and topmost battlements were complete and armed with their catapults and trebuchet. Armorers from the great city of Pinitera had laboured long, crafting the weapons from local timber. The castle walls were built of large carefully quarried blocks of limestone that would be perfectly smooth on the outside and almost impossible to scale. Siege ladders would be difficult to place on the jagged rocks below the walls.

In the top level of the keep were the new apartments where Norri now lived with his new wife. The apartment next to them was occupied by Tom and Lettie and their baby son, Dillon. Tom had been inducted as Warden of the Southern End, the last strip of arable land before the mountains bent inland to meet the southern sea.

Sir Brian and Lady Gillian had the apartment on the other side and the fourth was free for the many guests who often seemed to come and stay at the castle these days. The rooms below were reserved for other guests or were armories and store-rooms.

The bottom floor of the keep had a large dining hall and a big friendly fireplace with a chimney that rose through the centre of the castle to warm the rooms above. Work progressed quickly now on the lower fortifications which would house the townspeople and militia and their horses if the town was attacked. Once the lower fortifications were complete, the castle would be impregnable to any known kind of warfare.

As Norri walked briskly down the street, he passed the numerous, new, wooden buildings that housed the many workers for the building of the castle. There were also new taverns that were already busy and rowdy at this time in the afternoon. Sounds of laughter and conversation poured out through the doors as he walked by. He passed several of the locals as they headed for the old tavern. The farmers and original artisans of Egleton still preferred the old stone tavern that Gorigond kept much the same as it had always been.

Norri noticed that he was universally treated with respect nowadays. He dressed better, of course. That was partly Kirin's influence and partly because he could now afford to. He also usually wore his sword and the silver clasp on his cloak that indicated his new rank. Even under his cloak the sword was evident, and he looked much the part of a royal official. He nodded politely to the farmers and artisans as they greeted him and continued down the street towards – home Cair Egleton.

The town seemed to have grown in recent times and much of the less seemly side of life was evident in its streets. Norri also suspected that what they did was being watched and reported to their enemies. It was more a feeling and the odd expression on the faces of some of the passers by. There were many strangers in the village now – more like a large town. There were workers of all kinds: masons, carpenters, tilers, cement makers, some for the work on the new fortifications and others taking up the opportunities that the new work provided. There was more demand for everything. The fishermen at Greyton worked longer to supply the demand of the taverns and guesthouses. The farmers had expanded their flocks and herds and put on extra staff in their dairies. As the town became more populous, so the amenities proliferated: taverns, gaming rooms and worse spreading down the side streets of the town that seemed to have sprung up overnight.

As Norri walked down the main street, he noticed a small bundle on the narrow verandah of one of the taverns. As he came closer, he realised the small bundle was human. He could just make out a small face. It was shrouded in a thin cloak and huddled up to avoid the chill of the late afternoon wind. Norri approached and the boy looked up. Norri guessed he was less than five years old.

"What are you doing here?" The boy pointed inside the establishment.

"My Daddy inside."

Norri could hear laughter and the clinking of tankards and the glow from inside indicated a roaring fire. He didn't like the boy being alone, out here in the wind; shivering.

"Are you hungry?" The boy nodded hesitantly and glanced at the doors of the tavern again.

Norri knew the girl who ran the kitchen; she was a friend of Kirin's. He went down the side passage to the kitchen door and asked for Janina. Janina appeared at the door,

"My Lord, what can I do for you?"

"Janina, there is a little boy out on the porch. Do you think you could get him plate of something hot? Here."

Norri produced a silver coin. Janina shook her head.

"That won't be necessary, Sir."

Norri handed her the coin anyway.

"No. I'll pay for the food. I wouldn't want to get you into trouble." Janina took the proffered coin and slipped it into a pocket of her apron.

"I'll be but a moment."

She took longer than Norri expected but returned with a hot freshly iced cake and a mug of hot milk with Cocoa. Norri was impressed.

"Thank you, Janina, very good! I'll take this to our young man out here."

Norri rounded the corner and saw the small boy's eyes brighten at the sight of the cake and the hot drink. Norri sat down next to the boy and passed him the cake and the mug.

"What is your name?"

The boy looked at him with a happy smile.

"Mort," and took a big bite of cake. Norri then passed him the mug and he took a sip of the hot, sweet, milk drink.

"What're yer' doin' wiv' me son?" roared a burly, broad-shouldered man in his early thirties as he crashed through the doors of the tavern.

Norri got to his feet.

"…just got him something from the kitchen, he looked cold".

"Yer' sayin' I can't look after me' own kid?"

The man kicked the mug out of the boy's hand with a force enough to break his fingers. Mort shrank away from the force of his father's drunken anger, tears welling in his helpless eyes. The man then picked up the cake and hurled it at Norri.

"Git away from me' kid."

Norri now stood his ground before the other's anger.

"The boy was cold. I just got him something hot. You were inside; by the fire – drinking."

Just then the doors swung open again and Wenston the innkeeper appeared on the porch. He saw Norri being menaced by one of his patrons and the scattered food. Janina appeared around the side of the inn, having heard the commotion, "What is the matter, MY LORD?"

Norri didn't answer immediately. The use of his title and the sudden glimpse of his sword had given the man pause. Janina saw her chance to defuse the situation, "Lord Jung told me there was a hungry young man out here, so I brought him something to eat n' drink." Wenston took her lead. "All part of the service for our good patrons isn't it, Janina? Be good enough to get this young man another cake and drink will you love?" The big man relaxed at this and growled as he turned to go back inside.

Wenston took him firmly by the wrist, "You've had enough don't yer' think? Why don't yer' take the little boy and get some dinner?" The man grabbed the little boy roughly, dragged him to his feet and trudged off down the street. Mort looked back at Norri as his father led him away.

Wenston stood beside Norri, "Sorry, my Lord." Norri's eyes followed the two down the street, "Not your fault, Wenston."

Norri thanked the innkeeper and Janina and continued down the road to Cair Egleton feeling sad and helpless. Something about Mort had touched a chord deep inside and he hurt for the little bloke. When he reached the works, he was met and acknowledged by a group of guards who watched over the workings. Although the keep was finished – ahead of schedule, but the larger works on the barracks and stables and their surrounding battlements would still take some time.

Norri reached the entrance to the keep. Steps led steeply up to the heavy oaken doors that barred the front of the arch. You then passed through a tunnel to the next set of doors that were of oak, reinforced with iron. The doors were all open. They were at peace now, but the castle was designed as a refuge against future need and was very strong. It was also possible to have some measure of secrecy there.

Norri passed through the tunnel and crossed the small courtyard of the keep to the hall. The kitchen staff were working on preparations for the evening meal. The apartment that belonged to him and Kirin was upstairs, but he guessed he would find Kirin in the kitchen. He was right. Both of them found it hard to adjust to the fact that they had status, and their servants. Kirin was talking to the cook about what they would prepare for the evening meal.

Both Brian and Tom had been out all day on militia business. The local militia, under Brian's leadership had grown to three hundred and fifty strong of whom one hundred were horsed. There had been a flood of volunteers. The people of Egleton had suffered badly in the last Corrii invasion and another didn't seem so far out of the realms of possibility. Tom's wife, Lettie, was busy with a new baby. Kirin had just taken care of the running of the household because someone had to. Norri kissed her lightly on the cheek and drew her into his arms, "You are preparing a lot of food."

"Everyone will be back soon, and they will be hungry." And aside, quietly, "and General Gorian mentioned that the commodore will probably arrive tonight."

They chatted about his day. Norri had been arranging transportation for Kirin's mother and her belongings to a new house closer to the castle. If he had to go away, Norri wanted to make sure everything was organised for the two women in his life. Kirin would be happier having her mother closer, instead of two hours' walk to the outskirts on the other side of the town.

Norri was now glad of the treasure that was a gift from the emperor of Bernadia. At the time it had seemed a vast amount of money. But now furnishing their rooms in the castle had proven expensive. And the ongoing cost of running the castle, even though subsidized from the royal treasury, was proving considerable. He began to wonder, now, if his gold would run out.

Kirin walked back inside with Norri's arm around her shoulders. She noticed his somber mood, "Did everything go well with the house?"

"Yes. It is all organised."

"Did something else happen? You seem a bit sad."

Norri squeezed her, she knew all his moods already and it was such a short time that they had been married.

"There was a small boy sitting outside Wenston's tavern. His father was inside drinking. He looked cold so I asked Janina for something warm for him to eat. Janina brought him a cake, still warm from the oven."

Kirin smiled, "She's a softie that one."

"She came out with a warm cake and a cup of hot cocoa. The little boy had only just started to eat the cake when his father came out of the tavern, drunk and kicked him. The little boy spilled his drink and the cake fell in the mud. Wenston and Janina managed to diffuse the situation, but I was very close to drawing my sword and who knows what would have happened then. I was getting very angry."

Kirin cuddled him. She knew Janina wasn't the only one with a soft heart, "Was there any sign of a mother?" Norri was amazed at her perception.

"Not that I could see. Little Mort seemed to be alone; with just his drunken father."

"That is why you felt drawn to him." Norri smiled at her, "Yes ... I was once a little boy without a mother. But at least I had a father, who cared about me."

"You would have still been drawn to your little friend in the front of the tavern and I expect his father is better when he isn't drunk" Norri grimaced, "I wish I hadn't had such a bad start with his Pa. I might have been able to help a little if I hadn't mucked it up with my misguided charity."

Kirin wasn't so sure, "Give it time, there may be a time when you can do something. The man was drunk tonight. Tomorrow he will be sober and may see things differently. If he is alone with a small son, it will have been very hard for him." They walked through the hall together to the small room beside the kitchen where the platters and cutlery were kept.

Norri walked out with Kirin carrying large trays of platters to the dining hall. They were setting about putting the implements on the board when they heard horses in the courtyard. They put down their trays went to the entrance. Brian and Tom had arrived back and with them a tall, elderly man in a naval officer's tunic. Kirin indicated the tall man.

"That will be Commodore Denquinar. They say he defected from the Corriian navy and has won the trust of the king."

One of the guards took hold of the horses while the three dismounted and led their mounts to the temporary stables to the side of the courtyard. When they returned from the stables Tom introduced Commodore Denquinar to Norri and Kirin, "I presume you all know of one another. Commodore, this is Norrimae Jung and his wife Kirin. Norri, Kirin, Commodore Denquinar, former Grand Admiral of the Corrii Navy, now *transferred* to our forces."

Denquinar bowed and kissed Kirin's hand, "Honored my lady." Then, turning to Norri, "I am glad to finally meet the one who caused my former countrymen so much ah …consternation."

Kirin curtseyed as best she could and invited them all inside, "You have been on a long journey Commodore, you will be glad of refreshment. I will show you to a room where you may wash. And we have dinner almost ready." Denquinar smiled gratefully, "Dinner sounds most welcome as is your kind offer of hospitality. I did think to stay at one of the taverns."

Norri indicated the door of the hall, "The village is not as safe as it once was. It would be better if we kept all comings and goings as secret as possible. And we would insist you stay with us anyway. I am afraid General Gorian has the best room."

Denquinar thanked him, "A mat and a meal is all I require. My needs are simple these days. I am on my own and my son is with his ship." Kirin indicated the side door of the hall. "Come this way, Commodore. I will show you the way to the room I have prepared for you."

Denquinar followed Kirin and the others made their way to the front of the hall where tables were set for dinner. Norri and Tom drew some wine from a large barrel and placed the cups on the table. Hot bread was being placed on the table already and there was the unmistakable smell of roasted beef coming down the passage from the kitchen.

Soon Denquinar came down the steps again, having changed into fresh clothes and Kirin emerged from the kitchen with a huge haunch of beef. Norri took a great knife from the mantle and began carving. A lass from the kitchen brought vegetables and condiments of mustard and horseradish sauce and they all sat down to their dinner. Denquinar enjoyed his food and listened to the happy banter about the state of the fishing industry in Greyton, the jibes about the shortage of orkya nuts these days, because neither Norri nor his father had much time to gather them, and the general talk about the comings and goings of Egleton.

After dinner, Tom suggested that they see his work on the battlements. They took a pot of fresh coffee and some cups and climbed the four stories to the fighting tops of the keep. Denquinar looked around with approval. Four ballistae were mounted on the battlements, facing toward the river channel and six trebuchets behind them were likewise trained to fire on any ship that entered the harbour without proper signals. Chests were provided for the cordage that powered the huge ballista bolts and two flights of stairs led down to the magazine where the ballista bolts with their exploding oil canisters were ready in racks. All was prepared to deny the river channel to any wooden ship brave enough to try an assault of the town.

Away to the north on the promontory of Thornton, a watch tower had been built. It was a strong tower of stone and oak with a secure entrance like the castle. Defenses were not much good unless you had enough warning and there was always the danger of the signal tower being overrun to prevent any warning reaching the Cair Egleton. The Thornton militia there had a roster to man the tower and keep watch. It was a large commitment and took all available manpower. The village had suffered badly in the last war and its men were willing volunteers. They had arranged for the tower to be well provisioned to make the task of watching the ocean and the beaches for eight hours bearable.

The lights of the watch tower could be clearly seen in the gathering dark. They sat in the quietness of the fighting tops and discussed the plans for the voyage south. Kirin didn't like thinking about Norri going away. She finished her cup of coffee, stood up and turned toward the staircase, "I'm going to bed, Darling. I will stay awake as long as I can."

Norri wanted to go with her. Time with his wife seemed so precious now. Denquinar noticed him shifting on the bench.

"Go to bed with your wife young man. Leave the strategy to us who have nothing better to think about." Norri smiled. He didn't need too much encouragement. He bid them a good night and after finishing the last sip of his coffee, followed Kirin downstairs.

"What do you think of Cair Egleton, Commodore?" The general lifted his bad leg up onto the bench that Norri had vacated to relieve the ache.

The naval man looked around at the weapons and fortifications. "Its best advantage is that it is situated on this naturally defensive place. This rock outcrop overlooking the river will make it hard to attack with siege towers and the walls are too high to easily scale with ladders. Your builders have done well." Gorian poured another cup of coffee.

"I hope you're right. They have built a timber fort on a rise outside the village. It currently serves as a store for weapons and stables for the 50 or so horses they have here who are not kept by their owners. That place is better than nothing but would be easier to take and this may be the last stronghold if the fort fell."

Denquinar nodded. "All defenses are better than none. The problem will be the strength of numbers that the Empire can mass against them. They will have learned lessons from the last attacks. They will not underestimate Herelstrom again. They will attack in many places to prevent forces being marshalled against them as they were last time."

"Do you think they will come again Commodore?"

Gorian put down his leg and looked intently across the table at Denquinar. The Commodore thought through the proposition.

"They will come, certainly. The only question is when. The Empire thrives on war. It holds the fabric of its society together and provides the resources to sustain the social structure: the gold, the slaves and of course the heroes. And the young Emperor will need some victories if he is to cement his position against the discontented nobles who supported his father and who no-doubt suspects the untimely death of Entilates VII was somehow contrived."

Gorian stroked his grey beard. "Will we have much warning do you think?"

Denquinar shook his head. "They made that mistake last time as well. You can assume the Empire's commanders will not make it again. They will not assemble an armada. They will assemble at sea and find any landings they can. They will not risk trebuchet and ballista fire from your forts again. The arrogance will have gone out of Entilates. He is a good general and he was humbled last time. His successes were probably just enough to keep his hold on power. The dismal failure of the dog-soldiers also helped. They were sent by his mother to prevent him from the sole hero of the campaign. In the end they failed and Entilates had some measure of success. It appears now that the old emperor's return was all that saved your capital. Entilates had taken its walls and if he had not been recalled by his father you would now be just one more outlying province of the empire; ruled with ruthless brutality to quell any last thought of resistance.

Everything of value would have been taken to Corrimar and half the people of the country enslaved. That is the pattern of things. But he will be eager to renew hostilities now his father is out of the way. He has a point to prove. It was always his lot to conquer Herelstrom. The empire has always seen it as an unseemly blemish on its history of conquest – the more so now. If they know young Norri downstairs was at least in part responsible for their problems, this may be where they will strike first; for revenge!"

In the anteroom of the temple of the god Melekah the coven masters met to finalize their plans. They were determined to use the information that Ingwit had gained at great personal cost to the greatest benefit of the covens.

High Priestess Ingwit stood with the hood of her black and silver robe thrown back. Her hair hung in golden ringlets around her shoulders. The edge of the robe almost covered the purple bruise on her neck. She was not afraid to show what her relationship with Emperor Entilates was costing her. The masters needed her.

Coven Master Groemelian looked at her with a look that was part hunger and part respect. He knew the news she would present to the others. She had done well; surprisingly well. He smiled to himself. She was a sharp tool in the hand of a master craftsman. And he was the craftsman. He was producing … power: power for the coven of grand masters and he was its head. He was the true ruler of the empire though few knew it.

"Step forward, High Priestess, what news do you bring us from the central seat of power?"

Ingwit lifted her chin and stood proudly among the mightiest men of power in the world.

"I have convinced the emperor to allow the raid. I argued cogently that we had found the place where those who most upset our plans lived, happy and successful, building a strong place where they think they will live long and safe, far from the reach of the empire. I told him that a quick blow and the sudden destruction of their heroes will be a key strategic stroke. It will weaken morale and make the final blow easier. I told him that we have intelligence and a man that will recognize the ones we seek."

Groemelian smiled to himself, the arguments of a beautiful, naked girl always seemed cogent to the rulers of the empire. They were so predictable! That part of the plan was easy.

Also in the room was Bentonius Velonia, master spy. Even with his recent promotion he stood in the back of the room and deferred to the greatest of the masters.

Curled up in the corner of the room were two great dogs; more than dogs, more than mere flesh and fur: the archgrimulves Scriei and Voniock lay with their heads on their paws; listening to all that was said with an almost casual interest.

In the temple the chanting of priests could be heard. They processed in a long line through the great building. Their censers gave off fragrant incense that rose up to the great flying arches and the high windows that allowed filtered daylight into the vast hall.

The masters conversed in hushed tones. Master Groemelian spoke again. "In honour of his excellent work, Bentonius will accompany the raid on the south of Herelstrom. Your task is to bring terror to our enemies. That is why we send the wyvern and the unnamed ones with the cult soldiers of Ba-al Giborachir. We wish the fools of Herelstrom to know they cannot toy with us and slay the great masters without incurring our wrath. We do not know how they resisted us; much less, escaped after killing our people but we can make them pay and pay dearly.

How go the preparations, Velulf?"

A small, wizened man spoke with a slow sickly voice and a heavy accent.

"The dragon men have departed Dorphir Sunde. Their blachships are at sea. They carry the giborach urns."

Groemelian smiled, savouring the thought of the horror about to be unleashed on their unsuspecting enemies. No-one humbled the Coven-masters without paying a terrible price.

"That is well; Bentonius can join them as they pass Orsimater." To the spy, he nodded approval. "We will send you in a swift ship to rendez-vous with the Dorphirmen at sea. Search for the infiltrator, Bentonius: the one who hurt us so badly and is now living happy and safe with his new wife in Egleton. You know now whom we seek. If you find him set the wyvern upon him. Few escape their jaws or their poison but if you manage to capture him, all the better. Killing an enemy's heroes usually serves as the best first step in subjugating a country."

The grand master pulled up the black hood of his robe and led them out. They all bowed their heads and covered their faces as they left. The masters came out of the anteroom followed by the two great grimulves. They walked briskly to the front doors of the temple and dispersed quickly to set about their agreed tasks.

2

Bells

*I*t was just after dawn. Tom led Lettie down a narrow secret passage. The entrance was a locked grating at the back of the granary that looked like others in the castle designed to provide some ventilation to the lower rooms. The walls of the small passage were rough hewn, and the passage was very small and close. Tom went ahead with a candle to show the way. They came to a hole with a ladder that led down into a cave. Once in the cave, the passageway was only large enough to crawl through. Tom was struggling to crawl and hold the light. It took some time to reach the end of the tunnel. This was bricked up but there were picks to dig through the roof. Tom explained that the entrance brought you out among the scrubby bushes behind the bluff. These were high and dense enough to facilitate an escape – especially at night.

"If it seems certain that the castle will fall, this will provide an escape route for you and Kirin and Dillon. Norri has already shown this to Kirin and you both have keys to the lock."

Lettie thought that it would surely be safer inside the keep than risking flight in the open country if Egleton was overcome and the Cair was besieged, but she didn't say anything. Tom and Norri had obviously gone to great trouble and found discreet workers who could be trusted to build this secret entrance. She didn't ask the obvious question, "Wouldn't you be here anyway?"

They retraced their steps and closed the secret door. Lettie didn't like anything about this. It meant that Tom really thought they were all in significant danger. She comforted herself with the thought that Tom nearly lost her in the last invasion and he was taking even more precautions than necessary; but the thought would not go away: why wouldn't he be with us?

When they came up from the storeroom, they found Gorian, Norri, and Denquinar setting about getting some breakfast. Kirin was organising food for everyone. The kitchen had prepared hot bread and there were pats of fresh salted butter and pots of steaming coffee. Tom joined them while Lettie checked on little Dillon. Kirin saw that everyone had what they required and then joined them for breakfast.

When they had finished eating Lettie took her leave to see to Dillon's breakfast and Kirin left to keep her company. They poured fresh coffee and Denquinar took a large leather map case from under the table.

"And now gentlemen: to business. I have all the information I have been able to glean from the archives in the palace library. Luckily these were in part of the library that survived. The Corrii set fire to it before they left and I gather the king's councilor was much aggrieved at the loss of many precious volumes. This old map, however, has survived."

He unrolled the old parchment on the table. It crackled with age and the ink was faded.

"You can see from this chart that the mountains meet the sea a little to the south of here. They meet the coast here and continue out into mountainous islands well out into the sea. We will have to sail around them. They are likely to be rocky and there are no reefs marked. I would guess there will be hidden reefs, however, and we should sail well to seaward of the islands. It will be further south that we will need a landfall to take on water. Both the ships will be well provisioned, but we will take any opportunity to hunt on islands or shores that offer to extend our stores."

Denquinar moved his compasses over the map with an ease born of years of navigation.

"You see here there is a long coastline drawn; it stretches some two hundred leagues, but it does not show any mountains. It may be that the map maker simply did not draw them. He marks no streams on his map or harbors which you would expect if he had found any. They are the first thing a sailor marks on any map, after any reefs or shoals but those that discover shoals often don't get to bring their maps back."

"I am glad Kirin isn't hearing this conversation," said Norri looking intently at Denquinar's parchment.

Denquinar smiled. "I am under strict orders from the king to bring his forester back. Fear not, young forester, we have built the ships out of the best oak of Herelstrom, sailors of my old country would have given much to have such materials for their ships. The Swiftsure and Suresafe are very sturdy ships. We will brave the wild seas rather than stay too close to shore. Better be tossed about in the ocean if your ship is up to it."

"That is all very well for you, Commodore, but the most my stomach has had to cope with is a swaying treetop." Denquinar chuckled as he thought about this.

"It might be much the same feeling, forester. We can put you in the crow's nest. You can just imagine you are on a swaying branch, and you should be fine."

Norri didn't seem much comforted. He stood up, "I am going to get some more fruit. I will enjoy it while my stomach can handle it. Would anyone else like some?" Gorian accepted and Norri went to the side table and returned with a wooden bowl full of apples and another full of nuts.

Denquinar, looked at the assortment of nuts, "None of your famous orkya nuts I suppose?"

Norri shook his head, "I have some in the storeroom but we will need to set up my old brazier to roast them. I will roast you some to tonight if you like." Denquinar smiled in anticipation, "That would be wonderful; I have found them to be one of the wonders of my adopted country. Harder to get these days, though: the local nutter hasn't been working very hard I hear."

Norri laughed, "Hard enough to have a good personal store for my guests."

Tom was looking over the map on the table, "I notice that there is not much detail at all farther south; only a line indicating the direction of the coast by the look of it." Denquinar nodded. "Indeed, and this is the best map we have. It was made by one of your naval captains some four generations ago. You have no living officers who have explored these southern seas."

"That sounds like a bit of an accusation Commodore," said Tom. The tall seaman shook his head. "No accusation intended. In the Empire we had many keen young officers willing to explore unknown seas; I was once one of them. A commander of a small ship could hardly make a name for himself in battle, so exploration was one of the few courses available for such an officer to get noticed."

Tom looked at the map again, "I am a bit envious of you and Norri and Gordy going on this voyage. It will be a great adventure. What are the plans?"

Denquinar opened his map case again and drew out several sheets. "There are the recognition signals for the two new ships. They are leaving Cair Neren several days apart so as not to arouse any suspicion. The Swiftsure will sail down to the Erne River and take on whatever fresh supplies she needs in the harbour here. She will then leave harbour and stand off to seaward. The Suresafe is due to leave the Neren River and arrive here three days later. We will board her and rendezvous with the Swiftsure at sea a day later."

A deep-throated bell rang from the tower above!

The resonance seemed to reach every corner of the castle. The warning bells would only ring as a call to arms. Already the bell of the fort was responding. If it was only the sighting of the Swiftsure that they were expecting the sentries would have come and informed them. All those around the table looked at one another with something like shock. They had been preparing against this pass for months; now it was here they were almost frozen into inaction. Tom rose slowly to his feet, "We have rehearsed for months, now the play begins." His words called them all instantly into action. They all scrambled for their swords.

Lettie and Kirin appeared in the stairwell almost at the same time, Kirin ran to Norri, "What is it?" Norri put his are around her trying to slow the beating of his heart and calm them both, "up to the tower!" Then, trying to slow his voice, "Let's find out what is happening."

They all scaled the stairs in record time. Tom ran to the guards, who were still ringing the bell, "What …?"

The sergeant who had reached the tower before them pointed north in the direction of the watchtower at Thornton, "The bell of Thornton tower was ringing. We could just hear it but it has now gone silent. There is a strange mist or smoke over the ocean. It has completely obscured the tower."

One of the guards pointed toward the mouth of the river, "There are sails coming around the heads." The sails of a ship could be seen. Signal flags were flying from her foremast displaying her number, but she was clearly the Swiftsure. She had just cleared the headland when more sails appeared: another ship that was almost identical.

The two sailed down the river toward the Cair with more signals running up their masts. Denquinar read the signals, "'Enemy ships in sight: Sixteen vessels.'" This is not an invasion. It may be a raid.'

Tom turned to the crews who were now uncovering their catapults and ballista, "Setup for our maximum range! We may need to cover our ships as they come up the river!"

Gorian reached the top of the stairs last of all. He had been straining to hear what was said on the battlements above as he struggled up the last flight of stairs with his bad leg. Norri saw him and joined him at the top of the stairs.

"General, the guards say that they have seen a mist or smoke that is obscuring the signal-tower at Thornton. The admiral says the Swiftsure has rounded the point and signaled there are sixteen ships in sight."

Gorian walked slowly, dragging his gammy leg to the battlements, and looked out at the mist.

"It is smoke, not mist. It is not natural. Tom, is it like the dwimerinds that were used against us at Pinitera?"

Tom shook his head.

"Like and yet unlike, the dwimerinds were very dense; this seems more like a thick fog."

Gorian put all the pieces together with dispassionate military precision.

"It sounds like a raid! They are trying to intimidate us. We need to counterattack quickly and inflict as many losses as possible. Brian, assemble your cavalry and inflict as many losses as possible as they land.

Tom, gather together the mounted archers and give orders for the infantry to assemble and march as quickly as possible to Thornton."

Then turning to the sergeant in command of the Cair's defenses, "Sergeant, man the tortion weapons and close the gates once the cavalry have left, there may be an attack from the river."

There was furious activity, Tom, Norri, and Brian rushed downstairs to put on mail and saddle their horses. Horns were blowing in the village. Brian was met by Gillian at the gate of the Cair.

"Be careful, darling. Think like an officer, save your men and yourself and don't take unnecessary risks: that just plays into their hands." Brian nodded. His hands were shaking as he tried to buckle on his sword. It was not for himself that he was afraid, now. Many others would depend on his decisions. Gillian's words calmed him a little.

One of the guards had already saddled their horses. Brian leapt into the saddle and urged his horse out the gate, "I love you Gill!" he shouted over his shoulder. Tom embraced Lettie who was standing at the entrance to the hall shocked and trembling with Dillon in her arms. He kissed the little boy, held his mother close and rushed out after Brian. Norri hesitated a moment longer. He was just a plain soldier and had a bit more time. He held Kirin close and whispered urgently into her ear, "I love you! Whatever happens, I love you."

She held him tightly and could feel the tension in his muscles.

"Go, darling! Keep safe." Norri rushed out after Tom. His horse was already saddled by the guards. He slipped his foot into the stirrup and mounted. A guard passed him his shield and lance. Norri glanced at the straight, Bernadian blade at his side and wondered if it would get some use sooner than he had expected. Norri looked around at Kirin; raised his lance in salute and urged his horse forward toward the gate. Kirin managed a weak smile in return.

The last to leave was general Gorian. He limped to his horse and was aided into the saddle by a castle guard. After the general had left the keep the guards ushered in all the workmen and masons who took up weapons from the stand in the courtyard or ran to help shut and bolt the gates. Kirin and Lettie ran up the stairs to the battlements to see what they could see. The artillery master tolerated them but his scowl as he aimed the trebuchet made it clear that if they saw action, he wanted them off the battlements. They found Gillian, in chain mail with a sword by her side, stringing a bow.

By the time Norri reached the town there were already seventy horsemen assembled and about another fifty bowmen and spearmen. Many of the horsemen also carried bows slung behind their saddles. Brian ordered the lancers to the front and mounted archers to the rear and led out the cavalry at a brisk trot. They had no idea what was before them, and mounted militia gave them more flexibility. It was a full twenty minutes before they reached the outskirts of Thornton.

He led his cavalry at a steady pace. They had to arrive with strength to fight. As they rounded a forested bend at the approach to Thornton, Brian reined in his horse and gagged at the sight before him.

There were bodies scattered like fallen leaves along the road; killed as they fled; dismembered and disemboweled and over some still stood long winged, lizard-like creatures, all red and black with occasional scales of gold. Their reptilian jaws dripped blood and the torn flesh of their victims, but their eyes, even at a distance looked at the approaching horsemen with of more than animal intelligence: a calculating malevo-lence; intent on cruelty: they were devourers; living on terror; feasting on death. The creatures spread their wings as one and rose from the sav-aged bodies of the women and the small piteous forms of the children who had been their most recent victims.

Brian might have hesitated; he had no idea what these creatures were, but the sight of the murdered children so raised his ire that he cried out with a ferocity that would have given any enemy pause. His horse was used to this. He flattened his ears and sprang forward. Brian lowered his lance and charged at the creatures. There was a great beating of wings as they sought to evade the lances of the charging horsemen.

He was the first to reach the place of massacre and as one of the monsters rose into the air with wings beating frantically and long tail lashing the air, his lance struck its strangely armoured belly. There was a gush of black blood; the creature screamed in anguish and then van-ished leaving only an eerie red and black smoke where it had been and what seemed like a ragged scrap of leather fell to the ground.

There followed a terrible time where the horsemen circled around trying to reach the creatures with lance and sword and the monsters dived on the men and clawed at their faces and eyes. Norri drove his lance into the ground and drew his sword. He judged it was a better weapon to fend off the creatures. He held his shield over his head and scythed through the air with his sword as another of the beasts dived at him with claws extended and needle-sharp yellow teeth protrud-ing from its red mouth. A stench of death followed it; its underside gleamed rutilant and gold as it veered to avoid the flashing steel blade and lashed him with its whiptail as it passed. Its tail had sharp down-ward-sloping, barbed fins dripping with anaesthetizing poison. The blow all but knocked him off his horse; only his good armour protected him and turned the poison quills. One fallen rider was savaged by two of the creatures and lay prone; covered in blood before others could drive them off.

Tom and his archers fired at the flying reptiles. Some they hit and they burst in a spray of red, bloody smoke. But for the most part they hovered just over the horsemen so that Tom and the others dared not shoot. One dived on Tom. He swung in his saddle and released his arrow just in time. The red smoke of its destruction blinded his eyes, and his face was torn by a flailing claw before it completely disappeared. As the smoke and the blindness passed Tom remembered the dwimerinds that had attacked the fort at Pinitera.

Tom caught Norri's eye as he wheeled his horse seeking new targets. As their eyes met a silent communication passed between them. They had both been in such a pass before. Norri had told Tom about the one word that he had to speak in the prison hold in Corriamar. Tom had told Norri about the garments that saved his men from the terror of the dwimerinds in the fight for Pinitera. Both spoke a quick, earnest prayer that began, "Father, help us ..."

Tom wheeled his horse again as he spoke and saw a line of soldiers running toward them – only some fifty paces away.

"The creatures are sent to distract us," yelled Tom and dug his heels into his horse and rode to warn Brian. Norri sat his horse and looked at the men that ran toward them, they were fierce and wild looking. They had red emblems of the winged creatures on their shields and their armour was laced with red ribbons that hung in tassels the colour of blood. Their helms had long red plumes that added to the theme which was all of a wild lust for blood.

Tom galloped to Brian, who was, indeed, so caught up in the wild battle with wings and claws that he had failed to see the new threat.

They just had time to order their troop and ride away from the immediate danger. Tom's archers seemed to make more hits now as the cavalry retreated. And the red creatures hung back as each feathered shaft cracked through the air, its tip flashing deadly in the sunlight that now broke through the clouds and shone brightly around the battlefield. Even the wild men in their red armour halted their charge. Militia soldiers had arrived from Egleton.

A young man stood next to a general who was arrayed in red and black armour, trimmed with gold. His own armour was black and silver and he carried a fine scimitar by his side. He also wore ankle-height black boots that seemed out of place with his armour. Bentonius turned to the old soldier beside him, "What now, general?" A cruel smile made the general's scarred face look even more evil, "You will see, spy! Just keep a look out for our quarry – the one we were specially sent to kill or capture."

Bentonius scoured the field with his eyes. He knew the one he was looking for. He was small in stature and no great warrior, "My guess is that he will be with the horsemen, general, I know he purchased a horse." The general turned to a small group behind him and spoke orders in a guttural language that Benton did not understand.

A small group of magicians, dressed in the skins of strange animals took the lids off several wicker baskets they carried and three gordrills leapt out, they were impossibly larger than the wicker baskets that had contained them. The huge beasts stood on their hind legs, testing the air and after passing some soundless communication between themselves turned and capered toward the battle. The baskets sat smoking on the ground where their magical inhabitants had left them.

Denquinar rode up next to Gorian and pointed toward the black and gold winged shapes that circled above the ranks of their enemies, "I believe the red creatures are Wyvern, General. They are creatures of magic, very ancient and deadly to all men. They are not really alive as we know it. They are called up by incantation – in some foul rite the men Ba-al Giborachir from the far eastern island of Dorphir Sunde call them up to fight for them in their wars.

Once they fought against the empire but some of the coven masters have made a covenant with them in blood and they have become allies of a kind."

"Do you know how we can fight them, Commodore?" asked Gorian even as he indicated the commanders of the militia should order their man into ranks.

Denquinar saw how Tom's archers had managed to pick off almost half of the wyvern, "Even as you see young Tom has done. I had heard that they did not succumb to arrows but somehow Tom had managed to destroy them. That young man has something about him; that is certain." Gorian watched as the horsemen reined their horses on the wing of his infantry and wheeled awaiting new orders.

They looked across the field. On the grass of Thornton Green stood an army of some 260 – 300 warriors and above them flew more wyvern: perhaps as many as thirty of the winged creatures flew back and forth over the warriors. The red soldiers seemed to carry small shields with pointed blades protruding from the edges. They stood in a long line as if they were about to begin a foot race, not with closed ranks as men ready to defend themselves against cavalry. A sharp command was given, and they began to move forward. They carried their shields by their sides as they marched – seemingly heedless of arrows.

Above the charging soldiers a line of wyvern formed in the air and dived toward the militiamen.

Gorian rode up to Tom, "Tom here, wipe the blood from your face with this" and passed him a cloth from his saddle bag which he wet from his water-skin. Tom wiped his bloody face and then tied the cloth around his forearm. Gorian then pointed at the row of archers Tom had trained.

"They are the best archers in the kingdom Tom, can you help them deal with those?" he pointed at the rapidly approaching creatures. Tom nodded and rode along the ranks of archers, drew his sword and pointed it at the lines of red and black winged monsters, "May you feel the bite of the arrows of the army of God!" The bowmen and horsed archers all fitted arrows to their bowstrings with trembling hands.

The light that broke through the clouds at that moment seemed to become brighter. The black and red winged phantoms seemed some-how smaller in the bright clear sunlight.

None felt he had any strength or skill against the creatures that now menaced them, but each drew back his arrow to his chin and picked out his target.

A great shout came from the red lines that opposed them and the wild men surged forward, grim; wild faces screaming their battle cries as they came on.

As the dragon-men came into range with their spears the wyvern folded their wings and dived on the hapless militiamen. Gorian ordered the spearmen forward to protect the archers with their wall of large, oval shields.

The wyvern, wings folded back, made small targets but Tom's bowmen were good shots. Tom waited. Then gave the order: "Shoot!"

More than half the arrows found their mark. In moments more arrows were on the string, "Shoot!" the volley was more ragged this time but effective. The air was filled with smoke as one wyvern after another exploded in blood-colored smoke.

Some of the militia men were attacked by the winged creatures and fell in agony when they were pierced by the poison barbs. Gorian ordered them forward and the gaps in the ranks were filled. Gorian yelled at Tom, "Shoot at the men!" There wasn't much time. Tom yelled at the lines of archers, they took several steps forward and stood behind the ranks of spearmen who were standing, legs braced, and teeth clenched in their lines.

It was only moments before the lines met that Tom ordered the bowmen to shoot. At this range they were deadly. Many of the red-clad soldiers fell with arrows through their throats or unprotected parts.

This did not even slow their charge but the wyvern for the most part had failed to break the lines of the militia. The Dorphirmen met lines of slashing spears. This cost them but they used their shields with frightening effectiveness and knocked the shafts of the spears out of their way in their haste to get at the militia soldiers. Once they did, they were quick, skilled, and deadly.

Many of the Egleton militiamen fell to the short swords and the wicked blades on the four points of their shields. The ranks of thesouthern enders wavered; it was only fear and a desperate need to defend themselves that kept them close together, thrusting at their assailants with their spears and swords.

Brian had withdrawn his cavalry far enough on the right flank of the battle to rally them for a charge. He formed them into a tight group and charged again.

As they rode across the grass toward the main battle and the relief of the infantry, three enormous shapes ran onto the field between them. They stood taller than a man. Their front legs were longer than their hindquarters and their head and shoulders were covered with thick, black hair. They stood menacing the horsemen who reined in their mounts at the site of the new monsters. They had cat-like muzzles and huge teeth. And they seemed to be looking for something.

There was a momentary standoff until the gordrills reared up to show their extended claws and then raced at the horsemen, as if the lances and swords held no fear at all. Brian urged his horse forward, but it was reluctant. In moments, the monsters reached the cavalry and leapt into the air landing on the horsemen with claws and teeth extended.

Norri saw a gaping mouth coming at him and felt the shock of the creature's weight hitting him and reefing him out of the saddle. His blow was only defensive, but it seemed to bite. As he rolled over, he saw the huge hairy shape standing a couple of paces away, blood issuing from a large gash in its chest. It was preparing to attack when a yell from Brian and a blow from the shaft of a lance distracted it. Norri's horse was nearby rearing and terrified. He took the chance to rush to him and grab the reigns. He swung back into the saddle and urged the horse away. It didn't need much encouragement. Norri's chest hurt and he gasped for air. He needed to catch his breath. The force of the monster's charge had winded him. For his trouble, Brian was attacked by the gordrill. It lunged and grabbed his leg in its claws while it gnashed at his arms and body with its teeth.

Norri saw Brian pulled from the saddle and was about to ride back when he heard horns. He looked north and saw two lines of horsemen in bright yellow and red livery forming up to charge. Many of the veterans of the last conflict with the Corrii recognized the horsemen; they were the knights from Cair Neren in the north. They wore the bright gold and vermilion trees that symbolized the trees of the Neren Valley in autumn. A shout went up from the Egleton militia at the sight. The knights formed up their lines and charged. The shout and the thundering hooves halted the assault of the Dorphire-men, and they broke off the assault to form up in a line to defend against the horsemen.

Norri noticed how disciplined they were. They stood in lines with wide gaps. Not carrying spears or pikes they could not protect themselves from the lances. They stood ready to die on the heavy blades or try and duck aside and slash at the horsemen as they passed.

Tom saw the wyverns grouping in the air and urged his mounted archers forward. His shoulder hurt and he could feel the sticky blood on his clothes; his blood he was sure, but he knew he had to protect the charging knights. His twenty or so horsed archers rode to the flank of the fresh knights and shot at the wyvern as they tried to unhorse them before they could join battle. Only one or two fell. The rest of the knights crashed into the red-clad ranks with dramatic results. These soldiers had clearly never fought this way, and many fell in the first charge. Ordered battle then became an affray. Gorian ordered his spearmen to charge, and they surged into the broken ranks of the Dorphir-men.

The battle continued with small bands fighting all over the field, but the red-clad soldiers and their flying allies seemed intent on withdrawal and none of the warriors from Herelstrom had much strength left to chase them. The two remaining gordrills stood between them and the retreating Dorphire-men and none felt much inclined to do battle with these things to get at their retreating adversaries. The monsters, for that is the only way to describe them, stood on their hind legs, a full eight cubits tall, with their black manes bristling; huge incisor teeth and long black claws exposed, snarling; daring any to come at the retreating soldiers; none did.

A smoke lay over the battlefield. The sun still shone. Tom grasped Tillion's hand. "Again, Tillion, again we are in your debt."

Tillion grasped Tom's hand warmly.

"There has never been any debt. You have aided us and we, you, when need was great. The red men seem content to continue their withdrawal. What are these things?" He pointed a large pile of smoking hide. The substance of the monster has blown away on the fresh wind that had blown up from the sea. The other two had drawn back with the red-clad soldiers.

"I think I can answer that." They both turned to see the ex-Corriian admiral, poking at the smoldering pile of fur with a broken spear as if loath to get any closer.

"They are gordrill: magical monsters from some other place, called up by the foul incantations of the priest-magicians of Ba-al Giborachir on the eastern islands of Dorphir Sunde at the edge of the empire. They are the only part of the empire not conquered. They asked to join, at least the all-powerful priests of Baal Giborachir did and no-one else had any choice. These things are servants of their god, as are the wyvern, but these are far more fell."

They all looked at the retreating host, not beaten, just retreating in order; outnumbered. A large number of red shapes lay on the battlefield. The lances of the horsemen from Cair Neren had turned the tide of the battle. Had they not come Tom felt they would have been beaten and he dared not think of the consequences. He had a young wife and a small son. He didn't think even the guard at the new castle could hold out for very long against these determined, disciplined soldiers; especially with the wyvern to help drive the defenders from the walls. They were called out of their reverie by Norri who knelt over Brian, lying covered in blood on the field, "Quick! Help me with Brian."

Brian lay on the field with bleeding punctures in his leg and thigh from tooth and claw and a sword slash across his arm and chest that had rent the chain of his armour. His breathing was shallow, and he was very pale. Norri folded his cloak and placed it under his head and sought in his bag for bandages to stem the flow of blood from the deep wounds in his leg. Tom helped Norri as much as he could, but he was also wounded. Tillion left them to marshal his horsemen to prepare another move against retreating enemies.

Those with the worst wounds were placed on stretchers. Those who could ride were taken back to Egleton. The sun rose very slowly in the east. By midday the field was cleared of wounded, and the Dorphir-men were embarking their boats for the trip back to their ships. Gorian and his spearmen with the mounted knights watched over their withdrawal.

The battle had petered out into a draw; many had fallen on both sides and the hale were carrying or dragging their wounded comrades from the field. Many still lay on the grass groaning from their injuries, too badly wounded to move. Norri looked about at the horror of battle and wondered why; what evil could conceive this abomination? He looked down at his friend Brian, lying on the grass that was stained with his blood; breaths coming in shallow painful gasps, and he knew that Brian fell trying to save him from the black monster. Tom appeared at his side, bleeding from a couple of wounds that he seemed to barely notice as he looked at Brian, "We have to get him back to town." Norri nodded. "We cannot put him on his horse. He is too weak." Tom began to struggle with some pieces of broken lance to make a stretcher. Norri noticed he couldn't use his right arm properly, "You're hurt as well. Let me do that." Norri completed the stretcher. He had to make it so that it could be towed behind a horse because there were too few to carry all the wounded. Gorian and Tillion had rallied the bulk of the militia and cavalry to watch over the retreating Corriian formations. They dared not show any sign of weakness. It took too long for Norri's liking but soon a rag-tag procession was formed with all the wounded on horses or on stretchers moving off on the slow journey back to town.

They had struggled on for one merciless hour after another. Norri felt every bump in the road and ached for the pain it caused the injured. Brian had slipped into a stupor and had stopped moaning. Tom rode beside Brian's horse and held the reins while Norri walked beside the stretcher and tried to keep it as steady as possible.

After a couple of hours Tillion rode up beside him.

"How fares my cousin's husband?" Concern was written all over his face. He had ridden hard back from the battle to see how Brian was as soon as Gorian had felt the situation allowed. Norri didn't need to say anything. Brian was pale and silent on the rough stretcher. Tillion looked as desperate as Norri and Tom.

"Is there any way we can bring him back quicker?"

Tom shook his head, "His breathing is laboured; if we try and carry him across a horse he may die. This is the only way to get him back."

"I will send some of my riders to the town to get wains and horses and more people to help with the wounded." Tillion called to his aide, "Gwenran, go to the town and bring back anything with wheels. Even hand carts will be a help but get wains and horses if you can." Gwenran had been fetching bandages from his saddlebag for Tom whom he saw was bleeding.

Tillion took the rolls of cloth, "I will do this, Gwenran, it was well thought of. Tom, why didn't you say anything?"

Tom shrugged, "There are many with worse hurts than this."

Tillion helped him down from his horse. "No doubt, but it is still a way to town and we will do what we can here."

He helped Tom out of his hauberk and bound the arm while Norri dabbed some water on Brian's forehead. Brian's eyes opened and looked at Norri gratefully, but his eyes filled with fear a moment later as he looked over Norri's shoulder.

"Behind you, Norri!"

Norri turned and looked up. He and Tillion drew their swords. Two gordrills stood on the edge of the forest. One of the monsters reached his hand behind his back and drew a wicked curved blade from amongst its mane of black hair.

"Weegh cumm tooo slaygh therrr weeverrr orrf spellls."

They looked straight at Norri. "Therrr deestroyerrr weeell bee deestrroyed."

One jumped with impossible speed and landed right in front of Norri. The creature swung its ugly scythe-like blade and Norri barely had time to parry the blow. Then instead of pressing its advantage, the gordrills looked to the side and hissed fiercely, "Sss-servents of the err-rnemy," and drew back.

The two monsters turned and ran off through the forest at incredible speed with their manes bristling and their tails held high in the air.

As the monsters disappeared into the woods, they heard horses and a wagon came around the corner. David Goodman appeared around the corner, driving a wagon with Gillian and Kirin.

They waited as they drove up. David reined in the team and Gillian leapt from the wagon and ran toward them. In a moment she was on her knees beside Brian, "Darling, you're hurt!" Norri stood by her side, "It was one of those …" He pointed into the forest but the gordrills were gone. Kirin was at Norri's side moments later.

"Are you alright?" Norri nodded, "I might not have been. There are great monsters that the Corrii have brought with them. They are like great apes of some kind, but they can speak, like the grimulves. Something must have scared them off. They seemed to sense some enemy but then no-one came around the corner except the two of you and Pastor Goodman. Maybe they thought you were reinforcements."

The old village pastor, older and wearier with age than the girls, tied the reins to the wagon rail and stepped down, immediately a look of concern spread across his face when he saw Brian lying on the stretcher in pain, "What's this about great apes?"

Norri went to help lift the stretcher, "They did this, big black creatures, like the small apes that traveled with the Bernadians, but of much greater size. You seem to have scared them for some reason."

David was thoughtful, "It would not have been me they were scared of. But all of us have been praying for your protection; perhaps there are other beings here that we cannot see. Come help me lift Brian onto that wagon."

Brian winced as they lifted him onto the bed of the wagon. It was filled with a layer of straw to make it more comfortable for the wounded.

The march back to town seemed to Gillian to take much longer than the journey out. She walked by the wagon trying to encourage Brian all she could and not seem too worried. But she was worried. Their first aid had stemmed the bleeding for the most part, but the bandages were soaked with blood and Brian looked very weak and pale.

When they reached the road to the castle more people hurried out and helped with the wounded. The dining hall became a hospitalis and everyone with any skill at healing hurts was there. There was old Janice, renowned for her knowledge of herbs - both culinary and healing. She had brought many bunches of dried leaves and was busy soaking them and binding them in poultices to place on the wounds. The activity was frantic. Gorian arrived at the castle with a hogshead of his best brandy and began to distribute it liberally to any who were in any pain. He knelt next to Brian's stretcher and helped him take a drink from a cup mixed with the strong brandy and some wine to make it easier to drink. He noticed the worry on Gillian's face and smiled at the young woman fearing for her husband. "He will be fine. My brandy can cure anyone." Gillian smiled back weakly.

Gill stayed with Brian even after the brandy had worked on the pain and he was asleep. Kirin came and lifted her to her feet.

"Come and have something to eat yourself. He will need you when he wakes up. He is asleep now; and that is a good sign."

Gillian let herself be led away to a table where Kirin had provided hot soup and fresh bread. She sat on a bench by the board and picked at the bread and soup which seemed to have no savor. All she could think about was Brian.

David, the old village pastor, was busy going from one injured soldier to another with cups of Gorian's fortified wine and words of encouragement. His wife Patricia and Kirin were busy bringing food to all who were up to it. Kirin had ordered the kitchen to prepare lots more of the soup. Norri had told her about Tillion and his horsemen. They would probably be there soon as well, and she would have more mouths to feed. He watched her work. She had her sleeves rolled up and the recalcitrant strands of her long brown hair hanging in her face. He loved her. Everything about her made him proud to be her husband.

Gordy went from soldier to soldier warning them not to look too poorly or they would "forced" to eat Kirin's soup.

"We'll get you out of here and get you some proper food that hasn't been drowned in boiling water".

All around, between Pastor David's cheerful words, Gorian the inn-keeper's "fortified" wine and Kirin's soup (which many ate in spite of Gordy's dire warnings) the hall became a little more cheerful by the time evening approached.

The horsemen returned last having ensured that the Corrii had boarded boats and returned to their ships. Tillion saw that his men had food and shelter and came in last of all to seek something to eat. It was now quite dark. Norri had recovered enough from the battle to assist Kirin serving food to the horsemen in makeshift tables in the courtyard. The horses were tethered outside the castle; watered and foddered in a sheltered place where they could rest.

Tillion was standing by the door of the kitchen with a bowl of pottage and a hunk of bread. Norri spotted him as he returned from tending the horses. "My Lord, we all owe you a debt of thanks for your timely arrival today."

Tillion dipped the bread in the soup again and ate a large mouthful. "As I said to Tom earlier today, no thanks are required. We all do what we can. The ships were sighted many days ago, but they were well out to sea. They tried to slip past our defences by staying out to sea. Fortunately, some of our fishermen saw their sails. They lowered their own to remain concealed and once the Corriian squadron was passed, raced into Cair Neren to give a report. We have shadowed them as they sailed down the coast. But they sailed faster than we could ride. We ended up having to take the inland road and had to hope that we could arrive in the south in time to intercept them."

3

The Men of Ba-al Giborachir

anks of red-clad soldiers assembled on the beach. Bentonius Looked at the men's faces as they assembled in their legions, "The men show no sign that they are defeated, General, even though many of their number lie slain on the battlefield, it seems more a sort of resolve."

"My men are campaigners, Bentonius. We are used to wars where there are many indecisive actions." General Groeballas walked among those who had wounds and were receiving aid from the camp servants and those, tired from the battle who were taking bread and wine that had been brought ashore in the boats that were to ferry them back to the ships.

Bentonius was not pleased, "The horsemen have spoiled a complete rout. It would not have taken long for us to destroy the motley militia. Then we would certainly have killed the spell-weaver, the strange forester who has power that hurt us so badly in Corrimar. Now we don't know whether we have succeeded or not. I want to be able to take a positive report back to the masters."

His mind played with possibilities, "Do we dare send parties on ahead to ambush the retreating militia?"

The general shook his head, 'Not until the horsemen withdraw. They have too much of an advantage. Our sorties would be run down and destroyed to no purpose.'

Bentonius was pacing about agitated, "Perhaps we could wait until the horsemen withdraw and search the dead for any sign of the nutter…. But there is no certainty that they will not take their dead for burial."

He saw the magician-priest standing with his fellows and acolytes. "Perhaps the Gordrills can find him for us?"

Bentonius approached the priests. At their head stood a large man dressed in furs like the others, but still having the bearing and aura that chilled Benton every time he met him, "Legrarff, can the gordrills sense the power of the spell-weaver?"

The priest spoke with a deep, guttural voice, "They come from a place where power is not measured in strength and weapons, even though the creatures they indwell have the power once we bring them back to life." Bentonius was not sure what the answer meant but persisted, "You know the one we seek. What we do not know is whether he has the power or is just the pawn of one who does."

For a moment Legrarff seemed uncertain. He looked at the two huge gordrills. They were eating, tearing at long strips of dried meat with their sharp teeth. A smile crossed his face and he spoke to the creatures in a language that Bentonius didn't understand. The creatures dropped their food, looked at each other and with an expression like a smile, loped off toward the forest.

On the beach the general moved among his men, glad of a break from the querulous coven master. His lieutenant passed him a wooden cup with wine and took one from the servant himself, "I hate having to withdraw like this. We would not have needed to if those horse-boys hadn't turned up."

Groeballas was a seasoned soldier. "There will be many battles, Cerios and only a fool fights on to the death against greater odds." He would encourage his men and bide his time. He looked at the ships tossing about on the choppy water. He pointed to them, "They are the key. We can move faster than horses and strike wherever we like; then have the advantage again."

He stroked his beard. "Perhaps a feigned withdrawal will work to our advantage. There are forests to the north where we can rest and await the reinforcements if the weather will ease a bit. The reconstitut-ed-dog soldier regiments are following. Some of them have fought in this strange little land before. They were all but destroyed then. They will be less arrogant and more cautious the second time. Their over-confident officers are dead by all accounts. I will be more patient and not make the same mistakes."

His lieutenant looked in the direction of the trees, "It was said that all their officers perished; they paid with their lives for their arrogance."

"Yes Cerios, we will be more cautious, ruthless but cautious. And there is usually some fun to be had in that."

The young officer smiled.

"We will keep our men alive. Our task was not to conquer but seek out weaknesses, harass and if possible, help Master Bentonious find and break the people who had foiled them before. We were chosen because we had proven his skills in other campaigns. They know the Dorphire-men are masters at the art of attack, hurt and withdraw; weakening the empires enemies before the major attacks that deal the crushing blow."

"The people of Herelstrom will all be afraid after today. They will fear to venture far from their defended places with the wyvern and the gordrills about. Once released they must be destroyed or remain a constant fear."

General Groeballas smiled at the thought, "Every pathway, every clump of trees, every dark lane may hide a nightmare. We have turned the tables on them. Once, a hidden power in the forest destroyed our people. Now we can root it out and destroy it."

"It is said that one young officer from that action is now sailing to join us."

"Yes, young Captain Baubacus is obviously a capable officer. I asked for him specially. That he had got any of his men out after the failed attack from the underground river showed that. He will know only too well the capabilities of local archers. I always like to have men in my command who have a score to settle."

"He will certainly have that, sir."

The general looked away east at the beginnings of the great trees, "The report on Baubacus said that he had brought up the rear, trying to ensure that they were not being pursued. When he reached the entrance to the underground river all his men were gone. He and his two companions got into a boat and rowed for their lives. They were all of the raid and its reinforcements that survived. Aparently his father is a noble."

"It is amazing how they seem to be the ones who survive."

"Probably a sense they have that life owes them something. Not only does he survive but gets a promotion. Anyone else would be flogged as a deserter."

"He can hardly be blamed for running away – with unseen enemies all around them in the trees. We know now who hides in the trees. Bentonius managed to poison some of the tree-people, they can't be too clever."

"So, he says. When Baubacus arrives, we can put our minds to the problem of the archers. As it is, this first attack of the new campaign has gone reasonably well. Our force is intact, and the enemy was blooded; badly blooded if I am any judge."

He looked at the magicians in their strange garb, "They have made a big difference. I am glad they are on our side."

One of his aides pointed to the boat standing ready for him. He hated being at sea, especially in these heavy conditions. They had built a temporary, hidden camp in the forests to the north. It was in dense forests well away from the road. The last campaign had shown the north road was poorly patrolled and the forests rarely at all. If the confounded seas would die down, they could land and await the rest of the ships. Let the navy ride out the heavy weather, he liked feeling the earth beneath his feet.

The boat was in knee-deep water and Groeballas waded through the wash to take his seat on the stern by the sweep, the seamen plied their oars, and they were away. He looked behind and saw horsemen patrolling the shoreline. He smiled to himself. The next attack would be where they least expected. This was just the beginning of the war.

Three days later Groeballas sat with Cerios in the large stern cabin of the Battleship Argamaro. The forests of southern Herelstrom were just a dark shadow out the port windows of the stern cabin. They showed no lights, and the meeting was being held by moonlight which came in through the starboard side of the cabin. The Argamaro was rigged for the night: just enough sail to give her way and there were other ships sailing astern in strict formation.

"I am looking forward to meeting Tribune Baubacus, Sir. He has been preparing for this invasion for a year now. He will have left nothing to chance. This is his chance to make up for the last debarcle and show that it was very much the fault of others. I believe he lost a couple of good friends to the ambush by the secret people in the forest."

Groeballas stroked the smooth wooden hilt of his sword which lay in his lap. He always kept it with him since he was surprised by the Arionites of the south while at a staff meeting. They had fallen on his legions at night in huge numbers; none of the officers had so much as a dagger and the savage warriors killed them all. Only Groeballas, who managed to pick up a sword from a fallen guard as he dashed through the flap of the command tent managed to defend himself and survive.

The sword in his lap was the same sword. He never went on a campaign now without it. It was just a common legionary's blade, but he kept it razor sharp and valued it above any other weapon. It had saved his life; it was lucky. In the manner of soldiers, it never occurred to Groeballas that it hadn't been lucky for the soldier who had been slain outside his tent.

There was a knock on the door. A tribune entered first, Groeballas assumed this was Baubachas. He was followed by Bentonius and Admiral Norrens.

Cerios stood in deference to the senior persons who had entered the mess. "Tribune Baubachas, I presume. This is general Groeballas. I presume you have been introduced to Spymaster Bentonius and Admiral, Gastuss Norrens?"

Baubachas snapped his fist on his cuirass in salute and took the seat the general indicated.

"I am pleased to meet you general. I am pleased to hear that the first battle went very well."

The general frowned. "I wouldn't exactly say that Tribune. We got a bloody nose, I would have said."

The tribune smiled. "From what I have heard you even encountered more of the enemy cavalry than was expected and still inflicted serious losses leaving them retreating from the field carrying their wounded with the wyvern feasting on their fallen."

"It's as you say but I have *not* taken the south of Herelstrom as would be the case had the reinforcements not arrived."

Baubachas looked out the stern windows at the lines of ships. "I also failed to take the southern part of this country because we had too few men. I have brought you plenty of men for the final assault, General; your initial attack will have weakened and terrified them. It will make the final assault easier."

"The red men took significant losses."

The tribune smiled a not very pleasant smile. "They have yet to prove themselves. If they wish to be taken seriously by the empire they will need to shed some blood and have some victories."

General Groeballas was warming to the young tribune. Here was an officer willing to take risks but also one who had a keen sense of strategy. What was more, he had learned the hard way that the best way to win battles was not to take unnecessary risks.

"In that respect their rulers are like ours. No senior officer survives many defeats. Those who are the true rulers of the empire see to that, even if the military courts exonerate you."

"I have tried to ensure that we cannot fail this time general. We have six legions. Many times, the numbers that Bentonius says we will face here in the south of Herelstrom. We have engineers and siege equipment aplenty, and we have the wyverns and the gordrils...and the grimulves as usual. We will overcome any who stay to fight, and we will have the creatures that are with us hunt down and kill any who escape. Their southern town will be a byword for terror."

Admiral Norrens leaned forward at the other side of the table. "What are your plans for the tree people, Baubachas?"

The tribune sighed. "They are a more difficult problem. It is not with numbers that we will defeat them. We can never bring them to battle. I have discussed the problem with Bentonius."

The spymaster smiled. "The way to defeat an enemy who depends on a particular resource is to remove that resource."

The general smiled. "Cut down their trees?"

Baubachas sat back in his chair with the glass of wine the Admiral's cabin servant had provided. "It does not have to be tomorrow. But we want the trees, do we not, Admiral?"

Gastuss Norrens nodded, "More than you know. Even boards of reasonable quality to repair our ships are in short supply."

Baubassus sipped his wine. "So, we occupy the coast and fortify it. We send the wyvern to hunt at will in the trees and when their homes are no longer safe, we bring the forest people to battle. As with all our enemies, we win a war of attrition by persistent campaigns as we ever have."

"You do not think the forest people will come to the aid of the militia here in the south?"

Bentonius put down his cup. "I cannot say for sure, but I do not get the impression that they are very numerous. Their strength is in the forest, and I do not think they would come out to do pitched battle with our legions."

Gastuss Norrens had been thinking of the Battle of Cair Neren in the last invasion. "We had five legions at the battle of the Neren River and most of them were lost. The tree people (at least that is who we think it was), came under cover of some strange mist and annihilated them."

General Groeballas smiled. "I know what you are thinking Baubachas. 'Dog Soldiers. Ha! Coven men, not regular legionaries' and you are right, but the admiral was there at the river Neren. We must not underestimate them, and we have to prepare for the unexpected. And as much as we may not always get on with the dog soldiers and their methods, they were all seasoned men and a loss to the empire for that. What can you tell us of that evening Admiral?"

Admiral Norrens put down his wine cup and the slice of cheese he was eating, sat back in his chair and tried to remember the night.

"It all started in the evening. We had been working hard all day preparing for the attack of the castle at the Neren River mouth. The dog soldiers' legions had been conducting continuous attacks in the previous days, and on several, almost managed to take the walls. Each time the defenders managed to fight them off, so they had spent five days constructing siege towers.

This meant my men were busy ferrying the wheel rims and tools ashore and my carpenters were ashore assisting the military engineers construct the towers and the traces to pull them as well as cutting and trimming timbers and constructing the things. I lost all but a couple of those men."

Baubachas was leaning forward on the table. "When did you have any idea that a surprise attack was coming?"

"Not until evening. Everything was progressing as we expected, and the defenders were fighting hard in a battle even they must have realized they were losing. I was on the poop deck of my ship watching the progress. I had teams of sailors ready to take anything ashore that might be urgently needed but apparently General Etequinator was supremely confident. He believed that they had weakened the defenses and the defenders were exhausted with constant fighting while he had fresh men keen for the kill and the loot. I had been asked to prepare a secure cabin in case there were captives that were to be transported to the capital. Apparently, it was thought that the ruler of the southern part of the kingdom was there and maybe even their king who had somehow escaped the capturing of their capital, Pinitera. The Thane as they call the local lord was supposed to have very beautiful daughters. Aparently the empress had some interesting plans for them when they were captured."

Baubachas smirked. "What plans? Do you know, Bentonius?"

Bentonius also had a wicked grin. "Let me tell you later, after the admiral has finished the story."

The Admiral gave the two of them a disapproving look and ignored the interruption. "The first sign that anything was wrong was that the grimulves began to howl at something nobody seemed to be able to see. From the ship we could hear them. They seemed angry and then...."

Baubachas gave up thinking about the possible unhappy fates of the reputedly beautiful girls that had the misfortune to be the daughters of a defeated ruler and gave his full attention to the admiral. "...What?"

"If I am any judge, Tribune, I would say they were terrified. And rightly so because survivors said that they began to leap into the air and fall to the ground dead – smouldering, reeking, piles of fur.

Then the mist came. It was a bright mist as you sometimes see in the morning in the north when there is a fog, but this seemed to roll out of the forest across the greensward below the castle; that is about all I know. There are reports and rumors as I am sure you all know."

Baubachas scoffed. "Yes; of ten cubit high warriors, that glowed and had swords that cut men in two and the rest."

The admiral nodded. "I know what you mean. I am as skeptical as you. I saw no such warriors. What I can say is that seasoned warriors were taken off the beach terrified; and the losses were huge."

Baubachas shook his head. "I lost my men in the forest as well. I don't know about ten cubit high warriors. Bentonius assures us that their tunnels would not accommodate warriors of such size. It must be their weapons and even that makes little sense. More wine...."

A servant quickly refilled the tribune's cup. The tribune's mood was completely changed. He had more sympathy for the Admiral who has kept his ship in the Neren River all night while his sailors brought aboard men telling stories of huge warriors with impossible weapons. He had tried unsuccessfully to save his men, who conducted the raid through the river under the mountains; and failed."

The mood in the room had soured. Baubachas stood and looked out the stern windows of the Argamaro at the lines of dark shapes: ships blacked out and rigged for night sailing but keeping station on the flagship expertly. He mused that they had brought unexpected weapons of their own this time and he would never make the mistake of underestimating an enemy again. There were thousands of men in the ships. Ten times the number of those they planned to attack.

4

The Swiftsure

There had been no more signs of the Corrii for some weeks. Brian was back on his feet, if a little shaky. Their ships had sailed back up the coast and there was no sign of them from any of the watchtowers.

Work went on apace now that they had received a scare. The walls on the lower defenses of the Cair progressed quickly but there were many cubits of stones to go before the main wall reached its full height. Brian supervised the work. He had the big stones laid in on the east wall where the castle was most exposed to attack. Even there it was near impossible to use siege towers because the land sloped up to the bluff on which the castle was sited. It would be ladders for sure if the castle was attacked and height made all the difference.

Tom met him at the works as he was supervising another great stone being raised while leaning on a crutch Norri had fetched for him from the forest.

"There is no real way to get it done any faster is there?'

Brian sucked his teeth as the great block slipped a little as it neared the top of the wall.

"The blocks take time to cut, that's the trouble. And then they have to be brought on wains from the quarry. There is no use in building with bad stone. They have to be able to resist catapult fire."

"Gordy is supervising the building of two more heavy wains. They have been working day and night."

"He will be a loss when he goes with Norri," said Brian saying what both were thinking. Tom nodded, thinking how loath he was to risk losing his friends again. If their situation was not so dire, he would never have allowed them to risk it.

"To make matters worse we lost a wagon crew. They were found by their wagon when they didn't arrive this morning. All dead, men and horses; all cut to pieces. The men who found them said they seemed to have teeth marks as well. They didn't stay around long. I have sent more men out with weapons and archers to investigate and bring the wagon in. They said the horses had been partly eaten, raw."

Tom felt a cold chill, "As well as the castle we need to strengthen the defenses of the town. When this gets out nobody will feel save in their beds. What is that wagon coming down from the main road?"

As he spoke there was a wagon with two men in it escorted by four knights. They were too far away to identify the heraldric markings.

"They don't seem to be from Cair Neren, and surely Tillion would have said something if the Thane was sending someone else. Maybe it's a message from the King."

They both started down the stairs but before they reached the bottom Norri and Kirin had been told and they saw them by the gate awaiting the small wagon.

When it pulled in through the gate an old man climbed slowly down from the seat beside the driver. Norri did not recognize him but for courtesy sake offered his arm to the old man, "Welcome sir, to Cair Egleton. I am..."

"I know who you are, King's Forester. It is you I have come especially, to see."

Norri was bemused, "Then you have me at a disadvantage."

The old man laughed, "That is the trouble with fame, Forester. Many know you but you will often be at such a disadvantage. I am Eli Varmanor. I am one of the King's counselors, as you are, in your own way."

Norri was unsure what to say so he thought food and drink was a good idea. But, before he could say anything, Kirin made the offer, "Sir, we are honored, will you come inside the keep and refresh yourself? I will organize water for you to wash and some hot food as soon as it can be organized."

The old man smiled at her, "They say at court, that the King's Forester has a gracious and beautiful young wife. The rumor is understated. Thank you kindly, Kirin, is it not? I would welcome a little water and some bread and that will suffice. I came here against the will of the king but with his blessing and we are in a time of war. I heard tell of war and strange stories as we journeyed south."

Tom and Brian came up with Brian using his crutch to support his wounded leg.

Tom had met Eli during the siege of Pinitera. He reached out his hand to the old counselor, "My Lord, you have journeyed a long way to visit us."

Eli shook Tom's hand and then Brian's, "Here is another heart stealer. Hello Brian. I see you are hurt?"

Brian shook the old man's hand, "Yes, but I am becoming hale again. We encountered strange creatures in the last raid. Not only are they dangerous but they seem to have some power to weaken and terrify. And we fear they are still at large somewhere nearby."

Eli nodded, "We will encounter many such enemies, I fear, in the days to come; we will need to learn how to fight them."

At this point Kirin interrupted. "Come inside all of you, we will arrange water to wash off some of the dust of the journey and refreshment at least."

The knights that had accompanied Eli had taken their horses to the temporary stables that were really just a shed inside the walls and returned. They eagerly accepted Kirin's invitation.

She and Gillian with the help of the castle staff set out water and towels and chilled drinks. These were followed by sweet rolls and coffee and soon everyone was sitting back relaxing and asking questions. The knights were asked if they had seen any signs of their enemies on their journey south. They had not.

They in turn wanted to know all about the raid and the creatures that had come with the strange fighters from Dorphir Sunde.

As evening fell, Eli took Norri and Gordy aside, "Gentlemen, you are knights of the king and I know of the journey that is being prepared. My part is lore and the writings of old that have come down to us from prophets and men of wisdom in the past and to try and discern what truths we have been told that bear on our current struggles.

I don't know how much you know of the history of our land, but ten generations ago King Terrean, Terrion's son, went to great efforts to set up and train pastors who would teach the words of God spoken through His prophets in all the regions of the kingdom. Many generations later, such men still faithfully carry out their appointed tasks in the kingdom, though it is weary work betimes." He sighed. "Sorry, I digress. In the time of Terrean, there was a man of God known to hear truly the words of the One God. Many of his oracles predicted events which, in time occurred and he was held in esteem by some, including the king.

But some of his oracles did not seem to have any particular importance at the time.

Now it came about that I was reading the old scroll and attempting to make a copy for a pastor at Neren Keys and I found a passage that seemed important. I cannot exactly say why but I knew of your plans, and I thought I would bring the scroll to you.

This is the oracle:"

The old man unrolled the parchment on a table and read the words,

> "A father's love protects you,
> Though you cross the storm-tossed sea,
> The eagle's cry will save you,
> From a most dread enemy.
> His Mari will come to you,
> When your heart has no more strength,
> When fear of foes besets you,
> And your faith is at full-stretch;
> You are not then forgotten,
> For your plight is surely seen,
> And the Son, the One begotten,
> Will be there in your need."

Then he handed Norri a copy on a smaller piece of parchment, "Do you read, Forester?"

Norri nodded, "I read a little, my father took me to Sunday afternoon classes with our local pastor. I am not very good, but I think I can read this."

Eli nodded, pleased, "Words written on velum or paper are precious. You don't have to be a great reader to get much benefit and much guidance from them. Words of our old prophets and teachers sometimes seem as though they are written for a particular situation, perhaps many particular situations.

When I saw these words, I read them to the king, and he also thought of you. We do not understand them all. There is more in this scroll that we understand even less, and I will not bother you with our theological speculations. It is one of the most ancient books in the king's library."

Norri looked at the old scroll and was somehow drawn to know more, "Could I try and read more?"

Eli was pleased, "Of course. If you wish, I will read it with you."

Norri seemed pleased, "My studies with Pastor David have helped me in ways I cannot fully explain. I would like to study more and there is little time before we sail south. Would you spare me some time after dinner tonight?" He looked at Kirin working clearing away some plates, "But we mustn't be at it too late."

Eli caught the look at Kirin and pretended to look tired, although he was rather looking forward to discussing the scroll with this eager young man, "Yes I have had a long journey, but we could spend an hour or two if that would suit."

So, the time for a theological discussion was made and Norri went to talk to his wife.

The river was quiet. Norri and Gordy had their bags sitting on a pile of boxes and barrels of fresh produce and local wine stacked in the old boatshed by the river.

The plan had been for Tom to go with Norri and Commodore Denquinar, but his injuries needed time to heal, and Gordy had offered to take his place on the long journey south in search of a way to Bernadia.

Norri wore the finely made sword given to him by the Emperor of Bernadia as a gift of thanks for saving his son from a Corriian prison. The sword was a token of friendship that they hoped they could turn into an alliance. The trip had now become urgent.

They were expecting the Swiftsure to arrive at the mouth of the Erne this morning. The plan was to rendezvous with her sister ship at sea. They would sail south until they came to a region where the mountains along the coast seemed less formidable. Norri and Gordy then planned to take the inland route some three hundred leagues to the outskirts of the Bernadian provinces.

Kirin stood next to Norri, holding his hand fiercely; every sinew of her trim body said that she didn't want him to go – but she didn't say a word. Norri knew he was loved, and she judged that a young man who knows he has a wife at home longing for his return, will do all he can to do so. She also knew he had to go, and she respected him. Both these things, she knew, helped her husband to be brave and sensible. Jenny was laughing and acting the goat with Gordy. Kirin knew that this was Jenny's way of doing the same thing.

Kirin was shading her eyes to look out through the heads of the river when she heard bells ringing from the tower of the castle. All four of them looked at one another. This was not right! The warning bells would not sound for the arrival of the Swiftsure.

They looked up toward the castle and saw the commodore and his son running down the hill toward them. Kirrikanatus arrived first, breathless.

"We were watching for the ship from the battlements. We saw her flying down the coast under all sail. The Suresafe was with her. There are ships chasing her, Corrii naval vessels and four gothships of the coven. There are also some smaller craft that look like Ungarvarian Dows."

Gordy's mood changed in an instant.

"Kiri, what is your father's assessment?"

"Possibly enough ships for a serious attack – especially if there are transports following."

Now they could see the king's ships flying for the harbour. The Swiftsure trailed smoke from her main deck and her sails showed damage from fire and catapult – it had clearly been a struggle to get this far. The small ships Kirriakanatus described were making darting runs at the bigger clumsier ships and firing their weapons before tacking away and attacking again.

Denquinar came running up looking at the unfolding drama as he came.

"The captains have done well. Ungarvarian Dows! They are very fast if handled well; and if they can sheer off a stay or a spar with a bolt from a cheiroballista they will have our ships. The galleys will catch them and use rams or borders."

Norri caught the naval officer's eye. "Is the mission over, Commodore?"

The former Corriian Admiral glanced at the ships entering the river. He stroked his beard and seemed deep in thought. In his mind, he evaluated all the tactical information they had.

The Corrii were clearly not going to give up their ambitions toward Herelstrom.

The attack by the men of Baal Gibrochir meant that the covens were involved and believed they had a score to settle. In the last battle they had suffered much damage to their prestige that needed to be repaired.

They knew that the old Emperor whose unexpected return had saved them last time had died; unexpectedly. Denquinar knew Corrimar was a dangerous place; even for an emperor, if he crossed the wrong people.

Denquinar knew that young Norri's escape with the son of the Bernadian Emperor from the Coven masters' hold in Corriamar was a stroke of enormous luck. He didn't even know how he had managed it.

Now Herelstrom needed an alliance with Bernadia. Working together they might withstand the Corrian might. Apart, Herelstrom was doomed and Bernadia would ultimately succumb. The Corrii would invariably make peace with one while they crushed the other and then tear up the treaty. It was the usual way.

Their plan had been to sail south to where the mountains were passable. Norri and Gordy would be put ashore to attempt a landward crossing.

At the same time, he would take the two ships and search for a seaward passage to Bernadia via the unexplored southern seas. If he found no passage, he would find safe anchorage and await Norri and Gordy.

The current attack was the problem. But his calm strategic mind assessed the benefit of their few swords in the coming fight against the difference their current plan could make if they succeeded.

Denquinar knew clearly in his own mind what should be done – or at least be attempted. Norri was a knight of the king, and the king knew this task was one they must attempt. He looked at the young couple, married barely six months and felt pangs of pity.

All these thoughts passed through the commodore's mind in moments. He was about to speak when Kirin, reading his face, said what had to be said.

"Commodore, I see by your face that you think we should still go ahead with the plan."

Norri looked at her in surprise. He had just been thinking that everything had now changed, and his responsibility was now to stay and protect his wife, his home and his friends; especially now that Tom and Brian were hurt.

Denquinar smiled a rueful smile at Kirin, in his mind he was comparing her to the women he knew in Corrimar, officers' wives mostly. They all knew their husbands had their duty but that was where the similarity ended. He fixed Kirin's eyes with undisguised admiration, "You are right. The journey should go ahead."

He looked at the clutter of sails in the river mouth. "We will have to get past these. But as ever, surprise will be the key."

Norri saw Kirin screwing up her resolve to help him decide. They had made this decision already; it was just more dangerous now. All he could do was nod.

Kirin pressed her body close to him and leant into his embrace. She saw by the look in his eyes that he wanted to stay and keep her safe. She also knew that she was strong and capable and had as much chance of surviving the coming struggle on her own. Her mind scrambled for words to say until clarity, not her own, cut through her surging emotions, "I love you Norri and I will love you just as much when you return."

Norri had nothing to say so he kissed her, clutched her tightly to him and then ran to join Commodore Denquinar who was carrying his kit toward a boat that was approaching from the Swiftsure, "I love you so much Kirin."

The girl stood on the greensward by the river, steady in her resolve to show her husband that she was not afraid and make him believe she would be all right. She wanted to give him courage for the tasks that lay ahead of him.

The Swiftsure had come about a bare cable's length from the jetty near the boatshed. Her captain had his boat in the water in moments and his best crew dispatched to pick up their passengers.

Gordy clapped Norri on the shoulder and they both ran out onto the jetty with just their bags, there was no time for the extra stores. Gordy jumped into the boat behind the Commodore and his son, mouthing words to Jenny that only she would understand.

As they rowed away both Gordy and Norri looked back at their wives. Gordy looked at the look on Norri's face, "It is a big thing for a man you know."

"What's that?"

"To be respected by your wife."

Norri didn't answer. He knew it was true but the pain of being separated from Kirin hushed him into silence. He watched as Jenny pulled Kirin away and they both ran to the castle Kirin turning and waving as she followed Jenny up the hill to the castle.

5

Flight

*C*aptain Reynolds was making ready to depart. He also felt that the mission for which his ship had been built should continue. It was just harder now. They knew there would be difficulties; they had just begun sooner than anyone had expected. He stood at the poop deck railing watching his officers. Each knew his orders and there was no more to be done. Seamen stood ready at the braces, weapons officers were standing by their charges, and they were as ready to run the gauntlet as was possible.

The captain saw the boat approaching, in the stern was an elderly man in the cloak and tunic of a Commodore in their navy. Reynolds recognized the former Corrian grand admiral and his son. He guessed the other two were the Lord Forester and Tom, the Warden of the Southern End. He was unaware of the battle at Thornton and the changes to those he was to take on the quest. The plan was that they would attempt a nine hundred league trek across mountains and God-alone-knew what in an attempt to reach Bernadia.

As soon as the boat was unloaded it was taken in tow and he nodded to his first officer. The sails were loosed; billowing and cracking as the wind filled the canvas. The Swiftsure gathered way. Now the first task began. They had to fight their way through the Corrian armada. Their aim was not to engage but to escape. Reynolds and drilled his men for hours every day for months, first he had used a clumsy merchant ship and once the Swiftsure was ready they had driven her to her limits in her sea trials. She had proven that the careful choice of timbers and solid design were worth the effort. Her masts and spars were cut from the best pieces of blue pine and ash available. They were strong, supple and forgiving. She was tough, she could lie close to the wind and she could handle well in heavy seas. As Reynolds looked out the heads at the massed sails of his enemies, he remembered that he had once lost the ship that was his pride and joy to the Corrii. He would not let it happen again. The Swiftsure was not a two-deck war-galley like his first command. This ship would survive because she was swift and maneuverable, like her name, not because she was dangerous.

Reynolds saw that the Commodore and his passengers were being taken below to the cabin they would share. The Suresafe was under way also. He nodded to Henderson on the poop of their sister ship. The obvious tactic was to separate. They would try opposite sides of the river. And split their attackers' ships.

Denquinar nodded to the captain as he was led below. He knew Reynolds would need all his wits to pass their enemies and escape to the open sea. Even then, he knew, the Corrii wouldn't just let them escape. The armada he had seen had ships of many classes: some smaller than the Swiftsure and some larger. The faster ships would run them down and try to cause enough damage to allow the bigger ships to catch up. Then it was just a matter of time.

Denquinar and his son Kiri along with Norri and Gordy were shown to their cabin. It was small with bunks, benches and a table.

Denquinar and his son wasted no time. They opened their bags and drew out leather armour. It had strategically placed plates at the front to protect against arrows and was thick enough to turn any but a determined sword thrust. Norri noticed that the armor had ties at the shoulders, waist and armpits. He guessed it was so it could be removed easily in the water. He guessed the rig would be deadly if the wearer fell overboard. He noticed that Denquinar and Kiri assisted each other to do up the ties. Over the armor they both strapped sword belts.

Norri and Gordy both had leather jerkins on over their clothes. His own jerkin had buckles. Perhaps not the best design for a sea voyage but there it was – it was too late to change them now.

Denquinar noticed that Norri had been observing his armor, "I have seen many armored men drown because they couldn't get out of their gear when they fell in the water. Kiri and I have been working on this design. It is just a matter of sewing in ties instead of buckles. If we survive today, I will help you with yours.

For now, we will probably be needed on deck when the fighting begins. Gordy, I see you and Norri have bows. You will be needed first.

Kiri go to the captain, ask him where he wants us. We will obey his orders in the battle. Tell him to consider us as two archers and two swordsmen. If there are spare boarding pikes, get them."

Turning to Norri and Gordy, "Have your bows ready to shoot boarders as they come up; particularly those with grapnels. They will attack with Ungavarian dhow. These are very swift boats. It is a miracle of sailing that they got them through the straits of Geitor. They are seaworthy craft, but I would have said too small for a long voyage in heavy seas. For one thing they cannot carry the supplies.

These ships will try and grapple and board. We must stop them. If they succeed, they will be trying to disable this ship. That will be disastrous. We are too far outnumbered. The Swiftsure must be able to carry full sail if we are to escape to the open sea."

Gordy and Norri looked at each other. They checked their gear, strung their bows and got more nervous before Kiri came below with pikes and boarding axes. "The captain's compliments; he sends these weapons and bids us supplement the men amidships if one of the dhows attempts to grapple and board. He bids us stay low and keep a hand hold. He will try and out-maneuver them as he has all the way from the Neren River where they were first sighted. He says if we can sail through them, we should get away; the heavy seas will be to our advantage."

Denquinar hefted the boarding pike. It was a long vicious weapon designed to push would-be boarders away from the ship, most likely into the sea. "They say the best way to win a close fight is to kill an opponent before you get into one."

Gordy tested his bow string; "Given my skills in swordsmanship, the farther the better. Let's get to it."

When they came on deck, they found a worried-looking group of sailors strapping on leather jerkins and cutlasses. Others were already at the railings tying quivers of arrows to railings and bollards.

Norri watched his friend at his best. Gordy took a place next to a young ship's archer who was looking with alarm at the massed sails approaching the river mouth, "Gordy's my name. (The young man said his name, but Norri could not hear) The wind is from the east, is it strong enough to affect our shots at close range? I've only brought twenty arrows and they tell me I have to kill thirty Corrii with them." The young man pointed out several quivers full of arrows ready at hand. "I see. Well, they have a problem then don't they." All the sailors nearby laughed.

Gordy winked at Norri. Norri knew he was just as concerned but Gordy's ability to make a joke of dangers was a powerful weapon.

None too soon the first test of their defenses came. One of the dhows that had been clearing Tom's ranging buoys swung toward them. She would be attempting to cut off the escape of the Swiftsure to the sea. It seemed an impossible task. Her lighter planking would not survive a collision, but her commander probably guessed correctly that Reynolds could not afford getting his bowsprit tangled and hoped to cause the Swiftsure to turn into the wind and give him and another approaching dhow a chance to catch her.

Captain Reynolds was up to this task. He waited until the last possible moment then tacked in the other direction.

All the dhow could do was come about. But she did so too early and made herself an easy target for the artillery officer on the Swiftsure. Durken Smith whipped the spray-cover off his weapon while a sailor slipped the bolt with its burning fuse into the weapon. Durken and the crew on the second ballista fired their torsion weapons within moments of each other and immediately rewound the weapon for a second shot if their captain could give them time.

The range was too short for them to miss in the calm water of the river. The two bolts flew across the gap between the ships trailing smoke from their fuses and crashed into the deck of the Corriian vessel. There were two flashes as the oil canisters in the head of the bolt exploded. These were small versions of the defensive weapons mounted on the castle above, but the burning oil caused enough consternation to distract the crew of the dhow from the attack. This was all they needed.

Seeing their first attacker foundering, Reynolds pointed to the next target and Smith swung the deck-mounted weapon in the other direction. The oil-filled bolts were counterweighted and heavy, which limited his range, but against the small, lightly built vessels they were effective. Still Smith judged he had time for several shots at the second dhow which was now closing fast, lying closer to the wind on the same tack. Her captain wasn't making the same mistake the other had made. On these converging tacks, the Swiftsure could not easily evade her and her companion ship was back under control and coming up behind if he managed to grapple. Smith could see the captain on the raised, stern platform that was all the small ship had as a poop deck.

He quickly ran to the other weapon to give his orders. Both weapons were rewound and ready. The sailor loaded the plain steel headed dart while Smith aimed. There was too much swell to be really sure, but he had practiced and practiced. He nodded to the other ballista crew and again both triggers clicked moments apart. Smith watched through the sights. One man on the poop of the dhow screamed as the dart passed right through him and threw him overboard with its force. The second missed everything and tore a hole in the railings.

The steersman threw himself on the desk in his surprise and others had to grab at the tiller.

Smith now re-armed the ballista with oil-filled bolts and waited. The captain of the dhow knew he was in danger now. He and all the officers were crouching around the tiller.

She was coming closer now and he wouldn't miss. When they were ready, he nodded at his captain who gave orders to change tack as soon as the weapons were fired.

A seaman touched the wick-fuse with a torch from the holder. "Click": and the weapon flew with amazing speed to the poop deck of the dhow. With the other crew's bolt, they burst into flames and all the officers on the small ship were covered with fire.

Reynolds shouted his orders and the Swiftsure came around. But somehow the captain on the other ship had survived, little hurt and came about behind him.

They now had two of their adversaries behind them closing very fast and there were black sails ahead.

A man stood on the bow of one with a line and a grappling hook. Norri pointed him out to Gordy. "That man with the grappling hook and the line, do you think we can shoot him?"

"The archers on the dhow will shoot at us in we stand too long over the protection of the planking.' As if to confirm Norri's words an arrow thudded into a hatch cover nearby.

Gordy set an arrow to string and knelt ready to draw his bow. Norri did likewise.

"Now!", said Gordy. Both stood, took aim and shot. The man dropped his rope and pitched overboard with an arrow in his leg and another in his chest. The grappling hook went overboard as well. With any luck it would pay out and drag on the bottom.

Gordy reached for another arrow. "The one in the chest was mine." Norri Smiled.

Reynolds was standing at the poop-deck rail ignoring the arrows that passed perilously close to him; smiling down at them, "Will you two stop wasting arrows shooting the same man!"

Gordy leant against the wall of the quarterdeck fitting another arrow, "Can't please some people...."

They both popped up and shot again but the two Dows were now much closer. It was an easy shot, and both hit an attacker, but it was swatting gnats, the forward decks of both ships were swarming with boarders.

"Ware borders!" the captain shouted moments later. Several grappling hooks clattered over the sides of the Swiftsure. Gordy reached for an axe and hacked at a rope, but it was not yet taught, and the axe couldn't bite. They could see the big lateen yards looming closer on both sides it would be hand to hand stuff soon.

Norri drew his sword. He had often practiced on parade days with blunt practice swords, and he was a bit surprised by how light it was.

"Stay down!" whispered Gordy urgently.

No sooner had he said it than the hulls hit, and a surge of men jumped onto the Swiftsure's deck. Two attackers fell with vicious upward thrusts of their swords. Norri cut one down and then stood up and used his sword and shield to block another who fell back screaming between the hulls.

The boarders kept coming even though the men on the Swiftsure had killed and thrown back many.

Reynolds slashed at a Corriian sailor with a cutlass that lay on the deck and shouted an order to the helmsman who hauled on the wheel. The Swiftsure had been sailing as close to the wind as she could. He had let the helm come off a couple of points, now he let her come back onto course. The effect was amazing, the first attacker on the starboard side drew away and many of their boarders fell or clung to the sides of the Swiftsure as the distance between the hulls increased.

On the port side, they came crashing into the other ship and with their greater weight, smashed her planking and threw the boarders backward onto her deck.

In minutes they were free and sailing clear. Norri looked up at their undaunted captain as he snapped orders to shorten sail, change tack and watched the consummate skill as he maneuvered their ship through the press of attackers.

The gothships used no magic against them and passed down the river; only leaving the warships – big Corriian galleys and four-deckers that the Swiftsure could easily out sail.

As they passed clear of the headland and into the open sea, they saw the Suresafe pass the Corriian navy as well. It was odd. It seemed that the Corriian fleet was mainly bent on attacking New Castle. At first this was a relief, but as more and more ships turned into the river, now heavier transport ships with large square and trysail rigs, both Norri and Gordy thought about their wives, left behind in the castle; without them.

6

Voniok

Kirin and Jenny ran up the hill to the castle. They slipped inside the outer gates of the entrance tunnel just as they were being closed. Many of the town's people had come to the castle, including much of the militia. The people from the southern part of the town would most likely flee to the wooden fort built by and for the militia.

What Kirin saw when she came through the race and into the courtyard of the partly finished castle was fear. It was everywhere. You could see it on people's faces, the way they stumbled as they ran.

Kirin looked around her, conscious that Jenny was at her elbow. What could she do? Something must be done. These people couldn't defend the keep. They were falling over one another in their fear. What did Norri say? God was like a Father. He could speak order and courage where no other voice could. Kirin felt completely helpless, young and unimportant but someone had to do something.

She saw a sergeant of the guard running past with armloads of arms. "Wesley, have you seen Tom?"

Wesley pointed to the new wall. "Over there, by the workings." Kirin saw Tom, shirt sleeves rolled up directing workers to make the unfinished part of the wall as strong as possible. She ran toward him then stopped herself. She was the wife of the King's forester, the savior of the country, lauded by their king and even by foreigners. And now he was gone on a vital journey – to save the country again. (It was so unfair.)

She stopped herself. She had to think clearly. If she panicked, others would be watching. She slowed to a walk. "You men - over there! See the sergeant. He will get you weapons."

She crossed the courtyard in what seemed to be half a day. She spoke to nearly everyone she passed; gave directions, made decisions (She had no real idea if they were right.) and finally came to where Tom was working. She stood there waiting for him to have a moment to speak with her. Finally, Tom finished passing a load of bricks up to the top of the half-finished wall to make parapets and noticed her.

"Kirin, has he gone?" Tom looked at her. He saw her loss and pain and that she was holding it all together because she was needed. He stopped for a moment to admire the young woman his best friend had married.

"Are you doing all right?" It was a stupid question. Of course, she wasn't. Tom climbed down of the pile of boards he had been standing on and drew her into a cuddle so that she could compose herself in safety.

"I am almost finished here; I will go to the battlements and see if we can do something with the artillery to give them something to think about. Can you keep things moving here?"

Kirin picked up her skirt and started giving instructions again.

"Take those children to the main hall - through there in the keep...

How old are you, lad?" (The boy was probably only a few years younger than she was.)

"Fifteen, Maam."

"What's your name?"

"Steve, Maam."

"Steve, through that door then downstairs on your right you will find bolts and oil for the ballista crews. If you carry these it will mean they can work faster, and you will help damage or destroy the ships that are attacking us. Can you do that?"

The boy didn't even wait to answer. He was off down the stairs.

Tom was heading to the turret of the keep after hastily pulling on a hauberk and taking his sword from Lettie. He smiled at her and then kissed her and ran for the stairs.

Kirin saw the fear on her face. She knew it was different being a mother.

"Lettie, you need to take care of Dillon. Is he in the keep?"

"He is upstairs asleep."

"All this noise will probably wake him."

Lettie was looking around at the chaos.

"There's so much to do here."

Kirin turned toward the entrance of the keep.

"Go. We will have everything under control soon."

Lettie nodded and started toward the door, then hesitated.

"Kirin, what about Norri?"

"He has gone. They will be on their way by now. They are probably safer than we are. Now, go!"

Lettie ran for the door of the keep. "Lettie, walk...." Lettie understood and slowed down. She smiled at several people as she passed them.

Kirin felt wobbly at the knees, but it didn't show.

Tom reached the battlements of the keep, to find the ballista crews at their posts with the torsion weapons ready and bolts standing by with fuses primed.

Behind the line of five ballista stood two catalo trebuchets also loaded and primed and awaiting his orders as to targets. Tom surveyed the harbor. He could see their own ships setting sail with his friends on board and six sleek low Dows racing to intercept them. But they had other plans as well and two turned into the wind and came alongside one of the marker buoys that Tom used for ranging his weapons. They hooked the buoys out of the water and were trying to cut their moorings.

He would make it hard for them. One of the Dows was trying to remove his farthest buoy. It was at extreme range but worth a try. Tom spoke to the trebuchet officer and then in turn to each of the captains of the ballista. They turned their weapons to tried and tested settings and fired. A bit ragged thought Tom, as six ballista bolts traced an arc from their oil-soaked fuses toward the small ship.

They toiled for an hour. Their weapons took a toll on their enemies and became more accurate as more ships crowded into the river to disgorge men and equipment and soon the side of the river was teeming with sailors and boats ferrying men ashore.

Tom focused his fire on the black and silver trimmed ships that followed after the Dows in the attack. There were also others that were painted red and orange. Tom made an educated guess that these were the ships of the magic-wielders they had encountered. His guess was soon confirmed as red and gold shapes left their decks and flew toward the castle.

As soon as Tom saw these creatures he yelled for archers to the parapets, but he was soon faced with a new menace. Several large warships, quinqueremes, had rowed into range with their catapults and began to hurl burning balls of oil-soaked cloth at the castle. The three long, war galleys with two torsion catapults each fired their weapons intermittently. Tom's ballista crews never knew when one of the deadly projectiles would fly over the battlements. They were heavy with lead centers and burning oil-soaked cloth wrapped around the lead.

There was a double danger, the harm the lead projectile could cause and the fire which spread from the burning oil on impact. One hit a ballista crew. The weapon was damaged, and four men were badly hurt.

Tom set the archers to shoot at the wyvern and warn of incoming missiles. "Down!" called a watcher and a missile roared overhead. As they all ducked for cover two of the vermillion and gold dragons swooped on the battlements.

The last flotilla to arrive in the river was made up of slow, heavy, transport ships. Tom guessed that these were the most dangerous of all because they would carry troops and siege engines.

Tom's men on the battlements were under constant attack from the flying creatures and the sea-borne artillery. Their own fire was barely half what it had been. They were being worn down.

Tom looked out from the parapet at the scene below. A well-planned attack was in progress. He could see some of the troops they had fought two weeks before at Thorton Green, but there were others, legions of the same men they had seen before at Cair Neren: dog-soldiers named because of the devices on their shields and their wolf shaped helms, but also for their companions. Already ashore were two great dog-shaped creatures. Tom knew what they were, Goroths from Geitor in the far north, in-spirited by the Jungari in foul rites by the covens; the height of a man and the weight of two. But Tom knew it wasn't just their power in battle that was to be feared.

This was no raid. These armies were intent on their destruction and conquest. Tom turned to see General Gorian standing behind his left shoulder, 'What do you think this means General?'

The elderly soldier had a bad leg and had taken a while to reach the battlements. He stood now like a rock amid the confusion on the battlements as men fought off the attacking wyvern and screamed with pain as Corriian artillery crashed among them killing and maiming his defenders

"This is an invasion, Tom. I have feared this, since the Corrii were driven off last year."

You need to give orders for the cavalry at the fort to get mobile. We need their help but they should not be used defending walls – their real value is in remaining mobile and hitting the enemy where they are weak. Tom's heart sank. Tillion, the young cavalry officer from Cair Neren was below organizing the defense. Tom knew they would need his help. And he had to admit he hoped he would be beside them in the battle that was to come. Every skilled soldier was needed. He nodded.

"Can you give the orders, general? What about Brian and his cavalry?" But he knew the answer.

Below there was confusion as the horsemen in the castle were getting mounted and the gate was being opened long enough for them to sortie before the castle was besieged.

Brian still had several wounds that were not fully healed but he could ride. The horsemen were formed up ready for the sortie when he noticed his wife on a horse behind him.

"Gill, you cannot come with us!"

Gillian nudged her horse forward. "If you can fight them mounted, I certainly can. And somebody has to look after you."

The gates opened and Tillion led out the cavalry, there was no time to argue. They were surrounded by moving horses. They followed the others out.

Tillion rode to the town. He halted his battalion behind the hill overlooking the river, temporarily out of sight of their enemies as they made their landing. He went forward with his lieutenant and saw parties of dog soldiers moving up the hill from the river. They had a chance to strike hard now before the companies were ordered into defensive formations that could form a shield wall.

Tillion returned to the line of horsemen and began to give his orders. Then he saw Gillian.

"What are you doing here?" Gillian could see her cousin was none too pleased. She stuck out her chin and looked him straight in the eye.

"If I am going to die today, I will die with my husband." Tillion noticed she had a bow over her shoulder; there wasn't time to argue.

"Use your bow; stay with the archers! Neren Company to the right; New-castle company to the left. Form up! Charge!"

The horsed companies came over the crest of the hill, Tillion leading his horsemen from Cair Neren and Brian leading the local cavalry.

The invaders were not prepared but reacted almost instantly and closed ranks with lances forward but there was still time for the horsemen. Their enemies were still in scattered groups and although their centurions shouted orders and hastily pushed men into line. They had not expected a cavalry attack.

The cavalry crashed through the ranks with fearful effect. Lances splintered as they tore through the packed soldiery and mounted archers took a toll on the men that tried to reform. But as the cavalry tried to form up for another attack, grey forms came out from among the ranks and ran into the space between the soldiers and the horsemen. There was one very large grimulf. He stopped and stood in the middle of the strand. There seemed to be a faint glow around him. The Archgrimulf Voniok bent all his thought on them. Terror came from him in waves and the horses went mad in their fright. Some threw their riders and fled, Gillian managed to keep her seat, but she could not make her horse turn back he was careering away from the thing as fast as he could run. She didn't know where Brian was, and she couldn't slow her horse. She clutched handfuls of mane and dug her knees into its sides. She felt sure that if she fell, she would certainly die.

Somewhere in the back of Gillian's mind quiet words were trying to get through but her terror brooked no intruding thoughts. But then the quiet voice said more loudly, "Brian." and Gillian heard.

She clutched at the reins that were flying loose and tried to slow the horse.

Tom stood next to general Gorian and the two watched in dismay as their cavalry fled from the eldritch, canine phantom standing alone on the strand.

"What is it? It is driving the horses mad."

Gorian sighed, a resigned sort of sigh that was not yet without hope.

"An enemy Tom, just another enemy. And you and I have fought many enemies before. Come on, let's go below to the wall and see that the fortifications are as strong as may be. That is where the next assault will come."

Gorian turned to the artillery captain. "Terry, do your best. Try and reduce the artillery fire from the ships. If you cannot stop it, make them pay for being in your range."

"Will do, Sir! Good luck Tom!"

Tom detoured to his apartments in the keep and sought out Lettie. He found her with Kirin. She had her arm around Kirin who had tears in her eyes.

"Lettie, Kirin, we have to talk."

Kirin wiped her eyes on her sleeve and waited for Tom to say what he had to say.

"The cavalry have been driven off - toward the forest; hopefully some of them will escape. It doesn't look good. We haven't had enough time to send messengers to Cair Neren for help and it would probably take too long anyway.

The help they might have sent would have been cavalry and they were here; already beaten and chased off by the Corrii. I am going to join the defense of the walls. We will hold out as long as we can.

I want you to take Dillon and get out the secret way."

"Lettie looked pale; she had no answer. He couldn't be serious. She wanted to ask what he proposed to do, but she knew. He would stay and fight and give them a better chance of escape."

Kirin read all this on both their faces.

"Tom we will not be the only women. There are lots of women in the keep – some with children as small as Dillon."

"Yes, there are. But they are not the wives of Tom Roper and Norrimae Jung. They hate us; particularly Norri and they will take out their hate on you. There is danger for the other women but even the Corrii will surely not kill helpless women and children."

"Are you sure of that?" said Kirin.

"No, but that doesn't change my mind, you two and Jenny should get out before the Corrii are too numerous and even the secret exit is discovered."

Lettie picked up Dillon who had been silent, maybe sensing the tension in the room. She looked at Tom in despair.

"I just want to stay here; with you and take what comes."

Tom looked at her and smiled a rueful smile.

"I know, darling. But we have Dillon to think about. And I cannot leave." Lettie threw herself into Tom's arms and pressed her face against the hard rings of his chain mail until it left an imprint on the cheek.

Then Tom released her.

"Go, both of you. It's the best chance. Take Jenny if you can find her quickly and get to the tunnel. Try and get into the forest; then go north."

Tom set off down the stairs with Lettie watching him go.

"I love you always, Tom…"

He ran down the stairs two steps at a time, knowing that it was very probably the last time he would see his wife and son.

7

Gillian's choice

*G*illian dragged with all her strength on the reins; when she looked back Tillion was also struggling to control his mount, glancing back at the fallen men. The rest of the cavalry were in full career towards the forest.

Gill turned her horse with difficulty and came up close enough to Tillion to see what he was looking at. Then she saw Brian and she also saw Voniok. The Archgrimulf was coming up the strand toward the men who had fallen from their horses. Some were limping and struggling to get away from the canine phantasm that now glowed an aerie green in the afternoon light.

She saw Brian, struggling to get to his feet and then falling again on his bad leg that appeared to be broken.

Gill dug her heals into her horse and with a force of will that neither she nor the horse knew she possessed, directed it toward her husband. The great grimulf came toward them and as it came closer opened its mouth in what could only pass for, a grin, "Despair, daughter of a prince. The hour of your death approaches. You have no power or weapon against me."

At that moment Gillian became aware of something strange. The fear had lessened. No, that wasn't it. The fear was still there. The *terror* had gone, and in its place, the quiet voice spoke strongly. "You do not face this evil alone, Gillian".

She slipped off her horse still clutching the reins in her left hand; she drew her sword. She had no idea what she could do against this thing. She led her horse toward it.

Then several things happened at once. There was some sort of confusion among the landing troops. It seemed that a launch full of troops had struck a rock or submerged branch and was sinking with much confusion.

There was a large eagle soaring over the troops and they didn't like it for some reason. The great bird gave out its long screeching cry which seemed temporarily to unnerve the Corrii and especially the Archgrimulf.

The beast turned its head and looked at the sky. For a moment it just looked like a mangy, worn-out old dog. Gillian roared at it. "Get away from my husband, or I will kill you."

Voniok turned and stumbled away down the braeside. Tillion looked at Gill with new wonder. "What did you do?"

Gill looked at him and with the simple honesty they had always known together since their shared childhood at Cair Neren. "I don't think I actually did anything. Something has distracted it!"

Gillian ran to Brian and helped him up. She knew she had to get him onto her horse. She pulled on the reins and the frightened beast stood still enough, trembling. Tillion wound the reins of his own horse around his wrist and together they half lifted, half helped Brian onto Gillian's horse.

"You ride behind me Gill and keep tight hold of the reins. We will try for the forest and then decide what to do", said Tillion. Brian was in obvious pain but managing to keep his seat on the horse. Gillian climbed nimbly up behind Tillion, and they turned the horses for the forest hoping to make their escape while the grimulf was distracted.

But no sooner had they begun to follow the other retreating horsemen than they heard screams coming from the forest. Something was in there. The screams seemed to be from their own men. They veered north, by unspoken mutual agreement and kicked their horses into a gallop. Brian was struggling to keep his seat, but they had to escape.

When Gillian looked back. She saw two men running from the forest and a third still mounted. Behind them two huge ape-like beasts gave chase. One leapt and caught the hapless soldier from behind swinging him around to face it with terror. In a single swift motion, it drew a scimitar from within its mane and cut off his head. Gill didn't wait to see what happened to the other two. She cried out to Tillion and spurred her horse onward.

The tunnel was dark and wet, Kirin went ahead holding a lamp with a lighted candle; Lettie followed struggling with little Dillon in the dark cramped space and Jenny followed behind with another light. They had brought little food and few weapons. Kirin brought her bow. Norri had spent hours with her teaching her how to use it and she was passable with it at a pinch. She had a light sword that Norri had made for her. Bow, quiver, and sword were draped over her shoulder to prevent them catching on the rough stone of the tunnel walls. Jenny had also brought a long knife and was carrying the bag with their food and water-bottles. It was all they had been able to find quickly. Fortunately, they had managed to get to the storeroom with the entrance to the secret tunnel unnoticed. Kirin felt bad. She would have liked to help the other women and children escape but knew that Tom was right. They were the main targets: she and Lettie. The Corrii would love to capture the wives of the heroes of the last conflict. The commodore had warned that this was the Corrii way.

They struggled along the low narrow tunnel for what seemed a very long time and came to a stop at a solid wall. There was a shovel against the stone and the roof, which seemed to be made of earth, was supported by wooden beams which were locked into culverts in the limestone.

Lettie looked back down the tunnel. "I think I can smell smoke".

Kirin gave her lamp to Lettie and put her shoulder against the closest beam. She pushed and it would not move. Lettie lay Dillon down on the stony floor and came to help. With both of them pushing the beam moved a finger width. They continued to shove, and Jenny held up both the lights. Finally, one end of the beam was free, and the large piece of Oak crashed to the floor. They all stood silent for a long while. What if someone heard the sound of the falling beam?

When there was no sound, they worked on the second beam. This time they got it free more easily and laid it beside the other. Kirin took the small shovel and began to dig at the earth roof. Fine soil fell down all around her and got in her eyes. It did not take long before a crack of daylight appeared, and they stood still, listening. There was no sound, so Kirin dug away a bit more earth. The roof was too high for her to climb out so she propped one of the beams against the wall of the tunnel and pushed her head out through the leaf litter. There was no one in sight. So she climbed out and reached down to help Lettie out. Next

Jenny passed the baby out who was fussing. Jenny passed the bag out and then climbed out herself. Kirin slipped the bow off her shoulder and bent it. An enemy could appear from anywhere and Dillon was making just enough noise to give them away.

Jenny had just climbed out of the tunnel when they heard a voice. "Aarh sohh ther fleeing rarrts harve finnarlee cummm. I harve hard arr lorng wait."

The three girls turned toward the voice and a huge, grey grimulf stepped out of the bushes. Kirin reached for an arrow and tried to fit it to the string with trembling fingers. Jenny drew her knife and stepped in front of Lettie and Kirin to give her friend time to draw her bow. But the monster did not attack at once. They could see every muscle was tensed ready to spring but it only kept low and stalked almost casually toward them with its unblinking eyes fixed on Kirin. It had a knowing grin on its canine face that showed it had little fear of the three girls. Since the pup had been taken from its dying mother on the slopes of Mount Onfrening in Geitor the grimulf had encountered many enemies, all far more dangerous than these. Before the he-grimulf attacked it would cripple its adversaries. Its eyes pierced with a power that mesmerized and terrified its victims. Kirin found she had no strength to draw the bow string. Jenny felt the strength ebb from the hand that held the dagger. Cold paralyzing terror griped them, and Lettie clutched the crying baby to her breast.

The grimulf took two paces nearer. It looked at Kirin.

"I aarm queeck arnd yoo harve burt warne shot. Cumm weeth mee arnd yoo weell leeve arnd bee arr slaave, meess arnd yoo weell arll dee. Ther child ees helpleess – I weell tearrr eet aparrt larst."

But a sound from behind it distracted the grimulf. It stopped and looked around and gave Kirin a moment to draw her bow. Somehow, she knew that if she didn't shoot now, she would not be able to and released her arrow just as the grimulf turned back toward them. The sun broke through the clouds and the tip of Kirin's arrow seemed to gleam brightly in its short flight. It flew true and straight and struck the grimulf in the side of its chest. It rounded on Kirin again; the look on its face was of surprise. How had this weak, insignificant enemy struck it such a blow?

The arrow had not killed the grimulf, but it was uncertain. There was the sound again. The *Archgrimulf Verchimore* felt it was surrounded by enemies. He turned but saw nothing. Then as he turned back to his prey, Kirin and Jenny attacked and two flashing blades bit into the sinews of the Corriian warrior-dog. It gnashed at its attackers, but Kirin was too quick, and a second thrust of her weapon drove through its neck spraying blood everywhere.

Kirin jumped back away from the huge canine teeth and watched in shock as the brute slumped down in the leaves emitting foul smelling smoke from its mouth. The three girls grabbed their bundles and ran, not waiting to see any more.

They ran up the hillside into the dense scrub that covered the cliff-top above the river. They kept low and did their best to stay hidden. The dense scrub was almost impassable. The short distance took most of the morning. Lettie struggled on holding Dillon who seemed to have fallen asleep in her sling. But he was a dead weight around her neck.

The branches of the coastal heath were so tangled that they made plenty of noise anway. And when Dillon woke up, he fussed and cried, and they had to stop long enough for Lettie to give him a drink. Jenny gave Lettie some water from their water bottle and stinted herself and Kirin by my mutual agreement. They did not know how long before they could get more, and Lettie needed to drink so that she could feed the baby. If he cried, he could give them away.

Once Dillon had fed, he seemed more settled, and they started again. The scrub gave way to larger trees and the going became easier. They also felt more exposed.

Then they saw the north road ahead. It was clear. They decided to risk the crossing. Kirin strung her bow again and had an arrow ready. She left Lettie with Jenny and moved as quietly as possible from tree to tree wrapped in her green cloak. Norri had said it was the only colour for the wife of a forester. It was a good choice.

As she approached the road she watched for any movement. There was none. Had she known it there was a Corriian picket not three hundred paces north, but they were around a long bend and well out of sight of that part of the road.

Kirin watched for a while and then, when there was no sign of enemies returned to Jenny and Lettie.

"The road is clear. But there is a bank on the other side that is quite steep. If we want to get deeper into the forest, we need to go a bit south. That means, back toward the Cair but I cannot see around the next bend and the road seems clear south."

"We'll have to chance it," said Jenny. "Come on Lettie, while Dillon is quiet, we'll make a dash for it and try and get deep into the forest before nightfall. We could use a stream, to collect some more water."

"Is the water low," asked Lettie. She had not noticed that Jenny and Kirin did not drink.

Kirin forced a smile, "We only brought one water bottle. I was more worried about getting away than supplies for the journey. Maybe that was a mistake." The truth was that her mouth was very dry since the encounter with the grimulf.

They worked their way through the forest so as to come out further down from the place where Kirin checked he road. As they came to the edge of the trees, they saw a body on the opposite verge and a small dark bundle beside it. They slipped behind the bole of a large oak tree and watched but nothing moved. Kirin thought she heard a sniff and a little sob. On an impulse she slipped out from behind the tree and quickly crossed the road.

A man lay there, dead. Beside him a small, tear-streaked face looked at her from under a thin cloak. The little boy made no effort to move. Kirin wondered about this. Perhaps she didn't seem very threatening.

She stepped closer, scanned the road in either direction and, then knelt down beside the small child.

"What is your name?"

"Mort." Kirin had almost guessed already. She remembered Norri's description of the little boy at Wenston's tavern.

"Is this your Pa?"

The little boy nodded. The man lay prone on a dark patch of earth, soaked with his own blood. He seemed to have been cut down fleeing. There was something underneath him. Kirin pulled at a leather strap and removed the bag.

Then she signaled to Jenny and Lettie to come. Both emerged from the trees, crossed the road.

Kirin took the small dirty hand. "Come along Mort, we cannot do anything for your Pa now. We must try and get to safety."

Mort obeyed and allowed her to lead him into the trees with a lingering glance back at the prone body of his father.

When they were deep into the trees on the eastern side of the road, Jenny gave her a worried look.

"Who is the little boy, Kirin?"

"He was lying with his father. It seems that his father died trying to escape with his son. I believe he is the little boy Norri tried to help. Norri had a run-in with the little boy's father as a result."

Jenny saw Lettie's face and said what she could see Lettie was thinking, "Won't he slow us down Kirin? If the Corrii were going to harm him surely, they would have done so already."

"Maybe, but I won't leave him behind. Norri came home very worried about this child and if he were here, he would want me to help Mort."

Lettie shrugged. "Let's get deeper into the forest and try to find some water."

Kirin led Mort by the hand, and they trudged deeper into the trees.

As the day waned, they stopped to have a bite of their food. Kirin gave Lettie the water bottle first and then offered it to Mort. The little boy was obviously very thirsty but seemed to judge the situation and took only a small gulp of their precious water.

Lettie then offered the water to Kirin. "You have to drink Kirin, or none of us will manage to get away."

Kirin took a small sip to moisten her lips then gave the rest of the water to Jenny.

"We need to find the stream. It flowed east to west and came out near Norri's cabin on the Brae. It should be south of here."

At this point Mort who had been watching them and reached for the bag Kirin had put down when they stopped. He runtled around and found a water skin which he passed to Kirin with a smile.

Kirin smiled back. "That's wonderful. What else have you in there, Mort?"

Mort searched through the bag and brought out a small knife, a few small loaves of bread, a ham bone wrapped in a calico bag and some small pannikins.

Jenny ruffled the boy's head. "What a champion you are, Mort.
We will eat this food and keep the rest in reserve."

They ate their meager rations, a little bread and a slice of ham followed by a mouth full of water. It wasn't enough for three adults and a child who had walked all day but better than nothing.

When they had finished their food, Mort picked up one of the pannikins and crawled off under some bushes.

He was gone long enough for Kirin to become worried, but he returned with the pannikin full of sour-berries which he offered proudly to Kirin and then to Lettie and Jenny.

All the girls praised his resourcefulness and were even more impressed when he produced some fallen orkya nuts which he had tied into his cloak.

Kirin found a couple of stones and helped Mort break the open the hard shells. The nuts would be nicer roasted, but they had no time or means for a fire and the nuts were rich and nutritious as they were. Mort's berries and nuts made them all feel better. Lettie felt very mean now remembering that she had thought the little boy would be a burden.

They settled down in a pile of leaves. Mort pulled his thin cloak tightly around him and lay down beside Kirin. Kirin felt a genuine affection for the little boy and wrapped her cloak over him as she sat propped against the tree trunk, making an attempt to keep watch.

She woke hearing Dillon fussing. Mort was awake also and seemed to be listening.

The place where they had bivouacked was a small space underneath an orkya tree and was reasonably concealed by the ferns. This was good as they heard voices not far away. Lettie quickly put Dillon to her breast to keep him quiet, while Kirin and Mort peeped out over the top of a fallen branch surrounded by ferns.

There were soldiers and grimulves tracking something through the forest. The beasts were crashing through the ferns followed by a party of Corriian soldiers, heavily armed; making no effort to keep silent.

A stone launched from a trebuchet struck the hastily erected wooden palisade on the top of the defenses and reduced it to kindling.

Soon after, another struck part of the wall and stove in several of the stones not yet set with mortar. Tom knew they could not withstand this punishment for long. He looked out from the walls of the castle at the troops formed up below.

They were attaching siege ladders to small carts and dragging the carts toward the walls. This meant they had to man-handle them over the rocks and around the stunted trees below the walls. These obstacles only seemed to slow the Corrii down, not deter them. Tom ran down the steps to the courtyard. He ordered all the men available to take shelter beneath the walls and await his signal that the attack was beginning, to man the battlements.

He then returned to the top of the wall, hunkered down and watched as the Corrii prepared their attack. When the siege ladders were almost within range of the walls, a hail of missiles were launched at the defenders: catapult stones wrapped in burning, oil-soaked cloth, ballista bolts and arrows with oiled wadding, lighted and trailing smoke as they flew over then walls.

Fires sprang up inside the castle and men looked anxiously at one another as they gripped their weapons, awaiting the order to man the walls. They could hear the shouting on the other side of the defenses and knew that battle was imminent.

As the ladders approached the walls with guys attached to draw them up, Tom gave the order, and a horn was blown. The defenders rushed for the stairs and ran along the top of the wall under the Corriian barrage.

Smoke rose all around them from fires burning in the courtyard below. It seemed that there were even fires in the keep. Tom saw fires in the slat windows. He hoped Kirin and Lettie had gotten away in time.

He saw a place where the top of the wall had been torn away by a hit from a catapult. A couple of dozen Corriian legionaries were lifting a ladder up against the gap. Tom nudged the young soldier next to him and they ran to the place to reinforce the defenses. Even as they ran the other soldier was struck in the hip by an arrow and fell. Tom reached the gap and called for others to assist him.

As he looked over the parapet, he saw that the legionaries were better equipped than the last time he had fought against them. They were better armored. They had helmets with visors to protect against arrows and better shoulder armor. They also had large oval shields that offered better protection. They could stand before walls and be impervious to arrows. This was not the armor of troops planning a long march. It was made for the assault of his castle.

Their information about the state of the building works was obviously up to date. Their ladders were mounted on small carts and had grapnels at the top so that they could be pushed up the steep uneven slope below the castle. They were not very long but could easily reach the incomplete walls of the castle. It was all perfectly planned.

Tom had little time to think about Lettie. He was on his own! Brian had gone with the cavalry, Norri and Gordy had taken ship with the

Commodore and Lettie would be trying to escape through the secret tunnel with Kirin. But he was Warden of the Southern End; entrusted by the king to govern and protect its people. Tom looked out at the forces massing against them and began to despair. How could they hold them off? He had seen the phantom-like dog on the battlefield and its effect on the horses. Surely it could do the same to his defenders. Tom began to feel the despair of an animal that sees that it is going to die; his arms felt weak, and his mind recalled good times with Norri when they were boys; he remembered dancing with Lettie at the summer dance and the celebration of their wedding that soon followed; the birth of Little Dillon and the wonder of holding his son in his arms.

At the thought of that little boy, something stirred in Tom that changed the nature of his despair. It was obvious that Cair Egleton would fall. The wall was not finished; their enemies had come too soon. The stones of the keep were strong but once their enemies had the outer wall, trebuchet would batter them down. But for the sake of the little boy and his mother, Tom would fight. The new feeling crept into his mind without him noticing at first; the weakness in his arms went and he felt an irresistible urge to draw his sword. The blade slid from its scabbard with the ring of metal on metal. The soldiers around him heard and all looked at Tom. His face was hard as he saw his enemies forming up on the strand for the attack.

He turned to his own men and he saw face after face filled with fear and despair.

There was a young man there in an ill-fitting hauberk with a sword at his side. He was obviously unfamiliar with the spear he held.

"What's your name?"

"Gavin, my Lord."

"See those short battle axes? Get yourself one! When we fought the Corrii at Cair Neren, we found they were most vulnerable just as they came over the walls. Stand behind the parapet and lop them like a tree.

Have you chopped trees before?

"Yes, my Lord." Gavin didn't sound too certain.

"It's just the same." Everyone around them laughed. Gavin picked up an axe and made a few swings. He smiled at Tom.

Tom liked the young man. "Gavin, let's make them sorry they ever came to threaten us and ours!"

Below there was a sound of trumpets and yells as the legionaries surged forward.

The first two legionaries that came over the parapet were hacked down by Tom's sword and Gavin's axe.

Tom turned toward the wall to see another ladder crash onto the parapet. Moments later a Corriian face appeared over the top. He struck the man across the shoulder, and he fell. Moments later another legionary appeared. He hurled a burning torch at Tom to give himself time to gain the wall.

Tom fell back as the pitch from the torch spattered over his chest and face and burned his skin. He recovered enough to raise his shield against an axe blow and then everything went suddenly dark....

Tillion rode as fast as he could with Gillian trailing behind. Brian was obviously in pain and looked as if he would fall off the horse at any time. Blood pounded in his temples. It was urgent that they reach help as soon as possible and let the Thane, Gillian's father and the king know that the south was under serious attack; perhaps had already fallen.

They had no food or water and Cair Neren was four- or five-days' journey. After a couple of hours with no sign of pursuit they reined in their horses. Gill and Tillion dismounted and together helped Brian off the horse.

They laid him down on the grass beside the road and examined his leg. It was hard to say whether it was broken or not. Neither of them had any skill in healing. It was painful to the touch, and they decided to strap it as tight as possible and continue on. They helped Brian up onto Tillion's horse and led both horses deeper into the forest keeping the road in sight. The horses were too spent for anything else. The fear-filled flight had worn them out and the best they would be able to manage for a while would be a walk.

Gillian's hastily wiped tears were noticed by her cousin. "We should be away from danger by now. I have a flint and steel and we can make a fire to warm him when we stop. These trees are Orkya trees we may be able to find some fallen calyxes." It was lame, but Gillian needed some hope. They had a long journey ahead of them. Neither of them felt much up to scaling the huge trees to get the nuts the way their friend the forester did.

Some hours afterwards as evening fell, two dark shapes came to the place where they had bound Brian's leg. They dropped to all fours and sniffed the ground. Several gruff words were exchanged, and they continued along the trail that led deeper into the forest and on northward.

Gill and Tillion became increasingly worried about Brian and finally had to stop before he fell out of the saddle. They found a thicket nestled behind some larger trees. They tethered the horses and gathered some stones and wood for a fire. It took Tillion a while to get a spark to take in his tinder but finally the crushed wad of grass caught and Tillion blew them gently into a flame which he slipped under the pile of twigs and dry leaves he had prepared. Gill tended the tiny fire until it took, and they had a pile of glowing sticks and flames licking around some larger wood.

"Who are they?" said Inglamora as he sat high on a branch in the tops of an orkya tree.

"They are people of the valley," whispered Vinsolore. "It seems that one of them is hurt. Surely, they wouldn't risk a fire else."

"Is there any way we can help them without betraying our presence?" said the younger Driadora warrior.

"There are some bunches of nuts in this tree. When it is darker, I will take them down and place them where they may most easily be found." Then we will do all we can to protect them. The smoke from the castle in the valley that has been seen does not bode well. Maybe the people there have fallen to their enemies and these few are survivors. If so they may be pursued."

Inglamora walked lightly and easily out to the end of a long branch and returned with two clusters of orkya nuts. "Will these serve?"

"Well," said Vinsolore. "You are the lightest of foot. Can you climb down to the foot of that tree and lay them on the ground by the bole without being heard?"

"I think so," said the younger warrior and slipped over the edge of the branch.

Tillion reached for his sword hilt as he thought he saw a silent shadow slip behind a tree. He dropped his armful of firewood and watched silently for a while but heard nothing. He carefully explored the place where he had seen the shadow and saw nothing. On the ground he did find two bunches of orkya nuts in their characteristic grey-green calyxes.

After watching for a little longer, he returned to Gillian and Brian with his prizes and more wood for the fire.

"Close, but well done, Inglamora," said the other warrior.

"I did not expect he would stray in my direction searching for firewood before I could get back into the tree. But he has found the nuts. Else they may not have found them till morn or not at all."

Vinsolore smiled. "Well that it was you. I would not have been so quick. Now let us stay high and out of sight and see if we can guard them from their enemies. My spirit forebodes that their foes are not far behind them."

Both driadora warriors strung their bows and went quickly through the tops of the orkya trees to a lower place where they could hide and watch the approach to the camp below.

Tillion returned to the fire triumphant. "I found not one but two clusters of fallen orkya nuts. I don't know why Norri finds them so hard to gather. I just picked these up at the bottom of the tree. We can crack them and roast them. We will not have to sleep on such empty bellies." So saying he heaped more wood on the fire heedless of the danger and when it had burned down somewhat removed the orkya nuts from their calyxes hit them with a stone to make a crack in the hard shell and placed them on the coals on the very edge of the fire. The crack in the shell was to facilitate easier opening once they were roasted. If cracked, they would split open more in the heat and they could get at the nuts.

It wasn't a large meal but much better than nothing and even Brian seemed to appreciate them. Tillion gave Brian water from a skin he always carried behind his saddle and Gillian fetched her own. They knew that water was almost as important in a battle as weapons. So at least they did have water- skins tied to their saddles.

Later that night Vinsolore's words proved true. The foes he feared found the camp. Inglamora was the first to see them, no more than shades that blended into the glaucous tangle; hidden from the moonlight. They walked sometimes upright, sometimes on all fours as they approached the camp where the fire had burned down to a pile of grey ashes speckled with glowing red embers. Gillian was supposed to be on watch, but she had fallen asleep, slumped against a damp log she had chosen to make herself uncomfortable enough to keep sleep at bay, but to no avail.

Moments after Inglamora's warning both the driadora warriors had fire hardened arrows ready and watched for an opportunity to draw and shoot. But the two creeping figures stopped, whether aware of being watched or simply sizing up the situation it was not clear. It took a long time for them to move. Inglamora's fingers became cramped as they held the arrow to the bowstring.

Then the two figures began to creep toward the three sleeping travelers. Inglamora saw Vinsolore draw his bow. The well-oiled forest ash did not creak as it was bent. Inglamora also drew the arrow back to her chin. Both released together.

In the silent forest, the passage or the arrows could easily be heard but there was only a moment to react. Both gordril flinched, but too late. One was struck in the leg; the other lifted its arm just in time to deflect the arrow aimed at its heart and was pierced through its sinewy arm. Both cried out in shock and fury.

Two more arrows were on the string in moments but the gordrill slipped behind trees which they guessed would hide them from the unexpected attackers.

The cries aroused Gillian and she had her bow strung and ready and hid behind the bole of the orkya tree, calling a warning to Tillion and Brian.

Gill scanned the forest for signs of her attackers. She could hear a hissing sound coming from a clump of oaks and looked for a target. Seeing movement, she drew her bow and released. She missed but not by much. The gordrill were searching the branches trying to see their hidden enemy but could see nothing. What was more their quarry was now aroused and dangerous. They were also badly damaged. Even their magically restored bodies could be damaged and impede their ability to fight. They withdrew nursing their wounds.

The two driadora warriors shunned sleep and guarded the three travelers until morning when they mounted and rode off through the forest.

"What do we do now?" asked the younger.

"Report to commander Velarentes and if we can, warn other scout parties to help as they can." The two ran along the branches, silently communicating with the trees that their help was needed to send the message to other warriors watching the north road.

8

Ibinithy

The *Swiftsure* was handling the conditions well. Reynolds had all possible sail set to try and escape the Corriian vessels that were following in a wide arc: some further out to sea; some closer inshore so that there was no possibility of escape by out-maneuvering them.

The *Suresafe* was a cable's length behind and inshore to stay out of Reynold's wind. They were making for open sea in the hope that their better ocean-going construction would enable them to carry more sail than their pursuers and escape. It didn't seem to be working. The Corrii were fine sailors, and the sleek Dows were fast even with reduced sail. They could see the waves crashing over their decks – but they did not seem deterred as the hunters closed on their quarry.

Several of the small ships were painted black with strange devices painted on their sails. That meant *gothships* of the covens and coven magic users. They all knew the dangers if these got too close. In the last war the *gothships* had sunk Reynold's own ship the *Seastorm* using a black cloud that blinded and terrified the men and set fires all over the deck. Now the ships that followed threatened to do the same to his new ship.

Gordy stood at the poop-deck railing watching them; trying to work out whether they were gaining at all on their pursuers. It was difficult to tell. The black hulls rose and fell in the heavy seas. For a while they seemed to be falling behind, then reappear closer. He turned to Norri, "We need some more arrows."

"We should talk to the marines. What do we do again if they send the black cloud against us?"

"Cover your face with a garment made by someone who loves you. You have to completely cover your eyes, nose and mouth. Tom worked that out. I don't know how he did it."

Norri looked back at the black ship with the strange image painted on its foresail, "I wonder if they will use the same weapon again or some other."

This seemed to shock Gordy, "I never thought of that."

"One thing about the Corrii, they are no fools. They will not use a weapon if they think that we have a good defense against it."

Gordy slumped against the bulkhead. "That's a cheery thought. We are being chased by enemies that probably have weapons we haven't ever seen before."

"I guess at least they are following us which means that whatever they do it will be against us and not against Jenny and Kirin."

"You do have a knack for summing up a situation, Norri. If they keep chasing us – I will be worried what they are going to pull out of their nasty bag of magic tricks, and if they stop, now I will be worried about what they will do to Jenny."

Norri smiled a rueful smile. "Sorry."

Gordy chuckled and slapped Norri on the back. "At least the longer they follow us the further they are away from the people we love."

Gordy looked back and pointed to the closest of the black ships. "Look! I think they are up to something."

On board a black ship in their wake, two cowled figures stood talking to three priests in horned masks and animal skins. The small group radiated power and menace. Even the crew of their own ship kept their distance. The priests smelled terrible as if they kept something dead upon their person.

Their ship was the newest and fastest of the vessels of the covenmen. They were making good speed and looked to overtake the fleeing *Swiftsure* which was now behind the *Suresafe* that had gained more advantage from a freshening northeast breeze that had reached her first.

At dusk, just as the last golden glow of the sun disappeared from the horizon, Denquinar was standing at the poop deck railing watching the closest of the gothships that was now just a dark shadow in the growing darkness. As he watched, he saw a small fire kindle into flame. The fire ran down the bow of the gothship and crept toward them like a flaming rope across the water.

Captain Reynolds looked enquiringly at the commodore. Denquinar went pale. "It is the gorefire. It can turn any living thing or anything that has been alive inside out and burn it to ashes by the power of the magic alone."

The rope of fire ran across the waves toward them, gaining speed as it came. The two magicians of the coven, Morimner and Gamlosser were deep in their trance. They could see the beloved Jungari *Be-el Corrimi*. The Jungari too concentrated its power. It could feel power resisting it, but that power was weak and dissipating. In the minds of the coven masters the spell was reaching out to the wood of the *Swiftsure* and the hemp of her canvass. It would consume all. The wood of her planks still had the oils of life drawn up from the warm earth: and then there were the men, the spell sought their very lifeblood; it would make it boil within their veins.

Bentonius said the men of Herelstrom had found a defense against the dwimmerinds that had so confounded their ships at sea. But no-one could resist the gorefire. Morimner and Gamlosser had spent months perfecting a spell, once only the specialized skill of a few, used rarely and kept secret. It was used mainly as an instrument of torture when there was a need to cause unremitting pain while leaving little external evidence, save the red weals on the skin which eventually healed. To make it a weapon of war - they had to learn to send the fiery rope long distance in search of living things to burn and this required deep concentration.

The masters stood on the bows of their ship deeper and deeper in the trance and the rope of fire sped across the remaining distance to the *Swiftsure*. Denquinar looked at Norri. His face was white. He knew what the spell could do. Was this the fate that Benhaust had predicted – the day of his torment and death? What of his son…

Surely after all that Norrimae Jung had done this could not be *his* end.

Norri saw Denquinar's consternation and thought about Eli's prophecy. He looked up and saw a speck high in the evening sky and the barely audible cry of an eagle.

At the moment, when the fire approached their ship there was a great stirring in the water. A great serpent head, all draggled with seaweed or what looked like it, rose out of the water near the bows of the gothship.

Gordy, Denquinar and the captain were all watching the fire. It was Gordy who first saw the head. "It looks as if another player has just joined the game."

They all looked up. The head rose out of the water on a neck like a huge tree trunk and the creature's huge mouth opened to reveal rows of needle-sharp teeth. The crew of the gothship saw the monster and cowered behind masts and bulkheads. Only the coven masters were left – still deep in the gorefire trance.

With frightening speed, the great head darted down, and the jaws closed around the cowled figures on the forecastle. When the head came up again, legs and arms could be seen hanging limply for a moment before disappearing into the giant maw. The gorefire was gone.

The creature turned sideways to reveal a body almost as long as the ship, with a tall, spined fin on its back. A great tail rose out of the water and crashed along the rear deck like a whip. Great spines on its tail drove into the trysail mast and pulled the ship over so that water flooded its deck. Crewmen were caught in the rushing water and thrown into the sea. The black ship had turned into the wind and lay dead in the water. The monster dived and churned in the water finding and consuming the hapless crewmen, throwing them high into the air and catching them in its jaws.

Norri watched for a while in horror. He saw that Gresham had all sail set and the Suresafe running as close to the wind as he dared. He turned to Denquinar who seemed deep in thought. "What is it, Commodore?"

The question seemed to jolt Denquinar out of his thoughts. "Jokes! They like Jokes! It is an ibinithy. I have never seen one, but stories hold that if they are not hungry, they will exchange jokes with sailors." Saying this Denquinar ran to Reynolds at the tiller, "Come about! We don't want it to give chase. Our only hope is to converse with it. Signal the Suresafe to do the same."

Then turning to Gordy, "Gordy, think of your best jokes. Hail it when it rises and shout Yo. Ibinithy. Yo, ho, ho; as loud as you can!"

Gordy whistled through his teeth. "No pressure, Commodore, easy to be funny when you are about to be eaten."

They looked around at Denquinar who was arguing with the captain. "Come about, Captain. You cannot outrun it. It can swim much faster than we can sail. We are closer than the Suresafe and the other Corrii ships have turned tail. We are its closest prey. If we run it will give chase. You saw what it did to the gothship!"

Reynolds was unconvinced and stood clutching the side rail in consternation but there was a slight eddy in the waves between them and the stricken gothship. There was little time.

"Come about!" he yelled to the men on the tiller. The *Swiftwure* turned into the wind and her way fell off her. Every eye scanned the waves for the telltale flurry of the beast rising.

Then it came. The great head with green and purple scales and a mop of draping seaweed-like flaps of skin rose out of the water a cable's length away.

Gordy leaned over the rail and called, "Yo Ibinithy, has eating those magicians given you indigestion?"

The monster swam up close to the ship, its green eyes the size of dinner plates, deep and sentient as it swam up and came close to Gordy - who did not flinch. Its jaws opened in what could have been a smile. It held Gordy with its eyes and in a very deep voice said, "Yo, man, they wore too much clothing by half. I think I have a piece of cloth stuck in my teeth."

Gordy looked up. "I will try and hook it out if you promise to try not to eat me for my reward."

"I will promise to try, friend but you must remember that I am both the devourer of all living things and a soft-hearted soul who shrinks from causing anyone any harm. I can be one in one moment and the other a moment later. Whales and fish are my food, but I do enjoy a juicy sailor for a change."

"Gordy kept his eyes fixed on the green dinner plates. "That is well, friend, for in truth, I am no sailor. Captain, pass me that boat hook?"

Reynolds signaled to the main deck and a sailor ran to Gordy with a long pole. Gordy reached up and hooked a piece of black cloth out of the Ibinith's jaws. He tried his first line. "Yo, Ibinithy. Is it not a great joke that the Corrii magician who wore this robe sailed so far – just for dinner!"

The Ibinithy laughed a deep throated laugh that rocked the ship, "Indeed friend, served hot and sizzling as well."

"Was the meat juicy, Ibinithy, even if the pastry was tough?"

"Very juicy, man, with a delightful hint of spice."

Gordy was almost overcome by the foul breath. "They are not all magicians, Ibinithy. Other ships contain fat soldiers, brought here by us, at great trouble; for your dining pleasure."

The Ibinith laughed again. "You have good wit, human. Such a wit should not be eaten. Shall we be friends?"

Gordy saw something in the monster's eyes when it said this, and his fear evaporated. Instead, pity rose in his heart. "Ibinithy, I am a man who makes jokes at times of fear and sadness. So, I venture, are you."

The Ibinithy bowed its head and did indeed look sad. "You are very wise, human. Indeed, once I was such a MAN."

Gordy was surprised but drawn to the big sad eyes. "How came you to be an ibinithy, friend?"

"I was wise and yet a fool. In seeking ever greater wisdom I dabbled in things no man was meant to know. In finding the answers I sought, I trusted spirits no man can trust. I gained great knowledge but lost my humanity. I became like the great spirits of the watery places, but I could not transcend to their realm. Instead, I was cursed to dwell in the oceans of this world, hungry and friendless until the coming of the end. I eat but am never full; I long for companionship but find none."

Gordy reached out his hand toward the creature. "Are you able to be a friend Ibinithy?'

"In truth, man, I do not know. This I do know - those with the black robes sacrifice too much to gain the little power they have, and they will not like it now that they go to meet the masters that they serve. I have lived many years in this form and yet I am glad that I have been spared their fate. Now I hunger and seek for some other answer.

I seek; I seek,

I hunger and I seek.

Not for food for this great belly,

But for other food, I seek."

Gordy turned as Norri suddenly spoke. "Ibinithy, is it the True Father of all men that you seek?"

The ibinithy turned suddenly and gazed at Norri. "I know your voice!"

Norri was abashed. "How so Ibinithy? How could you know my voice?"

The great brown eyes were fixed on Norri. "You spoke the word that shook the world!

Never was there a more passionate word.

I have learned to hear the voices in the world of the spirits, where sometimes also the shining ones come.

I heard you call on the One, the true Father. The word was followed by the earthquake and the Mari, the shining ones, came. I felt it in the waters and in the earth under the waters.

For a while your voice penetrated the sound of the earthquake and I longed to hear the passion again. It was the passion of the one who is called, answering the One Who called.

Well met stranger! I will die before I harm the one who has found the only answer."

Norri felt an ache in his soul. "What *have* I found Ibinithy?"

The strange expression spread across the terrible jaws. "You have found the one truth that all men were made to seek: that there is One Father who cares for men. Only with passion can He be sought they used to say: a passionate whisper or a passionate cry. For passionately He seeks men and only with passion can He be found."

"Have you not sought Him, Ibinithy?"

"I am no longer a man as you can plainly see, and I have dabbled in evil that clings to the soul; polluting even what is left of what I once was.

I have committed sins of pride and arrogance and cruelty. This is my punishment."

Norri considered what the creature had said. "Perhaps the One Father can find a way to forgive even these sins, Ibinithy."

"I do not know how He may do it:

- How can one seeking power in forbidden places be forgiven?
- How can He forgive one who has opposed Him in every way and sought the powers that hated Him more vehemently than any man?
- How can such a monster stand and look in His face, ever?"

There was a silence and the wind rose whipping their garments about them and the monster stood gazing at Norri with sadness… and fear.

Norri shouted over the wind. "I, Norrimae Jung have this to say to you, Ibinithy.

The old pastor of my village has always said, 'Turn from what you are doing that is of evil. The One God will see your repentance and turn aside from the punishment He has planned and redeem you with those who call out to Him day and night for forgiveness of their evil and their crimes.' For does not every evil thought and word cling to a man's soul like those tendrils cling to you. And do not all need forgiveness as you do, Ibinithy?

Turn now from the evil thoughts you cherish and turn to Him Who is your only hope!"

The great head rose higher out of the water. There was a glint in the brown eyes. Norri wondered if he has gone too far. Maybe this monster knew it was beyond forgiveness; maybe it was. Norri knew that at any moment the huge jaws could strike down and crush out their life.

He stood in dreadful anticipation.

The great head rose still higher out of the water. The great scaly neck bent over, and the tendril-draped head came close to the ship. Words came out like sobs. "Pray for me to your God, Norrimae Jung. Long have I thought I was beyond forgiveness and still do so think, but if there is a God Who has some hidden way to redeem those who are evil, I will repent and await the day of His salvation."

Feeling great pity and hardly knowing what he was doing; and almost with a voice not his own Norri spoke over the wind. "The Holy One has seen your heart, Ibinithy. Even the worst sinner who repents, can be saved. Await the day of His salvation!"

A great cry was heard and looking up they saw two great eagles wheeled above them in the circles of a great dance.

The monster looked toward the sky in amazement. "The Mari have come!" Above the eagles, lights played in the sky like shooting stars.

9

Graveloren

Kirin was exhausted. She knew that they must keep moving. Other grimulves would be hunting the woods and the road. She knew she had to get Lettie and Jenny and the two little ones to safety. The question was – where was safe and how could they find food. Lettie was breast feeding and needed food. There was nothing much in the forest. There were nuts but they were not easy to find, and she had no rope for scaling trees.

All these thoughts wore Kirin down. She had to find food, or their strength would fail; Lettie and Dillon first, then little Mort then she and Jenny.

Kirin looked at Mort he was tired, obviously, they all were but he seemed to have a toughness about his little frame. He plodded and stumbled along and occasionally he would look at her with a worried look. Kirin smiled at him at these times to try to reassure him that she knew what she was doing. She didn't of course. How could she. They were safe this morning in their home in the castle and now they had barely escaped with their lives and were lost in the forest, hunted and hungry.

The trees grew larger. She had not noticed this at first, but they were wider spaced and massive. The rough, gnarled trunks of the orkya trees provided a way up but Kirin was not certain she could find nuts or even that she could climb high enough to get to the canopy where they could be found. And she judged it would take more energy than she had. Those nuts that they found fallen had all been eaten by the benjiri. Mort had seen several bunches and optimistically turned them over to find only calyxes where the orkya nuts had been.

As they walked, Kirin began to feel a sense of unease that grew stronger than her tiredness. She began to shiver inexplicably. Fear grew like icy fingers reaching out to them through the trees. But where could they hide that they could not easily be found. She lifted her pace. Lettie gave her a look of concern; she must feel something too. Neither of them spoke but Kirin noticed that Mort walked closer to her side and gripped his stick that he had found.

Just ahead of them, where a thicket of mountain ashes grew close to a giant orkya tree there was a small tangle of branches and saplings that offered an inadequate hiding place – but it was the best available and Kirin turned toward the thicket. The others followed, unquestioning. They had to struggle through the unyielding stems and Dillon's blankets got caught.

They tore the blanket in their rush and pressed close to the trunk of the great tree as if it could somehow comfort and protect them. Dillon began to whimper. Lettie opened her blouse and pressed her son to her breast. He immediately began to suckle but his sucking seemed to make an inordinate amount of noise. Kirin wondered if Lettie's milk supply was failing. She must be famished! She just hoped that Dillon would not give them away.

As she peeped out through the thicket, she saw two large shaggy shapes moving through the trees. Between canine panting she thought she could make out words.

"Thee wunes wee hunnt harrve cumme thees waay. Theey harrve arr cheeld weeth theem."

"Ween wee deescuvrr theem, well feast orrn therr fleessh."

"Therr yunngerr, therr sweeter."

The two great shapes seemed to cast a shadow – even in the dim, glaucous light of the trees.

They came into a space between the trees; barely twenty paces from where the girls were hidden. Then one stopped and seemed to hear something away through the trees to the south.

"Theey harrve gorne thees waay."

"Goord! I hunger forr the taste orf freesh meat. Therr foolls, Therr soljerrs harrve onnlee staarrl meat – norrt feet forr eating. Wee murrst feend ourr arnn meat een thees garn feerrest."

One of the creatures looked around as if ill at ease and they both turned and loped away to the south.

Kirin and the girls peeped through the stems of the shrubs and didn't dare to move for a long time. Lettie was terrified. She clutched Dillon to her and quaked with fear.

Kirin had had no space to use her bow and had drawn her knife. She saw that Jenny had done likewise. She was certain that the creatures would not have come at the two little ones except that they first dealt with the two girls. She didn't know what they could have done but they would not have gone down without a fight. On the other hand, Lettie was in a state. Kirin wondered if that was how it was with hunted animals; that there came a time when fright and despair caused them to surrender to their fate. But courage welled up in her heart – she would save them – even if it took her last bit of strength and she died in the attempt.

As Kirin stood there, she thought of Norri and his great task, and her courage grew. If Norri could attempt his given task, she would do her part. She began to struggle out of the bushes.

"Come. We must keep going."

She didn't know quite where but they had to keep going or lie down and give up. Then if the grimulves came back they would be easy game for them. Something told Kirin they would be safer deeper in the forest.

They struggled out of thicket that was covered by creeping vines with tiny purple flowers that Kirin might have considered pretty if she were not so shaken and tired. Her stomach was complaining as well. They had eaten the last of their food over a day ago and she had stinted herself to give more to Lettie and Mort.

They struggled on for another hour and finally stopped in a clearing where they all slumped down feeling weary and hopeless. Kirin tried to stay awake but could not. Her head drooped and her eyes finally closed.

She woke to find she has slipped sideways and was lying in the leaf litter. She saw that Lettie was asleep with Dillon also asleep in her arms and Jenny was resting against the bole of the tree, also with her eyes closed.

Where was Mort? Kirin looked around but could not see him. She became concerned, stood up and began to look around for the boy. She called his name softly.

Then there came a response from above. "Up here," a small voice whispered back.

Kirin looked up to find Mort sitting high in a branch of a forest ash. He was eating something.

"Come down here, Mort! What are you doing? You scared me."

The boy seemed to hesitate and was putting something in his pockets as he came down.

"What have you got, Mort?

"These." The boy handed her a pocket full of small green shoots with sprouting seeds at the top.

Kirin tasted one and they were sweet.

"What is it?"

"I don't know but they taste good, and I have eaten some and they are good. They grow in the grooves of the old branches."

Kirin tasted some of the small green seeds. They tasted good, sweet and a little nutty but there was no indication that they were not edible.

"Are there more?"

"Plenty and there may be more in other trees. There are other trees like this one. Maybe they all have food."

Kirin ate a few more seeds. They did not satisfy her hunger, but they were certainly better than nothing.

"Mort, can you gather a few more handfuls? They may be fine but in case they make us sick we will not wake the others until we see that they are alright."

Mort nodded and climbed back into the tree. He began to fill his pockets with his new find and felt very clever. He so wanted to please Kirin.

An hour passed and both Mort and Kirin were suffering no ill effects from the food, so they woke the others with the news that Mort had found something to eat.

Getting even enough of the seeds for them all to have a little took time that Kirin regretted wasting, but they needed enough strength to go on.

When Jenny and Lettie had had a few mouthfuls of 'Mort's special food' as Kirin called it, they talked about going on.

The truth was that they all felt much revived. The seeds seemed easily digested and it wasn't long before Lettie, who was the most tired of all of them, was looking much brighter. They gathered up what little they had in the way of possessions and Kirin led them deeper into the forest where the orkya trees grew even larger and rose out of the earth like towers.

David Goodman and his wife Patricia walked through the trees together hand in hand. They had gathered all the people who had fled south when the Corrii had come. Now they were hiding deep in the forest. They had a rough camp with shelters made from fallen branches. Some five families had fled with them and old Gorigond the innkeeper and his brewer were also with them. It had looked very bad when they ran for the forest with the little food and water they could grab. David had looked back to see smoke rising from the castle at the mouth of the Erne and there were grimulves and Corrii soldiers rushing through the town killing anyone they could find.

David had heard screams of men and horses from the forest to the north of them where the cavalry had fled.

Now they were hiding here in the forest, lost and probably hunted. Gorigond had pushed them to go deeper into the forest and that had proved good advice. There were less of the small creatures that seemed to prefer the edge of the forest. Here they had been able to glean some food. Bunches of orkya nuts lay about the forest floor. Some had been opened and eaten but the ones with tougher shells were still good. They had cracked them with stones and roasted them. They didn't have enough but they had something. Now the families were hunkered down by the trunk of a great tree talking quietly and holding children many of whom were asleep.

"What do we do now, David?"

"Stay here deep in the forest for a day or two and then go back carefully and see what has happened to Egleton. If the town has been taken, we will just have to see if we can travel north through the forest."

"I don't know if I am up to a long journey through the forest."

"I know, love. But we can take our time and go as slow as we like. We cannot go very fast with the little ones anyway."

David didn't say it, but he thought their chances very slim. They had no skills for surviving in the forest. He was tired. He felt it in his bones - the tiredness that comes from a near escape and the tiredness that comes of old age.

They turned back to the fire by mutual unspoken agreement. Pat smiled at David. They both knew what they had to do. They would say little encouraging things, cuddle the children; encourage the mothers who were wondering how they would get enough food for their little ones.

David put his arm around Pat's shoulders and kissed her on the forehead as they strolled back exuding a calmness that came from long experience trusting the God they both loved.

Iigweell was perched on a high branch of an orkya tree. The sun shone on her golden scales, and she lifted her tail to sharpen the barbs on the bark of the tree. She was hungry.

Her kind were not particularly gregarious, but she wished for the comfort of the rookeries of her home world. She liked it here; there was much prey but also much that was different and unsettling.

She longed for the fire-mountains and the ashen plains where the runnemy ones scuttled from one hiding place to another to avoid the death-grip of her talons and the numbing poison of her tail. She could catch them and tear off their thick, fleshy tails. Then she would let them escape to nurse their pain and regrow their appendages for her to eat another day.

Once torn apart the weak creatures of this world did not regrow. They had to be eaten and their blood consumed, or they were wasted. What a strange place this was...and dangerous. Some from her rookery had been killed. It had been a surprise that these weak things could resist, but resist they had. And some of her race would never again return to soar in the red skies. The magic that brought them to this world was supposed to protect them, but the arrows and lances had not only destroyed them but those of her flock who had been struck had vanished in blood and smoke. Iigweel did not feel a sense of loss for the others of her rookery who were destroyed. It was not in her to feel regret for the others that perished. She was a creature of terror, a hunter and a devourer of prey. Death held no fear, a killer would, one day be killed. This was the way of things. There was no regret for those that were lost. What Iigweel missed was the freedom to roam and soar where she willed: free of the encumbrance of the priestly magic. Its black fetters tied her to the will of the priests; her wild will constrained by the invisible bonds of the spell that brought her to this strange world.

There was a high, wailing shriek; Iigweell looked blinkingly at the blue sky. Another gold and vermillion shape glided down to the branch on which she was perched.

"Iigweel! Why doo yoo tarry here? There arre norn food creatures in these treees. The'rr arll closer to the weede warves."

"They sent uss to sarrch the trees forr anee who harrve escarped and feest on theem at weell, Gryweel."

"Ire harv sarched therr treess and fornd norn. Eet ees teem t'reeturrn too therr preests. Wee'll diee een theees warld weethart the blark wartar."

Iigweell arched her long neck and hissed. "They beend uss heer by thee blark wartar of theerr altars arnd wee murst feend food."

"Th-ar maanee veekt'ms een thess warld. Wee weell neverr starrve. Carm; leet uss return to theem and drrink the blark wartar. Theen wee well hurnt. Ire leek ther taste orf freeshe blurrd."

Gryweell sprang off the branch and rose into the air on wide wings.

"Yoo arr ar fooll, Gryweel," hissed Iigweel after the other wyvern had soared into the air, "Yourr theerr slarve and yoo doo narrt noww eet. Withart the wartar frarm their altars wee weel weether and dee herr. Ire well feend arr waay to bee free. Ire weell hurrnt weeth ther dargs. Theyr free too harnt arrt weel."

Iigweell sprang into the sky to scour the forest again.

In a branch, listening, was a young warrior of the driadora. He lay silently on a branch with his living garment of leaves hiding him from any but the most discerning eyes. The Charnagra rustled and communicated with its wearer. It quivered at the horror of the evil when it had passed. Lefgild remained motionless, thinking. They had told him their secrets. Perhaps that information could be used somehow.

Norri stood with Gordy, Denquinar and Kiri on the main deck. It had been several days since the encounter with the Ibinithy. They had seen the creature again several times. Occasionally it seemed to come and frolic nearby. There was no other word to describe its play. It leapt out of the water and twisted in the air, crashing back into the water to create great waves that slapped against the side of the Swiftsure. Once it came close again and exchanged jokes with Gordy for a while before going off to hunt. They saw it hunting often and it seemed to consume great quantities of fish.

But as the days passed, they saw less and less of it and it seemed to have gone farther away in search of its preferred food.

The sea was empty and there was little wind.

The watchmen in the tops continually scanned the horizon for any sign of pursuit but there was none so far.

Denquinar did a sweep of the horizon himself. "The trouble is that if the Dows are following, they are faster than we are in these light seas, and they will catch us easily."

Norri looked at the horizon. "Will they follow us this far south do you think?"

"Denquinar turned to his son. "Kiri, what do you think? If you were a sea office, would you continue the pursuit?"

The boy thought about it.

"If my orders were to catch the fleeing ships, I would not dare give up the chase. If my orders were otherwise, I would have given up long ago."

Denquinar nodded. "So what do you think? Will they still be following?"

"Yes, they gave chase and would have caught us except for the Ibinithy. The captains will be afraid to go back empty-handed. Even the excuse of the Ibinithy will not be enough to save them from punishment for disobeying orders until it is clear that we have escaped and there is no way to find us.

I guess they are following now – just over the horizon hoping to come upon us at night."

"That would be my assessment as well."

There was a call from the tops. "Land Ho, on the port beam."

They all looked and there was a landmass: an island. It didn't seem too large but there was a large mountain and several smaller peaks rising out of forested lowlands.

Reynolds was beside them. "What do you think Commodore? Do we investigate it?"

"Yes…I think so. It may be a chance to get some fresh water and we cannot tell how long it will be before we can do that. The coastline is mountainous and there haven't been any suitable bays to land on the mainland so far as we have seen. And if the ships persuing us run low on water that will give us a significant advantage."

Reynolds climbed the stairs to the poop and gave orders to change course.

It took the rest of the day to reach the island and they saw no easy landing place at first. It wasn't until they got to the southern side that they saw a large bay open up before them.

It was a beautiful afternoon and still a couple of hours before sunset, so they decided to send boats to investigate.

Denquinar signaled the *Suresafe* to stand off to seaward and keep watch for pursuit while they sailed into the bay. The men got to work with a will, and many were envious of the boat crew, obviously keen to know more of this island only a week's sailing south of their homeland.

Denquinar was feeling the same. It was like the days when he was a young captain himself eager for new adventures and discoveries.

"I will go with the boat myself, with your permission, Captain."

Reynolds seemed crestfallen. Both senior officers could not go but he nodded to Denquinar. "As you wish, Commodore. I will send Lieutenant Campsey in command of the boat. We will load the empty water barrels."

He turned to a young eager officer waiting nearby whose duty included the command of the long boat. "Campsey, get the barrels up here and stowed, then lower the boat."

Once the boat was in the water and the crew were ready by their oars, Campsey stood aside for Denquinar to climb over the side and down to the boat. The bay was still, and it was easy to gain the back of the long boat. Campsey took the tiller and gave the orders to shove off. The twelve oars dipped the water with practiced precision and the long boat sped toward the beach.

Lieutenant Campsey pointed out a reedy patch on the shore that offered some promise of a stream and altered course toward it.

A midshipman on the bows shouted, "People on the beach, Sir! Away to starboard…"

All looked. On the beach were a group of about six people. It was hard to tell at the distance, but they appeared to be women.

Denquinar noticed an ever so slight increase in speed as the steersmen kept the ship a point closer to the wind. Soon they were able to see more clearly, and the people were indeed a group of women. They appeared brown skinned and wore grass skirts. They had shell ornaments on their arms and necks and were waving to the boat.

"They do not seem to be any threat, Sir," said the lieutenant.

"They may not be, but there may be men who will be less than pleased about your obvious interest in their women. Keep alert and keep your weapons at the ready."

"Yes, Sir." Campsey checked his sword. "Taylor, Dempsey, Bowen, ship your oars and string your bows don't be too obvious but be ready for any trouble and get up front with Jensen. Keep your eyes peeled!

The rest of you pull with a will and let's investigate. Ready oars…pull"

They swept toward the beach and saw no other people. The six young women seemed to be the only welcome and they were smiling and waving.

As they approached the shore break, Campsey called out, "Who are you? Are there any other people on the island?"

The woman who appeared to be the leader and who had the most impressive shell armbands and necklace, called back in stumbling words that they could none-the-less understand, "We are Ichtar. There are more of us. But men all gone and not come back."

Denquinar felt very uncomfortable with this answer. He also noticed the sailors grinning from ear to ear. This was going to mean trouble, even if it was just a matter of getting the sailors to leave the place. It seemed a paradise, a pristine, blue-water bay and beautiful women, probably plentiful food and good fishing.

"Keep up your guard." Was all he said to the young lieutenant who had the same silly grin as his men.

The boat ground up onto the sandy beach and the women approached. They seemed innocent enough.

Campsey asked if there was water nearby.

The head woman, who seemed to be called Chara, pointed to a silver ribbon running down across the sand and then in toward the forest. "We get water from pools in the forest. Water comes down from mountain and is good water. But we have water here come and drink."

They led the sailors up into the shade of the trees and there were shelters of branches and fruit in baskets laid out on trestles of lashed wooden staves.

Further up in the clearing there were other shelters without walls but only a few, perhaps enough for twenty people to sleep.

The women took shell knives and cut some of the fruit in half. They whipped out the black seeds in the middle and offered halves of the fruit to the sailors.

Then they offered water from small wooden bowls.

Denquinar's caution did not lessen but there didn't seem to be any immediate threat.

"Campsey, you had better send a sailor to signal the ship that all is well and that we will be returning with water."

Campsey lost his smile instantly. But he knew his duty and gave the orders.

The men grudgingly shuffled toward the boat and the water barrels.

Once the barrels were loaded onto small two wheeled carts they set off in the direction of the water.

The women came along with them and even offered to take turns pulling the carts. The men refused but seemed pleased to have their company on their trek.

The forest was not dense and there was a well-worn track to the rocky pools where they found the water fresh and good tumbling down over volcanic rock shelves into large pools.

The women indicated a place where the water cascaded over a small waterfall and filling the barrels was easy. The water then ran down into a larger pool shaded by large palms with clusters of enormous nuts and others with clusters of the large orange fruit they had been offered when they first arrived.

One of the girls who had introduced herself earlier as Gindra pointed to the lower pool. "We swim in the large pool when day is very hot. The pool is shaded and cool."

She was obviously pleased with the response she got from the sailors with that suggestion.

The barrels were much heavier when full and it took two men each to pull the carts on the return journey.

By the time they had stowed the water barrels daylight was fading. Campsey seemed disinclined to give the order to man the boat for the return to the ship, so Denquinar gave the order himself.

"Come on, Lieutenant, you may have a chance to come back before we leave. But we may still have enemies behind us."

The sailors began to push the boat into the water as the six women stood looking glum on the beach. The sailors were even less inclined to go, and it took a while for Denquinar to get them back to sea. The commodore also filed this small piece of information. Certainly, the women were beautiful and seemed hospitable but these were well-trained men and it took all the authority he could put into his voice to get them to obey a simple order.

He understood how they felt. It was a beautiful place. The fruit was delicious and their hosts delightful in every way. He turned and saw the women returning to their camp. They moved quickly; gracefully, but very quickly across the soft sand. He shook his head at himself. His experience of women had been singularly bad, maybe he was just conditioned to be skeptical. He was glad Kiri was still on the ship. These women seemed very wild, and he was glad he had been with the water collecting crew.

Denquinar knew that news of the beautiful inhabitants of the island would be around the ship in minutes. Navy ships were the same the world over. He decided he would have a talk to Captain Reynolds. If more of the men were to visit the island it should be for very short amounts of time. And they would have to leave the island behind as quickly as possible.

Once aboard he sought out the captain's cabin. He found Reynolds at his mapping table. He had taken the trouble to map the island and the lagoon already.

"Good evening, Commodore. You are back in time for dinner. The other officers will be keen to hear all about the island. We could see people on the shore who we take it were friendly. What shall we call the island, do you think? It isn't on any of the charts."

Denquinar sat at a chair next to the chart table and examined Reynold's map. He picked up a pair of dividers and measured the distance to the entrance of the Erne River and Cair Egleton. "Two hundred leagues... It seems odd that it has never been discovered before. I suppose it is well out to sea and any explorer heading south could easily have missed it to the east."

"I gather there was ample fresh water, Commodore?"

"Yes, we brought back full barrels and there was fruit which we have brought back as well. We will need fresh fruit and it will be good change for the men. We should be careful who we send ashore next. Pick an officer with a head on his shoulders.

The women on the island do not seem to have any men. They say they went away and have not returned. That worries me on a number of fronts. No men, no children and no evidence of any in recent times."

Reynolds was obviously intrigued.

"No men?"

Denquinar watched the young captain's response with concern. This news should have been ringing alarm bells for Reynolds, but he seemed to have the same silly expression as the sailors.

"Captain, we have a very important mission and the future of your country...our country (he corrected himself). We must not get waylaid on an insignificant island, no matter how pleasant the setting... or the inhabitants.

And I am worried about this absence of men. So far, we have only met six women, who seem to live there alone. They do not seem desperate to leave as you would think likely if they were stranded there with no men."

Reynolds was standing looking at the bay and the beach. There was no sign of the women, at this distance anyway.

"Perhaps it is just that this is their home and the men have gone away fishing or traveling to other islands and they are waiting for their return."

"Perhaps; it just seems a little odd, that's all. They were all young and quite beautiful. And there were no children either as you would normally expect."

Instead of sharing Denquinar's concern, Reynolds seemed even more intrigued.

"But only six you say...."

"Only six that we saw.... They said there were others, but we did not see any."

"We will organize the boats to go ashore tomorrow to gather such fruit as is available. There is no sign of pursuit, and the men can use a break."

Denquinar turned to Reynolds in surprise, "You cannot be serious! We have a mission that the future of your country may depend on, and you are planning a mission to gather fruit and fraternize with the natives."

Reynolds went red. "I think I know the extremes to which my men can be subjected, Commodore. They have fought their way south from Cair Neren under constant threat form the Corrii and you are going to deny them a few hours reprieve from danger."

"We are not sure we are out of danger yet, Captain,"

"Commodore, you may have command of the mission, but I command this ship and I have decided that my men need a short rest ashore. The island seems good and wholesome, and the natives are friendly and innocuous. Unless you overrule me, I am sending parties ashore in the morning."

Denquinar left the cabin without another word. He was fuming. Junior officers had rarely if ever stood up to him before. It was the uncertainty of the command structure. Reynolds was technically correct. Although the command of the mission was bestowed on him from the king, Reynolds was the senior serving officer. There was a conflict of authorities.

As he walked out onto the deck, Denquinar was bumped by one of the masters' mates who apologized and continued on his way. Denquinar mused that it would have been very different if a non-commissioned officer did that in the Corriian fleet. He could have been flogged. He could and often had, stripped men of their rank for smaller mistakes. It sounded harsh but it kept discipline strong and men so demoted would be reinstated once they had proven themselves again.

Here, Denquinar felt like a passenger.

He even had a smaller cabin than the captain. That would also not have happened in the Corriian navy. There was nothing for it but to be thankful that at least he was not under the thumb of the masters of the great covens and their cronies in government.

He stood by the railing and looked out at a calm sea. He looked at the island and his sense that something was not as it should be returned. He decided he would accompany the shore party in the morning and have a bit of a look around.

10

The Battleship Argamaro

*T*he ship was under half sail and progressed north at good speed with the wind off her beam. The duty officer and his helmsmen manned the giant tiller and the blocks and winches used to adjust her course. There was no foreseeable need to change the course unless this wind shifted.

Two officers stood by the railing and spoke quietly into the face of the wind so that no-one else on the top deck would be able to hear.

The Admiral Gastuss Norrens was a portly man well past middle years. His second lieutenant was also old for his rank. Both had been overlooked for promotion because they did not fit the requirements of the new navy. Events and policy had passed them by while they served the empire faithfully at sea. Now they were secure enough in their current jobs but unlikely to rise any higher. Both men accepted this as one did in all walks of Corrii society and services. You obeyed orders; that was all there was to it.

The lieutenant lowered his head almost to his hands. "I don't know why they could not have left her where she was."

The Admiral lowered his voice. "It is a strange measure. War or no, the rulers have never moved people around like this. It is hard enough for a woman to make any sort of life for a navy man's family without moving them off the family farms and housing them far away from relatives and friends."

"Leana is not the only one. Plenny says his wife has also been moved to the new naval settlement in the Verbigar hills."

"Is there any talk about who is behind this?"

"The talk is: Cherulia but it may not be only him."

"I haven't heard from Ghezia but last I heard she was still on our farm to the north Millaroth."

"Millaroth is a naval town anyway. Maybe they are trying to relocate all the naval families together."

"Perhaps, but why?"

"It has some advantages."

"Yes, but for who?"

"It is good if the seamen can see their wives and families when they are in port."

"So, you are suggesting that the rulers did this for altruistic reasons; to make our lives better? It would be a first."

The lieutenant's expression changed to one of concern as his mind went through the many ramifications of the idea. "You think they are keeping our wives as sort of hostages, Captain?"

"Perhaps we should not read too much into it. I just cannot see how it can help anyone to cram people together in naval enclaves and if we could figure out some good reasons, we would probably be wrong. Keeping track of the wives so they can be questioned or threatened if their husbands step out of line, is the sort of thing the covens might do."

"Do you think they suspect there is dissent in the ships?"

"I think the Empire always thinks that. They would expect it. No-one likes long campaigns, away from wives and family for years at a time. This may be just a way of ensuring it will never be any more than dissent."

"There just seems to be no end to these wars. What harm have the people of Herelstrom done to the Empire. Yes, we want their timber, but wouldn't it be easier just to buy it from them."

Lieutenant Cornelli lowered his voice. "I don't like being a part of a campaign that only seems to be about satisfying the grimulves thirst for blood and those other things.... The people of Herelstrom want no more than to live in peace and are not the slightest threat to the empire. All this talk of massing armies to use against us and a navy to harass our shipping is a lot of tosh; they could no more harm us than a butterfly could. As for being in league with the Bernadians against us – how could they do that?"

"The captain lowered his head and looked out over the water. "There is no honor in being a navy officer anymore. We spend our time transporting horrors to be let loose against women and children much like our own. I wonder what the price is of getting out."

Cornelli spoke louder than he meant to. "They will never let you retire while there is a war on, and good captains are needed. And the next push will be against the Bernadians, and they have many ships, they will need every experienced fighting captain they have."

Gastuss Norrens looked around and saw a movement on the stairs to the poop deck. The duty officer had moved so that he had positioned his own body between any possible listener and his captain. The young officer indicated the stairs with his eyes, and the captain and second lieutenant went silent.

Norrens moved quickly and indicated that Cornelli should take the port steps. As they reached the steps on either beam, they saw a figure disappear into the door that led to the officers' quarters. Both men followed through the door and found Bentonius in the hall bailed up against a burly sergeant of marines who was on duty guarding the door to the captain's cabin.

The captain smiled at the sergeant and pushed past Bentonius into his cabin, "Bentonius, just the man I want to talk to. Come into my cabin. You have saved me the trouble of sending for you. Will you join us as well, Cornelli, please?"

The sergeant made it clear that the request was not the sort that could be refused and closed the door behind Bentonius and the two officers.

"Norrens indicated a seat and Bentonius sat down while he and Cornelli remained standing. "Benton, you have an excellent reputation as a spy, I would not like to think that your skills needed to be used against your own people."

"Admiral, surely there would never be any reason for *you* to think that you would be accused of treachery or dissent?"

"Careful, Benton," said Norrens with a hint of a threat in his voice, "One should be careful about threatening a captain in his own ship when at sea and surrounded by all his loyal officers and men. Anything could happen to a spy."

"You know you wouldn't dare harm me. You know there are other spies on your ship and if you did anything to me it would mean the end of your life and that of your family. There are people looking to make examples of officers who foster discontent in the navy. You are already one who is being watched." Benton looked ominously at Cornelli, "... and we would not hesitate to complete any purge if once we started."

Cornelli ignored Benton's last words but picked up on those that were of more concern. "What do you know about threats to my family?" he raged as he grabbed Benton out of his seat by his tunic and pressed his face close. "Tell us what you know, or I'll slit you open and throw you to the sharks myself."

Norrens was coldly calm. "And this is a good place for sharks. The big ones with the white-tipped fins patrol these shores...hunting."

The coldness with which he said this, made Bentonius turn to him and stare. For the first time he wondered if the captain was actually serious.

"What do you know, Benton? If there is any risk to our wives, we have a right to know," said Cornelli, pushing Benton down into the chair and drawing a dagger from under his sea cloak.

Benton looked at Cornelli with eyes wide open and raked through his memory for something that he thought might satisfy the young officer who had clearly decided the world would be better off without him. He also quickly realized that the two officers had probably gone too far to back down now. Benton decided some honesty and a bit of diplomacy was what was required now.

"I have heard that there was talk of relocating navy wives to a couple of centers. The reasons were multiple. They wished for them to provide support for one another when husbands were away for long periods as was expected and they wanted the families accessible to the officers when they did put into port for short periods."

Cornelli gripped his dagger tighter. "What else, you piece of fish bait?"

"That was what they planned to say to the women. It was also considered a good way to ensure the loyalty of officers who are away from the control of the empire when at sea. Retribution could be swift and terrible against the families of any officer who deserted or committed mutiny. The empire's rulers have Admiral Denquinar in mind, not you, worthy sea officers; when this decision was taken."

"That's what I thought."

"It is no more than they expected you to think. You guessed this before I told you. What is more, I understand your sentiments but what can any of us do? Please put your dagger aside, lieutenant and refrain from threatening me with being the next meal of a white-tipped shark and let us all be civil and put these exaggerated discussions down to many long months at sea and too many night watches."

Norrens nodded to Cornelli, and the lieutenant sheathed his dagger again. "Leave us Cornelli and I will have a discussion with Master Bentonius." The use of his title seemed to calm the coven master.

Cornelli stalked out of the room and Norrens sat down on a chair opposite Bentonius.

"Not much of a way to elicit loyalty from good officers is it Bentonius? Did the masters *not* expect the men would react like this?"

"It was discussed."

"All you will get with threats like this will be skulking obedience. No naval officer will fight with a will for masters who theaten him and his family like this. What can you do about it? Not much, I guess. You are really just their spy. Get out of my office. If I were you, I would avoid lieutenants Cornelli and Plenny and restrict your walks on deck, at night. Good night, I can control my men. I hope you will be able to find a way to warn those who make these foolish decisions that they are not achieving what they obviously hope; and return an element of sanity. Please control your natural instinct to spy – while on my ship."

Norrens met Cornelli on deck several hours later when the young officer was on duty. "I was too aggressive with Benton, wasn't I captain?"

"Perhaps a tad rash to threaten one of the most powerful men in the empire with being fed to the sharks...."

"It was stupid; I don't know what came over me."

"I do. You were worried for your young wife and daughter."

"Yes. But my actions have only put them in more danger."

"It depends what Benton does when he is safe away from the Argamaro. He will never do anything on my ship; surrounded by officers loyal to me. What he may do when he is back in Bea-air Monar; with the resources of the covens at his disposal, who can know."

"I have been a fool. I have risked everything."

"Don't be too hard on yourself, Cornelli. I lost my temper as well."

"Am I a dead man, Captain?"

"Maybe we both are, but maybe you have just hardened our resolve to do what we should do anyway."

"What is that, Captain?"

"Get out."

"How?"

"That may take some thought and careful planning."

"Count me in and most of the wardroom as well."

"It may not only be this ship...." The captain's voice trailed away into the surge and swoosh of the water along the counter.

Gavin was cold. The hold of the ship was dank and dark. The cuffs on his shackles were loose but impeded him and clattered on the deck when he tried to move. He tried to stay as quiet as possible and not wake his companion. Tom lapsed in and out of semi-consciousness.

Gavin had tried his best to wipe away the dried blood on the side of Tom's head but had nothing much to do it with but his own torn shirt.

Tom was shivering in his fever. Gavin was worried about him. He liked his commander and willed him to recover but even with his limited knowledge of the Corrii, Gavin guessed that it would probably be better for Tom if he died of his injuries here in this dark unwholesome place than live on and endure what the Corrii would do to him.

Gavin thought there was a chance that he would be allowed to live. He would probably be sold as a slave, he thought. There was at least some chance that someone might buy him who was not too cruel to slaves. But Gavin had heard that the Corrii liked to make an example of captured enemies of rank; make them examples for any others who dared to stand against them. It would have been better if God had allowed the stone to kill Tom.

Gavin tried to cast his mind back to the few things he had heard Tom say but nothing would come into his head except the words his mother had said, 'Where there's life there's hope.' "What a ridiculous saying," he thought, "Tom was alive – but there was no hope."

There was another moan beside him. Tom was stirring again. Gavin put his arm over Tom's chest to stop him from hurting himself in his weak convulsions. He found himself praying that Tom would die and be at peace.

The ship rocked and lurched as it made its way through the heavy seas. On some days those who were fit had been taken up to the rowing decks and chained next to the rowers. These were actually ship's crew which surprised him. They sat beside the rowers on slightly lower benches and were forced to bend their backs to the oars. It was exhausting but now they had not had to row for several days. Gavin guessed that the wind had made it possible for the ship to sail.

The boards were hard and the cold kept sleep at bay but eventually he slipped into a fitful doze. What woke him was the sound of Tom rolling over and sitting up. Gavin sat up as well as the shackles on his ankle allowed. He looked at Tom in the dim light that came from the lantern hanging from a ring by the ladder at the end of the deck. Tom sat against the bulkhead; blinking and trying to make sense of his surroundings. He seemed to recognise Gavin which seemed like a good sign.

"Tom, you look terrible!"

"That's how I feel. Where are we?"

"On board a Corrii battleship, I believe."

"My head hurts. What happened?"

"We were defending the parapet against Corrii ladders, and we drove them off. I guess their artillery must have started up again and you were hit with a stone. It knocked you down and you didn't get up, but you were breathing. I stayed with you and tried to get you out of the way of more stones that they kept firing over the wall and at the defences.

Then they came again and beat us back from the wall. Those of us who were left were fighting by the outer wall because the keep was burning. Eventually the heat got too much and the Corrii told us to throw down our weapons. They then opened the door from the inside and led us out."

Tom tried to piece it all together. "Was anyone left in the keep?"

"I don't think so. The doors were open, and everyone had fled the fires."

Did you see my wife and child?" Gavin searched his memory for any hopeful memories. "I can't remember; it was all so confused. Groups of people were being gathered together, all over the town."

Tom leant back against the wooden hull. "I hope she and Dillon got out."

Gastuss Norrens and all his officers were on deck and the Argamaro was carrying her navigation lights as well as lights indicating her number to the forts on the southern point of the harbor mouth at Orsimater.

A line of lights appeared on the walls of the fort to indicate she had been identified by her coded number and was allowed to enter the secure harbor. Behind her four more ships were in sight; also signaling their number and there were also lights on the horizon. The Argamaro, Quinquereme and flagship of the squadron led in the proud line of battleships, back from a successful invasion of Herelstrom.

The lieutenants gave orders for her yards to be lowered as orders below simultaneously lowered the five banks of oars at precisely the right moment to maintain the battleship's even speed through the water. Men toiled all over the deck and others with the help of captives worked to lift the long oars out of the water, but to the eye of anyone watching she appeared impeccably precise and efficient. As she entered the harbor and turned to make her way to her allotted mooring, the lines of lights could be seen along her decks and in the windows of her stern cabins. She looked like the precise fighting ship she was, hiding the anxiety and confusion of her officers.

When they had secured the ship Bentonius appeared on deck and conspicuously did *not* salute the captain. He approached Admiral Norrens. "Norrens, will you organize a boat to take me ashore, immediately!"

All the officers on the poop looked at their captain with concern. The looks were not missed by Bentonius.

"Certainly Bentonius (Gastuss Norrens conspicuously didn't use his title, *Master*). Cornelli, have the jolly boat readied for Bentonius at once."

Cornelli smiled in spite of the tension. The jolly boat was so called because it was their smallest boat and would bounce about providing an uncomfortable and wet ride for the coven master even in the light harbor breeze.

"And Cornelli, instruct the boatswain to take Bentonius to the landsman's pier not the naval pier. It will be working barges to and fro and we don't want to have a collision and Master Bentonius in the water."

Bentonius nodded his thanks and went below to collect his gear.

Norrens turned away to Verna and Cornelli so there was no chance of Bentonius hearing. "It is also four times as far and over the most windswept part of the harbor."

Conelli smiled. "...and still a good walk; in wet clothes to the nearest inn."

Norrens grimaced. "Perhaps a small victory over the coven master.... But I fear a pyrrhic one. Still, it still gives me some satisfaction to know that self-satisfied little prig will have a good walk in cold, wet clothes and hopefully still think we have done him a favor."

When Bentonius returned on deck with his bags he gave them to the boatswain and called to Captain Verna on the poop. "Captain, you will continue to Bea-air Monar with as much speed as possible with the prisoner. The masters will want to interrogate him as soon as possible."

"Those are my orders, Bentonius, but we need to take on water and provisions first. We also need to ensure weather is favorable and that the straits of Geitor are passable."

"Get to Bea-air Monar as quickly as humanly possible, Captain; no unnecessary delays." Benton climbed down into the boat and nearly fell in as it tossed about in the swell.

The trip across the harbor was slow and dreadful. He was sick twice. He staggered out onto the old stone pier and had to sit for a time in his wet clothes before he could recover enough to walk. As he sat, he saw there were no barges working from the naval pier. Of course, there weren't, it was too late; surely Norrens had known that. Bentonius got to his feet. His anger had made him forget his illness.

11

The Empty Forest

I t was dark under the canopy of the forest now. Kirin struggled on with an empty grumbling stomach and a growing sense of being alone. She felt the burden of leading Jenny and Lettie and little Mort. They seemed to think she could save them, and she had no idea how she could so that.

It was only slowly that she became aware that she could hear voices and none of them were speaking.

She froze. The voices came from ahead. She couldn't make out any words. There were people in the trees ahead. Kirin felt her heart race. If they were enemies, they should hide immediately. If they were fellow refugees, they may find help.

She motioned to Jenny to be silent and hide behind the bole of a tree. That tree was huge, many times the width of any tree she had ever seen. Once the others were out of sight, she moved forward through the trees to try and find out who they had discovered.

She left the cover of one tree looked around and saw nobody, so she worked her way behind another tree and moved around the bowl to look at a small clearing, a space between the trees really. There were some people sitting around a small fire. The light was too poor for her to identify them but by their clothing they looked to be villagers.

"Kirin?" Kirin spun around and saw Patricia and David Goodman. They had just come around the tree from the other direction and seemed both pleased and concerned at discovering her in the forest.

"What are you doing here, dear?" said Pat concern written all over her face.

Kirin felt a wave of relief at the sight of someone she knew and ran to Pat who wrapped her in her arms.

David came closer and placed a gentle hand on her shoulder. "Are you alone?"

Kirin wiped away an unruly tear. "Jenny and Lettie and a little boy – back there in the trees…"

David took several steps in the direction Kirin indicated and called, "Lettie, Jenny, it's David and Pat Goodman."

The other girls came out from behind the trunk of the giant orkya tree and came cautiously toward them. Mort trailed behind sheepishly.

David looked at the sword by Kirin's side and her bow. "Have you encountered any Corrii in the forest?"

We escaped from the castle. And were met by a Grimulf! Jenny was not modest, "Kirin and I killed it!"

David looked impressed.

Kirin thought she should be honest, "I got off an arrow. It must have been a lucky shot and Jenny and I finished it with knife and sword."

Kirin saw David looking nervously about. "We have been traveling for four days. There has been no sign of Corrii or grimulves in the forest that we have seen."

Patricia looked at their bundles. "Do you have any food?"

"We had very little, it is gone now."

David patted Kirin's arm. "You have done well to get them this far."

Kirin saw Mort standing beside Lettie. "This is Mort. His Dad was killed by the Corrii. We found him by the north road. He was able to find a plant growing on the trees. It seems good to eat and we had some when we last stopped."

Mort beamed with pleasure at Kirin's praises.

David pointed toward the clearing. Come and meet the others. "We are only a small band of refugees, but we are alive and that is something. If young Mort here has found some source of food that is even better news."

Kirin patted Mort on the shoulder as they returned to the clearing with David and Pat.

The small group around the fire rose when they heard the voices. The men grabbed their weapons instinctively and then relaxed somewhat when they saw that it was just three girls and a baby.

One of the men, a short rough looking man with a wooden club in his hand rose and glared at them.

"Who are you? Have you been followed?"

Gorigond, the old innkeeper from the village, smiled as he saw Kirin. "It's all right, Bill. I know 'er well."

David held up his hand. "They are just people from Egleton like the rest of us, Bill. And they don't think they have been followed."

The words had just left his lips when a terrible shriek broke over the treetops. A gold and vermillion shape flew over the clearing and wheeling back, swept lower again and observed the people more closely.

Then it turned west with a long aerie cry.

The man called Bill went red with rage. "They have brought them down on us!"

David intervened, "It was more likely that they saw the smoke from your fire. I told you not to let it smoke."

Bill grumbled, "… have to try and warm the nuts for the children. They are bitter if you don't roast 'em."

Kirin listened to the cries of the wyvern as it few away over the forest. It seemed to be retracing the path they had come. "We had better move. It may bring other enemies down on us."

One of the women behind Bill screamed. They all turned.

Eight grey shapes appeared on the edge of the clearing. Bill rushed to place himself between the wulves and his family; club brandished. Another man drew a sword and placed himself between the people around the fire and two more of the monsters.

Kirin drew and arrow while Jenny had her long dagger out and pushed Lettie behind her.

David Goodman also has a large stave and pushed Pat and Mort behind him.

Kirin had learned not to wait for these creatures to stare her down she drew and shot and drew again. Her arrow missed its target. She released another that struck one of the grimulves in the shoulder. It howled in pain. There wasn't time for another shot. She threw down her bow and drew her short sword.

The man with the sword was attacked by the two grimulves together. He screamed as jaws closed on his leg and another of the beasts crashed into his chest knocking him down.

Gorigond stood in front of several of the children and swung his long cleaver at one of the beasts as it circled and backed away.

Bill was knocked to the ground but rolled over and struck his attacker with all his strength which gave him just enough time to regain his feet again.

Kirin lunged at one of the wulves as it attacked David Goodman. It dodged her weapon and circled for another attack.

Kirin was only peripherally aware of another sound. There was a sound of arrows as they thwacked the air in flight.

Grimulves screamed in pain and rage and figures dropped out of the trees. The newcomers were all clad in green and had swords that they used with great effect against the wulves. The remainder of their attackers turned and fled.

The green clad warriors gave chase and seemed to disappear into the forest. Kirin didn't think; she ran after the retreating warriors and found herself running next to a woman whose hair streamed behind her as she sprinted expertly through the forest, spear in hand.

Two warriors along side them, had speared a grimulf and several sword thrusts finished it. The warrior stopped and turned to Kirin. "We must go we have no wish to speak."

Kirin held up her hand. "I will not hold you. I only wish to thank you for saving us. What is your name?"

The warrior seemed uncertain. She looked at Kirin and seemed to be making a difficult decision. "I am Serelra, a branch leader of the southern arborites. We have been watching you and we had orders to protect you and only reveal ourselves if it was the only way to save you."

"Thank you. I am Kirin."

There was a stirring and another female warrior stepped out of the shadows.

Serelra was about to speak but the other warrior raised her hand. "I know whom we have saved, and I am very glad indeed, Serelra." She took several steps closer to Kirin. "Kirin, you do not know me, but I know of you. I am Isherri, now the wife of Baeri and the mother of your husband."

Kirin was taken aback. Isherri showed no such uncertainty. She leant forward and embraced the shaking girl who stood there in shock with a drawn sword limp in her hand.

"I did not know it was you, Kirin and as you heard, we may not reveal our presence unless there was no other way. In this case there was not, as Serelra has said."

"It would have been good to know that you were there. We were very frightened."

"It is only by secrecy that we continue to live in the forests. Even now you must keep the fact that you have found us a secret.

"We will do all we can secretly to aid you but there is only so much we can do.

"We saw that you have discovered the graveloren. We will help you find water and such other foods that you can gather in the forest as you travel. Where will you go?"

Kirin was not certain. "We have thought only of flight so far. I suppose we will be best to travel north if the castle in Egleton has fallen."

"I do not know if the fortifications have fallen but this we know. Smoke rises from the stone fort. Those of the soldiers that are alive are fleeing north and our people are protecting them as best we may. Fierce creatures are with the Corrii, flying monsters with poison tails and tall beasts that walk like men and are not, have come. The flying ones are hunting our people in the tree-tops, as if they knew we were there.

Kirin, do you know what has become of my son in the fight? Surely, he would not have deserted you if he lives."

Kirin smiled the first smile for a long time. "He has gone away, Isherri. He sailed south with the ships sent to find a way south. He was not there when the Corrii came."

Isherri smiled in turn. "That is good. I will do all I can to ensure his wife is alive when he returns. God go with you Kirin. We will shadow you as we can. I must go. Look out for any help we can offer."

So saying, she kissed Kirin and left her standing bemused, looking at the empty forest.

Kirin slowly returned to the cleared space to see how the others fared.

They seemed surprised to see her and in something of a daze.

They were tending the injured and seemed to ignore the smoking remnants of the grimulves. They packed up their few things and began to move again.

As they tramped through the forest, Kirin found David Goodman walking beside her.

"What just happened, Kirin? Did we get help from the tree people?"

Kirin put her finger to her lips to indicate they should speak of it as little as possible.

"They were the tree people; Norri's mother."

David smiled. "I see. Can they help us?"

"They said to look out for, 'graveloren', Morts's special food I should say. And other foods they will help us find them. They said they will protect us as they can."

"Mmm...," said David "The people who are not there help us again...."

Hidden in a tree high above, Serelra sat next to Isherri and caressed an arrow. It was no ordinary arrow. It was alive.

12

The Ichtar

*A*large flotilla of boats rowed toward the beach. Denquinar had confided his concerns to Norri and Gordy and now all three along with Denquinar's son were seated in the stern sheets of the launch from the Swiftsure. It had a sail and easily outpaced the longboat and the two smaller boats the ship carried.

The Ichtar women had assembled on the beach. There seemed to be more now, maybe twenty. Some were wading out into the water waving to the sailors. Norri looked at the faces of the men and then to Denquinar. The expressions on the men's faces were what Denquinar had mentioned. Norri could see exactly what he meant. The young women on the beach seemed pretty and the sailors had been at sea for a while; deprived of female company. Even so, it seemed as though they were over excited at the prospect of meeting new people.

Norri could see the beach now and it was as Denquinar had said, there were more of the women but no men and no children. They all seemed to be around about the same age: all in their twenties and lovely. The midshipmen and two of the sailors lowered the launch's sail and they continued the last distance to the shore with oars. Now the longboat was catching up fast and they looked as though they would reach the beach at about the same time.

As the boats ground up on the sandy beach the sailors jumped overboard and held the boat while the officers went ashore.

The Ichtar women were waving and smiling but were a little more reticent than before. Norri looked at Denquinar. He seemed happier about them being less forward. It seemed more normal, perhaps.

Denquinar then changed. He put on a smile and waved pleasantly. The seamen took this as a license to fraternize. Once the boats were ashore and anchored, they strolled up to the women and began to speak to them. The women then indicated the food laid out on the trestles at their camp. The partying began almost at once.

There were more of the women now and if they had recently returned, they had brought more fruits and nuts and there was a brace of suckling pigs roasting over a fire pit. The smells were intoxicating and soon all the guests were sitting on woven mats enjoying the array of fresh fruits.

Norri sat with a piece of a yellow fruit in his hand, enjoying its tart fresh flavor; watching Denquinar who seemed to be enjoying himself enormously laughing and speaking animatedly to one of the women.

The meal continued with the serving of the pigs and freshly roasted nuts. Norri took a professional interest in these and was shown the huge seed cases in which they grew.

The nuts were roasted on rocks placed on top of the fire pit and then seasoned with sea salt as he did with orkya nuts.

After the meal Norri and Gordy sought out Denquinar. The Commodore was arguing with captain Reynolds. They were discussing sending the men back to the ships for the night.

"It is a balmy night, Commodore; we need not send them back tonight. Let them enjoy their rest."

"Captain I am just worried that they will enjoy it too much. You do not want them to desert or scatter all over the island so that you spend a day recovering your crew before you can proceed on your mission. I think coming here was the most foolish thing you could have done."

"Perhaps you are right, Commodore. But it may already be too late. I think some have gone walking with the Ichtar women already."

"Very well then, Captain, we will wait till morning. Best keep all the remainder of the men together. Use the excuse that we do not know what creatures are on this island; it may be dangerous to be alone or without friends and weapons ready at hand."

"That I will do, Commodore; I will also post a watch of men with bows and swords as well. We will sleep together on the beach."

Reynolds went of to organize this and Denquinar sat down next to Norri. "That is better, now he is acting like a commander. What do you think, King's Forester, do you think I am being unduly cautious?"

Norri lay back on the sand with his head on his hands. "No... I also have some strange sense of unease. And my instincts have saved my life many times. We should be careful.

"If I may make a suggestion, Commodore, even though Reynolds is posting a watch, it is warm night and maybe we three should take turns to watch as well."

Denquinar looked at Gordy for agreement. Gordy looked around. "This lot looks like our apprentices on a Friday night. We used to say they could only walk straight if the road moved."

Denquinar followed his gaze. "Strange, isn't it? We have all eaten the same food and had no drink and they all do look like men who have been drinking."

They decided that Norri would watch first and he settled himself against a log. It was some hours later when he felt he could barely keep his eyes open any longer that Denquinar sat bolt upright.

"Nichtari!"

"What Commodore?"

Denquinar lowered his voice to a whisper. "Nichtari. They are only legends. They occur in old sailors' fables. I once heard an old merchant sailor telling tales of them in a tavern in Bae-air Monar. Beasts that are half woman and half-lion that have teeth and can tear sailors apart with their claws.

"Perhaps it is only another foolish sailors' tale."

Gordy had stirred and rolled over closer to listen. "What like Ibinithys?"

The three lay together and pretended to be asleep. Denquinar whispered, "Stay awake now! Do not give any indication that we think anything is amiss."

Gillian, Brian and Tillion had their last night in the forest and woke early; very hungry. They decided to saddle the horses and set out at first light. All three were anxious for a good meal and a rest.

They made good time along almost empty roads. By mid-morning the re-armed and re-fortified castle came into view. Gillian felt a strange mixture of odd feelings as she approached her childhood home. She longed to see her father. And yet she felt a sense of failure and defeat as they returned, just the three of them from the defeat and rout at Egleton.

The castle looked very different since the last time Gillian had been there. There was a new southern tower guarding the approach from the river. A great ditch had been dug and there was a drawbridge from the new tower spanning it. Large, pointed stakes had been set outside the ditch as yet another impediment to siege towers.

Workers were everywhere, building new stonework, bringing stores into the castle, and carrying loads of weapons.

Gillian and Tillion stumbled into the Cair. Brian sat on Tillion's charger, in obvious pain. Tillion led the horses and looked as dejected as a knight on foot could look. His demeanor spoke defeat more eloquently that any words. Susanna ran out of them as soon as news reached her that they were approaching the gates reached her. She stopped abruptly seeing their faces.

"Gillian, what has happened?"

Gillian wanted to cry and throw herself into her big sister's arms but knew this wasn't the time. "The cair at Egleton has been attacked and maybe has fallen. There was an army came from the sea. Where are father and uncle Taulin?"

"They are out inspecting the defenses of the town. I can send a messenger to get them."

"Do so. Sue. They need to know what has happened."

Sue looked at the state of the three of them. "Are you hurt?"

I am fine – filthy but fine. Brian is hurt. Can you help him? … And Tillion?

"Of course, Darling. You men! Help this knight from the horse; and be careful - he is injured! Quickly bring a stretcher from the refectory."

…Then, spotting a serving girl. "Justine, come and help Lady Gillian up to my apartments and organize water for her to wash and clean clothes."

Justine came running over, obviously very glad to see Gillian again, even in such circumstances. "Here my lady, let me help you with the shield?"

Once in the common room, Susanna quickly laid Brian down on a mattress brought from the storeroom. She examined the leg and the makeshift splint Tillion had made.

"You have done well Tillion. This is a fracture, but it had been kept well by the splint and though painful, will heal well. I will put and we will organize you some crutches, Brian so you can get around. You will be hale in a few weeks and fully recovered in six." on a new splint

Gillian was sitting with a tumbler of water and some fresh bread and cheese while several people fussed over Brian. Tillion had gulped a drink of water and asked for bread and cheese to be brought to him on the battlements. He had immediately gone to find the master of the guard to discuss the present threat and give orders for the defense plans for the Cair to be activated. Horns were blowing already as troops were marshalled. Crews were uncovering the large torsion weapons on the battlements.

Gillian heard the arrival of horsemen in the courtyard but was too tired to get up. Now, after days of struggling northward she felt she couldn't even get up from the table.

The Thane and her uncle Dillon rushed into the refectory and saw her sitting next to Brian. Taulin Ginroyal rushed to his daughter and threw his arms around her.

A quick look at Brian spoke his thanks for bringing his daughter safe back to him.

"What has happened, Gill?"

"Father…" she almost sobbed. "New Castle has been attacked from the sea. We went out with the cavalry to attack the Corrii as they landed but there was a great, black grimulf that seemed to send the horses mad. There are other things with them as well. Commodore Denquinar says they are Gordril from Ba-al Gibrochir. They are hideous monsters that walk on their hind legs like men and but look more like apes....

They attacked us in the forest and we were saved by the...

And they had flying creatures that can poison with barbs on their tailes..."

Dillon gave his niece a reassuring hug to show her how glad he was that she was all right and then sat on the floor next to Brain to get the whole story from a military perspective and discover the numbers and weapons of their enemies. He had to know quickly what they were up against. He and the thane would have to decide whether to shore up the defenses of the castle or risk an expedition south to try and help.

An hour later the decisions were made. They could not spare any more troops from Cair Neren. They had made that mistake before. They would send out expeditionary parties on horseback large enough to defend themselves and quick enough to report back on the state of the south.

Dillon and the thane left to organize mounted scouting parties and make their plans.

When Taulin returned to the hall, he had time to comfort his daughter and encourage her husband. It was all he could do to dissuade Brain from going with the scouting parties.

"Brian you are injured, and you could fall in a fight because you are not fit. Your country would lose a knight and a fine officer. I would lose a good son-in-law and Gillian would lose the person she loves most of all. You have done enough getting here and raising the alarm.

Rest and recover. All the evidence tells us there will be plenty of fighting to do yet. At least it seems that the ships got away before the attack.

I am pleased that you tell me they sailed. We need the alliance with the Bernadians desperately. Norri and Gordy will be in my prayers.

I have greater fear for our friends in Cair Egleton. Let us hope they have been able to hold out against the assault."

The next morning after sunrise, alarm bells rang, and two flying red shapes were seen in the sky over the castle.

In the wakeful hours of the night, Norri and Denquinar heard whispers. There was a little movement and at the same time the sand, warm from the day before, seemed to lure them to sleep. Norri leant against his sword so that the discomfort would prevent him dozing off. On one occasion when he felt that he just couldn't stay awake, Denquinar nudged him in the side gently and he rolled over again. There were shadowy forms moving on the edge of the camp but then silence.

When dawn broke over the eastern horizon with a breeze coming from land with the reassuring smells of trees and grasses, they noticed that their camp was much smaller. Men had gone missing. Denquinar hissed under his breath, "The fools have gone with them. It may be that our guesses were right. We must not let them think that we suspect anything is wrong until we are sure what is happening."

They stretched and got up. The Ichtar were fewer, and no explanation was offered but fruit and nuts were laid out for their breakfast.

Denquinar sidled up to captain Reynolds. "We seem to be missing some men. Do you think you could provide a bit of distraction? I will try and drift away and then go and have a look around."

Reynolds agreed and Denquinar took Gordy with him. Over a mouthful of fruit and a mug of water he whispered to Norri, "If this all turns bad, please get Kiri out of here if you can. Keep him close to the boats. And run for it if our worst suspicions turn out to be right."

Then he and Gordy strolled down the beach carrying their sandals and walking seemingly aimlessly along the beach.

Reynolds, true to his word had the sailors strike up a jig and draw as many of their guests, albeit reluctantly, into the caper.

Once out of immediate view of the camp, Gordy and Denquinar returned to the trees and made their way through the dense coastal scrub toward the end of the bay. There a rocky outcrop marked the end of an ancient lava flow and there were cracks and crevices a plenty for them to scale the mountain unseen.

After a couple of hours hard climbing, they came to a small ridge leading down to a wooded dingle. Opposite them was a path that seemed to lead down from the side of the mountain. They guessed it came from the middle of the island – probably the Ichtar camp.

As they looked over the top of the ridge, Gordy pointed out one of the Ichtar women and Midshipman Hinson strolling down the path toward the woods, hand in hand.

They ducked down behind the scree and rocks on the ridge and watched.

Denquinar was not impressed. "What is the fool playing at? I have noticed he is one of the more feckless of Reynolds midshipmen. In our navy that would probably indicate that he was the son of someone too important to be refused when he asked for a junior officer's berth for his son."

"It is the same in our forces, I would expect," said Gordy.

"The same the world over…"

"Shall we try and warn the fool?"

Denquinar shook his head. "Warning him may cost the lives of all of us if we are right; to say nothing of the success of the mission. And we don't know if there is any threat yet. It may be that the Ichtar girl is just after some innocent fun."

"She has brought him a long way if that was all she wanted. That fool must even have been wondering by now. I suspect her intentions are neither innocent nor much fun; especially for Hinson."

They scanned the slope below them and then turned back to the unfolding drama below. Whether by some trick of the wind or the geography, they could now make out words. The path wound deeper into the dell below them, and they noticed slight movements in the bushes. Gordy thought he saw a tail of some creature, but it seemed to disappear the next moment.

It did indeed seem that Hinson was nervous.

"Why do we have to go down there? We just came from the beach. This path just leads down to the sea on this side of the hill."

"I told you it be a surprise. It be just a little way further. You trust Neegi and get ready for amazing surprise." The scantily clad girl ran ahead provocatively.

The young officer followed meekly with a shrug of his shoulders.

Gordy and Denquinar could not take their eyes off the scene. Surely every warning bell in the fool's head would be ringing but it seemed that he could not hear them.

"Here up on these flat rocks there are pools of water." This seemed to cheer Hinson. He was thirsty after the long walk, and he followed her to the first pool and they both refreshed themselves.

The girl told him to cover his eyes and made as if to remove some of her clothing. Hinson complied and she took off a complex shell necklace.

Gordy could barely suppress a gasp of surprise. Neegi was suddenly larger and very different. She had a tail and the hind quarters of a great cat. Her arms had paws and claws and, as she opened her mouth, a jaw full of teeth. A hiss escaped her mouth as she opened fang-filled jaws.

Hinson looked up; too late. In moments seven other Ichtar had jumped onto the flat rocks. There was Chara, the largest by far. She bit down with slashing teeth on Hinson's leg when he tried to get up and run. Blood spouted from a ruptured artery and spilled down the rocks. The Ichtar had all removed their shell ornaments, and all looked alike. Hissing and shrieks of malign pleasure rose from the dell.

Denquinar sank back behind the cover of the scree. He whispered to Gordy, "Quickly! While they are engaged, we must get back!"

The climbed down carefully trying not to give themselves away by dislodging the loose rocks and then slid and climbed down to the forest below. As they stumbled through the tangled scrub, they came to a path heading in approximately the right direction. They needed speed and it offered the best hope.

Denquinar said under his breath, "If we meet Ichtar and they bar our way, we fight. One of us needs to get back whatever happens. If we meet them and our people are with them act as if nothing is out of order and we were just walking. We may only be able to save some of the men."

Gordy nodded. "I take it we act as if we are enthralled as well." Denquinar nodded. "There is someone coming! Slow down."

Around the corner they heard voices. "How far is it Ceti? It is hot in these bushes. You haven't got a uniform and a mantle to carry."

The feminine voice said, "It is a little way. We might meet your friend Hinson. He came here with Neegi for some special secret time also."

As they rounded the bend, they saw Gordy and Denquinar who seemed to be ambling along having a stroll. They walked past without saying a word, seemingly lost in their thoughts. Ceti giggled and ran ahead with Campsey coming along behind eagerly.

When they could no longer hear them, Gordy looked at Denquinar with angst all over his face.

"I feel like a traitor."

"It doesn't matter what you feel like it is how you act that makes you a traitor or not. Saving the rest of the men and the mission is what will prevent you from being one."

They saw the clearing of the camp was nearby.

"Slow down Gordy. Keep your voice calm. Go down to the beach and sit quietly with the men by the boats."

They came into the camp and casually went to the water gourds for a drink. Then Denquinar caught the eye of Reynolds and picked up a handful of nuts. He munched some casually and turned toward the beach and the boats.

Gordy saw that a couple of the Ichtar women were watching them; perhaps not suspicious yet but casually watchful. They strolled even more slowly towards the boats.

Just then there was a shout. Campsey came running through the camp clutching a shell necklace screaming. Monsters! They are monsters! Flee for your lives.

Ceti bounded into the clearing in her true shape and seeing her, the other Ichtar threw off their elaborate shell necklaces and revealed naked breasts but below that, a far more terrible sight. On all fours they attacked. Any men who could not reach the beach in time were savagely attacked.

Denquinar ran to the boats, shouting, "Arm yourselves, you fools!" Men seemed to waken out of their stupor and grabbed whatever weapon was at hand. In moments bows twanged and both Norri and Kiriakanatus shot.

Reynolds was throwing swords and boarding axes to his men who formed a semicircle around the boats.

Norri and Kiri shot again as Ceti came into the clearing, hard on the heels of the terrified Campsey. Norri had not lost his skill and although Kiri's arrow missed Norri hit the Ichtar in the middle of her chest. She collapsed onto her knees pawing at the offending shaft. Kiri was inspired and released another arrow. This hit one of the approaching creatures in the thigh of her foreleg and gave all the others a moment's pause.

Reynolds shouted at the men to man the boats and sailors pushed the tide-stranded craft toward the water again as if their lives depended on it. Gordy pointed out that they probably did.

"Do we make a sortie and try and save some of the fallen, Commodore?" shouted Reynolds.

His answer came quickly. Chara appeared in the clearing with thirty Ichtar behind her and many of these carried bows and spears. Her jaws and chest were covered in blood.

Arrows flew from both sides as the boats were manhandled into the water. The shore break was minimal and the men at oars and sail plied with a will and soon put some distance between themselves and the beach.

This didn't stop the Ichtar. They began to wade into the water, and some dived under the waves.

It what seemed too short a time, one of them rose out of the water with a spear. She hurled it and struck the man at the tiller of the launch who pitched over the side and screamed in terror as two Ichtar rose out of the water and bit into his body to drag him down under water.

The men rowed toward the ships while some stood ready with spears and swords in case the attack was repeated.

Kiri was working urgently with the box of small sized signal flags in the signal box. He quickly assembled the message from his father to the Swiftsure and then, in turn the Suresafe, "Under attack. Make ready to recover boats and sail."

Reynolds peered at their sister ship, hoping they had picked up the signal in the glare of the morning sun.

"Yes! They have seen us. They are weighing anchor and getting ready to take the boats in tow," shouted Kiriarkanatus.

As the boats approached the safety of the ship more of the Ichtar rose out of the water and attempted to drag men off the boats. Some paid dearly for this but the sight of the floating Ichtar corpses seemed to make the rest even more vicious.

Seamen scrambled up rope ladders thrown down the sides of the ship. The launch was taken in tow, and they began to unload the longboat.

The boat crews who stayed with their craft had to fight off several more attacks.

Once aboard Reynolds shouted orders. "We must winch the boats aboard as quickly as possible – the crews are exposed out there."

Even as he spoke a seaman in one of the boats screamed as an Ichtar rose with water streaming from her long hair and closed her jaws on his arm. His companion hacked at her neck with a cutlas, and she fell back into the water leaving a patch of blood in the wave where she had been.

The sailor's companion ripped off his shirt and tried to bandage the bleeding arm, when another Ichtar attacked from the other side of the boat. She had a long spear and the wounded seaman pitched over the side with the spear right through his body to disappear under the waves; leaving the remaining sailor alone in the boat; in terror.

"Pull them in! Recover the boats!" shouted Reynolds, as he watched in horror.

They could also see a group of about eight more Ichtar swimming in a course to intercept the ship. Reynolds ordered them to come about which also took the strain off the tow ropes and allowed them to get the boats in quicker. But the swimming Ichtar disappeared under the water, and they had no idea where they were.

By the time the third boat was being winched up the carpenter's mate came panting up to the poop.

Captain they are attacking the hull with iron spikes. They punch holes somehow and then another and another. Worsen and the other mates are trying to plug them, but we are taking water.

Reynolds gave orders for men to be sent below with an officer to help and gave orders for archers to shoot if the Ichtar came to the surface for air.

He looked over the side and could see the shape of one of the creatures below the water; he pointed her out to the archers who watched for their chance.

She was obviously busy attacking the timbers of the hull. When she rose to the surface several arrows struck her and she gave an unearthly scream as she bobbed in the water in pain. One sailor grabbed a spear and threw it well. It ended her agony and her body floated away behind the ship, all four legs and tail limp on the surface of the water.

The attack hadn't ended though; soon the other group reached them and dived under the water as soon as they were within bowshot. Again, the timbers of the ship's bottom were attacked with the punches. More water filled the bilges and the carpenter's mates were overwhelmed. The officer below decks called for reinforcements. He stood by the hull and waited with his sword drawn. One of the iron spikes punched through the oak of the timbers and then bent upward. He guessed the Ichtar was trying to remove it from the wood. He waited for the spike to be removed and thrust his long sword into the resulting hole and then withdrew his sword and grabbed some wadding to block the hole.

He looked at his sword lying on the half-decking above the bilge. There was blood on the tip.

The sailors got the idea and pointed out another punch being hammered in. He ran to the spot and repeated the process. Again, the attacker was driven off.

As the ship hauled up the last boat and gathered way, they passed the *Suresafe* who had bowmen and spearmen lining her sides to fight off the creatures and give the Swiftsure a chance to escape.

They made their way out to sea and saw the remaining Ichtar gather for the swim back to the beach.

There was a call from the lookout. "Smoke off the bows!" Denquinar looked at the white haze ahead and saw that there were indeed plumes rising from the sea.

Denquinar looked back and saw that the Ichtar were following and seemed to have stopped as a group and were bobbing in the waves, watching.

Denquinar ran to the bows with Reynolds only a pace behind him.

Denquinar called to a seaman, "Bring a bucket and rope".

Reynolds looked at Denquinar. "What do you think it is?"

The seaman returned with the bucket and rope and Denquinar indicated he should bring up some water.

"Steam. The seas are boiling!"

Reynolds looked at the water in the bucket suspiciously then put his hand in.

"It is warm. What does it mean?"

"Volcanoes under the water – making the waters boil." Denquinar looked back and saw that the Ichtar were still in the water behind them; not quick enough to catch the Swiftsure but able to intercept if they turned back from the boiling seas that seemed to block their path.

"What do we do, captain? Do we sail back to be entertained by Chara and her tribe, or do we risk the geysers ahead?"

"I think we thread the needle, Commodore: try and sail to the leeward of the islands and hope the Ichtar cannot swim fast enough to catch us."

Gordy had come to stand by the captain's shoulder. "Let us hope it isn't just a case of whether they get to eat us raw or cooked."

Denquinar chuckled. "I agree. Captain, give your orders."

Reynolds called for the carpenter to watch the seams for any signs that the pitch that made the oak planks of the ship watertight was giving way. To the seaman with the bucket he said, "Oaks, keep drawing water and give me reports if it is steaming when it comes up – don't put your hand in it."

"Yes, Cap'n."

Reynolds set a course to lay past the most easterly of the hot spouts and hopefully with enough width to pass clear of the Ichtar.

They signaled the *Suresafe,* and she turned to take position astern and on their port side, also in a position to shoot at the Ichtar if they made another attempt to attack.

Reynolds saw that they had armed the ballista on their decks. He thought that a good idea. Even if less accurate than a bow or spear, the ballista had greater range and may surprise their protagonists.

Oaks kept drawing water and indeed, as they approached the geyser the water in his bucket came up almost boiling. Moments later the carpenter sent a mate to warn that the pitch that corked the ship was melting.

Sweat ran off them and the sea appeared white with the steam.

They were taking water; and it was hot water.

Reynolds changed course almost due east. Ichtar or no Ichtar the ship would sink if she kept taking water like this.

Now the benefits of her careful construction showed its worth, her planks were well enough fitted that they were keeping out the boiling seas.

13

Masters of the World's Fate

*B*entonius was lying in bed next to Priscilla. There was only fear in her eyes these days. She must have known that he was behind the deaths of her young husband and her father. He had tried to hide his involvement of course but she must have guessed. Priscilla was the daughter of a noble family with significant power at court. She knew how things worked in the empire. She would have known that the covens were growing in power again and that they did so by eliminating all opposition once the old emperor had died.

He got up out of bed and poured himself a cup of wine. He offered her some, but she silently refused with a barely perceptible shake of her head.

Bentonius had paid dearly to get her. The assassination of her father and the contrived death of her husband had taken time and careful planning, to say nothing of money.

Now he didn't know why he had bothered. The vivacious, dark-haired girl he had fallen for, was no more than a compliant and silent drudge. He got no pleasure from her presence as he had before. It was as if she was resigned to her lot, hated it but was utterly powerless to change her situation. Without hope, she had become soul sick.

Bentonius did not know what to do. He remembered the happy smiling face of the girl he had known and mused, that girls were much prettier when they smiled.

He got his boots and street clothes and dressed quickly. The answer that came to mind immediately was Ingwit. She was dangerous – but she was alive; and she was in Bea-air Monar.

Bentonius asked a servant for paper and wrote a quick note to Ingwit to meet him in his room at the *Golden Kite* and ordered one of his servants to take it to the Coven Hall. The two had had many trysts. They both knew how vital Ingwit's relationship with the emperor had become and kept them very secret. It had been easy so far. The emperor had many concubines but like Bentonius, he appreciated her poise and confidence and she made for an excellent liaison with the coven people.

He was sitting in his little room at the *Kite* when there was a knock and Ingwit entered. She shot him a bright smile, but it quickly vanished.

"There are big moves afoot, lovely; you will see the complete destruction of Herelstrom if the present plans succeed. The emperor and his people are one with us in the desire to smash them. Their puny forts will be destroyed, and we will have more than our requirements of slaves… and wood for the navy. Then maybe admiral Cherulia will be able to build the ships that will smash the Bernadians."

"There will be plenty of sacrifices for those wild priests that are your friends."

"They are no friends of mine – they stink!"

"Perhaps, but whatever their hygiene habits, they are very useful and *very* powerful. I saw them at work in the first attack when we destroyed the new castle our friends at Egleton had built. The wyverns are deadly and the gordrills, ...they are incredible. If they can create more of these things there will be no army anywhere that will be able to withstand our might."

"They are very secretive though. I do not know how any of their spells work."

"They are willing allies and that is all that matters. Their society was in crisis – self destructive you might say. They need enemies and we were too big for them. So, it is just logical that they would want to join with us and fight our enemies."

"Yes. It all seems quite logical from that perspective. I would just like to understand what they do and how, so we do not inadvertently create for ourselves other masters. I just begin to wonder who is in control of the relationship. Are we using them or are they using us?"

"You worry too much, Ingwit. They do need us and we can use them against Herelstrom and against the Arionites. Once Arion falls and we have a clear road into Bernadia there will be no stopping the new armies. Eventually they will be a real asset against the big enemy. When we have done with these little powers, we can again turn the full force of our enmity against Bernadia. Then, Corrimar will rule the world; and we will control Corrimar.

Then Ingwit, you and I will be masters of the rulers of the world."

Ingwit stood looking at him with a quizzical smile; oh, he found her intoxicating. She stood there in the lamplight with her perfect figure and long blonde curls, the most amazing woman Bentonius had ever known. Priscilla seemed like a dark shapeless shadow in comparison.

"We should get some food, Ingwit before we go to meet Corrianasta and the others. It may be a long night. You know how they can talk."

Ingwit took his arm fondly; Bentonius liked that, and they left the room for the dining hall. They would eat and drink and they still had some time alone before the meeting later that night at the coven hall.

Later that night Bentonius would return to the business at the docks.

The coven hall of Bea-air Monar was set on a hill above the teeming harbor. At the military end of the harbor, Grand Master Groemelian could see ships of every kind that would carry their new armies to Herelstrom.

It was all part of the overarching strategy. They would finish the job they had started. Groemelian had lost some of his best people in that war. When everything seemed to be going perfectly, they had lost a battle they could not lose at the River Neren and the emperor, who everyone thought was dead turned up out of nowhere and regained the loyalty of the entire army. Groemelian vividly remembered that day. The empress was given her chance to lead in the ritual of the Kinbracher spell. The Great Jungari Lord had appeared, and the power of the spell was reaching forth when something broke; badly. Entiliedes died horribly, the old emperor they thought they had disposed of, returned; and killed several of the masters. Riok, the greatest of the grimulves was destroyed and he was beaten like a common criminal and kicked down the steps of the palace by one of the old emperors' officers.

Groemelian would make them all pay. He had not been idle. Although he liked to remain in the background and let others appear to be in control, he it was who stayed in the shadows and had the true power.

He had the new emperor completely under his thumb. Entilates VIII was no more than a puppet now. Groemelian had placed his people at the head of the administration. He controlled the money, ran the government, and guided the young ruler through the royal advisors who were now all his own people.

Ingwit had been wonderful. She had won the emperor's affection and played him like the fool he was. She had convinced him to appoint advisors who they wanted close to the seat of power.

Then gradually cause was found against the remaining nobles that Entilates trusted, and they were driven from court or found guilty of treason and executed.

Groemelian was more than happy for the emperor to enjoy all the trappings of power; it was necessary for the smooth running of the empire that the army and the populus had an authority figure. Now he surveyed his handywork: in barracks on the edge of the town there were thousands of troops ready to take ship. The army that would soon leave for the Neren River to join the forces that would by then have secured the far south of Herelstrom. There would then be little to prevent the consolidation of their control of the country. The two armies would then march north and take the capital. Pinitera had fallen last time to a quarter of the men they were now sending. He knew they had made mistakes last time. They would not do so again.

Below him in the courtyard were the priests preparing the carts to convey the giborach urns with their terrifying magical contents. The red and gold urns contained the dragons while the black ones contained the gordrill. In their magical suspended state, they were shriveled and curled up. When the priests dripped the black liquid into their mouths they began to revive.

The only concern that nagged at the back of Groemelian's mind was that he did not quite know how these priests did it. He would make it his business to find out. He did not like loose ends. He would consult the Jungari when they next spoke.

The priests also had their wild soldiers. These were housed in other barracks near the coven hall. There had been a few clashes in the town between the legionaries and the priest soldiers of Ba-al Giborachir. It had been interesting as both fought very differently. The Giborachites fought with wild jumps and downward slashes of their swords and bladed shields.

In the brawl more of the legionaries had been killed but once they grouped together in self defense the Giborachites could not penetrate their ranks. Groemelian thought that they had become dependent in war on using their magical monsters to penetrate the enemy ranks and they then followed with their slashing weapons. He could see how it would be effective. They had used the grimulves in the same way but these things were more ferocious even than the grimulves. And the wyvern could fly. They were a terror that could fall from the sky.

As if reading his thoughts, a large black wulf rose from the floor and sidled up to the grand master. "Thegh arr fierrce. Buut thegh cannorrt breeng terrorr arss wee carrn."

"They are tools only, Voniok, expendable. We are sending them against our enemies in the west. We will turn their safe little land into a place of fear where a monster may be hiding behind any tree or around any corner."

Scriei padded across the room and also looked out the window. "Vee eeverrn sennd terrorrss too invard therr skiess. Vee weell evern averng Keerrshemeerr."

A door opened at the back of the room and a middle-aged master entered.

Groemelian turned. "Ah, Corianasta, what news?"

"All the reports are confirmed. The Bernadians have been crushed with the aid of the priests and their 'er...companions."

There were uncomfortable chuckles around the room.

"They are utter filth, but they have their uses. If this continues, Corianasta all the sacrifices and struggles we have endured for so many years will be worthwhile. The strings that make all the puppets in the world dance will be ours to pull."

Corianasta smiled faintly. "I have many debts to repay. There will be many who will not like the payment they receive."

"Soon, Corianasta. You will have your share of fun; and revenge; after I have mine."

The grand master turned and crossed the room toward the door. "Come friends, we have a meeting to hold, and friends have reports for us."

Several masters and their acolytes were already in the coven hall. Groemelian walked in to nods of deference from all and mounted the podium. All eyes followed him to hear the news.

"Fellow masters of the grand lodge, we have news of the success of the attack on Herelstrom. No doubt you have all heard that the castle on the river Erne has fallen and that we have captured the ruler of that part of the country. Even now our reinforcements prepare to sail to consolidate our gains and prepare the final assault.

But we have other more recent news." Now every eye was turned to him. "The Bernadian northern army under prince Conamund has been defeated and is in full retreat westward where our forces are marshalling to deliver the final blow.

This changes the empire's strategy. We had planned to destroy Herelstrom first in a bid to gain timber to build a fleet capable of destroying the Bernadian navy.

Now we suddenly find they have faltered. Many of their best officers have fallen and our soldiers have carried off the prince of Bernadia from the field, perhaps dead. The remainder of their army is fleeing west away from the pass that is their route of retreat.

Elders, all our efforts and quiet work in the background have brought us to the point where with two deadly simultaneous blows on Herelstrom and Bernadia at the same time, we become masters of the rulers of the world.

Entilates VIII rode into Bea-air Monar in his chariot. The gold of his cuirass and helm shone in the bright sun of late morning. It was only in the gold that his armor differed from that of his legionaries. He took pride in using the arms of his soldiers. He drilled with shield, lance and sword and was said to be above proficient. He judged that good considering he bore the added burden of government.

Behind his chariot rode his honor guard. These were some of the finest soldiers in the empire, all decorated centurions; chosen for their skill and courage.

As he rode through the gates of the camp, he pondered the dilemma that recent events posed to his master plan.

The unexpected success the Dorphiremen and his southern legions experienced against the Bernadians had thrown his master plan into chaos. He had planned to keep the Bernadian Northern army tied up in a grinding stalemate while he finished with Herelstrom; then with his new army blooded and with new supplies of wood and slaves, build a navy that would crush the Bernadians who had always defeated them at sea.

Instead, messengers met him on the road saying that the wyvern and the wild dorphiremen had broken the Bernadian formations and that his southern army had them in full retreat westward; trapped on the wrong side of the mountains.

No sooner had he taken the report from these messengers than dust was seen on the road behind them. They stopped under a clump of trees and waited. Two naval messengers out of Orsimater, finding that he had left the capital had taken fresh horses and followed him. Now they breathlessly told him that the fortifications in the south of herelstrom had fallen and that General Groebalas was consolidating his hold with many fortified camps and naval defenses in the Erne River estuary. He was requesting more legions urgently to continue the conquest. Apparently some of the leaders of the southern town had been captured in the assault and were being brought injured to Bea-air Monar for *interrogation*.

So many things to consider! Entilates wanted to destroy Herelstrom. It was his life's task. His late mother would be very proud! She had met her untimely end when his father had returned unexpectedly when everyone was sure he was dead. Now, less than a year later, both his parents were gone: his mother by his father's sword on the day he returned, his father less than half a year later by a mysterious illness.

Entilates wished his mother was still alive to help him think through the ramifications of both choices: take the whole army to sea and crush Herelstrom like a nut or send part of the army to finish the job against the Bernadians. His thoughts turned to Ingwit, she had a quick mind; perhaps she was back in Bea-air Monar already and they could enjoy a little time of quiet over a cup of wine and discuss strategy.

Entilates felt a flush as he thought about how attractive a beautiful woman with a good mind for strategy could be.

The chariot wheeled and passed by troops on parade in his honor. He took the salute of his officers, but his mind was far from the parade ground. He absentmindedly fondled an amulet she had given him. It was said to have belonged to an emperor of old, the great Omrri Antarres. She said it might bring him luck; so far, it was working.

He closed his fist over the medallion. It seemed to help him think clearly. Perhaps it contained the wisdom of his forefather Omrri. Suddenly it was all too easy. He was surprised how effective the monsters had been: the gordrill and the wyvern in Herelstrom, the wyvern with the men of Ba-al Giborachir against the Bernadians. The creatures had changed the face of the empire's wars. Entilates had commanded the last assault on Pinitera, the famous *pink stone city*, the capital of Herelstrom.

Taking the walls had been the most difficult part but with the aid of the wyvern: the small golden dragons with their hard scales and poison tails, it could be much easier. They would be able to land on the parapets and drive off the defenders before the siege towers. It would be so easy. Ingwit was right. The alliance with the priest rulers of Baal Giborachir was to their mutual advantage. The empire gained useful allies with their terrible cohorts and the priests gained a share of the booty as well as slaves or sacrifices or whatever they were (Entilates didn't bother with the details). He had been told that each sacrifice was forced to watch the suffering of others to increase their fear. It all seemed very odd, but it wasn't his concern how a protectorate government chose to manage their affairs.

14

Mistress of the Coven of Avairs

*I*n the coven hall of Bae-air Monar, Ingwit, Mistress of Avairs, High Priestess of the Black Mountains, walked down a corridor toward the rooms at the far end of the complex. There, they had rooms where the masters could alternately house or detain those they wished to question.

She bore herself proudly. She was now one whom everyone in the empire feared, save very few, and even they respected her now. The coven guards snapped to attention and brought their pikes to salute as she passed.

She was bringing gifts to two small children in her care. They were important; very important. The bundles were tucked under her arm, wrapped in fine red silk cloth.

Outside the rooms where the children were kept stood a priest of Ba-al Giborachir. He smelled foul: of death. Ingwit thought it was probably from insufficient washing, but further reflecting, thought the spirits that gave him power may smell like this. The smell was hard to identify, Ingwit thought that if fear had a smell that would be what it would be.

But she had no reason to fear this priest. She was of higher rank by far and had more power. But they were allies and the empire needed them for the war. Herelstrom had resisted them before now and the masters in conclave had decided to send these priests and their soldiers against them.

The people of Herelstrom would never have seen anything like their magic and would have no answer.

But priest-rulers of Ba-al Giborachir in their turn, needed something from the empire.

The priest turned from one of the guards as she approached.

"Mistress, what do you carry?"

"Toys: a dolly and a soldier for our *guests*."

A smile spread across the priest's face that even turned Ingwit's stomach. Not much did that. She had seen more in her twenty-four years than most people ever saw. And she knew things both eldritch and terrible. But this priest....

Ingwit had no desire to speak with this man. She pushed past him and signaled to the guards to open the door. As she entered, she consciously changed the expression on her face.

Inside the room was warmly furnished and had a table set with food that had been little touched. Two small children sat on the hard floor holding hands. They seemed lost and scared even though Ingwit had worked hard to allay their fears.

She came and sat down on one of the beds. "Iroli, Gwendil, look what I have brought you presents." The two little ones who were about four and three years old, seemed to brighten. Ingwit held out the bundles and they came tentatively to her. Iroli unwrapped his bundle and discovered the beautifully made wooden soldier inside. It was not a Corrii soldier but a warrior like one of his own tribe. His face lit up and he sat on the floor playing with it. Seeing her brother's reaction, Gwendil also opened her bundle and found a beautiful doll with dark hair. Her eyes brightened and she looked at Ingwit with a smile for the first time.

Her smile moved something inside Ingwit. Feelings she thought long dead at the hands of fear and abuse, arose within her. Long she had hidden her feminine side under a fierce determination to become one who was: feared in turn; so that she could meter out pain and destruction on those who has used her so badly. She tried to suppress the rising feelings but the smiling, three-year-old girl had touched those soft parts of her feminine soul that she had forgotten since she was a little one herself.

As if sensing the growing warmth from Ingwit, little Gwendil put down the morsel of bread she had been eating and looked at her with pleading eyes. "Please. I want my mama."

Ingwit sat in stunned silence. The tiny girl's plea had touched the only warm spot in her heart that she had worked many years to make cold and hard with armor against the kind of hurt she had known as a child. That tiny remaining warm spot was the dim recollection of her mother's love. The flood of emotions that welled up took her completely by surprise, they rose up and overwhelmed her every attempt to keep them back. Ingwit had to get out of there. She dabbed the tears away from her eyes and headed for the door. She left the children with a servant girl and instructions for them to be given sweets.

She passed the foul-smelling priest outside but swept past him without even a glance and strode down the corridor to her own lodgings.

She let her blonde hair cover her face and wiped away the tears that defied her will and her self-control.

Her looks, her determination and her self-control had got her this far. She could endure anything.

"You fool!" she said to herself, "you spent too much time with them you allowed yourself to form an attachment."

That inner strength had enabled her to gain recognition in her coven in the north. It was close enough to the seats of power in the empire for her to get noticed and rise quickly to the grand conclave and the office of high priestess at an incredibly young age. Why did her self-control threaten to fail now? What was it about little Gwendil that aroused these churning emotions?

As Ingwit closed the door to her private chamber she let the tears flow freely and her mind flow back to the days as a small child when her mother was still alive. She barely remembered her father. He had gone away with the army and when her mother died, was not there to protect her. She was not yet five when she was taken into the household of a local noble; probably because of her looks, there followed years of abuse until she was noticed by a master of the black mountains coven. He had used her as well but he did introduce her to the coven life and eventually got her inducted. There she excelled beyond everyone's expectations.

Then her mentor died. She smiled at the thought of how she had engineered that. And she rose steadily to the role of high priestess, possessing great power and greater contacts in the world of the great Jungari: the spirits of the higher realms and the servants of the prince of the power of the air.

She was strong! So why did she feel like a tiny child again. She must not let these foolish feelings get a hold! She mustn't!

Bentonius walked along the docks with two men that seemed no more than typical dockyard workers. They had the look of men who would do anything or sell anything for money or drink. Both had the smell of liquor on their breaths and their clothes.

Bentonius slipped into the shadows of the building. "Is that the warehouse where they have agreed to meet?"

"Yes, my Lord. The entrance is at the side. Do you see those men – they are sailors, loyal to Captain Garlyon. They have been there all day. They have been watching for anything that may indicate that the conspirators have been discovered. There are two more on the other side of the building. They have also been strolling around the wharves; pretending to be drunk. But they are far from it. We saw a couple of thugs try and rob them, thinking them easy pickings: drunken sailors easily parted from their pay. Both paid dearly for that mistake."

"Do you think you have been seen?"

"No. We have been observing them from inside the warehouse over there. There was just a small crack in the wall. They would have had no idea they were being observed."

"Good. Go back to your hiding place and keep watch. If anything changes, one of you come to me at the *Gilded Kite*. I will be in the back of the common room or in my room: *number 34* on the second-floor landing."

The two men slipped around the corner toward the door of the warehouse and unlocked the door silently.

Bentonius continued down the street. He was alone in a dangerous part of the docks of Bea-air Monar. He checked his boot for the hidden dagger and then felt under his cloak for the more obvious weapon. He knew how to use these weapons at need, and he had others; more subtle and more powerful. Bentonius stayed in the shadows and was watchful, but not greatly concerned.

When he reached the inn, he slipped up the back stairs and went directly to his room. He would go to the common room later for a meal. Now he just wished to rest and collect his thoughts.

When he opened the door, he froze. There were men in his room.

Gastuss Norrens and his first lieutenant walked along a dirty alley by the docks of Bea-air Monar. They spoke little and stumbled as if they were drunk and on the way to their lodgings. Two younger officers followed. They were more wary as if they were watching over their more senior charges. They had their hands on the scabbards of their swords as if that gave some comfort in these dingy streets.

Norrens was elderly for a captain as was his first lieutenant. Both had been overlooked for promotion in the Corriian navy many times. It wasn't that they lacked skill or courage. Both had proved that many times and on many ships in the Empire's service. It was connections that they lacked.

The captain's tunic was of good stuff but dusty and draped carelessly over his frame which now tended to portly. He hadn't put on a clean uniform. That was not like him; he was usually fastidious in everything. Today was the very first time that he had ever been in doubt about what he was doing. Usually, duty in the empire was very clear cut. You might not like an order but there was usually only one alternative and that was to follow it. Initiative was tolerated and even encouraged but only within the context and scope of one's orders.

The navy had been good to Gastuss Norrens, on the whole. The admiralty had men of all kinds and all vices, but they were all seamen who had risen through the ranks and understood a seaman's life. They could be trusted to make sensible decisions and even when given tasks from the emperor that were impossible, they knew enough to subtly suggest alternatives or at least, contingency plans.

Denquinar had been an excellent grand admiral. He was canny and shrewd and an excellent judge of men. He also had an agile mind and could think several steps ahead of others, so he was always able to direct a conversation in a way he wanted it to go. He had argued for the resources they needed and successfully steered a course through the intrigues of court.

His desertion made no sense at all. He had everything a man could want. Gastuss Norrens was probably the last Corriian officer to see him. He was aboard an enemy ship and with at least some level of freedom. Norrens could not imagine what had happened to Denquinar. Something had made him snap. There was a rumor that it had been his son. Vice Admiral Cherulia had sent the ship in which the boy served on a suicide mission – probably to spite Denquinar. There was no love lost between the two it was said.

Denquinar thought Cherulia an arrogant fool who had gained his position in the navy because of his connections not his skill at command. He usually achieved what was asked but with the loss of too many men and ships. He wasted lives, or so Denquinar thought and Norrens agreed. With Cherulia it was worse than that. He seemed to take a perverse pleasure in sending men to their deaths. He even seemed to engineer it so that they realized that they were going to die and had no choice but to carry out the deadly orders or refuse; and be hung for cowardice and desertion in time of war. It always seemed to be the best officers he destroyed.

Bentonius froze in the doorway. His mind was calculating how long it would take him to draw and throw his dagger and get the door closed.

A cold voice calmed him. "It's alright Benton, it's me."

Bentonius knew the voice. He sheathed the dagger and slipped inside the door closing it behind him.

Vice Admiral Cherulia sat on the bed while two other men in nondescript clothes stood quietly by the window and occasionally glanced out at the street below.

"What have you found out?"

"Not much. I have had men watching the warehouse and there are guards loyal to them but no sign of the captains at all."

"The emperor will have my skin if I go to him with a half-baked story of mutiny among his senior naval officers and cannot provide any proof. He needs these men and their experience right now. You had better come up with some proof of the conspiracy or mutiny or whatever it is soon, or I will have your skin."

"You haven't got the power and you know it. I have contacts that could destroy you."

"Really? Ingwit? She may have the ear of the emperor, but you can hardly rely on that. And the grand coven has lost much of its credibility with their spectacular failures in the last war. No Benton, (Cherulia used Bentonius' alias to annoy him) I can dispose of you, if I wish. You may not think you need my patronage, but you will find that you do. And I can make use of your quite exceptional skills so let's not quarrel. I need to know if there is a mutiny or revolt among my officers as you think or assure myself that your first impressions were wrong. Experience would incline me to trust your first assessment – but I need some proof.

"If there is a revolt and we have to burn some captains alive to make an example it will mean that we will have undesirable delays while we replace these men and all the senior officers that are collaborating with them."

Bentonius was deep in thought, "You are right - we cannot let any escape the net. There will be many more than the chief conspirators who we expect at the warehouse."

Cherulia rose to his feet. "Think on it Bentonius. You are very good at this kind of thing. I am sure you will break into their conspiracy and find a way."

Cherulia nodded to his companions, and they left the room quietly, leaving Bentonius alone with his thoughts.

It was difficult. Loyal men were hard to buy, and it had been all but impossible to infiltrate the conspiracy. He had used all his skills to uncover details of what he had discovered. On his trip back from the sacking of Egleton, he had overheard some things that sounded strange, and he had spent the rest of the trip hidden, listening for any information.

There was plenty of discontent about the way the navy was being run. That didn't amount to mutiny of course. There was always discontent. It didn't matter as long as men obeyed orders.

The defection of that filth, Denquinar had sown the seeds of discontent in the navy. He was universally liked and respected as a very competent sea officer who could also fight the cause of the navy in the high command. His defection and the suspected part that Cherulia had played in it all, had started many tongues wagging. Bentonius began to wonder if supporting Cherulia was such a good idea.

His mind was too busy with all this to sit alone in his small room at the inn. He took his cloak and went back down the stairs to the narrow street. He turned toward the town centre and the old administration building that had now been taken over by the covens. He wanted to see Ingwit again, if she was still there.

Ingwit was something of a mystery. There were obviously depths of her that she kept very secret but in all their dealings she had been very open and even a collaborator. Bentonius longed for the company of a woman with a bit of fire. Ingwit was exactly the person he needed to think through the problems of Cherulia and his captains. She had an agile mind and they were well matched in wisdom and cunning. They had often talked until late into the night and their conversations usually ended with them waking up in each other's arms the next morning.

Ingwit closed the door. Tears now flowed unchecked down her face and her dress was wet.

She was shaken; more than shaken, she was distraught. She had lost all control and sat shaking and sobbing on the bed. The image of herself on a bed twenty years ago came flooding back. She had been horribly abused and her little body then seemed full of pain. She had been oblivious to the assault on her femininity, so absorbed was she with the fear and pain. The little girl she had now been forced to befriend had brought these feelings back.

It was obscene what they were doing: making little children trust them in order to savagely and cruelly betray that trust in foul, deadly rites that were designed to create the maximum fear in the tiny victims to feed the needs of the spirits of Ba-al Giborachir. If they were already afraid, they tended to go into a sort of morbid stupor with the fear. If they were not expecting anything was wrong, then they reacted in true terror when the intentions of the priests became clear. Terror was what the priests needed.

Ingwit was chosen to befriend the children on route to the island of Giborachir because she could be trusted, she was a master of the grand coven; she knew how much they needed these foul priests and their power; she could be relied on to do what no normal woman could do.

But it was destroying her. Her defense against her own abuse had been cold savage vengeance, but little Gwendil had slipped past all her defenses and shattered them from the inside.

Now she was a little girl again herself, bereft and without hope or any comfort.

There was a knock at her door.

15

Bernadia

From the docks of Bertola ran a straight road of stone slabs up to the steps of the palace of the emperor. In the harbor great ships rode at anchor. They were painted in bright red, yellow and blue to match the flags that fluttered from the turrets and domes of the palace. On the road and on the steps were officials, soldiers, and sailors and all busy at tasks to do with the administration of the empire. The mood was of a watchful major power, at peace.

All of Bertola seemed full of colour. The colours that adorned the great ships in the harbour, also adorned the clothing and turbans of the palace officials.

A tall young man strode along one of the docks, along the Via Altora and up the steps to the palace. Several others trailed behind him struggling to keep up. They all wore bronze armor and helms of bronze were tucked under their arms to allow the sea breeze to blow the locks of their hair freely in the heat of the day.

At the top of the steps, guards in the imperial livery saluted the young man and he passed into the palace.

They came to a wide corridor of black marble with mosaic friezes where it intersected with other corridors that led off to the right and left. At the end of the corridor great bronze doors stood open and the crowded throne room was beyond.

The marble columns of the great chamber were decorated with bands of gold, silver, crystal and lapis lazuli making it a place of wondrous beauty and great awe to any who visited for the first time.

There were many such visitors and emissaries in the hall, seeking audience with the emperor and looking about the glittering hall in wonder.

The young man made his way to the marble seat at the end of the hall where a portly figure, clad in jewelled robes sat surrounded by cushions, with servants, advisors and scribes all around him.

When he saw the young man approaching, he rose from his seat and took several steps toward him.

"Omari, you have returned; glad am I to see your face. How stands it with the twin cities, are they still allies, or have they succumbed to the pressure of the Corrii?"

The young man stepped closer and embraced the old man. "I am also glad to see you hale and able to continue the great work. The cities remain free and do not pay tribute to the Corrii, that is obvious. They gave us a cool reception though and there are clearly some who think that accepting our naval protection makes them more of a target for their enemies.

"They suffer from all the doubts you would expect from free cities standing between two great powers."

A young man in fine robes who stood several paces from the emperor stepped forward; in a voice of command and with a nod of deference to the emperor he interjected. "This matter needs more thought, and we will hear the full tale of Omari's emissary in council. For now, you should go to the palace and refresh yourself with water and food. Be back for council after the noon bell!"

Omari nodded politely to his oldest brother. He knew his place but wished for a longer audience with his father. He was not such a fool as to reveal anything of great strategic importance in court.

The emperor saw the exchange. He was only too aware of the tensions between his sons. He also knew that Omari was aware of the line he had to tread between his own authority as a general in the second largest empire in the world, and his lot as the youngest son.

"Omari is discreet, Anabund. He knows what can be said in this gathering. Be at ease. We will discuss our allies and their situations in council.

"Is there any news of Conamund?"

Anabund had been awaiting news all day and had send messengers with fresh horses to see if the messengers from the army were approaching the city. He shook his head. There was no sign.

The emperor rose from the marble seat. "Go, Omari, change your clothes and refresh yourself. Later we will take food and meet with the war cabinet.

"Anabund, could you send out fresh riders to see if there is any news from your brother and the army?"

Anabund drew closer to the emperor so as not to be overheard. "I have done so and there is no news yet."

"That is well thought of. Perhaps they will return yet before the cabinet meets. I am greatly concerned by the massed armies of the Corrii in the south. We thought one was being sent against the twin cities but if they have caved in to the Corrii negotiators, the two armies may have combined against Conamund.

"But let us speak of these things now. Go my sons, attend to what you must do, leave an old man to his worries."

They met later in the war cabinet room. There were four elderly generals, several civilian advisors, the emperor, his two sons and an elderly admiral. This meeting was of the utmost secrecy.

All the men stood in silence and waited for the emperor to take his seat at the top of the table.

"Well gentlemen, I take it there is no news yet?"

Anabund shook his head. "No, my Lord, there is no sign of messengers. I was on the walls until just a few minutes ago looking for signs of riders…. Nothing yet."

Then we will hear Mudubin and Omari's report.

The younger man nodded to the elderly politician on his left. "You had better give the report, senator. You have a better mind for these subtlties".

The elderly man stood up and looked around at the concerned faces in the room. "The citizen rulers of Venemar are as always, careful in every word they say.

"Their concern is ever for their wealth and security. They have high walls, and their trade makes them great wealth. With their wealth they employ the best soldiers but have no desire for anything except defense and prosperity.

They have had our protection against the Corrii up until now. Our ships have patrolled the coast and our better captains and ships have so far given the Corrii more than enough reason to stay well away from the twin cities.

The citizen rulers of Venemar and Solptor seem to have changed their mind about that alliance. They say they have enough ships of their own now to impede any Corrii offensive by sea and that they have strengthened the fortifications around their harbours."

The emperor was stroking his beard and thinking, "Do you have reason to doubt their words?"

Mudubin nodded to Omari. "I will let your son tell you about his thoughts on this." The Senator resumed his seat and Omari stood.

"My Lord, I took whatever opportunity was offered to search out the naval defenses of the cities. I asked for horses to ride out into the countryside but used the opportunity to ride along the coast. I saw very few naval vessels. It seemed that all the ships the citizens had were in the harbor at Venemar; probably to impress us. I also noticed that, although they bore no markings, I saw Solptorian officers on the decks of one. It was all intended for our benefit I believe and to make their arguments that they no longer needed our naval protection seem credible."

A tall soldier at the table broke the following silence. "So, you think they have been dealing with the Corrii?"

Omari had obviously been considering this on the voyage back.

"They would surely know the Corrii cannot be trusted. All here know that the Corrii have threatened them before and consider their status as free cities a challenge to say the least. Perhaps some news that we do not know has made them think that even a temporary alliance is better than nothing."

Anabund picked up a parchment with the last report from his brother and the army. "Conamund reports that the scouts have been able to observe the Corriian army and that it is too small to attack our forces in the north."

Omari nodded to his brother. "If that is the case there must be some new threat other than the threat of their legionaries."

Anabund looked annoyed. "That was what you were sent there to discover."

The emperor raised his hand. "What concerns me is the lack of information. We should have had two daily reports after this one, Anabund. And there is no news."

An elderly general who seemed to have been deep in thought and had been drawing lines on a wax slate on the table and counting in his mind spoke out his thoughts.

"There are at lest two places in the mountains where our messengers could have been waylaid. But they have swift horses and travel with protection so that it is hard to intercept them."

The emperor seemed to add this to his assessments. "It might be that the army has been attacked and cut off. I see none of you wish to advance *that* possibility; nor do I. Or it might equally be a typical Corrii attempt to distract us while they use their forces elsewhere. This would be typical. Corrii commanders like to strike hard and do damage to enemies that they cannot quickly defeat by the sheer force of their arms. This is more what I fear."

Omari had been considering this. "Do you think they might have other intentions such as our friends at Herelstron?"

"I had not considered that, but it may be as you said. The north is no longer passable to our ships now that the Corrii have become active again."

There were sounds outside the door.

All the officers leapt to their feet as the doors were opened to the war room.

A soldier was being half carried; half dragged into the room. He did not seem to be hurt. There were no obvious wounds, but he was obviously racked with pain and was struggling to breathe.

A sergeant who carried the man clumsily saluted the emperor while supporting the soldier. "I am sorry, my Lords but I knew you were eagerly awaiting news from the army and this man is one of the messengers. We were sent to look for the messengers and rode right past him. One of my men noticed him on our return. He was lying in some brush beside the trail and had not been able to catch our attention.

With some water we were able to revive him enough to get some of his tale from him and decided to bring him here to you and to get some remedy for his hurts – if there is any.

The emperor hurried to the wounded messenger as fast as his bulk would carry him and instructed that they lay the man down. He sat propped against the sergeant and lay long enough to gather his breath.

"My Lord, the army has been attacked by an equal force of Corrii and other soldiers in red who fight with strange creatures.

They have flying monsters such as we have never seen, who attack from the sky and use spines filled with poison to disable our men. They attacked those on horseback particularly, knowing these to be the officers.

My Lord, your son had been attacked and was gravely hurt. When I left, he still clung to life but he and many of your loyal officers have been attacked and poisoned.

The centurians in your army managed to rally the men and the Corrii were driven off in the end, but it was a very near thing."

The emperor took a towel that was handed to him, and he dipped it in water and wiped the spittle that foamed around the man's lips.

"How did this happen to you?"

"I was sent with news to the generals. On the way we were attacked by other creatures. Like great apes they were but they carried swords and could leap four times as long as any man. Most of our riders were unhorsed in their first attack and we battled three of them on foot.

I was struck and thought it to be the end but awoke later to find all my companions dead and me alone taken for dead, seemingly.

I began to walk along the trail hoping to meet other messengers, but my arm has been bitten here…" He showed them the swollen red bite marks on the inside of his arm. "It must have some evil in the bite for I have felt worse and worse since then and have fallen many times."

The emperor looked at the young man with pity. "That is enough for now, soldier. The news you have brought us, though very grave, is of great import. Thank you!

Take him now and get him help from the healers and have his hurts tended."

When the wounded messenger had been carried away the doors were again closed and guards returned to their stations to keep the discussions secret.

Anabund looked at the faces around the room. There was silence. Everyone felt the pain of the father and the brothers at the news that Conamund had been gravely injured and maybe was now dead. The generals also knew the young man to be a fine officer and a good soldier who suffered the depredations of weather and long campaigns with his men.

"I will take a mounted force north myself to see how it is with our brother and to see to the army."

One of the generals took his arm and shook his head. "My Lord, you cannot do such a thing. You are heir to the throne and if our worst fears prove true and your brother has been lost in battle or is badly injured, we cannot risk your life also. Let one of us go to see to the army and see what may be done for the young prince."

The emperor looked up; he had tears in his eyes. "It is as General Tumarind says, Anabund, we cannot risk you as well. Too often have I risked the lives of my sons, first I nearly lose Omari and now possibly Conamund. I will not willingly risk your life.

"But, Father, I am an officer and a general in your army. It is my place to lead the army!"

"One day, maybe in not too many days it will be your job to lead the empire. You would be a pretty prize for the Corrii, dead or captured... or poisoned and crippled like the poor soldier you just saw."

Anabund hung his head and did not reply.

Tamarind placed his hand on the prince's shoulder. "My Lord, I will go. I am an old soldier who has done too much fighting with words of late. But if I may make so bold, it would be good if the Corrii thought you were going to go to the army."

Anabund looked at him confused. "What do you mean?"

"Just that I think we may assume two things: The Corrii seem to have spies in the palace or at least in this city; perhaps both. And it does appear that they are targeting you and your brothers.

Would it not be wise to send another in your armor to the front? Then if the Corrii do have spies that are watching your movements and are targeting you in particular, it will be obvious, and you will be secretly engaged in other important business of the empire."

"What could be more important than leading our army?"

"Preparing another! My Lord, we may assume that the empire to our north is intending to destroy Bernadia. They are eliminating our allies and slowly weakening all our defenses. We must turn the auxiliaries into a serious fighting army and quickly. That would give us a second army that can be mobilized quickly."

The Emperor was roused out of his reverie. "That is good advice Anabund. I endorse what general Tamarind says. It shall be so. You have the best training of any officer in my army. You will find a way to make the reserves a serious fighting force if anyone can do it. They must be ready soon. Then you can quickly deploy them against any unexpected threat the Corrii can contrive. And we may assume they will devise new weapons and new strategies, they always have. Men and officers must be trained to be flexible and able to adapt to any new threat or new weapon."

Anabund was not happy, but it was clear that there was no other option.

Later that evening, after supper, Omari found the emperor in the garden of the palace by the fountain, drinking tea and deep in thought.

His father saw him and indicated he should sit.

"My son, I am glad to have you back. At least you and Anabund are safe for the present."

"You are thinking about Conamund, my Lord."

"Do not call me Lord when we are alone. Let it be enough that I am your father, and a very proud one indeed.

"Yes, I am thinking of your brother… and the other young men hurt by these evil creatures the Corrii have brought down upon us.

Where they come from who can know, I have never heard tell of such creatures and this world is full of many strange and dangerous creatures. But these obey the commands of the Corrii and fight for them.

They are trained, maybe. But can a wild creature be trained to fight with an army. I have never heard of such a thing."

Omari sat and poured tea into an extra cup - that just happened to be there. "There is some evil magic in it, there can be no doubt of that."

"We have long known that they bring the great wulves from the north and that these are somehow controlled by foul spirits that give them voice. Perhaps the Corrii have found a way to do this with other creatures."

Omari sipped his tea. "I have never heard of creatures with scales and long tails with poison spines that live anywhere in the world."

"Omari, please go and see to the soldier who brought us the news. Firstly, see how he fares and then if he is well enough to speak see if there is any more that he can tell us about the evil creatures they encountered."

The young warrior rose to his feet. "I will go to the infirmary in the lower city. I am guessing that is where he has been taken. The night is cool I will hurry and bring you more news if I can." Omari left the emperor to his tea and his worries about his son.

Below in the barracks general Tamarind stood by his horse. He was dressed in full armour. His cuirass gleamed beneath his cloak and his helm had a long black horsehair plume fully covered his face. A great wood and leather shield with a spiked bronze boss in the centre hung from the saddle. The old general was going to war again, in the prince's armour.

The rest of the mounted cavalry were of the emperor's guard to further the impression that it was the crown prince who was leaving the city. They were the best equipped and trained and the most experienced soldiers in the empire; they went on a mission to rescue the emperor's son and restore the morale of the army.

Forty mounted soldiers stood by their mounts. Horses champed and whinnied; their hooves clattering on the stones of the courtyard. They were war horses and were eager to be off into the cool evening air.

Several horses were being loaded with supplies sufficient for the journey north. Ten of the horsemen carried bows of Bernadian fashion: compound bows of acacia-wood and bone that had terrifying effect at short range. These, it was hoped, would serve well against both the ape-like creatures and against the scaled, flying ones.

Omari stood with the general. He had run to the barracks with all the information that he had gleaned from the injured messenger. He knew any information would be a help in reaching the army if these strange creatures were attempting to bar the way.

The general liked Omari, after all, he was the third son and very unlikely to be emperor, so he often got the less glamorous jobs and had none of the airs of his older brothers.

He knew the young man would have wanted to go but after refusing the crown prince the emperor could hardly have offered the job to his youngest brother. But Omari was the tallest and strongest and most proficient at arms of the three.

Outside the barracks, a tall, thin man in a baker's apron slipped back into the shadows. He had seen the young prince run into the barracks and has seen all the preparations for the sortie. He slipped back into the shadows and hastened down the street to report to his master what he had seen of the preparations.

It had been four days with no sign of the enemy and the troopers of the royal guard sat around their campfires and trivets preparing their evening meal and their tea. They had ridden up into the mountains and were just below the pass that would take them northward to where they hoped they would find the army. The men were resting and speaking together around the fires and enjoying the anticipation of the meal of beans and camp bread, when all looked skyward. A long, eerie cry came from the airs above.

High in the eastern sky, gleaming golden in rays of the sunset flew a creature none had ever seen before. Men quickly doused fires and ran for their arms, but it was too late to hide so large a company. General Tamarind looked in the direction of the cry and saw the large reptilian shape as it wheeled toward them. It had large bat-like wings spread wide as it glided easily on the mountain thermals. It also knew it had been seen and knew it could not attack so large a group of men alone - but it could make them afraid. The wyvern already knew that men fought poorly when frightened. It was the same with the prey in its world. It gave out its terrible shriek and swooped toward the camp where men scuttled about reaching for weapons.

Giriweel wheeled into a ravine that would keep her hidden from the men below until she was on them. She sped along just above the treetops and came out from a place the men did not expect. They were standing with their weapons pointed the wrong way when she appeared behind them and let out a screech that would freeze their blood. Before they knew what had happened and turned to shoot their puny bows, she was away out of their range. She reared up in the air and screeched again before rolling over and sweeping away with strokes of her huge wings. She would return; but not alone.

16

Unknown Valleys

*C*aptain Henderson of the *Suresafe* shadowed the damaged *Swiftsure* toward the coast. They needed a bay or some shelter from the weather to make repairs to her bottom and to re-caulk the planks – it was a full week's work if they worked in shifts day and night.

The *Suresafe* lay off her stern to windward. If they were overtaken by Corrii she would have to fight them off. The Swiftsure could not take much punishment. A day or so ago the lookout had spotted a sail. It was well out to sea and seemed to be tacking away from them. Hopefully they had not been seen. There was no way of knowing this. She may have simply turned closer to other ships of her fleet to rally them for an attack.

As both ships approached the coast, the mountains loomed up grey and menacing before them. Here the mountain chain that protected Herelstron reached right to the sea; there were barely even foothills. The snow and haze around the peaks did not provide much encouragement that they were passable.

Here the coastline bent away westward and there were some bays that would offer shelter from southerly winds at least but nothing better. In the end, the best that they could find was a beach sheltered from the north by a headland and a rocky outcrop and a plentiful supply of timber from stands of trees near the shore.

They would need wood to construct a slipway and winch to bring the Swiftsure far enough out of the water to effect repairs. Reynolds sent boats ashore to investigate and they returned with promising news. The timber was of good quality, a sort of pine they had never seen before, but which offered good promise and there was a stream nearby of clean water from the mountains.

Nobody was taking anything for granted but their situation was desperate. The Corriian navy was behind and even if they abandoned the Swiftsure there was no assurance of a safe return to Herelstrom. The mountains offered little hope of a successful journey east and the journey south by sea could not be undertaken without repairs to the *Swiftsure* all they could do was take all precautions possible and set to work.

They brought the Swiftsure in as shallow as they dared for a ship of her draught and sent boats ashore with men to begin the work on the slipway. Meanwhile the sailors began to de-rig her as much as possible and send the spars ashore to be stored until she was re-floated. All set to with a will but the work was painfully slow. Now, men slumped by fires on the sand at night to rest completely spent from the gruelling labor.

One night by the fire Norri floated the idea of climbing the nearby mountainside to see if there might be a way east.

They took thick cloaks against the cold they might find at those heights and set out early in the morning. By midday they had reached a spine of the mountain and had enough visibility to see down into the valley below. There was river surrounded by trees of some size which may offer a way through. It would certainly be worth a try.

Norri and Gordy climbed back down and arrived at the camp shaky with tiredness but bearing the promising news.

Denquinar, Reynolds, Norri and Gordy conferred later that evening over dinner aboard the *Swiftsure*, Denquinar did not like the idea of Norri and Gordy setting out this far north. He thought there may be better hope south but had no basis for believing this to be so.

"The mountains may thin out. That is the way of mountain chains that I know."

Norri wasn't so sure. "Yes, Commodore but these mountains are at least as high as those bordering my home and this may only be the middle of this range. It may go on and on further south and our journey east may be delayed by weeks."

Denquinar seemed to be calculating. "You are right of course, there is no certainty that we will find a better place for the eastward journey, and I agree the valley you saw offers some hope. You may find that you reach impassible cliffs or glaciers of course but that is always a risk. If you discover within a few days that the valley does not offer any hope, you can still return, and we will be here. This whole venture is fraught with risk. If you and Gordy think you may be able to do it, you may as well try. If we find the southern seas impassible, we will return to this place and see if you have returned. We will leave you plenty of stores. If you cannot pass the mountains, you may at least have some chance of hunting and there will be enough flour and dried fruit here if we can rig up some kind of storage cache. It will need to be inland and hidden in case those following us come ashore here. You can be assured they will take the stores or poison them at least – the former is most likely."

Gordy smiled. "Commodore you are full of cheery thoughts tonight. So far you have speculated that we will face impassible cliffs or ice, only to return here and be poisoned or at best to starve to death waiting for you to return to pick us up."

Denquinar smiled. "I'm sorry. It is the training of a sea captain to think of all possible contingencies. Often ships are at sea for many weeks and what you do not take with you, you must often do without. We will be here at least another six or seven days, making repairs before we can even begin to re-rig the Swiftsure so you may as well set out as soon as possible."

Norri had been glancing at the partly drawn map on the chart table. "That decides it we will try the way east for three and a half days and turn back if there seems no way forward. If there is, we will continue east."

Reynolds finished the plan. "If you are not back in seven days and we are seaworthy we will set off south leaving you supplies and a promise to return via this place at some time in the future; earlier if the southern seas are impassible. I will arrange a boat to take you ashore at first light tomorrow. Can you be ready?"

Gordy took his last sip of coffee, "Mmm. Endless days trudging thought country we don't know to find an unknown way to a place we have never been to...can't wait!"

Reynolds stood up and smiled. "Good. I'll organise the boat and send the quartermaster to help you with any stores you need." He left the cabin to find the quartermaster who was on deck.

Gordy called after him. "A bag of coffee... That, I am prepared to carry up mountains."

The following morning promised a hot day. Norri decided that if he had to scale a mountain that this was the way to do it. They took their packs and bows, and stout walking sticks they cut on the edge of the tree belt. They made their way through the pines and came to a couple of leagues of thick brush they had negotiated the day before. It was not until the sun was well up that they reached the bare slopes of the mountain. They stopped for a drink and morsel of food before they set out again.

They reached the spur by late morning and began the descent into the valley. It was steep and slow going but easier than the climb up. They decided to climb across the side of the mountain heading north so as to gain a better view of the valley beyond and maybe identify any problems before they spent days travelling through the dense forest on the valley floor.

This took about four hours and by the time they reached a point where they could see up the valley, it was dusk. They looked up the valley with the sun shining down from behind them. It was long and forested but turned around behind a particularly large mountain. There was no way to tell whether it came to impassible cliffs on the other side or not. But the water in the river ran slowly and there were no sign of eddies or rapids cascading over rocks so there seemed to be a good chance that it was like the rivers of their own country that ambled down from the mountains and across the coastal plain.

Gordy and Norri climbed down into the dim valley with the last rays of the day glimmering on the crags above them. They reached thin bushes and then to their surprise, coffee bushes interspersed with other shrubs. It was past the time of the year for coffee pods to be picked but they found a few handfuls of pods that the local birds had not plundered.

They had a struggle through some dense bushes that were taller than their heads and came to thinner cover under tall trees by the time it was too dark to go any further, so they chose a sheltered spot and made their simple camp. They had a small tent to provide comfort when it was rain-ing; just large enough for the two of them and their gear but this night didn't look like rain, and they made a small fire that quickly burned down to a pile of coals suitable to cook a damper and to roast a few nuts. They each tore off a strip of dried, salted meat and drank some water before wrapping themselves in their cloaks for the night. They would need water soon, but they decided to leave the search until morning.

They had kept half the previous nights damper for breakfast. It was less appealing cold but better than nothing and they revived the fire enough to brew some coffee to have with it. They were both tired from the previous day's exertions but knew their muscles would harden up with more traveling. They heaved their packs up and noticed how sore their shoulders were after the previous day's climb. They saw that the land sloped downhill and decided to veer downhill in the hope of find-ing the river to give them their bearings.

Norri decided that they should carry their bows strung in case they stumbled onto some game or even something less desirable. They had both brought ten arrows. This seemed a good compromise between too much weight and too few for the journey. It was easy to lose or break arrows hunting, and they didn't want to spend too much time searching for suitable wood to make more. Gordy did think to take a few extra hunting tips.

The ground began to level out and they startled a few fowl foraging in a patch of long grasses. Norri fitted an arrow but by the time he could draw his bow they were already on the wing and too difficult a target. The fact that they were there relatively undisturbed seemed promising and they decided to be more careful in the hope of spotting their prey and shooting while they were on the ground. They saw no more fowl until they reached the river. It was not much of a river really, barely four paces across in some spots and heavily overgrown on the banks. They struggled through the rushes and thick grasses to refill their water bottles but retraced their steps to the grasslands which were easier going.

They came to a copse with large bushes entangled with the prickly canes of sour berries. The wind was behind them from the sea and there was hope of a clean shot of any more of the speckled brown waterfowl were on the other side. They crept carefully around the edge with bows ready and saw that they had guessed correctly. There were about a dozen of the birds nibbling the seed heads of the grasses on the other side of the copse. Both Norri and Gordy carefully drew their bows and stood high enough to peep through the tops of the bushes. Norri winked at Gordy and both arrows were released, Norri's arrow a moment before Gordy's. Norri hit and the bird Gordy had shot at rose just in time and the arrow drove into the ground where it had been a moment before.

They skirted the copse and went to inspect their quarry. Norri had just bent to pick up the arrow when there was a snarl on the edge of the taller grasses ahead. A brown bear, very similar to the tree bears Norri had encountered sometimes near his home charged them. Norri dropped the bird and ran with Gordy close on his heals. Dropping the bird was a good move as the bear stopped to inspect the carcass. Then it picked it up and trotted back into the long grass.

Both of them stayed hidden behind the copse for a while but the bear didn't show itself. They thought they could hear crunching sounds.

"He's enjoying our dinner!" commented Gordy.

"Better that than our leg."

"Yes, but I already had that fowl sizzling over a slow fire."

"Come on he is probably full up now and won't give us any more trouble."

They continued along the river with arrows on the string in the hope of making Gordy's dinner a reality but by evening they still hadn't seen any more of the waterfowl and the terrain had become different again. The tall trees grew right down to the river now and Norri noticed a few Orkya trees among them. They were nothing like as large as the trees he was used to, but younger trees had more branches and were easier to climb. He tried a few and the result was encouraging. They took time to collect a few more bunches to make their dinner more interesting in lieu of roast waterfowl. The nuts were much smaller than the ones from the trees in the Southern End, but they seemed to be the same plant.

The forest became close, and the ground rose a little as they approached the large mountain, they had seen the previous day. The river was running in a deep ravine and seemed to be flowing faster. They had the pressure of the decision to go on or go back to the ships.

Now they struggled on slowly through a heavily forested rise with no visibility at all. The trees of a pine variety Norri did not know grew close together on the lower slopes of the mountain and became all but impassible. They eventually found a spot next to a larger tree where there was a little space for a fire and sat down for their evening meal. There was no shortage of wood, it lay about them everywhere and they threw on a few pinecones to make the fire blaze up quickly and burn some larger faggots. Soon a base of coals was ready for them to make some damper for their tea. It was fairly meager, and both wished they had had the waterfowl to make it more interesting. As it was, they wrapped themselves in their cloaks and slept by the dying embers of their fire.

They awoke late the next morning, and both were annoyed with themselves. They needed the extra hours to climb out of the pine woods and get a view of the valley below. They ate the remaining damper from their last night's meal as was their custom and clambered up through the pines. When they finally got into the clear there was still a spur of rock obstructing their view of the valley. They tried to get around it but the pines on the ridge were so dense that they were impassible. The only way was to climb out and over the spur. They had a rope and began the difficult climb. It meant taking off their packs and dragging them up after them with their rope. It was very slow going and it was afternoon when they reached the top.

What they saw didn't encourage them much. There was an equally difficult climb down the other side of the spur and more pine forests. The river at the bottom was somewhat obscured by the trees but from the sound was running fast over rocks. They guessed that it would take them most of the following day to get down and then there was no certainty they could get across the river.

Norri rested his tired arms on his pack. "Is it decision time?"

Gordy scanned the valley below and the steep hill on the other side of the river. "We still have till tomorrow night to decide."

"Yes, but it will take us until then to get the top of that next spur. Do you think there is any point on going on if this is the kind of terrain we will have to traverse?"

Gordy was thoughtful for a while. "Well...you know I think that Commodore Denquinar was right about this mountain range. It may go on south for a long way and we may have found a place where we can actually get across – even if it is a bit hard. So far it hasn't been impassible."

"I suppose you are right. Let's get on then and give ourselves time to get back if we cannot get past the next spur."

They climbed down; slid down in some spots because of the rough gravel and scree. The river below was running swiftly through sharp boulders but there seemed to be calm water further upstream, and they found a sort of path along the edge. Norri thought this was most likely made by animals, but they were wary none the less. It did take them to a place where the river was calm. The water was crystal clear from the mountains. There was a solid rocky bottom, and the current was slow. They decided to take off their boots and wade it. It took a long time, and the water was cold, but they managed it without falling in and getting their gear soaked. To their surprise the narrow path continued on the other side, and they followed it. Norri was looking for spoor. Any footprint of person or animal might give a clue to whoever or whatever made the path, but the path was hard and stony and there were no discernable marks. They continued until dusk. It was then that they had a bit of luck. They had been taking it in turn to carry a bow strung ready for use. It happened to be Norri's turn and as a pheasant was startled in a bush ahead of them, he drew and released and arrow. The bird fell into the bushes and after searching for a bit in the long grasses they found it with Norri's arrow right through it.

This meant that their evening meal would be much more interesting, and they plodded along with more enthusiasm. The trail left the river now and turned uphill. It was less discernable on the steep slope of the mountain side, but they were able to make good headway.

The light was beginning to fade now, and they began to look for a place to camp. There was a small rocky outcrop sheltered from the wind and they chose this to make their evening fire. There were still trees around, although these were beginning to be sparser. They gleaned enough wood for a fire and Gordy crushed up some dry grass and pine needles together to make a wad and struck some sparks into it with his flint and steel. He blew the embers into flame and slipped it into the small nest he had made for the flames under a pile of kindling. In minutes they had a good fire ready, and Norri slid a green stick through the bird that he had cleaned before they left the river. They found a couple of stones and suspended the pheasant well over the fire to slow roast. While this was happening Gordy mixed flour and water in a pan to make their damper and coated it with flour to prevent the crust from burning too much.

He sat this on a flat stone ready to slide into the ashes of the fire when they were ready and then sought out a couple of flatter stones to grind up some of the local coffee beans they had found.

He put the beans into the empty pot on the edge of the fire to roast and then cleaned the stones thoroughly so as not to get too much dirt into the grind. "I don't mind a bit of grit. That sinks to the bottom, but I can't abide coffee that tastes like mud. It is a good thing Tom isn't here his always tastes like mud anyway."

Norri chuckled but the roasting pheasant had taken his mind off his concerns for Kirin and Tom and their loved ones and Gordy's off hand comment brought all those concerns back. Norri didn't say anything but decided to continue with the small talk. They had a long journey, and it was very important to their loved ones that they succeed.

The bird was cooking well, and Norri took out a piece of vellum and began to draw the map of their journey so far. They needed to be able to get back, at least.

"The pheasant is almost ready, Gordy. Do you want to put on that bit of bigger wood, and we will get some coals ready for the damper and the coffee?"

"Sounds good.... I think I could eat three of those birds, but it will make a good appetizer."

They took the bird off the fire and laid it on a cleaned stone that Gordy had used to grind up his freshly roasted, coffee beans. Gordy poured some water onto the rough-ground beans and set the pot on the edge of the fire to brew.

They then set about getting every bit of meat off the pheasant. It was tender and delicious and as Gordy had said, it would have been better if there had been more of them.

When they had finished their meal, they drank the coffee. It was excellent. Gordy sipped some in his enamelled mug. "This is good coffee. Of course, we gave it its best chance by roasting and grinding it fresh, but it is still as good as anything at home; different though. It has a nuttier taste and is lighter. It would be quite a good seller in the market if we ever get back and have a chance to grow it. I will take some unroasted beans in my pack and try growing them when we get back."

Norri thought that it was most unlikely that Gordy would ever get to cultivate his alternative variety of coffee but didn't say so. He was hardening his will to finish their journey. He knew it would be hard and they would have to be ready for many dangers and surprises ahead.

They made pillows for their heads from pine needles wrapped in a piece of cloth and wrapped their cloaks around them for the night.

Norri lay quietly, thinking about Kirin. He did not know that the ache that came from being apart from her would be so bad. It didn't make any sense. He had lived alone for years and coped well. In those days he knew Kirin but had no idea she would be interested in him. He rolled over. The ache of missing her was like a physical pain in his side. Tears welled in his eyes against all his will to stop them.

His mind said that Kirin was clever and resourceful, and she would be fine, but he wished he was there to share her dangers and protect her with every ounce of his strength.

The morning brought a mist and as they looked down into the valley, they could not see the river for the mist that clung to the bottom of the dell. They didn't linger in their cloaks; the hard ground made any more sleep impossible. They got up had breakfast and a drink of water and began the descending of the slope. By midday they reached the top of the spur and saw that the path they were following continued down the other side. They both looked at one another. The decision was made.

Norri didn't say it but he was increasingly sure that this path led somewhere – the question was, where.

Commodore Denquinar had been standing with his son, Kiri on the top of a rocky outcrop at the end of the sandy beach where they had built the slipway. The work continued on the *Swiftsure*. They both searched the distant ridges with their shaded eyes. "I don't see any sign of them, Kiri, do you?

The thirteen-year-old shaded his eyes and scanned the forest and the mountainside beyond. "No, I cannot see them. Do you think it means they have found a way through the mountains, father?"

"Part of me hopes so and another, not. Part of me likes those young men and would like them to share the voyage with us. Another part knows we need to try both the overland and sea routes to get to Bernadia to try and forge an alliance."

He didn't say that he suspected it would be more difficult than he thought.

The boy looked sad. "I will miss Gordy, Father."

"I also miss him, Kiri, Norri also. Norri is quieter than Gordy, but he is a thoughtful young man who is always worth talking to. The road they have taken is by far the most dangerous. We do not know what lies between here and Bernadia. At least on the sea route, if we find it is impassable, we can turn back. Although we do not know if the southern End will still be defended when we do or whether it will have fallen.

I greatly fear for Tom and his wife and the others if their defenses do not hold."

"How far is it for Norri and Gordy to get to Bernadia?"

"It is hard to say. The distance will likely be as far as it would be to travel from Imrahall to Orsimater."

Kiri's eye's opened wide. "That journey would take many weeks marching."

"Yes. And on that journey, there would be well-made roads and clear signs. On the road Norri and Gordy have taken there will be many obstacles to cross and difficult places to negotiate. That is aside from the dangers."

Kiri looked out again at the forest. "I wish I were going with them, father."

Denquinar was pleased with that reaction. "So do I, Kiri. So do I."

It took another two days before the repairs on the *Swiftsure* were finished. Then they had to wait till the middle of the night to re-float her. The *Suresafe* had come in closer and had rigged a hawser to her stern.

Sailors had rowed out at low tide and driven long poles into the water astern of her, belayed in rows leading out to sea to rig with block and tackles to winch her out into the water again.

Everyone eagerly awaited the high tide and as soon as the water was high enough, the work began. The teams of sailors on the beach heaved on the ropes and the blocks came tight and groaned under the strain. The rowers on the *Suresafe* began to heave and take up the strain on the hawser. The *Swiftsure* began to move and her hull ground along the logs of the slipway. It took a good hour but she re-floated and the anchor crews secured her before turning in for much needed rest for the remainder of the night.

In the morning the work of refitting her began. The masts and spars were hauled into place. The main topmast was raised and set on a pivot before being hauled up to its normal height and lashed securely in place. Then the spars and rigging were set and sails bound on so that by the end of the following day the *Swiftsure* was sea-worthy again. The breeze was rising, and Reynolds was keen to take advantage of it and get to sea again. They dared not waste any more time and the heavier seas favored their ships over those of their enemies.

Denquinar and Kiri both climbed to the topmast crow's nest and looked out toward the forest for any sign of Norri and Gordy returning. But there was none.

Denquinar shook his head as a pre-arranged sign to Reynolds and the orders were given for the two ships to put to sea.

A day later, an ungarvarian dhow sailing close hauled along the coast spotted the slipway and immediately signaled two other ships astern and seaward of her. All three altered course toward the spot, weighed anchor and sent boats ashore to investigate. It seemed more than likely that a ship had been repaired here and it was likely to be their quarry.

Several captains came ashore in boats and examined the camp site and the temporary slipway. They soon saw that they had missed the ships they chased by barely a day. They also examined the edge of the forest and conferred with a group of wild priests clad in skins. The priests looked along the edge of the forest and found footmarks leading into the trees. They followed these long enough to be confident that a party of two or three had left the campsite and gone into the forest.

They returned to the boats and ordered the sailors to remove three very large, heavy wicker baskets. There was a long time when they stood over these chanting and then a sudden agitation and a snarling as three enormous ape-like beasts rose out of the baskets swiping at anyone close enough with their claws. The chanting became louder, and the priests managed to calm the creatures who eventually ran around the beach a few times and returned to the priests who seemed to give them some dark drink.

Soon afterwards the creatures were given arms and packs which contained their food and they loped off into the forest to follow the trail the priests had found.

17

Trapped.

General Bregarad surveyed the silent lines of Bernadian legionaries. They were the best Bernadia had, and they might be destroyed today. Rows of regulars with mail of bronze plates and heavy leather shields stood calmly behind the ditches and wooden spiked rampart.

Behind these stood the archers; they in turn were guarded by the remaining cavalry

Bregarad thought his defences would hold up the attack. What worried him were the wyvern. They attacked with the Corrii and these blood thirsty soldiers in red who now swelled their ranks. It was a difficult combination to counter. All three types of adversary fought differently; the legionaries were always looking toward the sky ready to ward off the deadly tails and claws of the wyvern and were vulnerable from the front.

Sometimes one of the dragons would sweep down and crash into the lines of his soldiers with lashing tail and deadly claws. One of his bravest men had killed one almost single handed but had been struck with the poison spines in so doing and now lay in a tent near the young prince who had suffered the same fate. The healers said that both were close to death.

His, were brave men but they were outnumbered, and if they could not now stand against the forces mustered against them, they would be cut off from the pass that was the only way to the south and home.

The general saw a young officer coming toward him His horse-hair plume flying in the strong wind. "How is Conamund, Degrarius?"

"Not well at all, sir. The healers say moving him will likely cause his death."

Bregarad scanned the hosts moving into position to attack. "It may come to a decision between that and leaving him behind. Have him wrapped warmly and a stretcher readied. Do the same for the centurian. I will not leave either of them to die here or fall into the hands of those foul priests we saw that march with the armies of Ba-al Giborachir."

"Yes, Sir; I will give the orders."

"Thank you, Degrarius, when you have done so, return here to me with haste we have a battle to fight."

The young officer left quickly and mounted his horse who whinnied and looked at the sky. Several more of the winged creatures had arrived. Now more than a dozen circled overhead like carrion birds over a corpse and the sky was dark with an approaching storm.

Degrarius looked at the clouds and shouted over the wind. "They say the god of Giborachir is the lord of the storm."

Bregarad scanned the horizon. "Then look to the true God, Degrarius. He is the true Lord of the storm. Pray that He will strengthen your arm against these foul things and their masters and the daemon who calls himself their god."

"I will pray as I go, sir; fervently."

"Good. Go quickly, Degrarius and return in time for the fun."

The young officer calmed his horse that had reared at the wailing cry from the air. He spurred the animal into a gallop and rode away.

The general scanned the lines of men below him. He walked his horse calmly along the lines, between the archers and the spearmen. The men looked back at him as he ambled slowly along; he was not afraid, and it encouraged them.

One of the largest of the wyvern saw him walking his horse and collapsed its wings to dive on the arrogant officer. A sergeant of the archers had been watching the sky. He quickly gave orders and ten of his best archers raised their bows and drew arrows back to their chin. As the dragon spread its wings again to control its dive, they all fired. Four arrows struck together, and the creature's life ended. Its world went dark, and all the soldiers saw of its end was an explosion of blood and red smoke. What the wyvern saw; terrified it. Death was not supposed to be like this. It was in a desolate place. Not like the plane it had come from but a place of desolation, of cold and fear. It heard voices, far away shrieks of terror. They were coming for it. It clambered away with claws that could not gain purchase on the icy ground. It could not escape them now....

General Bregarad smiled at the sergeant and gave a nod of appreciation. He continued to walk his horse along the lines.

The Corriian force did not notice the exchange. They were marshalling their enormous force to crush the Bernadians who they knew were trapped between them and retreat westward that offered no hope.

Their officers ordered the Dorphiremen to the left flank to attack with the wyvern. Then they would send a massive force of legionaries behind them and to the centre to break the Bernadian lines and collapse their formations in on themselves.

General Bregarad, saw this development and sent orders for the reserves to strengthen their right and centre and some centuries of the best men they had to strengthen their defenses on his right wing.

Then the battle began. The attack on the Bernadian left was a feint. It was quickly and easily repelled after taking some casualties from the Bernadian archery. As the attackers charged, the archers ran in behind the shield wall and shot at close range; straight into the faces of the oncoming Corriian legionaries. This tactic did not slow them, but it took enough momentum out of the attack for them to rebound off the Bernadian shield wall with casualties.

The main attack struck only minutes later as the best and most experienced of the Corriian legionaries and the Dorphiremen crashed into the Bernadian right.

The archers could not slow the attack because they were fighting off the wyvern who fell upon the ranks to smash places in the defenses. But Bregarad was there and sent his best centurions to plug the gaps in their line and it held, just.

The Corriian general still had reserves and threw in another legion of the Dorphire men at the weakened Bernadian right and this time they broke through and pushed the Bernadians off the top of their ramparts. The Dorphiremen seemed heedless of the arrows and spears and threw themselves into the ranks of the Bernadians in a wild frenzy that almost always cost them their lives, but broke the ranks open for others to get at the Bernadians hand to hand which was their strength; they used their bladed shields as additional cutting weapons and were most effective in a melee.

All reserves gone, all the Bernadians could do was fight back-to-back and try to hold back the flood of Corrii and Dorphiremen coming over their ramparts to destroy them. Their officers knew the shame and persecution that came to officers who failed to win battles. They knew they must destroy the Bernadians completely now they had them trapped.

Degrarius was now on foot trying to fight his way back to his general. The storm had broken, and the rain poured down. Men were fighting in small groups in the blinding rain and the mud. He staggered over a small rise and found a handful of men fighting to protect the prone body of the general. He could not see if the general was dead, nor could he get to him to find out he was assailed by two crazed soldiers in red. He dodged a blow from the first and slashed up with his sword and cut open his throat. The second fought on and the first staggered toward him lunging at him with his dying breath. The quick thrust ended his life, but he had to jump back to avoid the wild attack of the second soldier. Now fighting one on one he used his larger shield and parried several blows before slashing low and dashing open the other's thigh. He noted the shock on the soldier's face but then the wild, crazed visage of the death lust that seemed to drive him to one more attack that was sure to be his last. Degrarius was the better soldier unhurt and the other fell back with a loud exhalation of breath - his last.

Degrarius thought back to his last orders and retraced his steps to search out the prince and see if escape was possible. He found a large group of legionaries had formed a square defending the prince. They opened a way for him to enter the ranks and he rushed to the stretcher. There seemed little sign of life from the young man. He stooped closer and felt for a pulse. There there was a faint one. He indicated that the brave legionaries who had carried him should put down the bier.

"We may have lost him, and I will not sacrifice more lives to bring his body from the battle if there is no hope. Form up and order the retreat westward."

A centurian snapped a salute and gave the orders. But four legionaries who obviously loved the prince stubbornly stood with the stretcher on their shoulders. He shrugged and moved off indicating that they should follow.

Degrarius gathered as many of his soldiers into an orderly retreat as possible. As a gap opened between the exhausted Corriian soldiers and his men he sent the archers into the gap and whenever a Corriian officer tried to rally his men for another attack they got arrows for their trouble.

Degrarius marched in close order back to their supply wagons. They needed supplies if any of them were to survive. The camp servants had yoked mules to the wagons and whipped them to drag the heavy carts in the soft mud.

By the time darkness had come they had fled the battle with three in four of their soldiers killed or captured, the Corrii had given up their attack knowing that the Bernadians had fled from the only pass that led to home and help. They could reorganize and destroy them at will.

Tribune Degrarius had left the body of his beloved general on the field to be despoiled by their enemies. In the dark air overhead, he still heard the shrieks of the wyvern who were now well fed on the fallen and who eagerly awaited the chance to feast on them as well.

Degrarius walked among his men and saw that they all got some food and water and then roused them for another march. "We must move. If we stay here, they will fall on us in the morning. We must try and move up into the hills and fight them with the advantage of height."

As the men got to their feet, he saw that some carried another stretcher. He went to investigate and found that the sergeant who had fought the wyvern alone was still alive. He went up to the men who carried him. "Can you carry him?"

They looked at him stubbornly and one answered for all the four. "We will not leave him behind."

"Good. Bring him. If you need help, I will help carry him as well."

The men all smiled at him and they set off.

Degrarius got all his men and equipment moving toward the hills and came last himself with teams of archers who still had any arrows.

Perhaps there was no escape, but the will to survive drove them beyond hope into the dark night to an unknown tomorrow.

As they crested another mountain spur Norri looked back down the valley. At the far end of the valley, he thought he could see something moving. Three things. He crouched down behind a large granite outcrop and nudged Gordy. "Can you see anything down at the far end of the valley?"

Gordy stared for a long time. At first, he said nothing. "The movement is on the path we have come. We are being followed."

"Do you think Denquinar, or Captain Reynolds could have sent others after us for any reason?"

"No. Norri, I do not think the ones that are following us are human."

"Why did you think so?"

"They are very tall and not really the shape of men."

"Your eyes are better than mine but what does that mean?"

"Do you remember the things we saw at the battle of Thornton Green?"

"How far behind us are they do you think?"

"We were at that point a day ago, but they may go faster than us."

"I wonder if they can follow a scent like a dog."

"I don't know but we will have to get off this trail whatever happens. If we stay on it, they will catch us."

"There is another river on this side of the spur."

Norri followed Gordy's gaze down the slope to the river.

"I may be a place to lose them. There is no way of knowing how deep the river is or if we can wade it. There is no use avoiding them if we lose all our supplies. We might as well stay and fight as starve to death. If there are only two or three of them, we might have the advantage if we can ambush them."

Norri thought about this. "I am for trying to lose them at the river if we can. I don't think we should start a fight with Gordrills in a desolate place like this if we can help it."

The truth was that the creatures trailing them left them feeling hunted and desperate. Norri struggled against the feeling. They had to find a way to lose these things and continue on their journey.

They climbed down into the valley with amazing speed, all the time looking back over their shoulder expecting to see the shapes of the gordrill on the ridge. They had barely reached the tree line in the valley when they did. Gordy looked behind at the ridge and there were two shapes silhouetted against the sky. They crested the ridge and began to climb down into the valley after them. Both Norri and Gordy looked at each other began to run. All they could hope was that they were hidden by the trees but these were sparse.

Norri looked back and thought he saw one of the creatures bend down and sniff the ground. Had they found their scent? He didn't have any breath to mention it to Gordy. They both clutched the straps of their packs and ran. Norri saw Gordy fumbling with his bowstring. "Don't worry about arrows yet. Let's see if we can find a way to hide our scent and then hide ourselves. We'll fight if there is no other choice."

They ran on through the trees.

A mist from the river made everything surreal. They had no idea where they were going or where they might find any refuge from their hunters. They reached the river; it was still. The water was brown with silt and there were waterlogged branches partly submerged. It looked to be shallow enough to wade. The problem looked to be the soft sandy bottom. They had no idea how soft.

Gordy and Norri quickly pulled off their boots, pushed them under the straps of their packs and waded into the stream. The sand was fine, and they sunk into it up to their ankles but no further, so they continued to wade across constantly looking over their shoulders expecting to see the Gordrills on the far bank. When they were most of the way across, they waded downstream so as not to leave an obvious scent on the opposite side of the river. Norri knew little of tracking animals and was not sure this would pose any difficulty, but they had to try something.

They went maybe a hundred paces downstream before they turned and clambered up over the moss-covered rocks that lined that side of the river placing their feet where there was no moss to leave prints. Both had a sense of danger close behind and ran on with bare feet, not even waiting to put their boots back on. There was soft grass on this side, and they made good time, but they had no idea of where to go or where to hide. As the ground became stony Norri gasped, "Boots" and they stopped behind a boulder. As they pulled on their boots Norri peeped over the top of the boulder; there was no sign. If their pursuers had reached the river they were hidden by the trees.

They went on choosing the stony places now so as not to leave any prints in the sand.

Every so often, like hunted animals they stopped to listen for any sound of pursuit, but either they had given the Gordrills the slip at the river or they were quiet enough to avoid being heard.

They were climbing out the other side of the valley now and the ground rose steadily. They paused beside another outcrop of rocks and because of some trick of the wind Norri heard voices – coming from the river below. He signaled to Gordy who also listened and then increased his pace. Norri could see the sweat on his friend's forehead, and the fear. They rounded a clump of trees and were confronted by a wall of rock. The cliff rose hundreds of cubits above them and would take all day to climb even if they had that much time.

The rise they had already climbed came to a sudden halt and fell away suddenly becoming part of the cliff that confronted them.

Gordy stopped on the edge of the fall. "What do we do, climb of fight?"

Norri thought about it for a while. Both choices seemed very desperate. But they had encountered these creatures before and if there was any way to avoid a fight that was preferable. "Climb up through that fissure there. It might hide us as well and we may be able to find a place where we can shoot at them if they try to follow. Quick, go!"

Gordy led the way and they climbed as fast as they could. It was a long fall to the bottom now and the rocks were wet and mossy but both of them were good climbers and a fall seemed the least of dangers now.

They found their way into the fissure and as Norri had hoped, it did hide them somewhat, but it also gave them a good view of the rise below; and out of the trees came the Gordrills. They bent down often and sniffed the ground. That answered the earlier question about their ability to follow a trail. They were trailing them.

Gordy took his bow off his back, but Norri stopped him. "They know we have come up here. We cannot hide. We need to get high enough to be out of bowshot."

"Very well," said Gordy, "If you say so." So, they scrambled on up. Gordy was climbing faster than Norri would ever have thought he could but when he looked back the next time the Gordrill had seen them and were following them up the cliff.

Gordy reached a chimney in the rock; he took off his pack attached a line and squeezed in. He could inch his way up by pressing his back against one side and his feet against the other. There was no possibility of climbing. There were just no hand holds.

Norri stood behind him next to his pack and looked down. The gordrills were making incredible time up the cliff. They seemed able to jump from ledge to ledge and were able to climb up by ways that would have been impossible to Norri and Gordy.

They were away a little to their left in clear view now. They only had one more ledge to negotiate and they had them. Norri put an arrow to the string. He had run out of options.

The Gordrill saw him draw his bow and leapt for another ledge where it was out of sight. A second hid below a rock and watched him. Soon there would be one or more below and one above.

Norri yelled up to Gordy. "One is going up on the other side of that protrusion; it may get up before you!"

They heard a loud shout from above and a snort and a large deer with wide branched antlers fell off the cliff-top kicking wildly as it fell to certain death. It must have struck the gordrill near the top, for a moment later it too fell snarling and screaming down the cliff face.

18

Unexpected Friends

*T*he tribune snapped orders at his tired men. He kept them moving toward the higher ground. The mountains of Arion loomed before them. He knew there had been emissaries to the Arionites in the past. They had been received coolly and with distrust. The Arionites kept to themselves and the Bernadians left them alone. They lived in the mountain region that bordered the far north and protected that part of their northern border.

They were reputed to be fierce and merciless and brooked no interference with their affairs. Degrarius had no idea whether they would give them sanctuary or fall on them and with hosts of fierce warriors and utterly destroy them. Rumors had reached them that they had destroyed a Corriian expeditionary force decisively. They had used their knowledge of the heights and lured the legionaries into a place where they had all the advantages and then shot thousands of them with their strange, barbed arrows. The survivors had been harassed all the way back to the plains and returned to Corrimar to ignominy and disgrace. Apparently the Arionites had been left alone since.

It was a faint hope that the Arionites would see them as allies. He and his men might well suffer the same fate or worse.

He had positioned all his remaining archers around the marching formations. Whenever they came to a suitable rise in the ground the bowmen took up positions where they could shoot at the circling wyvern if they came too close. The men were edgy and watchful. They constantly looked skyward at the circling dragons and clutched their shields close, instead of carrying them strapped to their backs as was the usual custom with marching legionaries.

Degrarius moved up and down the lines encouraging his men. It was critical to keep them from despair. He mentioned nothing of his fears that they may be marching into a trap with aggressive Arionites on one side and the Corriian army with their red men and dragons behind: caught between the hammer and the anvil.

Dinki, Silip and Kilnin, warriors of the Ica Bica Baya, trudged up the steep slope of mount Carmeyen. Dinki wore the sword he had recovered from a spinney on the plains. It had belonged to the young warrior who had saved them from the dungeons of Corriamar: young Norrimae Jung. He had searched for the sword all across the plain. He had never been exactly sure where they had been captured and had searched through many thickets before he finally found it. Its weight had caused it to fall through the brambles and lodge under an old fallen branch. It was fairly dry under the canopy and the old sword had suffered little ill effect from the exposure. Even its leather scabbard came up alright with a little oil.

Trailing behind in a long line were the people of his tribe: women, children, and old people. Some had been unable to make the journey and had fallen by the trail. They had been forced to leave them behind to die. Dinky felt terrible. The old people would eventually die of exposure or fall victim to the packs of goroths. But there was no choice. The attempt to reach the Arionites was desperate. The Arionite tribes were distantly related but there was no communication. They might drive them off or even kill them all. But a Corrii army had come to the plains, and they had sent out scouts with their grimulves to scour the plain before them and kill any they found. He and his people had crossed the river in their few small deer-hide canoes and made for the mountains in the hope they could join the Arionites and fight with them. Dinki guessed the Corrii were going to Arion. They had tried to crush the Arionites before but now a much larger army had been sent.

As soon as mount Carmeyen had been seen, the old prophet of their tribe pointed it out and directed their course toward it. He had seen a vision of the mountain and the valley behind it and felt that they were to take their people there.

Biri Niri Miri had marched with Dinki tirelessly. The only time when he was not at the head of the column was when they were forced to leave an old person behind. Then he had stayed and prayed with them and given them assurances that their courage and sacrifice would be seen by the God who kept the fates of all in His hands.

Now the old man struggled on with every ounce of his remaining strength and led the people to what small safety they might find.

Shouts from above caused them to stop. Warriors with drawn bows appeared on the rocks above them.

Dust from marching columns could be seen behind and every time Degrarius looked at the sky there were the wyvern, watching their every move. There was no hope of remaining hidden. He had drawn in his scouts when the wyvern had attacked and killed some. Now they plodded toward the mountains with little hope. The army that followed them was marching quickly now, reinforced, and well supplied.

He had to see what lay ahead of them. Calling a centurion and several archers he formed a party and went on ahead of his army. The rest of his soldiers followed obediently. He was supposed to know what he was doing.

They were marching past a spur of the mountain range into a wide plain with hills and rivers.

Degrarius tried to keep his tired men in order. They had no idea whether they would meet friends or foes in these mountains. Degrarius had been well taught in both strategy and politics. His father, a member of the Bernadian Court often said, 'That you could not assume that the enemy of your enemy is your friend. They may oppose your enemies for reasons very different than yours.' Degrarius had learned the lesson well and now ordered his men to defend themselves in the case of a surprise attack. If that came, they would have enemies in front and behind, they would be caught between the hammer and the anvil.

But his men were physically and emotionally spent. He knew this – he could read it on their faces. They saw no hope in this mountain country. They had heard evil rumors about the Arionite tribesmen from their grandfathers. They were fierce and deadly and brooked no interference in their affairs and saw no need for treaties with anyone.

Norri climbed up the rock chimney to find Gordy on the cliff-top surrounded by warriors. They were mostly armed with large spears, and some carried torches tipped with burning hide and pitch.

A young warrior stepped forward. "Speak, strangers! What brings you into the lands of the Wangadilla tribe and what brings you unbidden into our lands?"

Gordy looked at Norri. He was not at all sure how much of their task he should reveal.

Norri clambered over the top of the chimney. He looked at the deerskin clothing of the hunters. He decided on a frank response as he had used when he had encountered the young hunters on this side of the mountains before.

"We came into your land fleeing the creatures you saw below us on the cliff-face: gordrill, the companions of the Corrii. They were hunting us; we chose the cliff as a last means of escape."

One young hunter looked over the edge of the cliff and pointed to the smoking remains of the gordrill at the bottom of the fall. He looked at the smoking fur and the scimitar. He returned and whispered something to the warrior who had addressed Norri.

The warrior indicated the chimney they had just climbed. "Our way is back down." He said this in a way that brooked no discussion. Take their weapons!" Several warriors came forward and took their weapons. Norri nodded to Gordy who was reluctant to surrender their only defenses. They handed their weapons to the warriors.

The leaders of the warriors led the way to the edge of the cliff and began to climb over the edge. Norri shrugged at Gordy and followed.

Gordy lowered himself over the edge carefully. "More rock climbing ...excellent."

They took a longer time to reach the stream at the bottom than Norri would have thought and the canyon they entered was gloomy and dark with a mossy stream at the bottom. It was cold.

At the bottom of the fall was the elkarn. Not far from it was the smoldering fur and broken scimitar that was all that remained of the gordrill.

When they were all at the bottom of the canyon the hunters examined the fallen gordrill.

The young man who was the obvious leader pointed at the smoldering fur. "What is this thing?"

Norri hoped what he had experienced in the past with tribespeople on this side of the mountains was also true of these hunters. He returned the unflinching gaze. "It is a gordrill. They must have followed us from the coast. They came with an army of the Corrii, and we have fought against these before. An ex-Corriian admiral told us they are from the island of Dorphire Sunde on the eastern edge of the empire. They are creatures of magic called up by their priests.

We have been sent from our land to try and find a way to Bernadia. We hope that it may be possible to make an alliance with other enemies of the Corrii. Some of these creatures must have come with the Corrii in their ships and they must have sent them to hunt us."

The hunter looked at the packs they had carried and at their weapons. "Give me some proof that you are not Corrii."

"I cannot give you the proof you ask. All I can tell you is that we left our homes and our wives when ships came into the harbor. We came south and nearly got into serious trouble when we stopped at an island inhabited but monsters who masqueraded as beautiful women. After we escaped from the Ichtar we stopped to repair our ships on a small beach on the coast. It was decided that the ships would continue and try to reach Bernadia by sea and Gordy and I set out overland to try that way."

"The tale you tell has the ring of truth although much you say is strange and makes me fearful. Our world is changing, and we may have to change with it. There are also rumors that strange creatures have been sighted with the Corrii."

Norri again looked the hunter in the eyes. "Can you help us find a way to Bernadia? It is for that purpose that we came into your lands."

"We know the Bernadians. They are not friends, but neither are they enemies. I will take you to the chief of the Elkarn tribe of the Arionites. So, we do with all our prisoners. He will decide your fate. For myself, I think that you speak truth, but I warn you, others may not be so inclined to trust you. My father will put much store in the words of the augurors."

"Who are they?" asked Gordy.

The young man struggled. They are strange and separate; living in caves in the mountains; apart from the rest of the tribe. They can read the signs in the skies and in the land and the animals. They go into the mountains for many days; to the God who made all the world and all the creatures.

If the augurors say we should do this or that, my father will move camp or do any thing that they ask. If what an auguror prophesies does not happen, then he knows that my father may order he be killed or at least cast out of the tribe and away from his family and everyone he knows. For this reason, they speak the God words little but when they speak people listen."

Some of the hunters began butchering the animal they had killed and cut strips of the fresh meat to cook, while others set a fire with all the dry wood they could find washed into the canyon.

As he held the meat skewered on a green stick which they gave him to hold over the flames to roast, Norri noticed that the hunters kept well clear of the remains of the gordrill. The remains of the creature had ceased to smoulder and only a blackened space lay on the rocks with the blackened sword.

Once it looked ready, Norri sat and munched at a strip of meat. The elkah meat was tough but savory. He ate it with relish as he sat and watched as the hunters cut the remainder of the meat into strips and pack it in the hide which they tied together with strips of leather and tied to poles for transportation. It was a messy business, but the hunters had clearly become skilled at the task, and it was soon complete. Norri noticed that they set apart some of the meat wrapped in scraps of the hide. He supposed that they kept it aside for the morning.

The leader of the warriors saw that he watched the process with interest. "Do you hunt in your land?"

Norri nodded. "Yes, sometimes and fish as well. But I also collect nuts from the trees near our home."

The hunter did not seem very impressed. Gordy noticed the look of distain and guessed he thought little of such work.

"We have seen trees with the nuts in your lands. But they were much smaller than the ones we have. In our land they grow many times as large and tower high in the sky. Norri is one of the few who can climb so high. But Norri has been made a great leader in our land and given great honor and has had little time to search the tall trees. He was the first to find that the Corrii had invaded our land and he alone found a way to defeat them."

The hunter seemed almost relieved. Gordy saw a slight raising of the eyebrows and he looked at the well-crafted sword that lay with their gear.

The hunter picked up the sword. "This is a fine weapon; well made."

Gordy decided it wouldn't hurt to blow Norri's trumpet a bit. "It is a gift to Norri from the Emperor of Bernadia."

The hunter looked at Gordy in disbelief. "Why would such a great chief give such a gift?'

"...because Norri saved his son from a Corrii prison."

The hunter looked at Norri with piercing brown eyes. "Did you save the son of the Bernadian High Chief?"

Norri knew to meet that gaze and answer as honestly as he could. This young man did not seem to be one who could be trifled with. "I did, in a way of speaking. I was captured by the Corrii when I tried to find how they were coming into our lands, and I was trapped on this side of the mountains. I was caught and taken north to their prison in Corriamar."

The word seemed to be something of a byword and the hunter looked at him with amazement, but not with doubt.

"The emperor's son was also in the prison and we escaped together."

The hunter seemed to accept the story but seemed confused by a detail.

"Bernadia is that way (he pointed east). You came from that way."

Norri cleared a patch of earth and drew a picture in the dirt.

"My home is here....

"We are here....

"The Corrii are here....

"Bernadia is here....

"The Bernadian Emperor came this way, in his great ship. It was when something happened to the Corrii.

"Now the Corrii are strong again and ships cannot go this way."

The hunter looked at the map as if he understood the vast distances involved. "Is it possible to go to Bernadia this way in ships?"

"We don't know. We need to try both ways. Some of our people are trying that way. We came this way into your lands. We have never been here and did not know they were your lands."

"Not lands of Wengenevy. Wengenevy belong to the land."

Norri noticed that the hunter used his name.

"I understand. My name is Norri. The land is greater than those who live in it."

Gordy noticed that the hunter had accepted them and that the young man was wiser than his companions and a natural leader.

Norri decided they needed to ask for help. "Wengenevy, can you tell us the way to Bernadia?"

"Cannot let you go through Wangadilla lands unless chief agree; other chiefs of the Arionitre tribes also. You must go through lands of many tribes to get to the far east.

"Wengenevy not as wise as father; but know that if you were a Corrii spy or scout, you would not say so to an Arion warrior.

"All know we fought and defeated the Corrii when they tried to invade our land."

"How would we convince you that we were only enemies of the Corrii?"

"No need. Your lives are in the hands of father, chief."

Gordy chuckled. "And I suppose we don't look like too much of a threat to the Corrii anyway."

Norri noticed a smile of the warrior's face which showed he was thinking the same thing.

19

Turbid Waters

*T*hey left Tom unshackled but Gavin and the rest of the prisoners were herded up to the rowing decks. Tom recognized some of the faces as they trooped past; stooping because of the cramped space between decks. He noticed their eyes in the light of the lamp; they all spoke of despair and resignation as they shuffled forward.

The Argamaro rowed ponderously down the harbor and Tom only knew they had reached some destination when Gavin returned to his place and his shackles were again linked through the ring bolts used to secure the prisoners. His head pounded with the pain of the wound on the side of his head, and he tried to sleep. It came in fits and starts as he wondered if Lettie had done what he had asked and tried to get out of the castle. He took some comfort in the knowledge that Kirin was sensible and would keep her going. The trouble was what would they do then? The only option would really be to travel north. He hoped they had taken some food; and water, he thought. Lettie was feeding Dillon and needed lots of water. Sleep finally overcame his fears and he dozed uncomfortably on the hard deck.

He was aroused by light coming from the hatchway at the end of the deck and Gavin was gone again. They were moving.

There seemed to be little wind and the fact that Gavin was gone made Tom think that they were at sea again and were rowing. The rocking motion of the ship as she rose and dropped in the swell seemed to indicate that as well.

On deck, Norrens and his officers tried to predict the wind in the Straits of Geitor. They had left as soon as the ship was provisioned. Norrens had told the quartermaster to request extra stores of water and food at Orsimater. The Argamaro had been ordered to Bea-air Monar with all dispatch. The supply officer knew what was at Bea-air Monar and didn't dare to argue.

They rowed north in a strong northerly, making tediously slow progress. It gave Norrens time to think. Perhaps they were dead men as Cornelli had said. Norrens wondered if they might survive a slight on a master of the grand coven - if they did as they were ordered but there was more to it than that.

The breeze in his face and steady drumbeat from the rowing decks below seemed to cocoon him in sound and his mind turned over all his concerns. Even if they did avoid serious repercussions from the argument with Bentonius, he kept asking himself if he could condone what they were doing, and the answer was always the same.

The coven masters had been moving the men's wives and children into enclaves. They all knew what it meant: "Do your job; obey orders unequivocally – or else."

Norrens had an eight-year-old daughter, Chloe and his incredibly patient wife, Ghezia meant everything to him. Norrens made himself an oath, if they ever dare to hurt his family, they will pay. He wasn't sure how, but they would pay....

A secret meeting on board in Norrens' cabin made it clear that all the officers felt the same. They agreed to subtly canvass all the ship's mates and master and see how they felt.

When they met again it was clear that all the seamen felt the same; especially those with wives and children. Many had also heard that their families had been moved to newly built houses in the Verbigar hills, not far from Biel Harfing the harbor port just across the gulf from Dorphir Sunde, the island of infamy and fear.

There were many sailors who had no wives or families, but these had become disillusioned as well. The stories of the foul priests and their human sacrifices were circulating below decks.

It was common to have discontent in the services, but the discontent had been fuelled by anger and disillusionment. The rulers of the empire were serving foul foreign priests and using their own people. Gone were the days when a man of courage and skill could make his way in the navy. Now they were bullied and threatened into doing their jobs. Everyone knew that spies of the covens were on board. A series of incidents occurred, and those crewmen suspected of being spies began to disappear over the side or had falls from the rigging.

What was more, coded secret signals from other ships in company told Norrens and his officers that the discontent was not only in their ship. It was beginning....

In the security of the captain's cabin on the Argamaro, they began to make their plans. The journey down the Geitor straits was expedited by the wind swinging around north westerly and they made good time along the coast under the shadow of the northern mountains.

Bentonius opened the door of Ingwit's room. They were very close now, and he was not concerned about walking into her room unannounced.

What he found shocked him. Ingwit, the brilliant woman of poise and insight, was gone. In her place was a distraught slobbering mess. Her dress was soaked with her tears, her eyes were puffy from crying, and she bled profusely from many cuts.

The ebony handled knife lay on the bed covered with blood indicating that the many cuts were self-inflicted.

"What are you doing here? Get out!"

Bentonius was stunned and shocked. He calmed his voice even though he was alert now for some new danger.

"What has happened, Ingwit?"

"Get out!" She wiped her eyes which only resulted in her getting blood on her face.

Somehow this stirred something that Bentonius did not expect. He felt a strange need to protect her from whatever had so disturbed and upset her.

"I may be able to help."

"You can't. Nobody can. I just want to die."

Bentonius was shocked into a rare moment of genuine concern. "I will help, if I can."

"You are just their lackey, filth like the rest of them."

"I have some influence, and so, do you."

"I have none. I am just their tool as you are, their stooge who does their dirty jobs."

Bentonius stood upright. "I have influence with Groemelian."

"Corrianasta says Groemelian is just letting you think you can aspire to the inner circle, while you remain useful. He already thinks you are getting above yourself and plans to humiliate you to keep you in your place. He has forbidden me to see you anymore."

Bentonius was shocked. "Why are you telling me this?"

"I can't play the game anymore. I just can't do it!" Ignoring his reaction, she again took up the knife.

Bentonius was horrified and shaken. "What has happened, Ingwit?"

"You won't understand." There was no emotion in her voice now.

"Try me."

She looked up with a mixture of hatred and vague interest. "They are going to torture and kill the two little kids next door."

"What kids?"

"Two children of the plains people."

"Who are going to torture and kill them?"

"The priests."

"I see."

"You don't see you scion of a donkey! The little girl is like I was, only what they are planning to do to her is worse; worse even than they did to me. They hurt me and laughed while they did it. They made me do things... and laughed."

Ingwit seemed to become resolute. She looked sternly at Bentonius. "I am finished with it all. I will free them and probably be killed. I will be glad it is over. I am still their tool and plaything; I want to die with a little self respect; I want to *not* hate myself even if it is only for a few moments before I die."

Bentonius stood, stunned. He watched as she took a towel to mop up the blood and went to the ewer to pour water over her arm. The water turned pink in the porcelain basin, but it stemmed the flow of blood.

Ingwit then bound a clean cloth bandage around her gashed arm and calmly chose a clean dress with long sleeves that would cover the injury.

As Bentonius watched his mind raced. What she said was true, they were just tools in the hands of evil men and what reward had they got so far: they had granted him the girl he lost, and now she was no more than a terrified slave. What real power he had he gained made him feel more and more a slave every time he used it so that now he hardly called up the jungari at all.

His lightening-quick mind made a decision. He loved Ingwit. He realized that now. Maybe there was a way to save her. He had uncovered the plot that Admiral Norrens was preparing and even as he realized what they were doing he had felt a strange longing to throw in his lot with them. He wondered if there was a chance that they would believe him. Perhaps it was a chance. He would be completely at their mercy. They could throw him to the sharks if he proved false.

"Ingwit...?"

She turned to him, hearing the strange tone in his voice.

"Do you want to leave the empire?"

"What, take a ship and sail away like Admiral Denquinar?"

"Sort of… I have uncovered a plot by Admiral Norrens and some of the naval officers. They are angry that the rulers have virtually imprisoned their wives and children at Biel Harfing to ensure they remain loyal and follow orders."

Ingwit looked up at the mention of the name. "If they don't follow orders...? They would send their families to the priests – our own people?"

Ingwit stood amazed at the growing audacity of the masters.

"I think they intend to sail soon; probably to Biel Harfing to try and rescue their wives and children. I overheard that place mentioned quite a few times on the ship. Then…I don't know – probably sail to Bernadia and ask for asylum."

"Why would they trust you? …Or me either? They know we are part of the Grand Coven."

"I know about their plan to defect. I have been watching them. How if I were to go to them and say we know what is happening and want to join them."

"They could just kill you."

"My men know what is happening, and you need not come with me at first. We could hide you and the children. The biggest problem is getting you and them out of here."

Bentonius knew there could be problems getting the two children out but saw the steely resolve on Ingwit's face and discounted the idea of suggesting they leave them. He looked out the window of Ingwit's room and saw that there was a drop of about eight cubits to the street below. Manageable.

"Can you bring them to your room so we can get them out this window?"

"If I can bluff those filthy priests and make them think that nothing is amiss. Nobody should suspect me."

We will have to time this right. Once I show my hand to the naval men, they will never let me out of their sight. We will have to have a way to signal you to come and join us or fetch you and the children."

"They may still kill us when we are on their ships and away from help."

"They may but we will be no worse off than we are now."

Ingwit shrugged. "I am finished, but what about you?"

"Without you I don't care."

Ingwit looked at him in amazement as the implications of what he said dawned on her. Here was somebody willing to risk his life – for her.

Then as quickly as the amazement, doubt replaced hope. "How can I trust you? You have much to lose. And you have Priscilla and your position in the conclave."

Benton met her eyes. He had no answer. He was a master spy, a deceiver by trade; he could easily be engineering her destruction; even on the orders of the masters. He was ashamed and lowered his eyes. He had indeed become something that he didn't like very much.

Ingwit saw it all and guessed his thoughts. She inwardly reviled herself.

"Bentonius, I am sorry. You are offering to risk your life for me, and I accuse you of falsehood." In her heart Ingwit had made a decision. If he was false, she was dead. But she was dead anyway. She decided as her last decision to trust him. How foolish trust was really but what was the alternative, vengeance, and hatred – that was worse.

Bentonius left Ingwit and went to the messenger service next to the stables. He spoke to a man there he knew could be relied upon. The Coven kept messengers that could ride quickly all over the north, to relay messages and deliver instructions to operatives.

Once he had made the arrangements he wanted, he returned to his own suite at the other end of the corridor. He opened the door to find Priscilla sitting in a chair by the window. She didn't cry any more these days, she just sat listless and vague, and the spark had gone out of her eyes. She looked up at him to see if he wanted anything from her. To her surprise he stood silent, looking at her.

This surprised her, it was not like him. "What is it Bentonius? Is there anything you want? Do you want me to bring some food or wine? There is some cheese and bread in the parlor..." Something was clearly wrong, and Priscilla began to be frightened.

"No. I do not need you to get anything, Priscilla. I am sorrier than I can tell you for the great harm that I have done to you. I cannot undo what has been done but I will do what I can.

Here is money. I have arranged for a messenger to be ready downstairs to take you wherever you wish. I guess you would like to go back to your family in the north, but you may do what you wish. I only advise you to be well away from here as quickly as you can."

"Bentonius, has something happened?"

"No. Not yet anyway. Go Priscilla and make yourself a better life. I don't expect forgiveness but maybe one day I will be able to do something for you that you need. You only have to ask, and if it is in my power, I will do it."

For the first time he could remember, the spark came back into her eyes, and she looked a little like the girl he has once admired.

She looked at him with a quizzical smile and kissed him. "Thank you – I will go to my uncle's home near Mount Orfing." She swept past him to grab her bag that was already packed to leave with Bentonius in the morning.

She stopped at the door and smiled at him once more before leaving and closing the door behind her.

The warehouse was only lit by two ships lanterns sitting on an old, dilapidated table. Fourteen officers stood around the room. They were the cream of the fighting sailors of the Corriian navy. Vice Admiral Norrens knew that many of them were decorated and experienced men whose loyalty had never before been questioned. Captain Vertori, the most senior post captain present and captain of the *Vorsero* stepped into the lamplight so all could see his face. The silver ship badge on his tunic glinted in the flickering light.

"I have always been a loyal officer of the emperor; for me to take this action has been the hardest decision of my life."

He drew his sword and laid it on the table. "My loyalty I transfer to this group. I take my orders from Admiral Norrens. He remains my commander, but I no longer accept the orders of the high command."

With a flourish all the officers in the room drew their swords and laid them on the table next to Vertori's gold hilted blade. Gustass Norrens said nothing he had no words. The confidence of these brave men and their courage brought tears to his eyes.

Before he could speak, the door opened. One of his men came over to him and spoke quietly, "There is a man at the door. He is disguised but I think it is Bentonius."

Several of the officers took their swords back off the table but did not sheath them. The Admiral thought for a moment, before deciding. "I will go out and speak with him. All of you stay here. We may have been discovered." All the faces looked grim. If their plot had been discovered, there would be no escape. They would face the horrible end of traitors. It would be better to fall on their swords now. And die quickly.

Norrens went outside. Two of his men stood with daggers drawn watching over a man who was standing there hooded and cloaked; apparently – alone.

Norrens approached the hooded figure. "Who are you?"

The other drew back his hood. It was not the silver trimmed, black hood of a master of the grand coven but just an ordinary woolen garment, old and repaired in some places. "Bentonius."

"Why do you come here, Master Bentonious?"

"Forget the title, it doesn't mean anything anymore. May I come inside? I already know all the officers who are here, and I have no intention of revealing your conspiracy. I have already sent away the men who have been watching this place with orders to speak to no-one until they hear from me."

Norrens ushered him into the dim room. Suspicious eyes from all corners of the wharehouse were turned toward him.

"I think most of you know Master Bentonious. I believe he wants to address this meeting."

There was no use posturing with these men he had to win them over and he had little time to do it. "Gentlemen, I have not come here to expose your plans but to ask if I and one other may join you."

He paused for them to absorb this information.

"This place has been under surveillance, but I have sent the men away who have been watching you all arrive. They have orders to wait to hear from me. That may give us some time – but not much."

Vertori was watching his face as he was speaking and employed every skill he had developed over his years in the navy. He always prided himself that he could pick a liar but before he could speak Cornelli asked, "How do we know we can trust you? I for one see no reason not to run you through and throw your body into a rubbish pit."

Bentonius looked at the grim expression and seething hate in his eyes. "I do not blame you, lieutenant but it would be better if you kept me alive. Admiral Cherulia knows of your plans and if I disappear, it will confirm his suspicions and he will move against you anyway. You need to sail immediately. If you wait until morning, it may be too late. And I am sure you know that Cherulia has spies on board your ships. You must suspect anyone who tries to leave before you sail."

Norrens wanted to understand the apparent change in the coven spy. "Why the change Benton? Why do you want to join us and who is this 'other' of whom you speak?"

"Ingwit. Something she has been required to do has caused her great distress. And I have found that I have not gained the power and authority that all my efforts deserved; on the contrary, I have discovered that I am also being used; I want no more of it!"

"Do you think we have time to get away?"

"As soon as you leave, they will guess; and they will find my men and guess that I have been killed. They will immediately send messengers to arrest your families. We must race these messengers to Biel Harfing where the rulers have been moving them to enclaves that are really no more than concentration camps with a few amenities for the look of things."

Norrens and the other officers looked at each other. If their plotting had been uncovered there was no choice. They all made their decisions without a word being spoken.

The Admiral spoke for all. "What you say has the ring of truth. Where is Ingwit?"

"She is at *The Kite* in my room second from the back stairs on the second floor She has two small children with her. If you have someone to send, please do. We both knew that I would need to stay as surety."

To Benton's surprise Cornelli spoke. "I know *The Kite*, Sir. I will go. Will any other come with me?"

"I'll go," said a lieutenant from Vertoli's ship who seemed to know Cornelli.

Norrens rounded off the meeting. "It is decided! Pray to whatever gods you know for westerly winds and a head start on the coven messengers. Benton, you come with me. I have more questions. Verna, what are the tides?"

"High. And already on the turn, Sir."

"We leave for Bea-air Monar in two hours. Rig for silent and black out the ships as we weigh. We will try and leave without anyone noticing; it might give us a few precious hours."

The officers moved with the precision of men used to obeying orders. Each went to do his appointed tasks and to ready the large ships for sea.

A man stood in the shadows by the back door of *The Kite*. He saw two naval officers enter Bentonius' room and leave with a cloaked figure and two children. He thought it suspicious and went to report it to his master.

The two officers picked up the two children and held them as if they were their own as they hurried through the dark streets toward the ships.

On board there was much activity but most of it was being carried out in the dark below decks. To anyone walking along the docks, it would seem that the ships rode quietly at anchor on the harbour, and nothing was amiss.

In his rooms at the most prestigoius hotel the naval town could boast, Cherulia was sitting with a glass of the best brandy and a large piece of the finest local cheese. There was a knock at his door.

Cherulia nodded to his two bodyguards who were instantly on the alert as he got up and went to the door.

A man enterred who was known to them all and the guards relaxed. The Grand Admiral was not pleased at the disturbance. "You had better have a good reason for disturbing my evening."

"I am sorry, my Lord. I have been watching over Bentonius as you instructed. A very strange thing happened, and I thought I would come immediately and tell you. Unfortunately, they wouldn't let me into this hotel, and I had to climb up the outside wall and into a window of another room. I am afraid they have complained and there is quite a stir."

"What happened at *The Kite*, you fool. I have no time for your prattle."

"Sorry my Lord, I saw two naval officers come to the room and soon after they left with someone hooded and cloaked. I do not think it was Benton. There were also two children."

"Children? How odd! What would Benton be doing with a woman and two children in his room?"

"I do not know, my Lord. I am not sure it *was* a woman, but I suppose it follows. The hooded person was not very tall, but if a woman not a short woman either."

"It all smells fishy. I will go to the coven hall and see if Corianasta has any ideas about what may be happening. I don't like this running about with naval officers in the dead of night. Something is happening and I intend to find out what it is."

In the hallway there was a gathering of people speaking with the hotellier. They pointed to the man who had invaded their room.

Cherulia called to the hotelier. "Deal with this intruder, will you?"

Cherulia's man looked at him, shocked, but Cherulia ignored him and left down the hall.

One of his bodyguards chuckled as they walked briskly down the hallway to the stairs. "Poor Sevil, he'll have some work to do to talk himself out of that."

"I pay him to think on his feet. It will distract them, so they don't think about our sudden exit."

20

Wyvern

*I*igweell soared over the forest. She was starving! The priests would give her dried meat, but she felt she would choke on it. It was dry and had no blood in it, she felt she would rather eat dust.

What was the use of the wulves if they couldn't hunt and kill? She had led them to the prey, and they had run away from a few feeble humans. These were the same kind they had killed in the first battle before the soldiers came. The soldiers had swords and shields and strong bows. They were a threat but the people she had found in the forest were just females and young and a couple of male ones trying desperately to defend them.

She had seen a few of the wulves run away through the forest. What a weak puny world this was, where a creature was not willing to die capturing its prey. She tested the wind for any hint of the ones she sought. Each stroke of her wings seemed to drain her remaining strength. She must find food!

Was that the smell of burning? She craned her long neck and scanned the forest looking for the source. The tiniest tendril of smoke rose from the forest where some particularly tall trees almost obscured it.

She banked into the wind and turned for another dive. The sun shone on her golden scales. She felt the exhilaration of the wind on her body and bent the spade of her tail to direct her course toward a clearing she had seen. It was really no more than a space between several large trees, but it was in the direction where she guessed her quarry had escaped. They were puny ones these humans, but she would get her own food.

Her keen eyes caught a movement. Automatically her body readied itself for attack. A gland secreted poison into the spines that lay flat against her flowing tail in flight; the sinews that that made them erect began to tighten.

Her claws uncurled on the hind legs that dropped down as a brake on her speed through the air.

The hunter made her silent, deadly approach.

Branch leader Serelra sat on a branch and stroked the shaft of an arrow as she watched over the camp of the refugees from Newcastle. In the camp a couple of the women and a small boy were trying to get some of the older people to eat something. The old woman seemed to be saying that she didn't need anything, and that the food should be given to the young mother.

Serelra heard the young woman say, "You must eat. If you don't eat, you will get tired and you will slow us down; we will stop if you do. We will not leave you behind."

Serelra listened. She liked the young woman and was glad to guard her. She even thought that they could be friends if contact were allowed. She and her warriors had been trying to shield several groups of valley people as they tried to make their way north through the forest after their homes had been sacked. She had wondered about these orders. The people they shielded were not warriors; she wondered that the arborites had not been assembled to defend their own country from the invaders.

All was quiet except for the sounds from the group below and Serelra relaxed in the branches. She thought about the living arrow in her hands. Others had teased her and said it would not work but she doubted her doubts.

She had found the charnorgara deep in the forest. It was a quite different creature to the living, moving plants that they wore as clothing. This kind was small and just looked like a twig of whatever tree they lived in with only a few leaves on one end to distinguish them. But he was clever! Serelra could feel him reading her mind and responding, becoming her friend. "Strange," she thought, "He seems to do what I want and order what he does and how he grows to please me. He is trying to be friends."

The other warriors who were guarding the group had gone to fetch food and water.

Serelra was alone when *she* came.

Iigwheel approached on silent wings until she was almost over the camp where she had seen the whiff of smoke. She settled on a branch directly above them and cried out with a shriek she customarily used to terrify her prey; then she hopped down off the branch and half glided half pounced into the middle of the camp.

The small group responded surprisingly quickly. One man came at her with a large cleaver-like weapon. She rose with one beat of her wings and grabbed him in her hind tallons before he could swing then crushed him in her jaws. She had tasted blood and it sent her into a killing frenzy. Nothing was now as important as killing. She would survive!

An arrow struck her in her hind quarters, but she hardly felt it. Two old people stood between her and some of the younger prey. She struck out with her talons to kill one and swung her tail so that the poison barbs struck the other on the back.

She saw more in the trees; one clutched an infant. It would have the sweetest meat of all. Iigwheel crouched ready to spring.

Serelra drew the charnorgara arrow to her chin to give him the maximum power in his flight. Her mind spoke to the shaft, "Can you kill this?"

"Yes, if you can launch me with enough speed." Serelra pointed the living arrow at the wyvern and released it.

The arrow concentrated on the belly of the living creature before him and sensed its beating heart beyond. He had to fly below and up. There! There! ...Hot blood and the beating thing above. He wriggled forward with the last power of the bow and pressed his sharp head into the beating thing.

Iigwheel reared and screamed and clawed at the arrow with her claws.

Serelra climbed down and jumped the last six cubits to the ground beside Kirin.

"Can we save it!" Kirin looked at her without comprehension. "What the monster?"

"No. The arrow. He is alive!"

Kirin drew her sword and approached the wyvern.

Iigwheel lifted her claw to strike this impudent creature, but she had no strength. The thing was inside her. It had pierced her, and her blood was leaking from a burst heart.

Kirin saw and swung her blade. She removed Iigwheel's head. Then, ducking under the falling wyvern, Serelra reached out and clutched the charnorgara. The living shaft shook in her hand as if with revulsion and pain. Serelra wiped it clean of the black blood on a tuft of soft forest grass and clutched it to her. The leaves and stalks of the Charnargra she wore, closed around the small arrow as if to comfort him.

All around them was death. Kirin stood with tears streaming down her face as she looked at Pat and David. The tears made tracks in the grime on her face. Her hair and dress were spattered with Iigwheel's black blood; all around her lay prone bodies. Pat lay silent and David was still. Gorigond's broken body lay with his famous cleaver still in his grasp. Several of the children had been struck by the wyvern and lay like fallen leaves on the ground near their parents who had died trying to stand between them and the flying death.

Kirin was drawn to the body of the old pastor. Whether it was some slight movement or sign or life or whether she was pushed by some unknown force she didn't know, but she left Serelra holding the arrow and knelt down beside David.

At that moment his eyes opened. "Where is Patricia?"

Kirin indicated the old woman's still form beside him. He turned his eyes and looked lovingly at her then looking back at Kirin's tear-streaked face, "Do not be sad for us dear heart, we are old and weary, and in need of rest."

Kirin was about to say something, but David silenced her with his eyes. "Stay strong and be here for Norri when he returns. We will all meet again." The old man's eyes closed, and he looked at peace like Patricia.

Kirin heard the voice of the driadora warrior behind her. "I see a great and ancient warrior who has fallen."

Kirin was bent over David and her tears fell helplessly. "He did not fight with swords."

"The greatest warriors do not."

Kirin looked behind her and saw Lettie holding Dillon close to her and between them stood Jenny with her dagger limp in her hand and Mort beside her with his stick, his face full of concern for Kirin.

Kirin got up and laid her sword on the ground. She drew the small boy into a cuddle. He made no attempt to wriggle away as he usually would. He clung to Kirin as if she were life itself.

21

Sargasso Sea

*D*enquinar stood next to Reynolds who had the watch. They had lost sight of the Suresafe hours ago but that was no surprise, visibility was now down to a few cables in this storm. For a while they could still see her rigging and riding lights, but they lost sight of her in the rain and spray of the gale.

The huge seas had torn and broken her rigging and the sails were rent and shredded. They had even lost an experienced topman blown off the main topyard while struggling to put in a last reef.

Now the Swiftsure was doing all she could to weather the storm with her big spanker-rigged mainsail to give steerage way she rose and fell on the waves that rose higher than the crows nest and deluged them as they crashed over her bows.

Denquinar was taking a share of the watches to give Reynolds another officer to share the watches. They were down an officer since the episode on the island of the Ichtar.

They both wore oilskins with hoods, but they were soaked through, nonetheless. All their kit was soaked now; the same was true for the sailors and Denquinar was glad he had insisted on woolen clothing to be added to the ship's stores. At least the wool still kept you warm even when it was wet. The men stood around in their oilskins shivering anyway.

Down plunged the *Swiftsure* into another trough and yet another huge wave crashed over her bows. That she was holding together under this punishment was amazing. Denquinar was pleased that the shipwrights at Pinitera knew their trade. He didn't think that any of the Corriian ships in which he had served could take this kind of punishment day after day.

He scanned the coastline; nothing but huge mountains and towering rocky cliffs. It was hard to tell but if they had passed any servicable bay or harbor he doubted it. He and Reynolds had been constantly on the lookout for some place to anchor and ride out the storm but had seen no structures such as islands or coves that offered any hope. All they could see were savage, rocky shores and shoals poking their black teeth out of the water as the waves passed foaming over them.

Denquinar figured it to be better to ride out the fury of the storm at sea and hope in the solid beams beneath his feet than risk staying too close inshore hoping for a harbor.

Two days later the coast disappeared. Reynolds sent a message to call the Commodore on deck.

"I noticed that the mountains seemed to get smaller and give way to sparse trees and low hills. Then all of a sudden there was just open ocean. My guess is that the coastline bends away eastward."

"Let us hope so, Captain. At least that offers some hope that we have reached the southern tip of the coast. Give orders to bring her onto an eastern tack. If you can get closer to the coast that will be good. Send men aloft to watch for shoals. If we have reached the southern tip, there may be submerged reefs. Try and do a depth sounding. We will see what this course brings."

A man was sent forward with the knotted rope and lead weight. The call came back, "No bottom!"

But Reynolds and Denquinar were smiling at one another. This could mean that they had found what they sought: the southern tip of the continent.

They ran before the westerly for half a day and saw no sign of land so altered course again to the northeast. There it was: the coast, sparse and windswept but running northeast.

They hugged the coast for another two days, but it got no more hospitable. The mountains seemed smaller and more wooded.

Midday on the third day since rounding the 'South Cape' as Denquinar had called it, there was a call from the masthead, "Land ho, on the Starboard bow!"

Denquinar who had been plotting the coast on the wax tablet, whirled around but Reynolds was at the railing before him. There was another coastline ahead running roughly parallel to the coast but, it appeared, clear water in between.

Denquinar stared at the new shore for a time before drawing it onto the wax mapping tablet on the poop deck for later transcription in ink onto their new map in the cabin.

"I may yet be proved wrong, Captain, but my guess is a large island."

"Then we may find some decent harbour yet."

"Let's hope so. We need water and a chance to make running repairs to rigging and sails. Still, given what she has been through, the ship has performed admirably."

Reynolds could not hide his little smile of pleasure at the praise for his ship.

As the seas became calmer and visibility improved. They could make a better map of the coasts on either beam. There was no mistaking it now, the coast ran northeast. They came to the end of the eastern coast, confirming Denquinar's suspicion that it was an island. They were able to map some of its shores and bays as they bent away to the east and south again.

A few hours more sailing brought them to another broad coastline off the starboard bow - probably another island. The two navigators could not resist the temptation to tack closer to each shore to map what they could see.

They did constant depth soundings as they approached the shores to record the depth in fathoms and from the measures of speed in knots, they had a workable map. They even estimated the distance between the islands and the shore and confirmed that although the straits were shallow; sometimes only a few fathoms, they were navigable.

A third large island came into view and the wind died. The *Swiftsure* was forced to resort to using oars and they creapt up the newly discovered coast at a sea snail's pace. What they did find was safe anchorage and decided to row her into a likely bay to see if they could find water.

All the while Denquinar was concerned about the *Suresafe*. It had been many days since they had lost sight of her in the storm. He would often spend hours scanning the horizon for any sign of a sail.

Shouts and the sound of ropes rattling through blocks signaled that the boats were away. The commodore looked around to see that his son, Kiri, as a midshipman on this voyage, was commanding one of the boats. Certainly, there were capable seamen on the boat and at the tiller, but Denquinar noticed with pride that his son was carefully watching the water ahead to steer them through the sand bars and weed beds.

They noticed a couple of sea cows sporting closer in. Denquinar pointed them out to Reynolds who had never seen the creatures before.

"They are quite harmless from my experience and shy of people, so they present no threat."

Renolds was watching the large animals with interest. "What an amazing voyage it has been with creatures never seen in our home waters."

"They feed on the reed beds and are very shy, perhaps the most peaceful creature in the oceans. They feed on the sea grass as our cattle feed on grassy meadows."

Reynolds watched one roll over with one flipper in the air and then disappear under the blue waters of the bay. "I would suggest a hunt if they were good to eat."

"Best leave them. They are shy and will keep out of your way. This bay will probably have plenty of fish. When the boats return with water, we can see about setting some nets. Do you have any men with fishing experience?"

"Yes several."

"Well, let's try that. There is no use trying to row through this calm. We would be better spending time repairing the rigging, doing a bit of fishing, and waiting for the wind to return."

But the wind did not return; neither did the boats. By afternoon on the day they anchored, Reynolds was concerned. He climbed the steps to the poop deck to find Denquinar also anxiously watching the beach. The boats were drawn up by a reedy section of beach that would normally indicate a stream and safely secured but there was no sign of their crews.

"I think I will take another boat and investigate."

"They may have encountered trouble. We don't know who or what lives on these shores, Commodore. I did send experienced men and they were armed and given orders to exercise caution."

Denquinar nodded. But he knew seamen; they were poor explorers on land. They would have taken none of the precautions that an army officer would take in a strange place. He could imagine them crashing through the forest with their carts and water barrels laughing and chatting. They wouldn't think to send out scouts.

Both officers were angry at themselves. After the near disasterous episode with the Ichtar, they should have sent an experienced officer to command the watering parties.

Denquinar looked down at the main deck, at the remaining boat. "We cannot afford to lose all the boats. I will take the jolly boat with enough men to bring her back and to secure the other two boats in deeper water, ready for a hasty departure if needed. Then I will go ashore with a couple of armed men and have a look around."

It took a little time to get the jolly boat crew assembled and armed and Denquinar went below to speak with the master armorer and returned with a heavy baize bag.

The boat was awayed out and lowered to the pristine blue water of the bay and the allocated crewmen climbed quickly over the side port and down to the boat. Denquinar followed with his heavy bag. He also had a sailor's cutlass in his belt.

The jolly boat approached the beach carefully but there was no sign of any trouble. The two larger boats were drawn up on the sand and the barrels and carts were gone along with the men.

They landed the boat and immediately set about re-launching the two larger boats. They put them out into deeper water and left them manned and ready.

Denquinar, Lieutenant Campsey and two armed marines waded ashore, and the jolly boat made back to the *Swiftsure.* They cautiously explored the beach. Denquinar stooped to examine marks in the sand and gestured the others to come and look at the spoor.

Campsey went white. There were several sets of tracks, and they were very large. They appeared to be several creatures walking side by side. There appeared to be more tracks through the seagrass on the edge of the sand.

"Do you think they are more Ichtar, Commodore," whispered Campsey.

"Perhaps. They are some large animal that travels on all fours; there are many of them judging by the multiple sets of tracks. That is about as far as my expertise goes."

Denquinar and the sergeant of marines opened the bag they had brought and took out a torch which they lit. Campsey saw that they had brought several terracotta canisters of fine oil with fuses. By way of explanation Denquinar whispered, "They may be useful if we encounter wild animals or even humans if they are not expecting them."

There were signs of the many footprints of the boat crews leading into the scrub and low trees; there could be no mistaking the direction the boat crews had taken. Their choice of direction made sense; they had followed the stream up the hill to where the water was fresh and hopefully running freely. The ideal would be a place where they could easily fill their barrels as the stream cascaded over rocks.

They split into two parties and made their way carefully through the trees trying to remain silent. It wasn't long before Denquinar heard sounds. They were animal growls and whines: there seemed to be much commotion just a little ahead of them. Knowing his son was with the landing party he wanted to rush forward but he had to be patient if he wished to get any of them to safety.

He reached into his bag and brought out one of the canisters and checked the direction of the wind. They were downwind and hopefully whatever creatures there were beyond the next clump of trees would not smell the burning tar. Denquinar moved forward through the scrub on a sandy track that looked as though it had been made by animals. The marine sergeant at his back strung his bow and fitted and arrow then crept along behind him.

The sounds of the animals grew louder. They looked over the top of a bush to see the dingle filled with wulves, huge goroths as large as any grimulf Denquinar had ever seen but these seemed to be a wild goroth pack; intent on their grisley meal. They were devouring sailors who all seemed to have been killed. What was left of their shipmates did not seem to include the boy, but it was hard to be sure. Then the sergeant pulled Denquinar by the sleeve and pointed to legs straddling the branch of a a tree. The uniform trousers indicated it was a sailor, but the leaves hid the owner of the trousers.

Denquinar guessed that they belonged to his son, and they could spot several other sets of legs in the branches that obviously belonged to others who had managed to make it into trees when the pack attacked. The difficulty now was to get them away without becoming prey themselves.

Denquinar's oil bombs had been brought as a weapon to startle and cause confusion to whoever they came against. They may work against these animals. They were their best if not their only chance. Denquinar pointed to a rocky outcrop in the bushes to the sergeant and signaled that it would be their path out and he aimed for the hard rocks in the hollow that would be sure to break the light terracotta canister. They lit their fuses and threw.

The goroths were distracted with their prey but a couple of the larger animals had looked up, perhaps sensing something amiss. The outcrop on the edge of the dingle burst into an explosion of flames. The wulves looked up only to be spattered with flames from Denquinar's grenade that burst in their midst.

At that moment arrows struck two of the largest of the beasts from the thicket opposite. He threw another grenade and then another. The whole dingle was in flames and injured wulves were thrashing about trying to roll on their burning fur, but the oil would not go out. They ran through the scrub even catching other bushes alight.

Drawing their weapons, Denquinar and his sergeant shouted and charged into the pack. The wulves were reluctant to give up their prizes but backed off a little as Denquinar swung both sword and burning torch in their faces. They snarled back and were beginning to circle around the new attackers, especially when it appeared they were only two.

Denquinar called to his son and the other men in the trees, and they shinnied down to join them. Things might still have gone badly but Dempsey appeared on the other side of the dell with the other marines and more lighted grenades. They hurled them at the pack and charged in among them to join Denquinar.

The flames were still licking up among the bushes on the edge of the hollow and Denquinar pointed to them. "This way, run through the flames!" They did and the goroths did not follow.

They ran through the low scrub and onto the sand. As soon as they reached the beach, they saw the boats pulling hard back to the shore to pick them up. Denquinar desperately looked for some hard object that would break his last canister open; finding none he pulled out the stopper and threw the canister and the torch toward the bushes which burst alight. Two or three more goroths were following them through the prickly coastal heath. When the oil burst alight in front of them, they drew back snarling, hackles raised.

They fled down the beach as fast as they could run and splashed into the water. The boats rowed in to pick them up and all were swimming before they were hauled over the gunwales into the relative safety of the boats. They all reached for oars and the sweeps steered them into deep water as quickly as possible. Several of the lerge goroths had skirted the fire and came bounding out of the undergrowth and stood on the beach, apparently unwilling to follow them into the water, or no longer hungry enough to do so.

Denquinar resisted the temptation to hug his son, not wanting to embarrass him in front of the men but the boy had no such concern. He threw himself into his father's arms; the pent up tears popped out of the corners of his eyes. "I thought they were going to eat us too...." Then as he got himself more under control, "I lost the men... I should have been more careful."

"You weren't to know you were being *hunted*." Still the boy remained in his father's arms. He was only twelve after all, and the sailors didn't seem to think it inappropriate. They had all barely excaped with their lives. Once they were in deeper water, they all slumped over the oars and caught their breath. Both Denquinar and his son pulled on the oars as there were too few men to properly row the boats.

Reynolds and the rest of the crew could clearly see the goroths prowling along the shore and now and it was obvious what had happened to their shipmates.

Once on board, Reynolds ordered that hot food and coffee be prepared for the survivors and he allowed Denquinar and his son a little time in the cabin he shared with the Commodore to settle their nerves. He knew water was now likely to be a problem; they had lost the carts and many of the barrels. He decided to ask the carpenter and the cooper if they had enough wood left to make some more. He decided to row on and soon the long oars were out again propelling the *Swiftsure* insect-like, slowly along the coast.

Two days later there was still no wind. They rowed on slowly taking two hour shifts at the oars; still the men were exhausted and had blisters on their hands. With the depredations of the Ichtar and the loss of the landing party, they were short of men and rowing used up more of their precious water. Even the midshipmen and the marines took turns at the oars.

About mid-morning a call came from the masthead, "Reef or somethin' off the port bow, Captain."

Reynolds and lieutenant Campsey couldn't see because of the mainsail and climbed the mizzen yards to see what the lookout had seen. At this distance it looked as if there was a mat of grass on the surface of the water as far as they could see and among the green there were large green spiked domes. In the distance they could make out another patch of land which might well be another large island.

They rowed on in barely a breath of wind and came up close to the green mat taking depth soundings all the while but there was plenty of water under the keel. The bowman called again, "No bottom!"

As soon as they were within a couple of cables, they could see that the mat was really long ropes of seaweed. Which moved and floated in the current, but which seemed to reach down to the bottom on long thick stalks.

They came up close to the weed bank. "Full fathoms six." Came the call from the bowman.

"Anchor aweigh, Mr Campsey." Then turning to Denquinar who was looking at the seaweed with considerable interest, "Do you know what it is Commodore?"

"Sargasso Sea. It is a legend: a sea so choked with long trailing weed that it cannot be navigated."

There came another call from the masthead. "Away off the port beam, Captain! More wulves; chasing people!"

They all looked and saw that a large pack of large shaggy wulves had seen what appeared to be a group of children on the beach.

"Sway out the boat if you please, Mr Dempsey. All armed crew...see if you can help."

The longboat hit the water with something of a splash as the men let the rope run through the winches too quickly in their haste to get her away; the marines followed the crew over the side carrying bows and handpikes. One had javelins which were his preferred weapons.

The children on the beach had seen their danger and ran for the water. They waded out far enough to be able to swim and began to make for the weeds. All seemed to be excellent swimmers for children. Dempsey was the last through the entry port and could see the wulves splashing through the water in pursuit. He had younger siblings and was appalled at the thought of children being prey to these brutes. He jumped down into the longboat and yelled at the oarsmen, "Backs to it, men! Let's get there and help those children." The stroke called out a brisk pace and the longpoat rushed to intercept.

By the time they were close enough to really see what was happening they saw that the swimming wulves were closing on the children who were spread out across the water with the smallest bringing up the rear and in the most danger of being overtaken. The wulves could certainly swim well, but Dempsey still thought they had the advantage being in the boat.

As they watched the wulves gaining on the last swimmer and looking to catch the child before they could get there, Dempsey called to the archers who drew they bows to their chin ready. The smallest swimmer looked behind him, terrified and desperately thrashed the water in his attempt to gain speed. It wasn't going to work.

Dempsey stood in the stern watching the drama. "Quick, sergeant, shoot!" But the swimming goroths were difficult targets and both arrows fell short and the hunting wulves did not even seem to be distracted.

"Again," yelled Dempsey but the marines were drawing more arrows as he spoke. They shot and one of the animals seemed to be hit. It stopped but several others continued the pursuit.

As the longboat rowed for all it was worth, another wulf was hit and a marine stood ready with a javelin. This was fortunate because while they were focused on the desperate race in front of them, they had not noticed that two wulves were approaching the stern of the long boat. One came within a couple of cubits of Dempsey's arm before the sweep warned him. He struggled to draw his sword, but the marine saw the danger and hurled his javelin.

The shaft struck and the animal emitted a howl of rage and pain as it struggled with the weapon that would no doubt cause its death.

This distraction momentarily took their attention off the chase and only some quick shooting stopped one grey shape from reaching the child.

The oarsmen now drove the boat between the goroths and the children. Dempsey reached down and lifted a small boy lightly out of the water. Realising the danger was not over a small girl swam over to the boat and was also lifted out of the water. The other children had now almost reached the reeds. They dived under the water and disappeared.

Dempsey had little time to think about the children. They had several of the brutes attacking the boat now, oblivious to the danger and furious at being deprived of their quarry.

The two children screamed as a huge head and paws rose over the gunwals and gnashed at them. Dempsey hacked at it with his sword and drove it off. One of the oarsmen pushed it away from the boat with his oarblade. Eventually the wulves gave up and those that could, began to swim for the shore.

Dempsey looked at the children. They were naked except for a green string around their waists and small skirts of a kind of seaweed. It was said that all people spoke some version of the same universal language of men and Dempsey tried to get answers to his many questions. "Who are you? Where are your families?"

They did not answer, and the boy seemed uncertain, so Dempsey tried again. "Where can we take you to be safe?"

The little boy pointed to the place in the weed where the others had disappeared. Dempsey gave orders to the sweep, and they rowed closer. As soon as they were within a cables' length, the two children stood suddenly, dived over the side and swam for the reeds. He didn't try to prevent them but watched as they swam to the sargassum and lifted themselves up onto a platform of weeds. They then ran around one of the green dome-like structures and disappeared. The lieutenant was a little stumped but decided that the affair had ended well and turned back to the *Swiftsure*.

As they approached the side of the ship and hooked the boat onto the side, Dempsey could see that the Captain and Denquinar were looking at something on the beach. He looked around and saw several of the injured wulves dragging themselves out of the water. One had a javelin right through its body and it seemed impossible that it could survive but once on the beach, it rolled over with a yelp of pain and snapped off the shaft of the weapon before following the pack into the scrub behind the beach.

The officers watched, amazed. Something about what they had seen sent a cold shiver down their backs. There was evil at work in the goroth packs.

Reynolds watched Dempsey and the boat crew climbing up the side and nodded his congratulations to the young officer. They could not have done themselves any harm saving the children. He wondered what kind of people these were.

As the day waned and they rode at anchor in the bay, they noticed lights appear in some of the green domes and it seemed there were more lights under the green mat of the sargassum weed that covered the surface of the water.

Then at sunset, they noticed some of the lights moving toward them. It was not long before a coracle appeared; it was paddled by two men. The simple craft came alongside and looked innocuous enough. Denquinar went to the entry port and looked down. A fine young man dressed in only a loin covering but of impressive physique looked up at him. "The king of the people of the water sends you greeting and thanks. The courage of your boatmen has been seen and you saved our children when we were too far away to help them. The king has sent a message that he would speak with you. He wishes to know if you are from the great emperor in Bertola.

Denquinar's curiosity would not allow him to refuse. "We are not from the Bernadian Emperor, but I have met him. We are from the northeast. We have traveled past the southern cape and so have come into your waters. We mean no harm and wish no offense to your king."

"You have caused no harm and prevented much; the boy you saved was the son of the king's son. I am bid to ask you to send your head person to an audience with the king if he will come."

Denquinar glanced at Reynolds and Kiri standing nearby. Unspoken words passed between them, "I will speak with their king. Look after my son while I am gone and if I do not return."

To the boatmen he said, "I will accept your king's invitation. Will you take me?"

"Yes. We are sent to convey you. Can you manage our craft?'

Denquinar looked at Kiri who was clearly chafing to go with his father but knew the protocol. Their eyes met only for a moment and Denquinar answered the boatmen by climbing down into the small craft.

He took the last step from the side ladder into the coracle with some trepidation, but the boat was surprisingly stable. And he seated himself somewhat uncomfortably in the middle of the boat on a floor that seemed to be of a living green plant. The two paddlers left the side of the *Swiftsure* and paddled toward the sargassum. As they came among the giant trailing seaweed, Denquinar could see that there were gaps between the long tendrils, and they passed quickly through the weed mat. He could now see that there were indeed many lights below them. The two sea men paddled up to one of the green domes and tied (Denquinar could not see exactly how this was done) the coracle to the structure. They then stepped through a flap opening in the dome and indicated that he should follow. Denquinar boldly stepped inside.

There was a small landing and a somewhat slippery rope ladder leading down to another landing below.

One of the watermen turned to him. "I am Sirgoron, and this is Virtor. We are messengers sent from the water king."

"I am Denquinar; I am a commodore in the navy of the king of Herelstrom in the far north. I am bearing messages to the king of Bernadia."

"You will perhaps find the Bernadian's beset with troubles and in poor shape to help anyone, if it is help you seek. But come and speak with the king; perhaps he will tell you things that will help."

They climbed down the ladder using the light from an iridescent green growth speckled all over the walls. The ladder below led to another ladder and then another and then into a tunnel that seemed to be comprised of a series of roughly circular chambers. They needed to step over ridges where each chamber joined onto the next and Denquinar found that they moved and shifted which was somewhat disconcerting.

As he followed his guides through the chambers, he could not help being reminded of the seaweeds he had often seen washed up on the beach which had many bubble-like floatation chambers. These appeared to be the same but much, much larger.

The undersea road eventually led them to a chamber where more people were gathered. There were two very impressive people who, by their bearing and sage countenances, had to be leaders.

Sirgoron led Denquinar into this larger chamber. "This is Commodore Denquinar of the navy of Herelstrom and an emissary of its king, your Majesty. Commodore, this is King Seor and Queen Semperor."

The messengers then bowed and left the chamber. Denquinar felt very much alone and could barely recall the way back to the surface and his ship. But he also felt an exhilerating sense of awe and adventure.

The king stepped forward and Denquinar bowed. The king nodded his acknowledgement but then smiled.

"Enough formality, we are a small people; driven by great tribulation to live in the sea. Please join the queen and I and our counselors in some food and drink. I hope our food is to your taste."

At a word from the queen, servants brought in long trays of various foods and squat containers of some kind of drink. The food trays were hung on ropes from the roof. The hanging ropes were also adorned with round globes from which shone the ubiquitous green light in greater measure so that those participating in the meal could properly see their food which was of cracked lobsters and crabs and large starchy lunps of something that looked like bread but was obviously not so. The queen led them to the trays and broke off a large piece of lobster and a piece of the spongy food and began to eat. The king did likewise and indicated that Denquinar should help himself. It didn't take much convincing; lobster was just about his favourite food and these lobsters were huge. They seemed to have been cooked in some form of fruit acid as he had seen done before and was lightly spiced with just a hint of the fruit acid remaining. It was possibly the most delicious thing he had ever tasted.

He pulled off a piece of the bread-like substance and found it had a spongy consistency and tasted something like a root vegetable; it acted marvelously to cleanse the palate after each piece of the lobster.

In the squat container was clear water with a hint of fruit flavor. Denquinar copied his hosts and took a long drink.

When they had all finished eating, they retired to a smaller, less brightly lit room and the king and queen sat around with Denquinar and the advisors. Denquinar was asked about their journey and recounted their many adventures since leaving Herelstrom in the midst of an invasion. As he responded to their many uestions, Denquinar asked himself if he was saying too much. His many years in the Corrii armed forces had taught him to be careful who he told what, but here he felt there was little threat these people were reclusive and secretive and very unlikely to be in league with the Corrii.

His thoughts were confirmed when King Seor began to recount their woes. They gathered their food on the sea floor and had developed ways of cultivating the tubers on the roots of the sargassum. They also caught fish, lobsters, and prawns but the food they were used to; that grew aplenty on the woods off the coast had been innaccesible for some time. The king explained that the episode with the children was typical of their problems. They had defied his edicts and gone ashore in search of the fruit and nuts that his people had often gathered, and which were an important part of their diet, to say nothing of their nutrition. The goroth packs had multiplied and become much more cunning; it was as if they were actively seeking his people and hunted them whenever they went ashore. Going ashore was now limited to a very few and done with great care.

Lieutenant Darson was on watch and stood at the poop deck railing keeping company with Kiriakanatus Denquinar who would not go to sleep. The boy had kept watch for his father since he had left, and it was now the middle of the middle watch of the night.

As they looked out at the strange fairylights of green and blue a couple of the lights began to move and it soon became apparent that they were coming toward them.

Kiri was tense and the palpable tension evaporated as he saw the form of his father returning in the small coracle. The craft came alongside long enough for the Commodore to grab onto the ladder and then paddled away again into the night and the lights on the coracle eventually merged with the field of small lights in the sargassum.

22

Midnight Wulves

*D*enquinar asked for the captain to be woken and the officers to gather in the wardroom.

"I have seen things tonight that make our journey more urgent. It will be best if I tell you the story so that you will understand the urgency of our next task.

I have gone below the surface of the sea and met with the king and queen of the water people. They have been forced out of the nearby forests and heath where they were used to gathering their food and have taken to living in homes they make for themselves in the Sargasso Sea.

This night the king and one of his warriors led me along a path within the seaweed. How they make these I cannot say but the path led us by a narrower and narrower way through the chambers in the weed itself and down to the ocean floor. At last, we came to what was the last passable chamber which had a door in the wall which was sealed in some strange way with many folds.

We could climb from the seaweed into a cave on the edge of the ocean. We had to wade a long way in water up to our waist that rose and fell with the ocean surge. Eventually the cave led up into the limestone and our way became dry. Somehow the sea people have found or made this way and it seemed that the limestone formations had grown for the very purpose of making a way for them to go underground a great way into the very bones of the hills.

The caverns were beautiful, but their purpose was other than to show me the caves and their secret way led up onto a ledge and we could look out into a waterfall of bright water that sprayed and glistened as it fell into a small pool.

The king pointed and said to me, 'Watch it is beginning again.'

I looked out of the small crack he showed me toward the pool, and I could see that a pack of wulves had gathered at the pool. At first, I thought it was to drink but soon many more began to arrive.

There was one very large goroth that seemed to be the leader and he would often climb up onto a large rock beside the pool and howl. His eerie cry brought more and then more wulves to the place and soon the space beside the pool was filled with them.

They began to look toward the waterfall. We looked also and saw that there was an image forming in the fine spray of the water. I knew who I saw. It was the image of Groemelian master of the grand coven. He is a shadowy figure at all times; he operates from hiding and lets others enjoy the limelight while he stays in the background wielding the real power, for all the grand coven people defer to him; he has the power, terrifying power and it seems to be growing not diminishing with the years whose depredations are visible in his body but clearly not in his mind or his skills.

His image shimmered in the falling shower. It was large and filled the space so that he must have appeared to the creatures as a god appearing to them out of the magic water of the falls.

Then we heard a voice; the voice I believe, of Groemelian. It came from nowhere and resonated in the dell formed by the waterfall and the pool. 'I see among you many who are injured and have suffered in a fight. Come forward!'

Several injured animals staggered forward; some dragging injured and festering limbs. A blue-grey mist formed in the dell, and it seemed many forms took shape in the mist and separated to become many small misty forms and they moved toward the injured wulves.

The ghostly forms seemed to coalesce with the animals and their hosts soon became hale and strong again, leaping and capering about with yelps of delight at being well.

I also saw many shapes gather around the head goroth and I could see an aura around him, and it was as if the shapes communicated with the aura not the creature.

As we watched it seemed that the image of Groemelian in the spray of the waterfall became brighter again, as if he was again putting forth power to illuminate his image.

'Now, take your rightful place as rulers of the south. Go and retake the lands that men have taken from you. Scatter and devour their live-stock to fill your empty bellies. Devour their children and eat the flesh of their females.

The great packs will run together again. You will not tire or falter until you have destroyed all the lands of the north; in every cot terror of your coming will be whispered and dread of you will spread like icy fingers over Bernadia, over all the lands of your persecutors.

No longer will they drive you from their lands with great bows. Now you are strong; and you are many and you will overcome them. Go Forth!'

As the words faded away into the air the wulves all looked again to their chief who stood and howled and spoke with a human tongue. 'Cum wee harve farrr tu trarvell and peeople to devourrr. Leet uss runn weeth th' weends and faarll upon them unawarres and unprepared.'

Then he leapt down from the rock and led his packs out of the dell and away through the heath.

I had to explain to the king that I knew to whom the image in the waterfall belonged, for I had seen master Groemelian several times before in the palace in my role as a Grand Admiral of the Corrii before I fled the empire seeking my lost son.

He seemed very surprised and not a little concerned that he had unwittingly revealed his secrets to a possible enemy. But I assured him that I am a fugitive to the empire; that my life is forfeit if I ever fall into their hands and his secrets are safe with me; even with the whole crew of this ship, for I could not betray his secrets even if I wished, for I know too little of them.

They led me back through the caves and through the weed chambers to the surface and two of them paddled me back to the ship. That is the end of my story."

Reynolds leant back in his chair. All the while, through Denquinar's story he had been thinking that they now had information that needed to be communicated to the Bernadians. The trouble was how to contact them to tell them about the threat.

"One important thing is that we now have some information that can be of some help to those we seek as allies."

Lieutenant Dempsey was fiddling with the handle of his coffee cup. "It seems that the Bernadians will have enough on their plate and may not have any resources left to help Herelstrom."

Reynolds knew that Dempsey has family at Neren Keys, his mother and two sisters and they were often on his mind of late as they sailed further and further away from their homes. "Perhaps what you say is right, Lieutenant but we do not seek an alliance with the Bernadians just to gain help for ourselves. Allies help each other and it is by coordinating their efforts that they offer the greatest resistance to their enemies. I feel better that we do not just arrive cap in hand but come with information that may protect the farmers and their livestock from a serious threat."

Denquinar had picked up a pair of dividers off the table. "The problem is to get the warning to them in time. We do not know how far it is."

Reynolds got up and pulled his partly completed map from the rack. "…looking at where we have come, Commodore, how far do you guess it might be before we reach Bernadian settlements or ports?"

Denquinar looked at the maps. "I don't have much more idea than you do, but I would guess that their coastal settlements reach a long way down the coast. You would expect fishing villages and the like in every sheltered cove and river estuary."

Reynolds looked over their drawings of the islands. "We will have to get out to open sea and look for some wind. Rowing is just too slow and this ship handles well in any seas. I want to feel her leaning into the wind again."

Denquinar looked at their chart as well. "I guess we can get to open water through these straits. There looks to be open sea beyond. We will have to try it anyway; we cannot afford the time to double back."

The captain stood up and reached for a bottle that was secured to a clip inside the chest under the seat below the stern windows. He then reached in for some glass tumblers in a wire rack. "We shall have a drink, gentlemen; then dine here in my cabin. After that Lieutenant Dempsey can give orders for the crew to be roused at first light. We need to make up the coast and find a settlement as quickly as possible."

They settled back to chat and enjoy their wine. The morning promised new adventures and new challenges. As they slept, they had dreams of terrible dogs chasing innocent unprepared villagers and when the officers of the *Swiftsure* woke to the sound of bells, they had all steeled their resolve. The ship was underway before dawn and as soon as there was any wind all sails were set and drawing, and the water surged by under her counter.

Her officers prowled the deck giving orders and everything was being prepared against unknown contingencies. The longboat was readied, and the crew was issued with their weapons.

They passed the Sargasso weed and came into a wide strait with a small island between two land masses. Reynolds sketched the islands on the wax tablet as they went to make a complete as possible map. In a couple of hours, they were in open sea and the *Swiftsure* was making fourteen knots.

They sailed close enough to the coast to be able to pick out any possible bays or signs of settlements. There came a call from the masthead. "Sail ho; off the starboard beam."

Even the captain climbed the rigging to look. There was no mistaking those sails. It was the *Suresafe*. She looked to be in good condition. Perhaps she had weathered the cape better than they had.

They had obviously been seen as well and their sister ship had changed tack to intercept their own course. Immediately they were within signal distance, Denquinar and his son began to send signals telling the Captain Henderson of their intentions. When they came within hailing distance, they were able to shout enough information across the small space between the two ships sailing in consort.

It appeared that Henderson had sailed down the other side of the islands and had stopped at a port on the seaward side of the island Island of Dirinar to make some running repairs. It was apparently a settlement of Bernadians and though the people were poor, mainly raising livestock on the island, they had been received well and given some information.

There was apparently a string of small bays to the north with some fishing and some trading activity out of one of the larger harbors, half a day to the north.

This sounded like the most likely place to find officials and they decided to search for the port that the islanders had said was called Margaritta River.

Armed with this information they sailed past a few small hamlets on the coast and made for this more northerly port.

They spotted the sails of a few small craft first and soon saw the river mouth with plenty of evidence of ships.

They hailed a passing fishing boat and when they explained they needed to speak urgently to a town official they were told they needed the chief warden who apparently had some militia troops at his disposal, but the fishermen were not clear on this point.

So as to indicate their friendly intentions the two ships sailed into the river and lowered their sails well clear of shore and lowered a single boat. Denquinar went in the boat with Reynolds, and they left Henderson and Dempsey in command if anything should go wrong.

As the boat approached a wooden pier, they saw that a crowd of people had gathered. One person in particular was a black robed individual with a beard that did not look at all friendly.

Denquinar was the first to step onto the jetty and he approached the robed man as he seemed to have the most authority present. They needed to find who was in authority quickly and wanted to avoid general panic.

The robed man stepped forward. "I am Bardleamun priest in Margaritta River. Who are you and why do you bring ships to our harbor and come armed into our midst?"

Reynolds spoke first. "I am Captain Reynolds, and this is Commodore Denquinar. We have sailed from the north, and around the southern Cape from Herelstrom in the north. Our land is being invaded by the Corrii and we sail to take a message to your emperor."

"And how is that any concern of ours?"

This took the wind out of Reynolds' sails. He tried again. "Commodore Denquinar also has reason to believe that you face a serious threat from the wulf packs in the south. He has seen them preparing to attack your villages."

"That is nonsense! There haven't been wulves seen in this part of the country for many years. Sometimes the villagers and hunters in the west encounter them but they are mostly shy and easily driven off."

Denquinar decided he would try; he guessed at the right form of address. "Father, I have seen the goroths being in-spirited with the spirits of the Jungari. The coven masters of the Corrii seem to have found a way to do this at a great distance. I think you may be in greater danger than you realize."

The priest nodded slightly at the appropriate address but was clearly unconvinced. "If this were true it would be useful to send messengers up-river to warn the farms and settlements."

"I believe, Father that there needs to be warning sent to all the people in the south. Do you have a head man in the village? A fisherman we spoke to coming in said you have a chief warden in the town.

"Yes, we have such a person, but he and his men marched out two months ago to join the new army that the crown prince has raised against..." here he gestured vaguely "some perceived threat in the north."

Denquinar was becoming increasingly frustrated. "Is there anyone else that we could speak to? Is there a way of getting a message to your southern towns that there is danger brewing?"

The priest was also getting exasperated. "Yes, I suppose so. You could try the taverner. He is the next in charge of the militia, but he has no men he can call on anymore."

Denquinar politely asked directions and led Reynolds up the main street of the town leaving the boat and crew waiting at the jetty.

When they reached the tavern there was a solid-looking man behind a bar and a young girl cleaning table. He looked at them enquiringly as they entered through the double, solid, wooden doors.

"You are obviously not from around here. Do I assume you gentlemen are from the ships in the bay?"

That sounded promising and they quickly repeated the story they had related to the priest. While they were talking the taverner drew two mugs of beer from a barrel under his bar and then picked up a plate of bread, cheese and pickles. Without mentioning any cost, he led them to a table and placed the refreshments in front of them.

Reynolds took out some money and offered to pay but the taverner shook his head. "There's no need, captain. If what you have warned happens, you will have earned much more than a couple of pints of ale. We need to get the word out as quickly as possible. Unfortunately, the town militia has been called up for service and is marching north with the prince. I have a horse and there is a boy I know who is reliable. We can send messages to the next couple of towns and ask them to relay them on. Jossy, run and fetch young Jonah as quickly as you can."

Denquinar gave a sigh; realizing that they had now found someone who understood the threat. "That sounds excellent. We should write the message down as best we can, so it is not transmitted wrongly." He sipped some of his ale.

"It should be fine. Jonah will remember the message if you ask him to repeat it to you. He has a good memory."

Reynolds sipped his own ale and smiled with obvious enjoyment which pleased the publican. "You should take precautions yourselves. This town does not seem to have any defences."

"You are right. This is the only place that is defensible. I will send messages out to tell anyone who is frightened that they should come and spend the night in the inn."

While they finished their drink and food the boy Jonah came in and was given his instructions to the taverners in the next two villages whom their host apparently knew well. He was soon on his way to the stables to saddle the innkeeper's horse. They heard him ride away up the hill a few minutes later.

Denquinar and Reynolds thanked him and made their way back down the street of the town to their boat. Now the word had passed around and everyone was watching them.

As they hurried along a woman with two small children hanging onto her skirts hailed them. "Is it true, wild wulves from the forest are coming here?"

"It is a possibility," said Reynolds, "if you have no sure way of securing your house you should ask for protection at the tavern."

She nodded and thanked them. It seemed that they may have got the warning out.

Back on deck, later that night, they did hear howls of wulves in the town as well as shouts and screams. The wulves of the southern forests had come indeed. As they watched from the safety of their ship, they saw a large animal walk out onto the pier and glower at them. Denquinar has seen this kind of creature before. Once possessed by the spirits of the Jungari the wild wulves ceased to have the fears normal to their kind. This wulf had stood unconcerned on a man-made pier, in the light of the moon.

23

The Grey Curtain

*T*he greased hawser made no sound as the capstan lifted the heavy anchor out of the water. It emerged covered with weed and slime from the bottom of the harbor and two seamen on harnesses were lowered to remove the weed as it cleared the water to avoid the great muddy tendrils falling into the water and making a splash.

Rowlocks muffled with old cloth and greased mountings kept the oars silent. Norrens' orders were for only one row of oars to be used and only the most experienced oarsmen so that their procession down the harbor would be silent and the oars would make only little disturbance as they rose and fell, caterpillaring the quinquareme down the harbor and out to sea – and freedom. With typical naval precision the other ships followed her out.

The riding lights on the Argamaro were doused as soon as they moved, and she was a dark shape in a moonless northern night.

As she passed the harbor fortifications there was no sign that anyone had noticed her. In fact, two watchmen saw them leave and one commented to the other that the navy was playing their games again. 'Let's see if we can slip away without anyone seeing us – just for practice'.

Once at sea the great yards were raised, and the sails banged and thudded as the expanse of canvas filled with the stiff northwesterly. The Argamaro picked up speed and her bows cut through the dark water. She was no racehorse, but in this wind, she could put on a fair turn of speed.

If anyone had seen them far out in the northern ocean, lights appeared in the three-deck sterncastle of the flagship as the officers retired to cabin and wardroom and the Admiral with his flag captain went to his cabin to study the maps and make plans. Dividers crisscrossed the chart as they measured the distance around the Northern Cape and south to Inrahall and Millaroth.

Captain Verna measured the distance for the fourth time and calculated the time required for the voyage from measurements of distance and speed. They heard the call from the poop and the speed in knots-of-the-rope relayed to the duty officer overhead.

"The coven messengers have a straighter road, but in this wind, we will still outpace them."

Norrens measured the distance between the two northern harbors on the map. "I will take a boat and land to the north of Inrahall. If I can get a couple of horses, I will make for Millaroth overland and see if we can free the families and make for the rendezvous at the Starvre Estuary."

"Do you think your wife is still at your home near Inrahall?"

"I hope so. If she is not, she may have been taken to Millaroth as well. That is where I will go next if I don't find her at home. But mine is an old family with many retainers loyal to my father. I have good hope that she is there."

"The other families are at Biel Harfing. Should we split up our ships and send one group to Biel Harfing?"

"Yes, I suppose so. My concern is having enough of our men when we get to Biel Harfing to win against the coven people if it comes to a fight – which I suspect it will. They haven't gone to all this trouble without taking some security precautions. We will follow as quickly as possible, and it shouldn't take long to pick up my family. We may even catch up with the squadron."

Verna put down the brass dividers on the map. "We have other problems. We must win over the crew first. Shall I send for the man from Egleton. We will see what help he and his people may be."

By dawn they had progressed further along the northern coast than any would have expected. The cold wind-swept cliffs of the North Cape were now already in sight. The ship's master had already altered course to give the cape a wide berth. The reefs and shoals along this part of the coast had caused many ships to founder in times past.

Norrens stood by the poop deck railing. "If this wind holds, we will be at the Starvre Estuary in a day or so," he sighed as he wondered what would happen next. "You had better assemble the men, Verna."

The flag captain gave orders and the call of, "all hands on deck" rang out around the ship and the lower decks.

Norrens saw the crew quickly assembling on the quarterdeck. "You had better bring up the prisoners too."

The sailors brought up the many prisoners from the lower deck. They came through the hatchway blinking like owls and looking around them to get some idea of where they were and what their fate might be.

Admiral Norrens stood at the railing as a couple of hundred faces turned toward him.

"As many of you know there has been much concern about the way the rulers of the empire have been treating the families of the men of the navy. Life in the navy is hard and we get little enough time in the quiet of our homes and with our family and loved ones, comforts which other men take for granted.

Now our homes and farms go to rack and ruin or are plundered by evil men, and we have to spend our time worrying about the well-being of our loved ones who have been herded together into enclaves at Biel Harfing.

More than this a terrible unspoken threat hangs over our families. If we rebell against authority; or even fail at some alloted task, they could ship our families across the water to Dorphire Sunde and the red priests."

There was a growing murmer of disapproval. He had them.

"Are these the actions of honourable men? Are these the desires of even the emperor himself? I think not. They are the the measured actions of devious, faceless men who now rule the empire in secret and have, in secret made pacts with the evil priests of Dorphire Sunde who practice their evil rites of torture and human sacrifice."

Norrens lowered his voice to add to the gravity of what he had to say next.

"Your officers will not accept this and have determined to sail to Biel Harfing to rescue all our families and get them away from the power and influence of these men to somewhere safe."

There was an uncomfortable silence as the men all looked at one another. Finally, the quartermaster spoke.

"Sir, you know there has been much talk about this as we do our work for this ship but what you are proposing has great risks; not just for us but as you say for our families as well."

"That is true, Dors. There are many risks, but we already know that Grand Admiral Cherulia and the coven people suspect dissent in the fleet, and this is their first move to counter that threat. We hope that we are closer to Biel Harfing than the messengers and we can try and rescue our people before orders reach the enclave from Corrimar or Bea-air Monar."

One old dailor spoke up from among the general mumbling. "Zir, I 'av no family but these overs 'ave. I for one will fight to 'elp their wives and little ones. But where would we go?"

"…Bernadia. I have spoken to Tom from Herelstrom who is one of the captives and was ruler of Newcastle in the south of their country before it fell. They have been trying to form an alliance with Bernadia against the empire. Tom also tells me that Admiral Denquinar is now a Commodore in their navy and is well respected."

There was general surprise at this and more murmuring.

"He is trying to find a way to Bernadia via the southern seas as we speak here."

Another seasoned master spoke up. "Aren't the Bernadians our enemies? Won't they just throw us into prison or chain us to rowin' benches in their ships till we die?"

Norrens had considered this. "Perhaps but probably not. Remember that for all the evil our rulers speak of them they have never attacked us. Perhaps Tom has something to say."

The bunch of prisoners pushed Tom forward. He painfully climbed the ladder and stood next to Admiral Norrens with his bandaged head. "Seamen of the Corriian Empire, I have met the emperor of Bernadia.

He travelled to my country this way after the last conflict. He came to bestow honours on a friend of mine who saved his son out of the prison of the covens. He is a good and noble ruler who judges men fairly. He will more probably treat you as allies, once you have proven yourselves true.

What is more the whole world is turning against these men who rule your empire. Why will you continue to fight for them against countries who mean you no harm?"

The Admiral put his hand on Tom's shoulder. "Will all the men of Herelstrom join us?"

There were nods and agreement from the group of captives.

"Now men, what do you say?"

There was much discussion and nodding of agreement.

"There is one last thing. We do not want men who are unwilling. If there are any who do not feel they can break the oath to the emperor we will put them ashore to go where they will."

The men looked about for any dissenters.

"Are there any men who would prefer not to join us? I will assure you no harm will come to men who can not join us because of conscience."

About half a dozen hands went up. And there was loud grumbling from the men on deck.

Dors spoke for the rest of the crew. "Of course, they want out. They are spies of the coven men and Admiral Cherulia. If they were good men, I would be for settin' 'em free but these …. I say let's tie them hands and feet and run them under the keel a few times. That'll get some of the hot air out of 'em."

Again, there was general agreement from the sailors.

"I don't want to summarily kill men who may be innocent…or even keel haul them, Chief Dors. We will put them ashore on Bil Mohol beach.

It is far from any roads and while they will not die, they will have a long and hungry treck to get any help.

...Oh, and Verna, maybe don't send Chief Dors with the boat. Don't let him take a knife at least."

There was laughter and the suspected spies were ushered below to be chained up until they were released.

Judging by cheers coming from other ships the other captains had succeeded in winning over their crews as well.

The stiff northerly continued and although it meant hard work for ther crew with constant trimming of sail and climbing rigging in the near gale, they were making very fast progress down the northeast coast.

There were constant signals from the other ships and Norrens was sending plenty of his own. It seemed to Tom (who was now allowed on deck) that something was brewing. As the admiral passed him on the deck he ventured to ask.

"Admiral, what do you plan to do next?"

To Tom's surprise Norrens was quite open. "I will take my ship on a small excursion to the estuary just north of Millaroth. My home is near there and I hope to find my wife and daughter and get them away to safety. There are several other families there also and we will bring away any who want to come. The other ships will continue on to Biel Harfing where the families of most of the seamen are being 'housed'. We will join them as soon as possible – we only hope to be half a day behind at worst."

They chatted for some time leaning on the railing watching the coast creep by. Norrens spoke about his wife and eight-year-old daughter. Clearly, he loved his wife and doted on his daughter. Tom spoke about his wife and son. Without giving away any details he said he hoped that they had gotten away when the castle was sacked. The two men both found they had much in common.

That evening Tom was below decks when he heard the activities and clatter of the ship changing course. Not very long afterward he heard the splash of the anchors and guessed that Admiral Norrens had sortied the boats. He wished he was back at home protecting Lettie and again wondered how she was. He just couldn't imagine life without her.

In the boat Admiral Norrens guided the sweep as they steered into the estuary and rowed up the creek that bordered his family farm. He could smell smoke; and dread filled him. As soon as they were close enough Norrens ordered the boat to the edge of the waterway and leapt ashore. He gave orders for his men to follow and ran across the fields and through a clump of trees toward the farmhouse.

Soon he could hear some of his men running breathlessly to keep up with him. The smell of smoke was stronger and as he emerged from the trees, he heard a voice. "Captain! Don't go there they are watching the house."

He spun around and saw an old retainer of his father's. "Mortel, what has happened?"

"I so glad to see you, sir. Men came this very hour and took your wife. They killed your father when he tried to stop them. There are lots now up at the farmhouse and there is a grimulf with them."

"What about Chloe?"

"They took her too, Sir and the wife of Admiral Denquinar who came to us for help some time back. She had arrived all in rags with bare feet and nearly starving. Your wife took her in, fed and clothed her. Now they have all been taken on a horse drawn cart away down the road to Millaroth."

"How long ago? Can we catch them?"

"Not on foot sir. They had horses."

"I have to try and catch them."

"Beggin your pardon, Sir but I kept hidden under the hay by the barn, they said something about Dorphir Sunde."

Norrens stood dumbfounded. He thought it had just been a threat – obviously it was more than that. At that moment his men ran up carrying their weapons. His sergeant at arms was a big man but he arrived first; with concern written all over his face for his commander.

"What has happened, Sir?"

"They got here first. It seems my wife and daughter have been taken to Millaroth and my father has been killed. Mortel says they were talking about taking them to the islands."

"Sir, we had better go back and follow them by ship. It's the best chance."

"You're right. Come on, Mortel. You had better come as well."

"No, Sir. I will stay and see to your father and keep out of their way. They don't care about me, Sir."

"Very well. Thank you Mortel."

Norrens ran back to the boat with tears running freely down his face, as much as he tried to stop them, they came.

Back at the small estuary, it took infuriatingly long to raise the anchors and get under way. Norrens begrudged every minute they lost to the coven people.

By the next morning they were in sight of the harbor at Millaroth, but they also saw a ship with black sails leaving the port. She had the markings of a coven ship. She was probably stationed there now on the fastest route to the islands of Dorphir Sunde and used to convey important messages. Norrens watched her with horror. She had twice his speed and he could not catch her. He was sure who was on board.

Verna stood silent, sharing his pain, watching her race away across the bay. "What now?"

"If they harm them…"

"Do we follow? "

…No. we will join with the other ships. We cannot follow her into the harbour at Dorphire Sunde with one ship. We would all die. It would be futile. Head for Biel Harfing." Norrrens knew that his captain's family was there. Verna didn't take much convincing. In minutes every inch of sail was set and the Argamaro was racing south again.

Verna took command. He guessed that the other ships of their squadron would have landed up the coast to the north of the town and entered the town from the landward side. But if they had met with opposition, they would need his help as soon as possible. He sailed straight for the harbour and gave orders that all the boats were to be reddied and every man armed, including the freed captives. He went to see Tom to beg his help as well. He also had to leave enough seamen onboard to be ready to leave quickly if needed. Tom thought he would slow them down but many of the fighting men from Newcastle willingly joined the landing parties.

Verna came out of his cabin wearing his sword to be met by Bentonius. "I want to help, Captain."

Verna thought for a moment. "Very well, join with a boat crew and come along. Get a sword! I presume you can use one." Bentonius just smiled in answer.

While Verna had been getting his landing parties ready Norrens and the sailing master had guided the Argamaro down the channel and brought her about ready to anchor but instead of lowering her anchors they had brought her alongside a harbor buoy so that she could be secured but could cut her cables and make a dash for the sea again quickly.

They came ashore to find the port surprisingly empty; they could hear fighting in the town. As soon as they had landed, Captain Verner sent armed marines and some of the Newcastle men ahead to assist with the fighting against the coven people. Bentonius volunteered to join them, and they reached the town just as a large band of assorted guards and ruffians were about to counterattack the sailors that had already killed or driven off their comrades.

The counter-attacking coven people forced a gate in the west side of the enclave and charged into the middle of the town. Sailors hastily gathered together to fight back and would have struggled had Verna's sailors and marines now unoficially led by Bentonius now charged into them from the side and cut them to shreds. The sailors in the centre of the town then charged in turn once Bentonius had knocked the wind out of the counterattack.

Verna arrived to see Bentonius and his band driving into the coven guards. He saw the skill and deadly speed the former spy employed in hand-to-hand fighting. He saw Bentonius attack with his sword and then kill numerous adversaries with the dagger he kept hidden in his left hand.

Verna's men joined the battle and soon the remaining guards fled down the main road and out of Biel Harfing.

The captain ran up and stood next to Bentonius who was wiping his dagger on the cloak of one of his fallen enemies and gave him a con-gratulatory pat on the back as a gesture of acceptance and appreciation.

The captain didn't know what to do next, so he sought desperately for any officer he knew. He spotted Scolli from the *Vorsero*.

"Scolli, have you found them?"

"Some are in the town hall – over there; all together and safe, but some have already been taken away in ships!"

Verna ran for the hall and looked at the crowd of terrified women and small children. His saw his wife and small son. She was to the right of the hall trying to comfort a younger woman. He ran and embraced her and then gathered up their little boy into his arms.

Their moment of tenderness was brief. It took a little time to explain that the other ships were off the beach to the north and there were boats waiting. Most of the women were married to sailors from their squadron and those who used to own farms came from the surrounding region. It had been customary to do this so that sailors when home from service could all get to their families in reasonable time before having to report back again for duty.

Finding which families belonged to which men and which ships was made easier by the fact that mainly those men with families had volunterred for the boarding parties.

Verna soon saw that many of their men were standing around looking distraught. They had soon discovered that many of the women and children had been taken away in a coven ship that had left an hour or so before they had arrived.

"Come on, all of you back to the docks and the ships. I think we are bound for Dorphir Sunde."

It still took too long to load the women and children into boats and get the ships under way and the coven ships would have outpaced them anyway.

Verna ran up to the poop deck to report as soon as they had recovered the last of their people and the boats.

"We have succeeded in part, Admiral. We have saved some of the wives and little ones, but the coven people loaded some on boats and left already for the southeast. What do you want to do?"

"We will follow them, Captain, to the very gates of the abyss if necessary. Give the orders!"

Verna saluted, "Aye, captain!" and ran down the poop deck ladder shouting orders.

Only just clear of the bay and the enclave of Biel Harfing, they saw the other six ships of the squadron all making a course for the the islands of Dorphire Sunde. No-one in the squadron had been there; it was a place of infamy. But that was where they were going. No-one questioned whether this was a good idea or not. The fact that some of their own families had been taken to the islands of the red priests was enough.

Ingwit came on deck as soon as she heard their course. She wore a sword and Bentonius saw that she also carried several concealed daggers.

The daylight waned and they sailed on into the night carrying lights to show the position of all the seven ships. Verna sent as many of their men to rest as possible, but it was crowded below decks now and not many rested. Who knew what the morning held? The shared sense of anger at the covens and the foul priests with whom they were in league kept men from sleep.

Dawn revealed the squadron still in formation and still moving southeast at a fair speed. The three smaller ships, a galley and two biremes, had reduced sail to keep station behind the big quatraremes and the Argamaro which was a quinquereme and one of the biggest ships in the navy.

And they were not alone. A row of war galleys were rowing toward them. There appeared to be five of them in front and five behind. They carried the colours of Dorphire Sunde.

Norrens smiled as he summed up the situation. "They are trying to fight like legionaries. It may work on the battlefield but not on the water, Verna. We learned a lot during the sea campaign against Herelstrom."

Verna smiled. He could also see the mistakes their adversaries were making. "We should get Tom the Roper. He will enjoy seeing the tactics we learned from his navy used now against these enemies"

"Good idea, send for him." There was a flurry of activity at the signal box as Norrens sent his orders to the captains.

All the rowing benches were manned and ready. They would need to row in this fight but as they attacked with sails set, they could attack from the windward. They had all the advantages of speed and maneuverability.

Norrens positoned his four heavy ships so that they bore down on the dorphiremen and send orders for the three smaller ships to tack away and attack from the rear.

As they came within a dozen ship's lengths the four ships came about and tacked away from battle. The ten ships of the red men could do nothing. If they altered course now to intercept,t they would run into each other. They kept steadily on in their formation. Once he was clear of their rams Norrens came about again and dropped their sails. The drums began to beat out a rowing beat and the five rows of oars on the Argamaro dipped the water. She and ther sister ships were speeding toward the starbord side of the enemy formation. The captains of the red ships saw their dilemma but could do nothing as they rowed forward ponderously into the wind Norrens' ships were coming at them from the side with fresh rowers and huge spiked rams bearing down with a terrifying inevitability. The captains of the redships gave orders to increase speed but it was too late. The Argamaro's ram sliced through the side timbers of the first ship with brutal efficiency. Verna shouted orders into the speaking trumpet that relayed orders to the rowing master below. The Argamaro's five banks of oars backed water and she pulled away from her crippled adversary. More orders and she turned toward the ship that followed. They were approaching bow to bow but the Argamaro had the wind behind her and picked up speed more quickly. They could see the warriors on the other ship crowd her forecastle ready to attack if the two ships grapelled. But Verna had no intention of allowing her to come alongside. At the last moment he gave orders for the helm to be put over. It just altered course enough for her battle ram to sheer away the bow timbers of the other ship. There was a terrible lurch and many of the sailors were knocked off their feet. The rowing deck was in confusion but after many shouted orders the Argamaro backed her oars and drew away. There were showers of arrows from the red ship and Argamaro's marines also fired arrows and deck artilliary but once she was clear the Argamaro only had to watch as her adversary filled with water from the gaping hole in her bows. What was more, the remaining forward momentum drove the water in faster and she dived under the water like a breaching whale.

The smaller ships had attacked the rear ships in the dorphiremen's formation; using the techniques they had learned from the king's ships of Herelstrom, they rowed in behind and smashed their steerage oars with their rams leaving them partially crippled and only able to steer using their banks of oars which was difficult and too slow.

The result was that by mid morning two remaining ships were rowing for their lives and the rest had been sunk or captured.

They put enough men on board the captured vessels to sail them and chained their crews to the rowing benches. They were told that if they didn't row the ships would be abandoned and scuppered. They would drown chained to their own ships. They rowed.

The harbor of Ba-al Giborachir now lay open to Norrens and in other straits he may have made elaborate plans for the assault but not today. His wife and daughter were somewhere on the island, and he intended to find them. He gave orders for Verna to enter the harbor and give orders for the other ships in the squadron to follow without delay.

By the time the quinquereme anchored Norrens had removed his cloak and was by the entry port ready to board the first boat. He left Verna to watch and protect the ship.

As he waited for the boat to be winched down from the main and formast yards, Norren's turned to see who the boatswain had put in the first landing party. To his surprise Bentonius and Ingwit were there. Verna came to the side and Norrens whispered to him, "Why are they coming?"

"They asked to, Sir. And from what I saw of Bentonius at Biel Harfing, he will be an asset. They may also have information about the island that you will need. Take them, Sir. I think it is a good idea."

The boat reached the water and the crewmen shinnied down the ropes to untie the blocks to be retrieved to launch the other boats.

Norrens grabbed a rope and climbed down into the boat. He was followed by several marines and Norrens found himself sitting in the stern of the boat with Ingwit and Bentonius. Well, he could ask them what they knew of Ba-al Giborachir.

He had no idea how to address these two former coven masters, so he addressed the two of them. "Why did you want to come?"

Ingwit gave him a look of fierce determination. "Admiral, the covens have done many vile things and there are many things that I have done that I regret but what the red priests are doing is an abomination. They must be stopped."

Norrens was surprised by her vehemence. "Where will they take the captives ... and my family?"

Ingwit had not realised until this point that the Admiral's family had been taken. "Do you have children?"

"They took my daughter Chloe. She is eight ... and my wife."

"I do not know for sure, but I expect that they will take them to the temple – somewhere in the temple confines at least. You can see the temple on the top of that hill. It is the great zigurat. The columned building behind is the rest of the temple."

The boat drew close to a stone jetty, and they leapt out. Bentonius saw Norrens desperate urgency and called to a sergeant of marines to gather their force and follow as soon as possible then he followed the Admiral along the jetty and up a flight of stone stairs to the roadway into the city. Norrens was out of control and even Benton and Ingwit struggled to keep up with him.

Clearly the guards on the gate were not expecting to see three people running toward the city on their own. They still had the great doors open to allow people time to come in from the docks, so they did not try and stop them as they ran through and along the main roadway toward the centre of the city.

Benton stopped as he realised the guards were trying to shut the city gates and doubled back. With some quick dagger work he despatched the guards and pushed the gates wide open just in time for re-inforcements to arrive. He then sprinted after Norrens and Ingwit. They had come to the great zigurat which had three smooth sides and steps to the side which seemed to lead to the high stairs that were used by the priests. In the piazza behind the zigurat women and children were tied to poles. They looked terrified and exhausted. Some slumped against their bonds as if they had hung there for some time. Norrens scanned all the faces without recognition and began to climb the stairs. Ingwit ran from one of the children to another and cut their bonds. They immediately ran to their mothers who Ingwit struggled desperately to free as well. Bentonius came up and began to help. He called out to her. "Where is the Admiral?"

"He went up the stairs looking for his wife and daughter." As others from the ships arrived, they ordered them to continue freeing the slaves and ran up the steps of the zigurat. Tom came up, struggling to keep up and saw them climbing the stairs. He called to one of the marines. "Help me up the stairs – it is important." The sailor did as requested, and they climbed to the top with difficulty. At the top there was a doorway and five priests stood barring their way into the shrine. They did not do anything – just stood clutching their staves with the strange devices on them and Ingwit and Norrens could not move. Benton also reached the top and rushed forward only to meet an inpenetrable barrier. One of the priests stepped forward his staff vibrating with power and began to force them back down the steps. Tom was now three quarters of the way up and could see something was driving Norrens and the other two back. He prayed a Norri prayer. It was all he knew to do.

There were cries from inside the temple. Admiral Norrens recognised his daughter's voice and cried out in fear and desperation. Something broke as another power tore through the high priest's magic. The black ebony staff broke and the invisible barrier gave way.

They passed into the temple. Bentonius thrust with his sword and stabbed with the dagger in his left hand as he enterred. Two of the priests fell backward. One tumbled down the stairs crying out as blood poured out from a slash across his throat.

Two priests held Norrens' wife and daughter. They had daggers in their hands. A third held another woman that Norrens thought he almost recognized but couldn't quite place. He stepped forward. "If you harm them, I will kill you; slowly. Let them free and you may go."

The two priests lowered their knives. Chloe and Elbeth ran to Norrens. They expected the priests to run but they did not. They positioned themselves in front of the altar and brandished their knives. These two seemed to be younger and perhaps didn't have the power of the high priest. Nonetheless they seemed ready to die rather than allow the intruders near the altar.

Inwgit and Benton nodded to each other. They stepped forward and with a level of skill that amazed Norren's, disarmed and killed the two priests who fell to the marble floor in a pool of their own blood. Ingwit looked at them with disgust. It seemed most appropriate that the priest's own blood now stained the paving stones.

They all looked up at the altar. On the top of a single massive stone block stood a silver altar stained with blood and smoke. It was shaped like a huge vase or censer and a fire of burning coals on the side wall was obviously used to supply it with burning coals. They climbed onto an observation platform and looked in. The fire still burned. There were human bones on the altar – the bones of a child.

At that moment the high priest came running into the temple with a spear he had acquired and charged them recklessly in his fury. Ingwit stepped aside and struck him in the back of the neck with her dagger. He sprawled on the tiles choking on his own blood.

Benton called to them and Ingwit and Tom climbed the stair behind the altar. A large silver chimney took the smoke from the altar and funneled it up to a window. Through the smoke of the window, they could see a strange scene. It was as if they were looking at a scene far away. Another place, perhaps even another world or existence. They could see a yellow alien sky and sulfurous vents issuing smoke. They could see creatures flying in the golden, misty sky. They were gold beneath and red on their backs making them difficult to see in the haze as they soared and glided over mountains and valleys. A path led down from the window into a deep valley with a river of black water at the bottom; nothing seemed to grow. They caught glimpses of human-like beings with strange bulbous tails and growths on their backs dragging behind them. They scuttled from one rock to another always watching the sky.

Four priests were climbing the path carrying a large creature tied on poles. It was alive but looked as though drugged or poisoned. They looked up and saw strange faces looking down through the window at them. They dropped the wyvern and began to run up the path leaving their charge struggling and squawking in its bonds on the path.

Ingwit ran and grabbed the priest's spear, placed the point against the silver censer on top of the altar and began to shove with all her might. Benton realised what she was doing and threw his weight against the shaft of the spear. The top of the altar began to move a little, then a little more, and finally slipped on the ash covered monolith and crashed to the tiled floor spilling its contents of coals and burning bones all over the temple.

The men in the other place, running up toward the window, screamed in terror and bolted for the top of the path almost knocking each other over in their haste. The first almost made it through the window but the smoke dissipated, and it was as if he was sucked back into the scene in the window as it faded and dissapeared.

Gutteral voices came from stone statues of demons at the base of the altar stone, "Bring us ourr food; bring us fearrr; bring usss terorr."

Norrens called to them all, "Let us leave this foul place and get our families to safety!"

They could hear shouts and fighting in the city below. It seemed that soldiers were trying to retake the gates. They finished cutting the captives free and searched for any more captives. There was a building behind the temple with many cells. They surprised a jailor and made him open all the cells. One heavy door swung open to reveal several children of the Ica Bica Baya tribes. They looked terrified and took some coaxing before they would come out. Finally, Ingwit knelt down and held the youngest who was quaking with fear and once she picked her up the others followed her.

They ran for the gates. Fortunately, Bentonius was with them, and Tom ran on the other flank to protect the group that was slowed by women and children. Ingwit was still carrying the little girl and Norrens' wife Ghezia picked up other children as they all ran for the gate. The other woman saw one little girl struggling to keep up and stopped to scoop her up. They reached the gate as more of the sailors and marines surged through and fought back the city defenders who had finally responded to the threat.

By attacking they gave the admiral and his companions a chance to reach the wharves and load most of the rescued women and children into boats.

It took several trips and was painstakingly slow. By the time they had got the captives safely onto the ships the marines had been driven back to the warves and were fighting for their lives against much greater odds. Bentonius was there with Tom who had brought his bow. He found several marine archers and they positioned themselves behind Bentonius and the marines and shot into the onrushing crowd of soldiery from the city. These were guardsmen and did not have large shields for use against arrows and they fell in numbers to each volley of arrows. This halted their charge and they backed away from the wharf again.

This gave enough time for the boats to come alongside the wharf and load the last of the marines. Tom and his archers came last with Bentonius and positioned themselves in the sterns of the boats to shoot back at the now crowded wharf.

As they rowed back to the ships, Bentonius turned to Tom. "That was nice shooting. I don't think you know me, I'm Bentonius. You can call me Benton if you like."

"Tom."

"Yes, I know who you are. I'm afraid to say I have been to your home as a spy for the covens."

"You may have fought well but don't expect forgiveness. Your people attacked my home and for all I know have killed my wife and child."

Norrens and his wife were trying to settle the last of children in the bottom of the boat. The other woman was still holding the little girl who clung to her like a limpet. Norrens looked at her, "I am sorry, I feel I know you."

"I am Kristina Denquinar."

Ghezia reached for her hausband's hand. "Kristina came to us to hide her last year. She was frightened the coven people sought her life after her husband had defected and died."

Norrens looked surprised. "Why do you think he is dead?"

Kristina looked intently at Norrens. "Do you think he is not? I heard he went south in a ship, perhaps searching for our son who was lost and was himself lost when the ship was sunk."

Norrens called down the boat to Tom. "Tom, you have seen the former Admiral Denquinar, have you not?"

Tom nodded. "Yes, he has aided our country greatly. The last I saw him he and his son were sailing on an expedition to find a southern way to Bernadia."

Kristina sat stunned; holding the little girl so tightly she looked up at her with a worried expression. There were tears in her eyes. "My son?"

24

Council of Chiefs

*T*he council of Arionite chiefs sat in a circle in a large brushwood hut. It was not unlike those used by the tribes on the plains but was built from branches of a leafy shrub that grew on the southern faces of the mountains instead of willow withies.

The hut had a flap on the roof that allowed the smoke from a small fire to escape. Seven chiefs and their attendants sat around the fire sipping coffee from small earthenware cups.

Morichii of the death serpent tribe spoke. "The army of the southerners has fled from the Corrii into the plains within our mountains."

Inadin of the mountain goat tribe sipped his drink as if it had no savor and sighed. "The warriors of the tribes together could kill them all if we so will."

Morichii stroked the iron sword that lay on his lap. "Our warriors have been successful before against armies, but it has been arrows not swords that defeated our enemies.

When the Corrii came we defeated them, but the scouts say these Bernadians have good armour and stay close together and keep away from any place where we could ambush them."

Chief Borgi offered, "I do not think these Bernadians come with evil intent. They flee the Corrii who are their enemies also. They cause us no trouble and if they stay away from our hunting grounds, I will not lift my hand against them."

Chief Waraheny of the Wangadilla turned to his auguror. "Bring Biri Niri Miri and the warrior with the iron sword." He turned to the other chiefs when the auguror had gone.

We will enquire of Biri Niri Miri, the great auguror of the Ica Bica Baya."

When the hide flap of the hut opened the auguror returned with a very old man and a youth.

Chief Waraheny nodded to the pair. "Please join the fire of the chiefs for a time, ancient one. We desire your wisdom." Biri Niri Miri sat in the space indicated and the youth with the iron sword sat behind him. "I am honoured, great chiefs."

Chief Waraheny gestured to the assembled chiefs. "We ponder the presence of the Bernadians in the mountain plain. They have come there fleeing the Corriian army.

We do not know whether to fight them as is our usual custom or whether to let them pass or what to do. What do you think?"

Biri Niri Miri stroked his bushy beard and then whispered to the warrior behind him who whispered something back.

"Would you not then have two battles to fight: first the Bernadians and then the Corrii as well? Why fight with the Bernadians. The Corrii will be hard enough to defeat even with their help. Our warriors will draw bow with you as well if you will allow us. We may stop them and do them enough harm to leave us alone for a while."

Chief Imadin spoke to his auguror and turned to the assembled chiefs. "We could give them safe passage through the southern rivers and guides to show them the way through our lands."

Chief Minmeri of the Vinverdo shook his head. "They would needs pass through my lands also, and I am loath to give up my land's secrets to the Bernadians even if they have caused us no harm in the past."

Chief Imadin agreed. "That is a concern as is the fact that the Corrii may simply follow them into the heart of our lands."

The flap of the hut opened and Wengenevy entered and spoke to his father. The other chiefs waited to hear the news. Waraheni sat silent for a time before addressing his fellow chiefs.

"My son brings much news. I will let him address the council if the chiefs allow." All the chiefs nodded and Wengenevy sat in the circle with his father.

"There is much news, great chiefs. I and my warriors have just returned from the hunt. As we entered the village, Orbanimi one of the warriors my father sent to watch the approaching armies met me with news. There is much to tell.

Orbanimi says that they watched the Bernadians come into the mountain plains with their blue and yellow banners. As you know we have many warriors watching them, but they sit by the stream silently waiting. Orbanimi believes they wait for us to speak with them.

He says also that three Corrii armies approach, and that the sky is filled with creatures we have never seen before.

The closest Corrii army does not pursue the Bernadians into the plain even though it is large enough to do so. Perhaps they wait for the other armies that approach. The one that follows the first is the largest. The sun shines on the tips of their spears as far as the eye can tell and the dust rises from a great host on the march."

"This is grievous news, Wengenevy," said chief Morichii.

The old Chief Imadin stroked his sword. "The doom of our time approaches! I call upon the augurors to tell us anything at all that they hear from God in their sleeping or waking hours."

Eliachar, the auguror of the Wangadilla spoke. "I have seen the great corlion again in my dreams he does not often speak but he seems to warn me with his eyes and often looks to the west as if looking for something ... or waiting."

No other auguror spoke so Wengenevy spoke again.

"There is other news, great chiefs." All looked at the young warrior again. "We have captured two wanderers while on the hunt. They were fleeing two horrible monsters. One of these fell when the elkarn we hunted fell off the top of the Ibirini Dell. It carried weapons." Wengenevy unwraped a leather bundle he had placed behind him. He took out a large, curved chopping blade and a bow and quiver and laid them in the circle.

Chief Borgi picked them up gingerly. "They seem to be Corii weapons, but they have a strange smell about them. What account do the strangers give?"

"They say, they are from a land to the north and are seeking a way to Bernadia. The Corii have attacked their land and they hope to make an alliance with the Bernadians. They did not know that the creatures who followed them had been sent after them by the Corii, but they had seen them in their land recently when Corii raiders came. They are called, 'gordrill'. They noticed they were being followed two days ago and they have been fleeing for their lives.

There is more also. The creature that carried this weapon can speak. I heard its cries and curses as it fell. They are now fighting with the Corii and there are others. Orbanimi says they have seen creatures with black manes concealed in the long grasses, watching the Bernadians and others have been seen on the slopes of the mountains. The scouts did not know what they were, and kept hidden"

Chief Borgi picked up the blade. "This is heavy; only a great warrior could wield it. None of our warriors could use it in battle. What do the strangers say about these ... 'gordrill'?"

"That they came with the Corrii when they raided a town near their homes and that they fought with the Corrii in battle. They believe that they come with priests who have allied themselves with the Corrii, from an island in the northeast."

All the chiefs sat in silence for a time pondering the news that the chief's son had brought.

Chief Waraheni slowly rose to his feet. "I am stiff from sitting too long in council; and my mood is not good. We will speak with these strangers Wengenevy has caught and decide their fate."

The chiefs filed out of the hut followed by the augurors.

Norri and Gordy were standing surrounded by warriors who carried their packs and their weapons when the chiefs approached. Waraheni stood at the head of the group. "My son tells me that you wished to travel to Bernadia."

Norri stepped forward and bowed. "It is true, great chief. My country has been invaded by the Corrii with winged creatures and great ape-like beasts as well as many men and ships. We sailed away as a great fleet began an attack on our homes."

"You left your homes and your people when they were threatened?"

Norri bowed his head. It was not something that sat well with him even now. He felt keenly the pain of leaving Kirin in danger. It was Gordy who met the chief's cold grey eyes. "He left his wife with my wife to protect her. Jenny is a match for any Corriian army!"

There were some amused smiles from several of the chiefs, but Waraheni still looked stern and waited for Gordy to continue.

"We have a token from the emperor of Bernadia." He pointed to Norri's sword that was a gift from the Bernadian Emperor for saving his son.

Chief Waraheni held out his hand for the weapon. He drew the blade from its scabard and examined the edge almost hungrily.

Then a voice called out. A young warrior had just emerged from a hut, "Norri!"

They all looked around to see a young warrior of the Ica Bica Baya tribe of the plains run toward them with an ancient auguror hobbling behind him on a bent staff.

Dinki Arumara of the Ica Bica Baya ignored the chiefs and assembled warriors and ran to Norri clutching his hands. Then turning to the assembled chiefs, "This man saved me from the Corrii and my friends also and the prince of Bernadia when we were captured and taken to Corriamar." He looked at Norri. "You have no sword. This is yours. I searched for it on the plain. I return it to its owner."

Biri Miri Niri came up and spoke to the chiefs. "It is as Dinki Arumara says. I can attest to the truth. I saw them taken away by the Corrii and Dinki speaks the truth."

Chief Warahini turned to Norri to hand back the sword, with some reluctance.

"You obviously speak the truth, but you will be sad to hear that there will be no help for your country from the Bernadians. What is left of their army is on the plains below hemmed in by many times the number of Corrii. We have yet to decide whether to aid them, as we are able, or leave them to be destroyed completely. We seek the will of God in this now. What do you say to this, strangers?"

"I cannot aid much in your deliberations, great chiefs but this I know. A prophet of God, respected among my people, gave me these verses before I left on this journey."

Norri fished in his pocket and brought out a piece of parchment. He unrolled the squashed parcel and read.

"A father's love protects you,
Though you cross the storm-tossed sea,
The eagle's cry will save you,
From a most dread enemy.
His Mari will come to you,
When your heart has no more strength,
When fear of the foes besets you,
And your faith is stretched full-length.
You are not then forgotten,
For your plight is surely seen,
And the Son, the One begotten,
Will be there in your need.

The old pastor of my people thought these words were applicable for our trip, although I am sure they were also written at a time of some past need...."

Just at that moment, before Norri had finished, a young arguror from the back of a group pushed forward. "It is as I saw in a dream...."

Eliarchar tried to stop him. "No Ibinichari! Be silent!"

The young man stumbled forward, and it was obvious to all that he had a bad leg and walked with a pronounced limp.

"It is as he says. I had a dream..." His words were cut short when Eliarchar struck him with his augurors staff, and he fell sprawling on the ground.

"He is a foolish boy. Pay him no mind. What he says cannot be. It is blasphemy! And these strangers speak falsehoods!"

Chief Waraheni stepped forward, standing over the prone form of the young man trying to get to his feet.

"Get up, boy. Tell us your name and what you know."

The young auguror staggered to his feet with a large lump already obvious on the back of his head. Tears streamed down his face; he was trembling. His words came slowly and with a stutter.

"I am Ibinichari, and you may kill me if I lie."

He now had their attention. "I had a dream two nights ago where I saw a huge corlion. He had huge incisor teeth like swords, a mane like a horse down his back, and hair like a beard on his chin. He come to me and spoke to me and said, 'I will help you.' I was amazed and said, 'Who are you, Lord?' He replied, 'I am the Son of the Most High, whom you serve.' And then the corlion vanished from before me."

Chief Waraheni looked sternly at the crippled young auguror who stood before him.

"Do you stand by your dream, boy?"

The young man looked up at the chief unflinching and nodded.

"If I believe you and commit my warriors and the warriors of these chiefs to battle and your words prove false, then you will surely die, by my hand if by no other. Do you understand this?"

"I spoke truly, great chief. What I saw and heard I have spoken to you. You must do as you choose."

"I see by your face that you speak what you believe to be true. The lives of many depend upon your words."

The chief then turned to Eliarchar. "As you value your life, old man, you will never hide a dream that you or your other augurors receive from me again."

Then, turning to the assembled chiefs, "Make ready all the warriors. Arion will go to war!"

Waraheni handed the sword that was still in his hand to Norri.

"Come. I will take you to the army of the Bernadians although I cannot see how it may help."

The Bernadians were sitting resting in whatever shade they could find under small bushes and clumps of grass. At least they had water from the nearby stream as it splashed and rippled over cobble stones.

They were aroused by the sight of lines of warriors emerging as if by magic from the grasses.

The chiefs and their augurors left the ranks of hide clad warriors who carried bows and spears and shields and all manner of other weapons as each was most skilled.

The ancient chiefs left the ranks and came forward. Norri and Gordy walked beside the chiefs; Dinki strode proudly beside Norri still wearing the sword that had belonged to Norri's great, great, grandfather.

Waraheni saw a group of centurions and a more senior officer judging by his ornate armor rise and come toward them. By the time they came close enough for speach, every Bernadian soldier was armed and in his battle position.

The old chief stepped forward and met the Bernadian Tribune who also stood alone in front of his men. Waraheni spoke an Arionite dialect of the language all men had spoken since the beginning of the world, for they were all descended from the same ancient tribe and on one level, both knew this to be true.

"Soldier, you and your men are upon our lands; at my command, my warriors could easily overwhelm you.

But I hesitate to give such a command. Many good warriors would die and the bloody work of the Corrii would be done for them."

Tribune Degrarius bowed his head in deference to the old chief before him who clearly led many more warriors that he did. "Great chief among many great chiefs," Degrarius let his eyes fall on the other ancient, lined warriors, "We apologise for trespassing on the hunting grounds of the warriors of Arion whom we ever respect and honour; we do so only to escape the Corrii and we have no other way of escape.

"Nor was it our desire to bring them down upon you. They have been driving us this way. Perhaps they hope that we may indeed waste lives fighting each other, instead of our common enemy."

Waraheni raised his hand. "Fear not, soldier. They were our enemies before you came and will likely be so when you and I have returned to the arms of our Father and our God. May it not be today!"

The tribune extended his hand in greeting. "Thank you, Great Chief. I am Tribune Degrarius of the Blessed Emperor's northern army, or what is left of it. I know I speak for the emperor in saying that we wish you no ill and are happy for the warriors of Arion to long be a bane to the Corrii on our northern border.

Degrarius was trained and skilled in diplomacy, so he again scanned the eyes of the chiefs as he spoke and noticed the slightest nods of approval at his words. It was so that he noticed the two young men in quite different clothes. He deemed that now was not the time to ask who these were until he noticed the silver hilt of Norri's sword and the emblem on the pommel. It was the last thing he expected to see on the plains of Arion.

"Great Chief," Degrarius said with more surprise in his voice than he intended. "Who is this that you bring with you who bears an Emperor's blade? Such a gift is only given very rarely; to those who are called friends of the empire."

The chief looked at Norri with renewed interrest. "He says he has spoken to your emperor."

Degrarius bowed to Norri, "Hail, friend of Bernadia. As a soldier of the empire, I am bound to do all in my power – including give my life and the lives of my men to aid the one who is honored with the gift of such a blade."

Norri went red and slipped the sheathed weapon out of its shoulder strap. "I did not realize that the emperor has bestowed such an honor when all I really did was escape the Corrii with Omari."

Degrarius's eyes widened even more. "You are Norrimae Jung. Your name was proclaimed all over Bernadia as the man who caused great consternation to our enemies. The emperor's son has told all about your valor!"

Degrarius turned to Chief Waraheni. "Great Chief, I think you may have brought us more help than you know. This is the man who it is said, caused the death of the Corriian witch queen and broke the hold of the covens on the empire."

Gordy looked askance at Norri. "It is always the quiet ones that you have to watch. At home you are just my friend. Everywhere else, you're famous."

Everyone now looked at Norri as if expecting him to do something dramatic, but he had not the least idea what to do. It was Chief Warahini who realized that he had to make the decision.

"Come soldier, we must sit by your fire and make our plans. What God may or may not do, we do not know. It is for us simple warriors to plan as we can."

As evening fell, Norri watched the warriors of the Arionite tribes file down into the valley. They came like living shades in the gloom; wearing strange armor of copper and bone that seemed serviceable and light at the same time. They had beaten copper arm bands and breast coverings of bone and hide. All carried large wicker shields with a covering of untreated hide so that the animal from which the skin was taken could be discerned. This identified the many tribes as they seemed to choose the hide after which the tribe was named.

They had their hair braided and tied with leather thongs and each carried his choice of weapon. Some had long-handled stone axes which Norri found later were incredibly sharp. These had wooden handles bound with wet hide to protect them against being damaged by swords. Some carried swords that looked to be Corrii in origin. Norri thought they might have been captured in past conflicts.

What Norri did notice that surprised him were the number of large drums. These were made of wood and stretched hide and the drummers beat these in unison as they strode down from the mountains. In the confines of the valley the sound was amplified and seemed to reverberate around making it ten times as great.

Bmm, bmm, booom

Bmm, bmm, booom

Gordy sat up listening with the remains of his coffee still in his hand. "Listen to those. I hope the Corrii can hear them. That'll give them something to think about."

The sound had a strange effect. Norri noticed that the Arionites were stirred and encouraged by it. Gradually as more and more campfires sprang up in the valley around them and the steady drumming continued Norri could see that hope was returning to the Bernadian legionaries. He also saw the faces of the Arionite warriors. They also seemed to be stirred as well. To Norri they seemed tall and strong; and grim.

Gordy looked at those camped nearby. "I'm glad they are on our side. I wouldn't like to have to fight against them."

Norri noticed one tall warrior nearby smile.

25

Cathedral of Lights

s the night wore on Norri saw the young auguror who had been sitting alone, rise and limp away from the campsite. He nudged Gordy and they watched the young man walk out of the camp. Gordy turned to Wengenevy, "Where do you think he is going?"

"I do not know, perhaps to the mountain caves. It is to the caves that the augurors of the Wandilla go to seek solace and wait on the presence of God."

Gordy watched the limping figure as the auguror disappeared into the darkness. "Do you think he is alright; he looks injured?"

"It seems to me that young man has always been injured. He was always watching our games as children because he was not strong enough to join in."

"I would like to follow him. I am concerned for him." Gordy said this in a way that didn't really leave much room for disagreement.

Norri shrugged. He didn't want to leave the warmth of the fire but roused his tired limbs into action and got to his feet. Wengenevy also stood. "I will come. It is a fine night for a walk, and it keeps one from thinking too much on what will happen tomorrow. This may be our last walk in the cool of the night, in this world."

They walked briskly through the camp that had been swelled by many new hide shelters. On the outskirts of the camp, they saw a path leading up the hill and a shadowy figure already well up near the top of the hill.

They followed at a distance and Wengenevy thought he knew the cave entrance to which the Auguror was heading. "There are several cave openings in the mountainside. There is one that is lower and two higher. The highest would be the most difficult to reach for an auguror who was crippled so he will probably go to the lower entrance."

They scrambled up the path which seemed impossibly steep for the young man they were following but when they caught a glimpse of him, he was high up the path and turned not for the lower entrance but the narrow path through the scree and rubble that led to the small entrance at the top of the mountain. Wengenevy showed them the way and they edged around the mountain on a goat track of a path.

The path turned upwards once away from sight of the fires below and they could just make out their way in the dark. The path climbed more and more steeply up. There were stones lodged in the packed soil of the track that were the only footholds. They found that their feet slipped and skidded on the path and the drop below did not bear thinking about. After what seemed half a watch of the night, they reached the top and came to a small ledge and an opening into an utterly dark cave. They wished they had brought some sort of light but there was no use going back for anything now, so they decided to try and feel their way inside. Gordy led the way with Norri next and Wengenevy last. The hunter seemed reluctant to enter the mountain and did so only under sufferance. Norri thought that he didn't want to be left alone on the mountainside. That made good sense with the wyverns soaring around the night sky searching for any prey that was foolish to move out of hiding.

Gordy reached forward and found that the cave continued on into the blackness with little change in height or width. So, he kept on, feeling his way carefully forward.

They only gradually became aware that it was getting lighter. Gordy first noticed that he could see his hands in front of his face but not the floor. Then the floor became visible, and they increased their pace.

The tunnel also became wider and higher; then finished. They came into a huge cavern. It was also filled with stalactites and stalagmites which glittered as a light from an unknown source glinted on the tiny crystals of the limestone making them shine with tiny points of light.

"Perhaps there is an opening above and some moonlight comes in," said Gordy as he climbed out of the tunnel and onto a ledge overlooking the great cavern. But even as he said that it, he thought it unlikely that this much light could come from the moon; even if they were still on the bare mountainside and there was no cloud.

Norri came out of the tunnel and stood next to Gordy looking into the glittering cavern in amazement. Following them, Wengenevy gasped in amazement and also stared at the chamber in awe. Tier after tier and dome after dome filled with columns and spikes of limestone in every color and hue, all illuminated from somewhere away to their left so that the light illuminated the farthest caverns least. Water could be seen trickling and dripping through the cavern making it alive with sound.

A narrow path led along the side of the cavern and up to some dome or opening at the top of the cavern. Gordy followed the path and climbed higher. They reached the top and there was a cave opening out on one side to the glittering cavern but otherwise unremarkable. It was just a small cave with a bare, sandy floor.

There was Ibinichary. They could hear him speaking as they climbed to the top of the path and thought he must be speaking to himself. Norri and Wengenevy were right behind him when Gordy glanced to his left and got a huge shock, "A corlion!" Gordy had heard rumours of such creatures. They were said to inhabit caves in the mountains. But this corlion was almost the size of a horse, but with huge neck and back and paws with claws the size of great curved daggers. He stepped back almost knocking Norri back into Wengenevy.

Ibinichari looked at the huge beast with a bright smile. "Not a corlion, The Corlion. He is the Corlion of Arion. We are called the lion-men; you have now met our Lord and God.

Gordy was awed and dumbstruck. He stepped into the cave and knelt down beside Ibinichari, unable to take his eyes off the corlion. He realized that the light in the dark cavern came from Him.

Norri also knelt down feeling awed and frightened and elated all at the same time. There was a big question that raced to the forefront of his mind and would not move. The Prophecy that Eli had showed him pounded out its words in his head. Not even knowing how even to put the question Norri risked asking what was on his mind. "Are you … the Son?"

The corlion looked at him with all knowing eyes; seeming pleased with the question.

"I am."

"Have you come to help us?"

"As commander of the army of the Lord, I have now come. What that may mean you will have to see. All that Ibinichari asked was that I come; I am here."

Then the light began to dim, and everything went dark.

Gordy knelt beside the young auguror. "Is he gone?"

Then words seemed to come from the path they had just climbed. "No."

Then the words seemed to come from a little further down the path. "In all the worlds I have made, I have sought the ones who will love me, even if I do not give them all they ask. I am trustworthy even when things seem at their blackest. Listen to my words and follow them; then wait to see my salvation."

They all sat for a long time and didn't speak.

Finally, Norri said, "I think He went back down the path. Perhaps we had best do the same."

Gordy could not see his hand in front of his face. "It is completely black and yet I feel like this is a place I never want to leave."

Ibinichari reached behind him and felt for his staff in the darkness. "It is time to go. I am used to the way. In daytime some light comes in from above, but I have often outstayed the light in my prayers and have learned the way by feel. You may take my hand."

So, they all stood, and the crippled young man led them back down the path and into the tunnel.

Emperor Entilates rode at the head of his columns in his great battle chariot. It was twice the size of the standard model normally used by the Corrii. It was also higher to give Entilates a better view in the midst of battle. He had seen the messenger riding swiftly towards them and had his driver stop some distance ahead of the legions so their words would not be overheard.

The messenger reined his panting horse and dismounted. He bowed before his ruler. There was some trepidation on his face. "My Lord Emperor, I bring a message from Tribune Orbinetti. He has the remainder of the Bernadian force bailed up on the plain under the mountains and has decided to attack. He has many times their numbers and wishes to inflict a telling victory before they dissipate and run deeper into the lands of the Arionites."

Entilates smiled. He did not mind boldness in his officers; he turned to his general, "Tribune Orbinetti has inflicted the first defeat on the Bernadians. Now he has chosen to finish them off before we can get there on a pretext that they will flee if they see our full might."

"He may be right of course. By the accounts, they took dreadful losses in the last encounter. The red men and their winged companions made all the difference. They may choose flight and risk the unknown lands of the Arionites rather than fight our combined armies in a battle they cannot possibly win."

"Let him attack. We will be another day before we reach him, and he is right. The narrow valley will prevent us using our full numbers to advantage. Praetor, return to your commander. Say to him that he may commence his attack, but he had better win."

The messenger snapped a salute and mounted his horse. "My Lord, I hope we will have a pile of enemy standards to lay at your feet when you arrive tomorrow." So, saying he wheeled his horse and rode back to his general.

"They very likely will, My Lord."

"That is all well. There will be many fights left before we fully sub-due the Bernadians and there is much glory ... as well as slaves and booty for my generals in Herelstrom."

The officer grimaced. He didn't like ocean voyages. He clicked his tonge against his cheek and said under his breath, "Just like Orbinetti to be in the right place at the right time."

26

The Battle of Arion

*T*hree days passed before they came; rank upon rank of spears filled the plain of Arion. The morning sun shone down on the glittering host. One cohort after another took its position on the field with their legendary discipline. Artillery pieces drawn by teams of horses were driven to their stations, uncoupled from the teams and heaved into their place where their fire would have the most devastating effect.

If all these preparations were not awe inspiring enough, red and gold winged creatures passed back and forth over the Bernadian position momentarily blotting out the sun and filling the trapped soldiers with dread. They sailed effortlessly on the thermals that whirled and eddied between the spurs of the great mountains of Arion.

The Chiefs, along with Degrarius had decided that the best warriors would take position on the Bernadian's left flank while the Bernadians would take up position perpendicular to the stream which would make any attack on the right flank almost impossible. Those warriors who were best with bows stood on the western spur of the mountain where their height would be an advantage shooting at the wyverns and they would be able to shoot over their own warriors into the ranks of the approaching Corrii.

They had decided that they would make the Corrii do all the attacking. The valley was narrow, and the entire Corrii host could not march between the mountain spurs. Since there was no way of outflanking the Bernadians it would be simply a battle of attrition and the Corri knew they had the numbers to say nothing of the help they had from the skies. Degrarius and the Arionite war counsel had agreed that the Bernadians would be the bait to lure the Corrii into the valley, so the tribune had set his legions in a tight formation well down the valley.

It was well known that the Corrii had respect for the warriors of Arion; even feared them. It was their speed that made them different and dangerous. The Corrii were used to fighting in tight battle formations. The Arionites on the other hand used an attack and withdraw tactic. They appeared out of the grasses or out of the rocks and charged the Corrii formations; showering them with incredibly accurate arrows and javelins only to fade away again into the grasses or rocky ourcrops.

Degrarius watched the crack Corrii legions enter the valley. He could see from their standards the many battles and honors they had accumulated. They had sent in their best first. The general clearly expected to rout this small army and had given the honors of the first blow to his best commanders.

Soon the fear game would begin.

The Corrii spread out into the widest formation the valley would allow and marched slowly toward the Bernadians. It was all about intimidation.

On the Corrii right were two legions of soldiers all in red. Degrarius knew who they were: Dorphiremen from the islands of Dorphire Sunde they were the men of Ba-al Giborachir, the dragon men. He knew the

Corrii had chosen them to outflank him on his right. They wore lighter armour and had smaller shields and attacked with great speed. He had seen their deadly efficiency and reckless bravery in their last encounter. And they were renowned for fighting with the Wyverns. That combination had almost destroyed their army in the last battle. All his men knew that you dared not risk becoming a captive of these men. Their priests were infamous for their ritual sacrifices. It would be better to fall in battle than be dragged kicking and screaming to the altar of the red priests.

The red men surged forward now on his left flank. Degrarius knew that if the Arionites did not stop them he would be overwhelmed.

Then with the timing of a great stage manager, drums sounded. Drummers hidden in the grasses started up a slow beat and a chant that spread all through the apparently empty grasses; warriors stood up in their tens of thousands clad in their strange armor. The drums sounded louder, and the chant grew.

Drom, Drom, Arion!

Drom, Drom, Arion!

Degrarius could feel the hope and courage sweep through his men as the sound of the chanting warriors. As the drums pounded out their challenge, the sense that the Corrii were marching to certain victory seemed to falter. The Legionaries ceased their marching song and the clashing of spear against shield and moved forward more cautiously.

The Arionite warriors moved into their allotted positions and stood, still and resolute repeating their chant.

Then the creatures came!

Out of the Corrii ranks one huge grimulf appeared. He seemed to be surrounded by an aura; and fear emanated from him.

From the ranks of the Dorphiremen ten huge black shapes emerged and ran at incredible speed to take up their positions in the middle of the field between the two combatant armies. The huge black manes of the gordrill bristled and their long tails lashed the air; their fangs spoke of their intent far more audibly than any drum. Even the grimulves kept their distance.

Shrieks from the skies warned that the winged hunters surveyed the field below with the hope of tasting fresh blood. They flew lower; their shadows and eerie calls made every eye turn skyward and every shield was lifted as if to ward off the lash of their poison tails.

Chief Waraheni turned to the young auguror and indicated the open space between the armies with his eyes. Ibinichari whispered under his breath so that only Norri who was right beside him could hear, "Did I hear you truly, Lord? They will eat me else." He took some tentative steps forward his hand sweating so much he could barely hold his bare auguror's staff.

Norri looked at Gordy and followed. Gordy drew his sword. "Oh, I'm coming. I wouldn't miss this! You know what I always say, 'Safe is dangerous and dangerous is safe.'"

Ibinichari walked out into the middle of the field - alone. Norri and Gordy forced their trembling limbs to follow him. Ibinichari took five more steps forward and then stopped. The armies of three nations watched and waited for something to happen but the Gordrill did not immediately attack the young man. They stood still. Their will somehow faltering. Was it the impudence of the solitary, crippled warrior with a stick? What could it mean?

One of the gordrill let out a howl of rage and moved forward. Ibinichari was about to close his eyes in anticipation of a quick death when he felt warm breath on his trembling left hand. Something that was invisible was becoming bright and real beside him. Ibinichari looked and sighed with relief. "You are here.... Are You the Son of whom Norri spoke?"

"I am." A mist seemed to rise up around the corlion and a warm bright light seemed to shine in the mist.

Then, as if it were only a small matter the corlion growled.

At the sound many other more corlions appeared out of a rolling mist that seemed to surround the One. The gordrill shrieked with what may have been anger or terror. The corlion and His companions spread across the field and approached the gordrill and the grimulf packs.

What happened next was hard to follow. It could have been a fight, but it was as if the corlions and the creatures were enveloped in the strange fog that now seemed to arise all over the battlefield.

When the fog cleared, the gordrill and the grimulves were just – gone. Norri who was closer thought he had heard audible cries of terror from the dissipating mist. He saw a bright presence return to the young auguror for a time and then dissappear. What surprised him was that the presence was no longer in the shape of a corlion, but a man.

Ibinichari raised his staff high and shouted in a voice that seemed overlarge for him. "Lion-men of Arion! Your God has come! Arise and destroy your enemies!" The staff seemed to shine brightly in the sunlight.

The drums began again,

Drom, Dromm, Arion!

Drom, Dromm, Arion!

Then they came, thousands upon thousands of stealthy warriors descended on the Men of Ba-al Giborachire and hurled their javelins. The shafts seemed to come at them with terrible accuracy and rank after rank of the red tasseled warriors fell. They looked to their priests, but they were terrified. They looked to the skies, but the wyverns had gone. They had just fallen out of the sky. They lay about the ground like heaps of discarded leather, twitching and flapping in the breeze. For some reason their life had left them, and they fell like broken leather gloves to shatter on the hard ground.

The Arionite archers appeared on the rocks of the mountain spur and began to shower the Dorphiremen's rear ranks with ironstone-tipped arrows and their ranks were torn open. Into the gaps the warriors charged. The tall Arionite warriors seemed to kill with astonishing speed and skill. Spears seemed to pierce armor easily. Battle axes struck with incredible speed inflicting terrible wounds or death.

The Corriian general saw his whole right flank break and collapse into his reserves who tried to hold their positions but were being forced back by their own retreating allies.

Seeing the enemy flank break open, Degrarius gave his orders and the Bernadian legions charged into the faltering front ranks of the Corrii formations. Bernadian veterans knew how to kill Corrii and now unhindered by the flying menace from above, they pressed forward and cut swathes in their ranks. The front legions were beaten back with more and more of the fallen lying on the field behind the Bernadian advance.

Norri and Gordy ran up beside the young auguror to defend him but when they stood beside Ibinichari they found that there was no need. He was safe and the battle seemed to surge around him without ever coming too near.

Once the Corrii front ranks were broken the fierce Arionite warriors attacked from the Bernadian right as well; along the edge of the stream as it turned away to the east below the eastern spur. They ran through the ranks cutting down legionaries too heavily equipped for fast hand to hand fighting; they fell everywhere.

The Corriian general, Tribune Orbinetti, gave orders for the reserve legions to form up for a counterattack. Orbinetti knew what would happen to him and even his men when it was discovered that they had lost a seemingly unloseable battle. Centurians struggled to push men into position. All knew they were going to die.

Two wings of the Arionite attack had spread out and were attacking from both flanks. Then out of the thick scrub beneath the opposite spur, came another army of warriors led by chief Borgi and his sons. Emboldened by the success of the other tribes, they charged across the plain and hurled their javelins at the hastily assembled shield wall that Orbinetti ordered to form up against the attack. The ranks formed too slowly, and the field broke up into a series of skirmishes.

Orbinetti looked toward the Bernadians and saw that his reserves were under attack from the front also; the whole front of his battle formation had gone. The cream of the Corriian southern army lay dead on the field of Arion. His foolishness in not waiting for the emperor to arrive with overwhelming force was now obvious.

Orbinetti drew his sword and jumped down from his chariot. He threw himself into the melee, but his life was short. He struck out at one Bernadian soldier only to feel the cut of a blade on the back of his neck. He fell with blood flowing down over his ornate cuirass and armor. He looked up as he fell and saw the cold eyes of the Bernadian tribune regarding him with cold, determined enmity.

Degrarius stood over his fallen enemy, his sword dripping with General Orbinetti's blood. Little bands of Corrii fought on but they were doomed and could not escape the fierce Arionite warriors who had no thought of taking prisoners.

The Bernadian tribune surveyed the field and the most unlikely victory. It *was* a victory; it was amazing!

27

Out of the Vale

*C*air Neren was not the little stone fort on the mouth of the river that it had been before the last invasion when the Corrii had proved how vulnerable it was. Now it had been strengthened by diverting the river into a water-filled ditch to form a moat at high tide and there was a wide outer wall with towers and fortifications. The towers on the outer walls sported ballista armed with explosive oil-filled heads.

But their enemies had come prepared. Spies must have searched out the land and identified the weakest parts of the defenses. The Corrii had brought engineers who devised ways to bridge the ditch and allow the siege towers to approach the walls.

But the light wooden construction of the siege towers had proved inadequate to the task. The ballista had wrecked them before they even reached the ditch and forced the Corrii to retreat and rethink their strategy.

Nor had the Thane left his cavalry in the castle. He had established strongholds in other towns three days march further up the valley. Although effectively safe from an attack from infantry, the cavalry could strike at will and harass the invaders. So Tillion Ginroyal, the thane's nephew and the commander of the cavalry had harassed and harried the Corrii and largely contained them to the head of the river. They dared not send out scouting parties of foragers as most of them did not return.

It was now a waiting game. The trouble was that the Corrii had complete naval superiority and the supply ships came and went at will.

Brian was now a trusted commander and the Thane trusted him with more and more of the defence. The trouble was that the Corrii had finally succeeded in filling in the muddy ditch that had prevented the siege towers from reaching the walls.

This had cost them many of their engineers. They had been shot at continually, but they had assembled wheeled carts with roofs and frontal screens to protect against arrows and had worked tirelessly to bring earth to fill in the moat. It had never been a great success anyway. It had silted up and never stayed filled with river water. Now the ditch had been filled in many places and the engineers continued to fill it in under the cover of every attack.

Brian's greatest difficulty was the wyverns. When the siege towers attacked - they came gliding in on the wind. They had hard scales on their belly so that only a shot from the side could hurt them. The wyverns had learned to attack front-on to the defenders so that the arrows bounced harmlessly off their thick scales or in the dark on moonless nights when they could attack silent and unseen.

So, the Corrii had now concentrated on attacking at dusk or at night. It meant that the wyverns could appear out of the dark and attack the defenders; often from behind as they defended the walls against the approaching siege towers. The outer wall had nearly fallen several times and nobody in the Cair could sleep any more. And worse, they were running low on all kinds of supplies. Arrows were in short supply, and they were the only weapon that had any effect against the wyverns.

Two days ago, Lord Dillon had fought valiantly against one of the creatures that had landed on the parapet and was wounded by the poison quills in its tail. He was now in the infirmary with a raging fever being nursed by Susanna, the thane's daughter who had charge of the infirmary and the many wounded, and was near to exhaustion. As more and more stretcher beds filled the infirmary and adjoining rooms, everyone could see that the defense was waning.

Brian had watched more and more of the strange priests arrive on the transport ships in the river estuary. They unloaded large jars that the defenders thought may contain the food for the wyverns – or the creatures themselves. The sky was often full of soaring wings and their eerie cries.

The thane looked out the window of the keep. He could see Brian as he moved among the defenders on the walls, encouraging the men. He was grateful that Brian had been able to take the place of his brother who was ill and near death. He had many concerns. The ditch had been filled or bridged in many places and the outer defenses were very vulnerable. The sunlight glinted on the gold and vermillion scales of the Wyvern who rode the thermals in the valley waiting for the sunset to strike at his men. Attacks were more and more frequent. The wyvern attacked silent and deadly on the evening breeze. They lashed some unfortunate soldier with the poison quils of their tails and then disappeared again into the night. The soldiers on the walls at night were in constant fear and prayed for moonlight to give warning of the silent menace.

They had no choice but to keep defenders on the walls because the Corrii would often come and attack the outer walls with ladders and siege towers in the dark.

Baeri climbed up into the high branches. As he climbed the tree, he thought of Norri. He had been gone most of autumn now; he missed him. He had been searching, the forest constantly for days now for Norri's young wife. The driadora had told him that they had found her, as well as Lettie and Jenny safe along with some others in the forest and had been guiding them north and protecting them from above in the trees but they had lost them when the warriors defending them had been drawn off to fight off a pack of marauding grimulves who were on their scent.

His wife who was a driadora warrior of renown was searching with others of her arborite and he hoped they would locate them in the forest quickly. Right now, he had other things to think about. He and a group of cavalrymen were doing all they could to harass the Corrii and take some pressure off the defense of Cair Neren. If the castle fell, the whole country was in dire peril. Baeri reached the upper branches of the great tree he was climbing. And saw the driadora arborite leader resting against the trunk of the tree. He was armed and carried a bow and quiver of arrows as well. Further along the branch were other warriors, also armed. They had shed their normal clothing of the living charnagara and wore hardened, wooden, scale armor with each piece in the shape of leaves.

"Lefgild, I am glad I have found you. A party of soldiers under the nephew of the thane of the castle want to attack the camp of the red men. It would be good if you and your arborite could assist by providing cover with archery as they retreat.

The driadora officer nodded and sat forward to speak in a hushed tone. "We will certainly do that, but I think I have some news for you that may slightly alter your plans."

"All information is useful in war, arborite leader, what have you discovered about our enemies?"

"Two evenings ago, I was resting in a tree, and I overheard two wyverns talking. I was a couple of branches higher; hidden in the canopy and I am sure they did not know I was there."

"Talking?"

"Indeed, I wondered if the creatures could speak to the red priests and to one another; they can!"

"What did you overhear?"

"It was hard to understand them; their voices were harsh and croaky, but it was clear that they hate the priests. They have been brought here against their will and need something from the priests to live. They spoke of 'black water' whatever that may be. The priests have to give it to them, or it sounded as if they would die."

Baeri thought about this. "If we can discover their source of this water and destroy it that may be a relief to the defenders of the castle."

"I have watched them from the edge of the forest and the priests constantly bring up black jars on handcarts from the harbor. They have a store of them in a camp by the river. The priests camp by themselves and seem to be shunned by even the red soldiers."

"Do you think we could attack their camp by night and destroy the jars?"

"It may be worth a try. We are assuming that the jars are used to store the black water."

'It sounds like a good guess. I think it will be worth a try. If you are right, it would be a very important piece of strategy.

If I bring up the cavalrymen to the edge of the forest could your people hold their horses and give us some cover as we retreat?"

"Yes, and we will join you in the attack. My king has given orders for us to harry the Corrii at every opportunity; I cannot think of a more important part we could play in interrupting their plans than this and you will need our archers. How long will it take to bring up your soldiers?"

"Four days. I will come back to this meeting place at this time of evening the third night and confirm that they will do it. We will work out the details then if their commander agrees. I am sure he will unless he can see any fault with our plan."

"Very well; that will give me time to bring down reinforcements. Much of my arborite has been looking for refugees. We are taking them to a camp near the mountains."

"How do you do that without revealing yourselves?"

"It is a skill we have developed. We use dark and light patches of forest. They always veer toward places where there is the most light. It means gaining the help of the trees. It is difficult but we can do it."

Baeri considered just how hard it would be. "We are grateful for what you have done. Thank you."

"There is no need of gratitude, we have as much to lose in this struggle as you do. We would like to remain as secret as possible however and resume our normal lives if it all works out the way we hope. Can the soldiers you are bringing be relied upon to remain silent if we show ourselves to them?"

"I believe they can be relied upon. You also have spells you can use do you not?"

"We will do that, but I have to answer for the decisions I make to my King."

"I will discuss this with Tillion. We will work out a way to shroud your involvement in as much secrecy as possible. Lefgild, have you heard anything of my son's wife?"

"No, we were shadowing her as you know when the fiend-dogs came, and it was all Isherri and those with her could do to to drive them off. After that they could not find her. Isherri will keep searching and others are doing so as well. It is difficult. The forest is full of the fiend-dogs, and we must also watch the skies. Some of our people have been taken from the trees by the wyverns. We hate them as well. It will be good if we can lessen the menace."

Kirin had been running and knew they could run no further. She was desperate for a place to hide. The howls of the pack following their trail were getting closer and closer.

She saw a dip in the ground that could be another shallow limestone cave. They had seen many of these, but they were typically too small and narrow to be of much use as hiding places. She left Mort to wait for Jenny and Lettie to catch up and investigated the cave. There was loose soil around the entrance in the flat ground and she almost slipped into the sink hole. When she knelt down and examined it, she found that she could climb down into it. The hole turned left, and she could follow it but soon found that it turned a corner and was completely dark. She backed out and called to the others. They had no choice; they had to find a place to hide. If they stayed among the trees they would surely be caught. She could clearly hear the sounds of many grimulves now as they followed their scent. She called to Lettie to give the baby to Jenny and get down into the hole. Mort was at the top of the hole looking at her with concern. She smiled at him to reassure him and then groped her way back into the hole. "Come after me, Mort. There may be a drop. If I fall warn the others. He scrambled in after her, unwilling to lose her.

It was very dark. She scrambled on all fours down the sloping hole; feeling ahead in the dark for where the cave went. She could hear Mort talking to Lettie behind him, "You can get down this way Lettie. It's easy." The instructions were passed back to Jenny who had now also entered the hole.

The howls of the grimulves were coming nearer. They could hear the sounds from above; amplified in the narrow cavern. Kirin could hear Jenny pass the baby ahead to Lettie. She guessed that Jenny was thinking she would have to block the way behind them. She suddenly had a horrible thought as she realized how Jenny might be planning to do that and scrambled desperately forward in the dark to find some place where they would be safe. Her heart was racing as she came to a much narrower place and thought the cavern may come to an end or be impassable. She fumbled forward and found that the place was just large enough to get through. It was only her fear that was driving her forward into this dark, claustrophobic place.

The driadora went first. The green-dyed hardwood armor that they wore and their ability to travel lightly and silently was needed for this kind of interdiction work. Behind them, trying to be as quiet as possible came the unmounted, cavalry troopers. They worked their way along the riverbank that was slippery with the oozing mud of low tide in the river estuary; the greelgrub trees that grew all along the tide flat gave them some cover. They soon came up under the camp of the priests; the flapping of leathery wings warned them that at least a couple of the wyverns were in the camp. As they peeped over the top of the riverbank, they could see fires a little way off and the priests cooking their evening meal. The driadora and the remaining troopers moved up behind the leaders. They had little time they knew before someone noticed a flapping garment or heard some sound that would give away their presence.

Tillion Ginroyal, the thane's nephew and Lefgild looked over the top of the bank. They could see two of the wyverns sitting quite close to them with heads covered by their wings. The Driadora branch leader indicated that a couple of his bowmen take up positions next to him and he pointed out the shapes of the creatures on the edge of the camp. All four bowmen drew their bows and with a barely perceptible nod from Lefgild, shot together.

A loud squawk from a mortally wounded wyvern caused panic in the camp. The priests sprang to their feet and two of the remaining wyverns began to beat their wings in a desperate attempt to get airborne where they had the advantage of height and speed over their attackers.

But the archery of the driadora was too quick and both wyverns fell back to the earth their serpentine tails writhing and twisting in their death throes. One was quite close to them and they drew back from its hideous squeals as it ripped and clawed at an arrow that stuck deep into its body underneath its wing; its poison-spined tail lashing around without specific intent but dangerous nonetheless. The thing crawled toward the bank its tail held high to defend itself. Tillion alone climbed over the bank and as the scaly tail came down his sword cut through it, severing it completely and causing the wyvern to overbalance. His second blow removed its head.

The priests were looking around dumbstruck and in moments the troopers were among them, cutting them down. Some fell defending the piles of stores with little but sticks and knives. A few ran off into the night blowing their horns as they disappeared into the night. Baeri called to Lefgild, "Have your archers watch the sky! They may be summoning more wyverns." Lefgild nodded and gave orders. Tillion ran to the tarpaulin covered pile and drew back the covering. There were many stores but among them were large jars marked with symbols that included a flying creature. He called to one of his men, "Geran, see if your axe will break these?"

The trooper swung his axe and shattered the porcelain; even in the dark, what poured out smelled foul, alien and eldritch. Baeri picked up an axe that had been used to split wood and went hammer and tongs at the jars as well, while Tillion uncovered other piles of stores in search of more.

There was a cry from above and Tillion turned just in time to see a man smitten by poison barbs from above. The wyvern banked and turned for another attack.

"You two men, get that man back to the horses!" He did not need to warn the driadora. They had their bows drawn and ready as the wyvern came again several arrows sailed ominously past its exposed flanks and it wheeled away into the darkness. They continued to smash containers until torches and shouts warned them that the fleeing priests had brought help. Tillion and Baeri put their shoulders to a remaining part of a pile of containers and pushed – they fell with a crash. They all turned and ran for the forest.

The dorphiremen were confused. They reached the camp to find dead priests, broken crocks, and no sign of enemies. When they came into the eaves of the forest seeking enemies all they got was a hail of arrows that confirmed the way their enemies had gone but prevented them from following. All they could do was return to the encampment where they found the remaining priests desperately searching among the containers for any that were unbroken. While organizing his men to take up defensive positions the centurion did not grasp the significance of the loss. He like most soldiers, didn't know or care much for the priests and their arcane rituals but one of the priests held up a piece of one of the broken vessels, "The wyverns…they must have this water, or they will die!"

The soldier knew the strategic value of the creatures. They engendered fear in the defenders, and they needed them to drive off the defenders and enable them to take the walls of the castle. He gave his men orders to assist the priests in their search for more unbroken containers. There were very few. The acolytes were carefully decanting the precious fluid into empty jars to save as much as possible.

One old priest came up to the centurian with a torch. He had been inspecting the losses. "They have struck us a serious blow. General Groebalas has been using the wyverns to help with the assault on the castle. I think we only have enough of the black water for a few days. Maybe the creatures can survive a week at most. There are more supplies coming but I do not know how long they will be. We brought ample stocks, but they have been destroyed. We must take steps to get more for the sacred creatures."

The centurion nodded. "I will go and report what has happened to the general."

He walked away; not at all unhappy to get away from the camp of the priests and the strange smell that now engulfed it. He might face discipline himself; he should have guarded the priests better, but they had the wyverns and the enemy had managed to deal with them. He wondered how their enemy had discovered this vulnerability that even he had not known about. The priests kept too much of their art a secret.

It was almost dawn when he reached the commander's tent and there was already much activity as tribunes came and went as the general gave orders concerning the day's attacks on the castle.

When he was finally granted an audience, the general listened to his report in silence. "Well, if new supplies cannot be obtained and we lose the wyverns it will be a loss but as you know centurion, we can take the castle with the traditional means at our disposal - catapults and seigeworks are our stock in trade; I will not change my plans because one weapon is no longer available to us. If the wyverns can be used, we will use them; if not, we have other ways of beating down an enemy.

I presume you have taken precautions against another attack?"

"Yes, Sir."

I like your efficiency, centurian. Where is your commander?"

"Fallen sir, shot with an arrow leading the counter-attack."

"It will be for your rulers to confirm this of course but I am promoting you as a battlefield promotion. Do all you can to protect the priests and report to me in two days as to the status?"

The newly promoted tribune snapped his fist to his cuirass in salute and left to attend to his many tasks. He had to move his own camp to the forest side of the priest's encampment and see what could be done about more urgent supplies of the black water.

Kirin found herself trembling and in pitch dark. Mort came next with the baby, and she could hear Lettie scrabbling through the tunnel. When the scratching sounds came closer, she whispered, "Lettie, is that you?"

"Yes. I can't see anything!"

"Where is Jenny?"

"I don't know, I think she is behind me." Lettie came out of the hole into the wider space and Kirin felt her fumbling for her in the dark. She took her hand and Kirin helped her to sit up.

"Here, climb over me. Mort has little Dillon."

When Mort handed the baby to his mother the little one settled a bit as if the dark was less frightening when he was against his mother.

Once they had rearranged themselves, Kirin felt her way to the opening of the little cavern. She could hear growling now and the snuffling of canine noses at the other end of the dark tunnel. Kirin could feel fresh air coming through the opening. She called quietly into the tunnel, "Jenny, are you there?"

The voice that came back was gruff and cold. "Wee harve Keelled Herr; wee weell nowr devourr herr. Cumme ourt arnd yourr weell die een ther light. Eef yourr stay, yourr weell perrissh een ther darrk arnd neverr see therr light ageen. Fearr well devour yourr een therr darrk."

Kirin felt little Mort trembling and she also felt a wave of black horror come down the tunnel. And the smell that accompanied it was like something dead. It was dark but she could see faces in front of her. The smell and the terrible faces made her want to get out and face whatever terrible fate awaited her outside. Staying in the dark with these horrors was beyond anything anyone could bear.

Mort was climbing into the tunnel. The last corner of Kirin's mind that was not filled with fear realized that the fear that came from the grimulves outside was driving him to go back out to the light, and certain death. She grabbed at him as he climbed into the tunnel.

"Mort, Come back!" She held him close to her and he buried his face in her dress to hide from the faces and the fear. His little body was trembling, and sobs came muffled from the folds of her dress that was now torn and filthy but a refuge for the little boy.

Kirin closed her eyes and prayed for them all.

Jenny stood up. She could not understand what had happened. She was still in the forest it seemed, but it was quite different, and the grimulves were gone.

She wiped her face and looked up to see a young man coming toward her. She stood trembling but not with fear. She didn't feel afraid and yet she did, sort of. When he came closer; in a voice that was as warm and happy as you could possibly imagine, he said, "Jenny, you are very welcome!"

Jenny looked all around her. "Excuse me, where am I?"

"In a place where you will never need to shed any more tears."

"Who are you?"

He smiled. "We will have a long time for every question to be answered in many different ways. For now, let me help you."

The young man looked at her with love and pity and joy in his eyes and reached up to wipe the tears from her eyes. At his touch power ...

joy surged through her; and with power came understanding. Jenny looked at her new acquaintance in amazement.

"Our friend Norri said he believed that our God and Father had a Son. Are you the Son?"

"I am. Come to the water with me and I will bathe your face. You will also meet some friends you have missed." He took her hand.

Jenny stopped still, "Sir?"

"Yes, dear heart."

"What about Kirin and Lettie and Mort?"

To Jenny it seemed as if their immanent danger was like a memory even though she knew all about the danger she had tried to defend them from. "Can you...are you able to help them?"

"I am and I can, and I have already sent help to them. Don't be afraid; come."

He led her through the trunks of huge trees to a bright bubbling stream sparkling with light and bent down and drank. Jenny did likewise and as soon as the water touched her skin, she felt life as she had never felt before rush through her body. She stood up and looked at the handsome young man beside her. "I miss Kirin."

She could see in his face that he understood but he looked behind her. "Here are some lost friends though."

Jenny looked around and Pat and David were there. They looked the same as before – but young again. Pat looked wonderful and David seemed to be wise and young and carefree as she hadn't seen him for as long as she could remember.

Then she suddenly remembered where she had been and thought, "I must look such a mess!"

Pat smiled, reading her sudden thought, "No, actually you don't."

Jenny looked down at her dress and instead of dirt and spattered blood it was perfectly clean – even glowing; the yellows and blue hues of the dress in better days were more brilliant and perfect than the dress when it was new. She felt her hair and it was clean and soft as if she had just washed it and brushed it dry in the sunshine on a spring day.

"Oh, Pat!" she said and threw herself into her arms for the longest cuddle. David put his hand on her shoulder and looked at the young man, "May we take her and get her some food?"

He just smiled back and the three of them went along the grassy edge of the stream to a table that suddenly appeared laden with wonderful fresh food and cups brim full of the glistening water from the stream.

Jenny looked around to see what had happened to the young man; he was gone.

Pat smiled at her. "He is gone, but he will be back".

28

Bertola Harbor

*D*enquinar sat with Reynolds and Henderson in the captain's cabin of the *Swiftsure* when a whistle blew, and they were called up on deck. Ships of the Bernadian battle fleet were ringing bells and making sail. Oars were out and the steady drumbeat of the rowing master reverberated across the water. Anchors were aweigh and eight quatreremes and quinqueremes left their stations and turned toward the open sea.

The battleships moved out of the harbor with evident precision. Denquinar could not but admire the professionalism, to say nothing of the excellent design of the ships as they swung their yards and took the wind making further rowing unnecessary once they were beyond the shelter of the harbor.

Signal flags fluttered from a tall mast on the long building that they knew housed the Bernadian admiralty. The Naval commanders had ordered their ships to sea.

Captain Henderson watched with the same kind of admiration as Denquinar. "Something is happening, but what?"

Denquinar looked at the answering flags on the big ships. "If only we could read their signals. Still if I may make a couple of observations: They moved out slowly, not as if an immanent threat had been detected. And they have not formed up in any kind of battle formation. They look as though they are taking up a precautionary stance.

Look over there. Other warships in the harbor that have not put to sea. You would think that if there was a serious threat, they would have deployed all their strength. The other ships do not seem to be making any preparations at all. Obviously, they think eight ships are more than enough for whatever threat has emerged."

Henderson seemed impressed by the former Admiral's quick assessment of the situation. Their questions were answered. A boat was seen approaching from the admiralty.

Tom and Kevin sat on deck with a group of the survivors from Herelstrom, complaining about the blisters on their hands from the oars. The winds had been almost nonexistent for two days. They had rowed well out to sea before turning south to avoid any other ships of the Corriian navy. Tom felt bad. He had been spared the rowing because of his injury. He had offered but his countrymen would not let him.

A Greyton farmer was nursing his blistered hands. "I don't mind helpin' out with the rowin' but I've never pulled on an oar before."

Tom had been called to speak with Admiral Norrens and now the wind had returned, and the men had been released from the rowing benches, he had a chance to speak with them.

"He is fleeing to Bernadia. He hopes to ask for asylum and if possible, to fight with the Bernadians against the rest of the Corrii fleet."

Brinman, one of the southern enders voiced the question several were thinking. "Beggars can't be choosers of course but will the Bernadians receive them and agree to giving them refuge?"

Tom had asked Admiral Norrens this and he did not sound too confident. "I think they are hoping for the best; they don't really know."

The southern enders were apprehensive and there was much discussion about how they might possibly get home and whether this would ever be possible. Some had wives and children who were separated from them when the survivors were herded together after the fall of Egleton.

The discussion came to an end when there was a shout from the masthead that land had been sighted and they went to the rail to see.

There was activity on the poop deck and flags were hoisted to the top of the main mast. When they broke and fluttered out on the breeze: a red flag of the Corrii navy with a white flag above it.

One of the southern enders commented, "You don't need to be a navy man to know what that means." All looked anxiously toward the foreign coast with its white buildings and walled coastal towns. Clearly these towns were considered under threat. They had enough wind to sail slowly south and now a white flag flew from the mast of every ship in the squadron, and they were close enough to the coast that the situation could be clearly seen from the towns. They hoped they would be seen and the Bernadians would decide that were not a threat. The last thing they needed was an engagement with those they hoped would give them succor.

Taller buildings on the shore indicated that they were nearing a major centre which the more knowledgeable knew would be Bertola. It was confirmed when the mouth of a large harbor came into sight and large warships were passing the heads and steering toward them. They were battleship class vessels with evil looking rams on their prows and armor glinting from marine soldiers on their decks. All could see the size of the vessels and the precision of those that manned them; it was obvious why the Corrii avoided a naval battle with the Bernadians.

Orders were given and there was an exchange of signal flags between the former Corriian ships and the Argamaro broke formation and sailed toward the Bernadian flagship on her own. They guessed it was the flagship. Strings of signal flags fluttered from its mizzen mast, and it was, in any case the largest ship.

When they came into hailing distance, Admiral Norrens picked up a speaking trumpet and called to the officers on board the Bernadian chip, "I am Admiral Norrens, formerly of the Corriian navy. We have defected and come to Bertola seeking asylum."

There was discussion on the poop deck of the Bernadian ship and then clipped orders came in reply for them to take position astern of the Bernadian flagship and follow her back into port.

There were more signals as Norrens ships followed her and the Bernadian force positioned itself to windward, obviously ready for any trick or the appearance of other ships.

But of course, there were not any and Norrens had ordered that his men wear no arms and the torsion weapons on deck were covered and securely lashed to demonstrate they had no ill intent.

When they entered the harbor, they were ordered to anchor next to the flagship and the rest of the former Corriian captains brought their ships into the same sheltered cove and anchored also.

They had barely secured the ship when a boat approached inviting their most senior commander to come on board the flagship - to explain himself.

Ghezia gave him a look of concern, but he smiled in return. "Don't worry, we represent a quarter of the Corriian navy, and our defection can only be good news for the Bernadians. I will try to return as soon as I can."

Ghezia nodded, obviously worried and watched as Norrens climbed down into the waiting boat. The coxswain gave a command and the boat carrying her husband sped across the water to the flagship.

The boat was hooked onto the chains at the entry port and Norrens climbed up to the deck. At the entry port he was met by an elderly naval man in a smart blue and yellow tunic wearing a sword.

"I am Con Vortez of his majesty's navy of Bernadia, of the Bertola squadron."

Norrens introduced himself as a former Corriian admiral and Con Vortez bowed as if he still held that rank. "Please come below Admiral?"

The latter led him below to a large beautifully furnished cabin and he was offered a seat.

"Will you have tea or some wine, Admiral?"

Norrens knew he had to keep his wits about him and requested some tea.

"Tea for me also, Vetson … and some cakes."

The steward left to arrange for the tea and cakes.

"Tell me your story, admiral?"

Norrens recounted the reason for their defection and the events that followed. He avoided any unnecessary details and confined his story to facts that the Bernadians would soon be able to verify for themselves.

Vortez listened carefully and only interjected with a few questions. Norrens noted that he took an interest in the fact that they had captives from Herelstrom aboard.

"This is all of great importance to our rulers, admiral. We have been wondering about the sudden disappearance of the wyverns that have caused us great difficulties in the field." (He kept back the information about the probable annihilation of their northern army.) "The army commanders will no doubt wish to ask you many more questions. For my part the loss of four battleships will lessen even further the chances of your former countrymen mounting a sea-borne attack on Bertola, unless they come here chasing you, of course."

Con Vortez inserted a deliberate pause. "Then they would have you *and* us to fight and one would think the balance would be against them, even if we were not already stronger at sea. Do you agree that we are?"

Norrens felt more comfortable talking general strategy. "Yes. It was to gain timber to build better ships that is the supposed reason for the invasion of Herelstrom. The empire knows that they haven't a fleet that can match yours yet. Of course, that doesn't matter if they defeat your armies. You cannot remain permanently at sea."

"Too true and that is the greatest threat."

Norrens smiled at the honesty. "Admiral Vortez, I am no soldier, and I don't know the current state of play on the ground, but I do know that the empire had hopes that the wyverns and the other foul creatures that they brought from Dorphire Sunde would hurt your armies in the field and turn the tide of battle."

"And they certainly have, Admiral. It is hard to fight against weapons you have never seen before. Our brave legionaries would have a difficult enough time fighting the Corrii without always looking toward the sky, fearing the lashing poison of the tails of the wyverns. What was the feeling in the Navy about these creatures?"

"As always there was a growing feeling that the rulers of the Empire were more and more in the grip of the covens and that these creatures of evil and magic were considered of much more importance than ordinary fighting men."

Vortez chuckled. "I must say I like your story about the priests getting caught in that strange other place where they catch the wyverns. Let us hope they like their new home?"

"Yes. There seems some justice in it doesn't there. I readily admit that I had not thought of causing damage to the priests and their magic. I was just trying to free my wife and daughter."

"Very well, Admiral, I accept your story and it all fits with other things we have observed like the sudden disappearance of the winged terror. I will plead your case with our government as well as the opportunity allows. Is there anything that you would ask?"

Asylum at first, of course, and succor for our families; then maybe a chance to do what we do – fight against the empire. There is no love lost between Admiral Cherulia and I and my men."

"We will have to see, but we are short of men right now."

Vetzon arrived with a pot of tea and a set of fine glass cups and an ample plate of cakes.

"Have a cake, Admiral. Vetzon has not brought milk. Do you take it?

"No thank you, only a little sugar."

Vortez smiled at his steward. "… a navy man Vetzon, no milk at sea."

Norrens sipped his tea and took a cake that the steward offered. They chatted about many things until Norrens had finished his tea. Con Vortez was particularly interested in the women and children and the captives from Herelstrom.

Norrens put down his empty cup. "Admiral, I would like to have something to say to my men. What are your orders concerning us?"

"There was no time to consult our rulers and there are … complications shall we say. I have authority here as regards all things to do with the fleet and the harbor. I grant you asylum for the present. You should convey to your men that they will be well treated and not enslaved. In that, we are unlike your previous countrymen.

The Bernadian Empire is a nautical nation and there is usually work for willing seamen. Do you have sufficient provisions for the present?"

"We have no immediate needs. Obviously if we are to remain in harbor for a time we will need to water and get more basic provisions."

"Of course. I will arrange for fresh meat and fruit to be provided to your ships and for your water parties to be assisted. You can send your boats to the naval service jetty after noon. By then they will have made all the necessary preparations."

"Thank you, Admiral, that is very kind of you." Norrens was surprised by the thoughtfulness of his host and knew the fresh produce would be received well by the men. They would take it as a sign that they might have lives in Bernadia after all.

The admiral glanced at the barely touched plate of cakes. "Admiral Norrens, did you not say that you had a daughter?"

"Yes, Admiral."

"Vetzon, wrap up those cakes and send them in a satchel with the admiral for his daughter. She has been through an ordeal for a small one - we will do what we can to provide a bit of cheer. Nothing cheers children up like cakes."

They left the cabin and made for the entry port and the boat that was waiting to return Norrens to his ship. Norrens smiled and cordially thanked his host before climbing down the side of the flagship to the waiting boat. He could see his wife and daughter watching from deck of the *Argamaro*. He guessed that Ghezia would be very relieved to see him returning.

He climbed up the side of the ship with care to keep his breeks and tunic clean. Who knew who he might have to appear before yet? As he climbed through the entry port and smiled at Chloe, he was met by Captain Verna. "Sir, look at those!"

Norrens turned to look at two ships anchored further down the harbor. He couldn't see anything remarkable about them, except their square sailing rig and three masts. "What is it, Verna?"

"Look at the insignia."

Norrens looked and as the breeze picked up the pennant at the mast-head, he could see the green and blue of Herelstrom on the foremast of the first ship.

Norrens took it all in. "Verna, get Tom the warden from Herelstrom, quickly!"

There was a bustle as Tom came up onto the poop deck. He had already seen the ships and seemed excited.

"What is it, Tom? Do you recognize those ships?"

"Yes, Admiral, I do. They left he river near my home on a quest to find a way to Bernadia from the south. The two ships are commanded by Commodore Denquinar. You may know him. He defected from your navy."

"Yes … I know Dursus well. I tell you the truth Tom, I never expected to see him again. His wife is here actually. She is with my wife below decks."

Verna was squinting his eyes in the bright sunlight. "I think I can see Admiral Denquinar, Sir. He is on the forecastle. Shall I go below and tell his wife?"

"Let us wait a minute and see what transpires."

They watched the two ships. They seemed busy on board. A boat had come alongside from the admiralty building with officers on board – probably messengers; then all the attention seemed to be focused on them.

On board the *Swiftsure* Denquinar turned to his son who was looking at the Corriian ships with amazement. "Do you recognize the ships Kiri?"

"They look like Admiral Norrens' squadron. What are they doing here?"

"That is what I intend to find out; right now.

Captain Reynolds, a boat of your courtesy? Would you like to accompany me on board a Corrii battleship?"

"It would be … interesting, Commodore. I take it the messengers from Prince Anabund were about these ships."

"Yes, he wants my opinion as to their true intentions. They have claimed to have defected."

"Let us go and meet them, Commodore. Lawkings, ready the cutter! The Commodore and I are going to the Corrii ships."

It took time to ready the boat and Reynolds made sure that weapons were secreted surreptitiously in her bottom in case all was not as it seemed. Once Reynolds and Denquinar were aboard Lawkings gave the order and the cutter skimmed across the water to the waiting Quinquereme.

A ladder was lowered down the high sides of the *Argamaro* and Denquinar led them up her side to the quarterdeck. As he climbed, he could see faces looking at him inquisitively.

As he came through the entry-port Denquinar saw an assembly of Corriian naval officers.

Denquinar saw Norrens and Verna and smiled. He waited for Reynolds to follow him onto the quarterdeck and made the introductions.

"Captain Reynolds of His Magesty of Helerstrom's exploration ship, Swiftsure may I introduce Admiral Norrens of the Corriian navy and Flag Captain Verna."

Norrens reached out his hand in greeting and amazement. "Denquinar ... Denquinar, I never thought I would meet you again."

Denquinar was enjoying their amazement at seeing him and in the uniform of an officer of the Herelstrom Navy when his own jaw dropped. Norrens followed his eyes to the hatchway and the person who had emerged, and he smiled in turn. "I think that maybe you are the one who is amazed now."

Kristina Denquinar stood as if rooted to the deck. Her husband had it appeared, come back from the dead. She had no words, did not even begin to know what to say.

Admiral Norrens broke the uncomfortable silence. "I'm sorry Denquinar, Kristina, it must have been a shock for both of you. Please come to my cabin where you can have some privacy."

Norrens led the way to the poop deck door and down the hallway to his cabin. He led Denquinar and his wife inside and then left them to get reacquainted. As he walked back to the quarterdeck, he couldn't help feeling a little pleased with himself. Denquinar could not have expected this in his wildest dream ... or nightmare. He wondered which it was.

Inside the cabin there was silence. Everything Denquinar thought of to say sounded lame and even callous or offensive. He had not ever hated Kristina. She was (had been, he corrected himself) a socialite with a keen sense of power and influence at court.

Kristina felt more alone in the world now she had been reunited with her husband. Finally, she decided on raising the one subject that they had in common – their shared loss of their son.

"Did you ever discover what had happened to Kiri?"

Denquinar looked up. He realized she had been suffering the grief of the boy's loss all this time. "I found him!"

"He is alive! Where?"

Back on the Swiftsure, anchored across the bay. Kristina ran to the window and looked across at the ship as if somehow hoping to catch a glimpse of their son.

"How did you find him?"

"It is a long story. Both of us nearly died in the ocean off Herelstrom, but as the people I have met from that country would no doubt say, *Someone* obviously had other plans."

"It is a miracle that you are both alive and both here."

Denquinar considered this. "Yes, and it is just as much a miracle that you are here. Kiri will be delighted to see you. He often speaks of you and never thought he would see you again. I think he misses you."

"What about you? Did you miss me – at all?"

"Kristina, I always thought I was just a marriage of convenience; that you needed an up-and-coming officer to justify your social position; because it was expected of a woman at court."

Kristina lowered her head and Denquinar thought he saw her whisk away a tear. "I suppose that was partly true, but did you not realize that I loved you and Kiri. I know I was not very good at showing it but since you left and since I fled the court, I have thought about you constantly, whether you can believe that or not. I have wished times beyond count that I may have a second chance at being a mother and a wife. Now here you stand, and yet that wish seems just as far away as ever.

Denquinar looked up and smiled. "Maybe not so far as you may think ... I also have thought of you and how I left without word and how cruel that was to you. I have often thought of you and the good moments we had together."

Kristina took a step closer. "It has been horrible since you left. A friend warned me that I was in danger; that you had apparently deserted your post and I would suffer retribution. I fled and made my way to Ghezia to ask her to hide me. She was the only person I knew that I thought I might be able to trust. Dursus, it has been horrible. They caught us and took Ghezia and Chloe and me to the island to be....

Denquinar looked at her in shocked amazement. "I am sorry. I didn't know that would happen to you."

Kristina's self control was now faltering, and she trembled as she remembered the island and the priests in the temple and the paralyzing fear. It was the best thing that could have happened. Denquinar saw her looking pale and took her in his arms and held her for a long time. She let him hold her and wept.

29

And the Darkness...

Queen Illuin of the Driadora sat taking reports from her people on the depredations of the wyverns. They hunted continuously over the forest. Their keen eyes could catch any movement and many of her people had been killed and devoured. This afternoon one had taken a child from a branch near the royal hall and flown off over the trees with the little one in its claws.

Illuin had cried for hours with the little girl's mother. She was angry and desperate when she went to her husband, but she found him busy with many other reports of troubles that the invasion has visited on their kingdom. Iubeth had paused in his work when she entered and when he asked what the matter was, she made excuses and left.

Her maids had told her that the gordrill that the Corrii had brought, had also killed many of their people. They were nimbler in the trees than the Driadora themselves and her husband had sent out almost all the warriors they could spare to hunt them, but they could retreat from the forest to their masters at will, and all they could hope for was a chance encounter for the warriors to kill them.

The king and his general were experimenting with a new arrow that Serelra, one of his branch leaders had bred. The trouble with hunting the gordrill was that they were able to hide in the trees, clambering around behind the thick trunks and it was very hard for his archers to shoot them. The charnorgara arrows may enable them to shoot around the obstacles. Their casualties to the gordrill and the wyvern had to be stemmed. He had lost dozens of warriors and many of his people. Illuin had seen the creases of worry on his brow and had not told him about the little girl that afternoon.

Illuin went with her maids to a quiet place near the underground river to pray and ask their God for help. At such times He was their solace. Not only did she wish to pray for her people, but her heart went out to the many refugees that had fled into the forest. She knew that they had heard rumors of the driadora and were afraid of them, but they had worked hard to usher them to parts of the deep forest where they could hide and be safe and she had sent food in whatever ways she could contrive to help them.

Iowa, one of her maids had brought a parchment with the writings of Twigroot to read and draw solace and inspiration. Illuin knew that Twigroot, the late prophet of her people, had a heart for the people of the lands beside the sea and sought his inspiration.

As she prayed, Illuin felt a great horror and fear come over her. It was as if a darkness of fear was closing in around her. She looked up at the light and it was still glowing with its faint green glow as usual, so why this feeling. She was reluctant to close her eyes again, fearing she would have the same experience but felt led to do so, nonetheless. The blackness came again, and she saw evil canine faces and smelled a smell that was like the excrement of dogs, but far worse. She prayed desperately, "Lord what are you showing me?" Illuin felt sure the image of the darkness was surrounding someone else and that it was urgent that she act.

The answer came with urgency, "Get up, Illuin and go where I will show you." She rose to her feet and made her way along a passage; led in some way that she could not quite understand, but as certainly as if she was being led by the hand.

As she followed the voice in her head, "Go here. Take the narrow passage to the storeroom. Go up to the end of the tunnel here." She took a lantern and went onto the dark tunnel with her maids following.

Illuin entered the narrow tunnel that led through the heart of one of the outer roots of the tree that towered above them. The tunnel was now narrow and close, probably a natural hollow space in the orkya tree's root system. The maids behind her followed obediently but looked more and more confused by Illuin's strange excursion.

Then as she could go no further, she heard the voice again, "Open a window here."

Illuin spoke to the spirit of the great tree and as if it took great exertion, there came a creaking and groaning, and a small hole began to open in the top of the root.

Kirin was trembling with fear and clutching an even more frightened Mort to her when a glimmer of light appeared in the impenetrable blackness of passage. It was only a little way further in and the light appeared where there had been utter darkness and worse - the evil emanating from the grimulves.

As they watched, the light grew and ever so slowly, they saw an opening in the side of the tunnel. Once the opening was large enough a voice came through the opening. It sounded to Kirin as if it was a kind voice. "Is anyone there?"

Kirin could not imagine anything worse than their predicament and replied. "I am Kirin. I am here with my friend Lettie and a boy ... and a baby."

There was a pause and the sound of muffled voices. After some moments, a face appeared in the opening. "I am Jemma, handmaiden to the queen. You are known to us, Kirin. Can you get down to us and climb through this opening the queen has made in the root tunnel?"

"I think so. Come along Lettie ...."

Kirin came through the opening, blinking she helped Mort out of the hole and then Lettie.

The queen stood before her, and concern was written all over her face. "How did you come to be underground?"

"We were hiding from the grimulves. Your Majesty, my friend Jenny is still on the surface or in the tunnel entrance. Can you help her?" Tears were streaming down Kirin's face and Mort held her hand and looked helplessly up at her.

The queen turned to her handmaiden. "Jemma, go quickly to the guard tower. See if they can get to the trees above us and see what has happened to Kirin's friend. Go quickly!"

Jemma ran back down the passage and turned a corner out of their sight.

The queen took a couple of steps forward and took the weeping Kirin into her arms. Kirin sobbed, "She didn't come in after us...."

The queen took the situation in hand immediately. She called her other maids "Summerwind, help with the child. Come follow me, we will get you some water and some fruit. Rilly, run ahead to our chambers and arrange the water and food!" Rilly dashed away down the tunnel the way Jemma had gone.

The queen herself picked up Kirin's bag and bow and her quiver with only two remaining arrows and led the two exhausted girls and the little ones to a place where they could receive help.

Anabund, crown prince and future ruler of the Bernadian Empire alighted from his chariot outside the admiralty building.

Denquinar and Vortez were already there as well as an elderly naval man whose lined face told of many years at sea and whose tunic and emblems of rank indicated he was senior to Con Vortez.

The prince was followed by two generals who ordered their aids to watch and see that those meeting inside would not be disturbed.

Anabund unbuckled his sword and laid it on the table. "Are the priests on their way? We have decisions to make that need more than military wisdom."

One of the generals nodded. "We saw them coming, Corscerrus, Wingerentus, High Priest Vernus and old Tiresius following last with his stick carrying more of his weight than his legs."

"My Father puts more store in the words of Tiresius than all the others. Commodore, you are an ally and have provided much needed services already. Can you Introduce yourself and then give us your report on the Corrii defectors?"

Denquinar bowed to the assembled officers. "I am Dursus Denquinar, now a Commodore in the navy of the King of Herelstrom but formerly Grand Admiral of the Corriian navy."

There were looks of amazement from the assembled officers which Anabund enjoyed. He liked surprising his officers.

The old Admiral spoke first. "Ah Denquinar, we meet at last. Often my officers have rehearsed plans for fighting you at sea and here you turn up - on our side. I am Von Etchens, Grand Admiral of the Emperor's fleet. Let me introduce our generals:

This is General Tumarind, returned but a day ago from the north.

This is General Costina, commander of the second army.

Con Vortez you know, Commodore.

Please give us your report?"

Denquinar cleared his throat. "It is only a year since I served in the Corriian navy as you know and the men on these ships now anchored in your harbor are known to me. I have served with and trained many of them personally. They are all good officers who might have served out their days loyally in the ships of the empire, had some extremity not forced them to rebel. Of course, there was always some discontent but it would never have amounted to anything unless something had driven them to it.

It was the actions of the empire's rulers in sending their sailors' families to Biel Harfing to ensure their loyalty that drove them to rebel against their lawful commanders.

They then sailed to Biel Harfing and attacked the militia to rescue as many of their families as they could.

What is also interesting is that they still have on board some of the captives from the campaign against Herelstrom. Some of these men, including Tom Roper, the warden of the southern province of Herelstrom, have been re-united with their countrymen aboard my ship."

"What do these Corriian sailors ask of us Commodore?" asked Tumarind.

"They have asked me to convey to you in the strongest possible way that they are refugees and asylum seekers who cannot return to their own country. They are extremely unhappy with the changes in their land and wish to fight against those who still side with the rulers and the coven people who are the real power in the country now."

Anabund looked straight at Denquinar. "Commordore, you know these men. Can they be relied upon?"

Denquinar met the prince's gaze. "Yes, your Majesty, I believe that they are genuine."

Admiral Etchens stroked his beard. "It may be one thing to say so now Denquinar, but what about in the heat of battle against their own countrymen when it comes to it?"

"It is a hard question, Admiral. Who can say what motivates a man to fight in the heat of battle. If I had the decision, I would say that they have no choice as to which side and many reasons to fight their countrymen who are still loyal to a regime they hate."

Anabund was clearly deep in thought. "What would you say we should do Commodore?"

Denquinar knew this was a crucial moment. He thought for a moment and sought to pick his words carefully.

"I cannot advise you, your Majesty, or your high command but I am commissioned by my king to ask for the aid of the Bernadians and I do ask for that.

Even if you will allow these men to return with me to fight against those that currently invade my new country and can do no more, I will consider it an honor.

I do not know the state of your army, but whatever the situation, a naval counterattack will reduce the pressure on your country and aid Herelstrom significantly. She has insufficient warships to hold back the tide of the Corriian invasion. With a few more ships to harass the Corrii supply lines at the least my king has a chance of defeating the Corrii in Herelstrom or if not, at least preventing total conquest."

Anabund nodded his approval. "Thank you for your report and your courageous offer, Commodore. You have answered our concerns by taking the biggest risk upon yourself. We will consider both and let you have our decision by tomorrow.

Please return to your ship. I have given orders for special foods and drinks to be sent with your boat crew and like supplies to the Corriian ships. Please assure your own men that we value the offer of an alliance in these difficult times."

Denquinar thanked the prince, saluted the officers, and left the room for the jetty.

There was a knock on the door and a naval officer entered. "Your Majesty, Sir, the priests are arriving."

"Show them in, Grinaith."

The four elders of the clergy entered in their ornate robes, Vernus the most impressively dressed of them all and Old Tiresius last. They bowed to the crown prince.

Vernus spoke. His tone was deferential but with significant personal authority, even over the prince.

"In what way may we help or advise your Majesty? Our military knowledge cannot be the reason why you have brought us all the way from the temple."

"No, Most Reverend, Vernus it is on a matter of ethics that I need your wisdom."

The High priest bowed slightly and barely concealed his pleasure at being asked about matters of national interest.

"I would have your opinion on the will of God for our deliberations. We have received defectors from the Corriian Navy who have been through great dangers in deserting their responsibilities and rescuing their families from the ghetto where the Corrii had sent them – under threat of being sent to the island of Baal Giborachir.

These men have also attacked that evil place and rescued the wife and daughter of their admiral from the hands of the foul priests.

What is more they have destroyed the altar of abomination in that place and closed the window that allows the priests to bring the wyverns from another plane of some kind to do their bidding and fight for them."

The oldest priest spoke first. "It would seem that the whole world owes these men a debt."

The high priest was a little dismissive. "Yes, Tiresius but so far, they have only acted out of their own concerns. That they may have aided us and our troops that have been harassed by these creatures of the red men may only have been accidental.

On what matter does your Majesty wish for our wisdom?"

"Captain Grinaith has briefed you about the coming of the ships from Herelstrom and their commander. He has offered to lead a naval attack against the Corriian navy with the squadron of former Corrii ships that now ride at anchor in our harbor and attempt to relieve Herelstrom which is now hard pressed by an invasion of the Corrii.

I have in mind to send the Bertola squadron to assist him.

My question to you relates to the requirement of protecting our people set against our responsibility to assist others not so strong as ourselves, who are oppressed."

Vernus frowned. "It might be a different matter if we ourselves were not so hard pressed. Surely every fighting man is needed to do his duty to defend the empire in these dangerous times. Wingerentus, what do the prophets say on this matter?"

Wingerentus looked uncomfortable. "I would have said that they condemned evil and spoke to the day when the Lord would destroy evil. When the Messiah comes, the one who is promised, he will likely lead us in a war that will destroy the perpetrators of these evils."

Corscerrus bowed to the emperor. "There are also many scriptures that speak of the king's responsibility to lead his armies against the enemies of our nation."

Anabund strode around the room. "You have at least clearly stated my dilemma – even if you haven't given me any real answer. Please return to the temple and study the prophets and the books of the emperors of our people and send me word as to anything that bears upon our dilemma."

The High priest made to leave but turned once more to Anabund. "Forgive me your Majesty but is this decision not still with your father, ill though he is?"

"Of course it is, High Priest, and I go to my father as soon as I have gathered all the wisdom on this matter that I can. I would not bother my father, *ill as he is*, until I had distilled the essence of the ramblings of all his councilors."

The suitably chastised priests bowed and made their way to the door. Tiresius was hauling himself up off a stool.

"Tiresius, you need not leave immediately if you want to rest before returning to the temple. Our discussions are at an end."

The old priest thanked Anabund and stayed on the stool while the others filed out of the room.

Soon only the old priest, the crown prince and the Grand Admiral and General Tamerind were left.

"What do you think old man? My father trusts your judgement more than any other."

Tiresius looked at Anabund with bright discerning eyes. "What has happened to the northern army, my lord prince?"

Anabund nodded to general Tumerind to explain.

"There is no sign of the army, Holy Father. I rode north and we were attacked by the flying menace day and night. Then one morning they were gone. It seems that the news of the Corriian Admiral and what he did at the temple is the truth for we found several dying wyverns as we continued our journey north.

When we arrived at the end of the northern pass, we found the sight of a great battle with many of our own men fallen but could not go further with many legions of Corriian infantry camped in the plain."

Tiresius considered this. "Your Majesty, is it not said that attack is oft the best form of defence? If our best troops have been destroyed as you obviously fear, along with your brother, would a strong naval attack with forces we believe to be superior to those of the Corrii be a sensible move? It would distract them and force them to put more resources into the campaign against Herelstrom and give us more time to train the troops of the second army against an attack in our north. This might be good military strategy even if we felt no compulsion to assist the people of Herelstrom in their need, would it not?"

"My father and brother feel the need to help Herelstrom. I cannot say I have that concern. But what you suggest makes good sense in terms of tactics. And I readily agree that it is better if the Corrii have two enemies."

"What of the twin cities, my Lord Prince?"

"Indeed, Tiresius that is another concern. Omari has discovered that they have some naval power; in fact, they have increased their numbers of ships. So far, they have been neutral and gladly accepted our navy as an extra defense against the Corrii but if they have been compromised ...."

Con Vortez looked worried. "My Lord, I must say that the Bertola squadron could do with some real battle experience and the possibility of a major attack on the Corrii squadrons assaulting Herelstrom is something I strongly desire, but if there is a chance of treachery by the twin cities, the absence of my squadron would leave our capital exposed."

General Costina had been listening in silence up until now. "Your Majesty, we will not be denuding the navy of ships and some of my legions of the second army could be deployed to provide extra protection for the capital. They will still be ready if any threat emerges in the north. I can train them just as well in the capital as in the countryside."

"Yes Costina, and it will give some comfort to the populace to see soldiers in the streets. Those glutinous priests have not added much to our discussions, but they did show us that there is fear among the people."

Tiresius chuckled at the description of his fellow priests. "Has your majesty formed an opinion? You are quite right to fear that your father cannot make such a decision on his sick bed."

"I think so Tiresius. Con Vortez is keen to take the attack to the enemy and I must say, I like the idea of our navy striking the Corrii where they least expect; from a purely pragmatic point of view, it is better if they must fight on two fronts. The fall of Herelstrom is not in our military interests.

Thank you, gentlemen, I should go and see how fares my father. Father Tiresius, would you like to shorten your walk to the temple with a ride in my chariot?"

"Thank you, your Majesty, I think my old knees would be better served with a quiet walk rather than bouncing along the cobbles in a chariot."

Anabund smiled and passed the old priest his staff which stood in the rack by the door. The stick was of dark wood with an ivory handle, worn smooth with much use.

"This is a fine walking stick, Father."

Tiresius took the staff gratefully and leant on it to take the weight off his right knee.

"Thank you, your Majesty. It was given to me by the people. Every shepherd needs a stick."

As Tiresius walked slowly along the street from the meeting, he mused that Anabund had promise. Certainly, he wasn't too concerned about the people of Herelstrom and that wasn't particularly surprising, but at least he could see the sense in having allies. Perhaps he might make a satisfactory ruler yet and in time might even develop a conscience as his father had done.

30

Allies

The old emperor sat in a comfortable chair propped on cushions to receive his guests. Omari and General Tumarind were helping themselves to refreshments at a table laden with fruit and cheese for the guests.

Prince Anabund was shown into the room.

"Father, they have arrived in the city. I have arranged accommodation and sent a message to the ships."

"That is good, do you think they suspect what we are up to?"

Omari put the last piece of peach into his mouth. "I don't think they have any idea."

The old emperor propped himself up higher on the cushions. "This is fun, isn't it? This is the best part of being emperor Anabund, as you will find. Many of the other tasks are dull and even painful, such as sending the sons of the empire to war but this part I enjoy.

Is Conamund coming?"

Omari passed the tray of fruits and cheese to his father. "Yes, he was hobbling down the hall on his crutches as I came in. He is determined to get here himself and prove he is not an invalid. I made sure there is a servant nearby if the crutches slip on the polished floors. That sounds like him now."

The doorman opened the cedar and bronze doors. "Prince Conamund, your Majesty! Also, Commodore Denquinar, of His majesty's navy of Herelstrom and Tom Roper, Warden of the Southern province."

"Good! Is the other party here yet?"

"They have been sent for from the waiting rooms on the west wing, your Majesty."

"Good! Sit down Conamund. We are not formal this afternoon. I don't want you falling over. It's unseemly."

Then the Emperor turned to Denquinar and Tom.

Good morning, gentlemen, Welcome to Bertola! I have read your reports and I must say that you ask a lot of an emperor whose armies are beset on every side by the Corrii. We would value an alliance and see value in co-operation but venturing my ships and men in time of war is a very risky business.

Commodore, my son has told me of how you aided us by bringing information about the gathering of the wulf packs and we are most grateful.

Master Warden, I have heard that you were injured when the Corrii attacked your town?"

Tom Bowed. "Yes, your Majesty. I am much recovered though, after a pleasant sea voyage."

"Mmmm ... I have heard about your voyage and what you and the former Admiral Norrens have done. Is he here by the way?"

Anabund smiled. "Yes, he is waiting outside."

"Then bring him in as well, Anabund."

Admiral Norrens was shown in. He was in his best uniform but obviously felt very uncomfortable, in the presence of the Bernadian royalty, who until recently had been his enemies.

He bowed to the emperor. "Your Majesty."

The emperor looked the former admiral over. Norrens felt as though even from a look this astute ruler could learn much.

The emperor seemed to be considering what he had to say and then thought better of it.

"Is the other party here yet?"

Omari went to the door and opened it. He went out and there were words exchanged in the corridor then he reentered the room. "May I present two people whom many of you know: Norrimae Jung, King's forester and Sir Gordinae of Herelstrom!"

The emperor and princes watched with pleased amusement as Norri and Gordy, Tom and Denquinar met in an anteroom of the palace of Bertola.

Norri and Gordy were obviously shocked to see Tom and immediately had many questions. The emperor could see this and gave them leave to speak.

Tom shook hands with Norri and Gordy and Denquinar. "I was captured Norri. I believe the castle has fallen and many of the men were being taken into captivity. I and the others have been freed when admiral Norrens here, and his squadron, defected. I can't answer your next question. I know from the other captives that many of the women and children were rounded up and taken to the town. They do not seem to have been harmed.

As to Kirin and Jenny, I asked Lettie to take them out via the secret passage. I had been injured and when I knew what happened I was on Admiral Norrens' ship. I am afraid that is all I know."

The emperor interrupted. "Let me fill you in on the events after the defection of the Corriian battle squadron if I may, Admiral. These men have not only removed a key battle group from the control of the Corriian navy, but they have also attacked a town and rescued their families. If that were not enough, they have attacked Be-air Monar in Dorphir Sunde destroyed the Dorphir navy and desecrated the temple of Ba-al Giborachire.

As all of you here know the priests of that place have been capturing and training Wyverns from some desolate place that may not even be of this world and turning them against us.

The destruction of the temple has destroyed the wyverns, and may I tell you saved what is left of my northern army.

Now, thanks to the King's forester here, my soldiers have been delivered, we have a new alliance with the wild warriors of Arion and a major part of the Corriian southern army has been destroyed.

And, personally speaking, there is one father in Bernadia who is beholden to a single man for saving first his youngest and now his second son."

The emperor turned to Norri with tears in his eyes. Knight of Herelstrom, you and your friend seem to have saved my son, Conamund when that seemed to all, most unlikely. There is no thanks an Emperor can give beyond considering how best to aid your country and return you thence as soon as possible with the hope of rescuing the ones you love.

You must understand that my personal gratitude does not override my responsibilities to my own people, but it certainly disposes us to consider your requests very favorably.

For now, please have some food and wine with us and become acquainted with your various stories. We will give much thought to your requests and decide what can be done most expeditiously."

As they spoke to one another, the emperor signaled that Norri should approach and spoke quietly. "May I ask you something, forester?"

Norri stood before the old emperor and bent to listen.

"They say you saw the Corion of Arion on the battlefield? Is it true?"

"More than that your Majesty, Gordy and I saw him when he came to one of the Arionite augurors as he was praying in a cave in the mountains."

"Did you speak with Him?"

"Yes, your Majesty. A little…"

"Can you tell me what He was like?" Norri seemed hesitant. "What is it forester?"

"Well, your Majesty, He was both gentle and awesome and not a little frightening."

"What do you make of Him, forester?"

Norri was lost for words. Gordy who had been standing close enough to hear, said, "Your Majesty if I may… it seems as though His plans are quite different from ours. But somehow it seems to me that He would value the returning of a son to a father; among many other good and wondrous things."

"Thank you. You have not answered my question and yet you have. His will is good. In the end that answers the one question I need to know. I am content."

There was more commotion in the corridor outside and the doorman opened the door to indicate to Anabund that more people he was expecting had arrived.

The Crown Prince nodded, and the doorman announced Admiral Con Vortez and his aide. Also tagging behind was an old priest.

The emperor indicated that the admiral should approach. "Have you and your captains all agreed to the plan, Admiral?"

"Yes, your Majesty. As you instructed, I asked my captains if they were willing to undertake a hazardous mission on your request. They were unanimous in their willingness, even eager."

"Good. We have a plan. Gather around gentlemen and my son will outline his idea."

Anabund drew a map out of a leather case and spread it on a small table where his father could see it from the couch. The men in the room looked on.

Norri was eager to see his home again. He stood gripping a stay on the forecastle of the Swiftsure which was among the fastest of their ships. They had been out of sight of land for many days; tossed by heavy seas that had put their seamanship to the test.

Norri was over adventures – but the adventure did not seem to be over. He longed to see Kirin and concern for her was never very far from his mind. The news of the sacking of Cair Egleton and Tom's capture had filled him with dread. He clung to the hope that Kirin, if she was captured, may not be identified as his wife, and would be treated as the other women but even that was a concern. The stories of how the Corrii treated captured women were horrific.

The plan was to avoid contact with the Corrii as long as possible and return to Herelstrom to relieve Cair Neren and then hopefully, Newcastle and his home.

Admiral Con Vortez with the Bertola squadron 14 war galleys including 8 battleships was sailing to windward of the Corriian defectors under commodore Denquinar, who all acknowledged as the most capable commander among them. They planned to throw all their naval force against Admiral Chereulia's ships now protecting the armies arrayed against Cair Neren. If they could interrupt the supply lines, it may give the armies of King Chadlyn a real chance against the Corriian invaders.

Norri with the *Swiftsure* and the *Suresafe* and a few of the smaller ships from Norrens' squadron were planning to make direct for Egleton. Newcastle, he corrected himself although he wondered if much of the new castle still stood and if it did perhaps it was now a Corrii stronghold. The *Swiftsure* was not designed for a fight at sea but was their most suitable long-range ship so they had some Bernadian troops and the returning captives from Egleton to attempt to retake their home.

Norri looked around and saw Tom chatting to the Bernadian tribune who commanded the mission. They had spent the long days at sea planning their attack so that it would give them the maximum benefit of surprise. They had no real idea of what they would be up against in Egleton and had to work out a way to attack the Corrii without harming any of their own people if possible.

Tom and Norrii with Tribune Fortinez had made the best plan they could and now Norri was anxious to land and try to find Kirin.

The wind was coming from the starboard quarter and the *Swiftsure* sluiced through the grey water making eight knots, but it was all too slow for Norri. He stood at the bows holding a stay and willing her forward with all speed.

Almost in answer to his wish the weather changed and grew foul. Grey billows came up behind them and the small ships were hit by a strong following wind. Captain Reynolds snapped orders and men raced up the ratlines to shorten sail.

The storm hit with shocking force. It was far worse than anything they had encountered in the Geitor Straights. Because the small ships were farthest out to sea, they encountered the worst of the storm. It drove them toward the coast and Reynolds commented that he was glad of the extra sea room. They ran before the storm for three days and managed to regroup over the next couple of days with the exception of one of the smallest ships, the Astica, and they had grave fears for her. Henderson on the Swiftsure signaled that he had last seen her astern of him and she seemed to have lost part of her foremast which seemed to be trailing overboard.

When the storm cleared Admiral Con Vortez gazed through the sleet trying to see any sign of the Admiral Norrens' ships. He hailed the masthead and after a long pause the reply was, "Ships in consort off the port bow, sir. Four in all, close hauled and on our course."

Con Vortez heaved a sigh. All was going to plan. Norrens' four big ships had weathered the storm and were still in formation. His latest measure showed them south of the mountains that marked the north of Herelstrom. Any day now...

The newly promoted, Corriian Grand Admiral Cherulia answered a rap on his cabin door. "Captain's compliments, Sir, multiple sail sighted to the north - looks like four ships."

Cherulia hastily threw on his cloak and clasped it tightly against the weather. He opened the door to the poop deck cabins and stepped out into the weather. It was a bleak day, and his cabin was much more comfortable. He was too old for this now. Better the younger men endure the harsh conditions on deck in this weather.

As he reached the deck above, he could see the officers gathered at the rail looking northward. "What do you make of it, captain?"

"The lookout says he thinks they are ours."

"Give me that glass, captain!" Cherulia scanned the horizon until he could make out the sails: two ahead and the tops of two more masts behind. Who were they? The supply convoys didn't need battleships as escort. Cherulia's mind ran through options. "Norrens! Could it be? Surely, he would not be so foolish! And the spies said that he was last seen taking refuge in Bernadia. How did he get here and what was he doing?"

Cherulia took up the spyglass again and stared long at the leading ship. "The Argamaro! Captain, we seem to have stumbled onto that renegade, Norrens. Signal the other ships to close formation! We have had a bit of luck. He won't escape us this time. I'll see that traitor kicking from a yard arm unless the masters have something worse in store for him. They may want to make such an example of the traitors that it will be remembered ...."

Bells rang and the Corriian southern battle fleet took up formation with seven ships in the front and four behind. Four additional ships tacked away to leeward to take up position to block the retreat of their quarry. Smaller ships of Admiral Cherulia's southern squadron were ordered to circle around the leeward side of the four oncoming battle-ships to take station to intercept them if they turned inshore and made a dash for safety.

Cherulia stood on the poop deck of his flagship. He had planned his strategy and deployed the pieces on the board. Now it was just a matter of watching the defeat and capture of the traitor Norrens and all that had gone over with him.

He watched as the rowing benches were filled, and the marines ran to their positions on the upper deck.

Cherulia gave orders not to use the new magical ballista bolts. They were the new secret weapon, and he did not need to reveal it. Two black-cowled priests stood by the ballista crews seemingly disappointed.

There was a hail from the masthead. "Deck ho! Signal from the Battleship Orcharhite!"

A young lieutenant picked a spyglass and read off the signal which he wrote on a wax slate that was kept by the signals box.

He handed the message to the captain who read it and paled. "Send: 'Confirm message!'"

"They are already re-sending sir – it is confirmed. They are asking for orders."

"Show this to the Admiral."

Cherulia had not moved in this time, but he had noted the concern on the usually stoic face of his captain. He waited until the lieutenant passed him the slate and then showed no immediate sign that it made the slightest difference.

"Lieutenant, send to the captains of the Orcharhite, Vendvora and Catavern: 'Engage with new enemy!'"

"But sir, they are outnumbered three to one by the Bernadian ships."

Cherulia seemed unmoved. "Captain, assign another officer to the signals: one who can obey orders!"

Another young officer stood before Cherulia and copied his orders onto the slate before rushing to the signal box where a young midshipman had already attached the flags.

The three battleships altered course a little to leeward and could be seen preparing for battle but now the new situation was evident to all: a line of large sails appeared on the horizon.

In a short time, they could be seen clearly, and their blue and yellow painted hulls gleamed in the morning sunlight.

As the Bernadian ships with a strong following wind bore down on them a line of vessels broke off and changed course as if they were trying to pass Cherulia's ships and then turned and tacked toward them again just as the king's ships from Herelstrom had done against them in previous battles when they discovered that the rudder and stern design of the Corriian naval vessels was weak.

Cherulia stroked his beard. "So, it is you behind this, is it Denquinar! All the better – now I will deal with you and Norrens together… Captain! Implement the strategy for attack from the rear! …And use the ballista bolts from the covens. We may have a fight on our hands."

Cherulia saw the face of the cowled man by the weapon and saw the smile. He nodded.

He smiled back. This day had portended nothing more than aimless patrolling – now he had a chance to make a name for himself that would be indelible in Corrii naval history for years to come. He looked ahead and saw the island that was called Lyre. The victor at the Battle of Lyre he mused – it had a nice ring to it. These foolish Bernadians had bitten off more than they could chew. He would see that some survived to take the tale back to their masters.

31

The Battle of Lyre

*A*dmiral Cherulia was doing the mental calculations – he was outnumbered but only just and he had some nasty surprises up his sleeve that would easily tip the ballance in his favor. He felt sure he could win this fight. Norrens and the traitors were first on his list to destroy or capture. Ah … capture now there was a pleasant thought….

He snapped orders and signal flags fluttered up the lanyards; high up the mast above the *Battleship Imrahall's* mizen sail.

He ordered the Orcharhite, Vendvora and Catavern to separate which would enable them to maneuver as much as possible to block the advance of the Bernadian ships and give him time to crush Norrens squadron.

The *Imrahall* and the other ships in his main force closed rapidly on the rebel ships.

Cherulia noticed that the former Corriian ships moved into a line and changed tack. What were they up to? Cherulia grabbed a glass and focused on the lead ship – Signal flags fluttered from the Argamaro's mast. A single purple triangle headed each string of signals, and the signals were completely different to the Corriian signals. Cherulia wondered….

He had heard from the coven spies that Denquinar had turned up in Bernadia. The purple triangle was Denquinar's old command sign as his was orange.

So maybe Denquinar had joined with the other defectors. That was a stroke of luck! He would get Norrens and Denquinar together.

Cherulia strode across the poop deck, down the steps and across the quarterdeck to the weapons officer and the coven-master who accompanied him. He spoke quietly to them and assured himself that there were plenty of the new ballista bolts ready.

He looked across at the *Battleship Overion* (the second of that name) and she was also making her torsion weapons ready. The *Overion* had a new rig that allowed her to use a trebuchet on her deck that could hurl a much heavier object further than was possible with a ballista. He could see a wire barrow being manhandled up the ramp to her forecastle where the weapon was being unlashed from its restraining mounts.

Cherulia could see seamen unlashing the crow ready for release as they came alongside the ships of their former countrymen. The crow was a long gang plank with a heavy iron beak (hence the name) that was hinged at the base of the mast and attached half-way up the main mast. When it was released, it fell across the deck of an enemy ship and punched through her decking timbers. Then armed soldiers could run across with the aid of a handrail and fight on the deck of their enemy with conventional heavy armor and weapons giving them a huge advantage over the sailors and lightly armed marines who avoided armor which was certain death if one fell overboard.

The crow would only be used if the battleship could come alongside their quarry; it was the coup de gras.

Cherulia could see all was ready for his orders and returned to the poop deck of the *Imrahall* to watch the battle unfold.

The *Arganmaro* fired the first shot of the action and a ballista bolt sheered *Imrahall's* foresail spar which crashed to the deck.

Cherulia ignored the screams of the injured men. He was used to blood; it did not bother him. It was a good first shot he mused. He set his mind on the big strategy as it unfolded.

After firing the Argamaro tacked expertly, and the big quinquereme came around onto a westerly tack immediately followed by the other three ships.

Denquinar stood next to Captain Verna and watched their battle plan unfold. As the ship came around and his view was not obscured but the huge sails, he could see the naval officer on the deck in silver trimmed leather armor. Denquinar had to control his emotions. There was the man who had consigned his own son to certain death on a whim. This would be the day, Cherulia. Today you would know that you have met your nemesis again. We will see how this day unfolds.

Verna stood by his shoulder. "We will lose speed Commodore, but we will not be so easily surrounded, and it will give the Bernadians time to come up. Admiral Cherulia would like nothing better than to cut us off and destroy us before the Bernadian ships can close."

"The rear ships are changing course to intercept. Cherulia will bring the front ships around onto us using oars. It will take too long. We will race these others toward the Bernadians and then tack across and see what damage we can do them before the main battle is joined. Then it will be every ship on its own."

"These four ships are attacking under oars and sail. They seem to be trying to get into range with ballista."

"Make it as hard for them as you can, captain. And if they come too close, we can try the maneuver the ships of Herelstrom used; attack their stern."

It was a slow process waiting for the ponderous quinqueremes to close. Several ballista bolts missed at the long range. The Corrian ships were rowing furiously trying to get into range. Denquinar thought this an odd strategy and tried to think through the possibilities. What was Cherulia up to? He could see black robed priests on the enemy desks. It had to be some evil they were brewing. It made no sense trying to fight an artillery battle in these choppy seas. There was a chance of some damage to sail and rigging but they could easily use oars to keep out of range of the crows and avoid grappling.

Denquinar was reluctant to use oars yet; men tired quickly at the oars, driving these big ships along at any speed was possible only for a short time before they needed to be rested.

The first of the Battleships was creeping into effective ballista range. Denquinar recognized her. She was the *Ilchorne*. he could not remember who had last commanded her.

Denquinar saw the ballista crew on her forecastle wind up the mounting screws to maximize the range. A bolt was loaded, and the smouldering projectile arced through the air toward them.

Denquinar tried not to flinch as the bolt thudded into the mast above him sheering a mizzen stay and sending a shower of wood splinters down onto the poop deck. From the canister fixed behind the head of the bolt came a brown tarry smoke. It poured out of the punctured head, down the mast and covered the deck. Denquinar heard the terrible shrieks that he had only once before heard when the Corriian coven people had used their dwimmerind spell against a king's ship who had rescued him out of the sea. His eyes were almost blinded to everything except the strange images. Somewhere, in the back of his mind he knew he had to do something. But couldn't think! A fire broke out on the desk, and he stumbled desperately forward trying to avoid the flames that licked along the deck and up into the rigging.

As if through a fog he saw Kiri. Every protective instinct he possessed pulled at him to drag Kiri to safety - maybe at the front of the ship – maybe into the ocean to escape the smoke. He grabbed his son's cloak, but Kiri pulled away and clambered onto the ratlines coughing from the smoke.

Denquinar saw that his son has a cloth over his face. That seemed important but he couldn't understand why.

A man ran into him clutching his eyes and yelling for aid. His clothing was on fire! Denquinar was knocked to the ground and quickly rolled over several times to put out the fire in his own cloak and then threw away the smoldering garment as he staggered to his feet. He looked up. Kiri was clinging to the ratlines and reaching full stretch for the shaft of the smoking ballista bolt. A final grab and he had hold of it and working it up and down wrenched it out of the mast. He coughed as he swung the thing over the side and watched it plunge tip first into the depths.

Men struggled to their feet coughing and gagging and wiping their streaming eyes.

Once his mind cleared, Denquinar saw that Kiri had his scarf that he had made for him for just this purpose over his face and remembered the Tom Roper defense against the dwimmerind spell: cover your face with a garment given to you by someone who loves you and the spell is neutralized.

Just at that moment Admiral Norrens shouted an order and they all looked up to see the Corriian quinquereme bearing down on them with her deadly ram dipping and crashing through the waves at her bows.

Verna snapped orders and the men at the tiller brought the *Argamaro* around just in time to avoid the huge double ram tearing a hole in her side. As it was the other ship swung around as well and her foremast crow smashed into their quarterdeck. Verna stood at the poop deck rail issuing orders and the greater way that the *Argamaro* had on her, enabled them to break away, but a massive hole was ripped in the decking before the crow fell back over her port side.

On board the *Vorsero* the situation was worse two bolts had landed on the deck and were pouring out their contents of acrid, magical smoke all over the decks.

Captain Vertori was on his knees trying not to breathe the smoke and not scream from the painful blindness. It was just then that a young cook's apprentice came up out of the hold with a cup of water mixed with sour fruit juice for the captain. He saw the ballista bolt protruding from the hatchway nearby and calmly pulled his shirt over his face, removed it from the panel and threw it over the side. Then unsure why others hadn't done the same he proceeded to throw another smoking bolt overboard.

Slowly the wind blew away the last wisps of the arcane smoke and men struggled to their feet.

Denquinar was close enough to the *Vorsero* to witness what the boy had done, and the pieces came together in his mind.

Both ships had been saved by mere boys - too young to know much fear and apparently much less affected by the magic of the coven masters' spells. He called to Kiri, "Run up this signal, 'The magic is only fear. Overcome the fear and it has no more power.'" Kiriarkanatus attached all the flags to the toggles and hauled on the signal ropes. Both Denquinar and his son watched the rope run cleanly through the pulley and run his signal up the mizzen mast of the *Argamaro*. The other battleships acknowledged and so did the leading Bernadian ship who transmitted the message.

Ponderously now, the big ships engaged. The wind seemed to die, and the melee continued with the big fighting platforms lumbering about under oars.

As one of the large Corriian battleships came alongside and released her crow, he and all the men on the Argamaro found themselves fighting for their lives. Men mad with battle lust ran across the crow that held the two ships in a grapple. Others swung across on ropes and hacked at the defenders with razor sharp scimitars and boarding axes.

Denquinar was grateful that as a young midshipman he had been taught hand to hand fighting by a couple of old ship's masters. One was a carpenter and the other a sail maker, both survivors of countless sea fights.

They had practiced with Denquinar in the long night watches and he as a young midshipman, had decided he would learn all the tricks he could. Now as he parried and kicked a barrel at two approaching seamen, he was glad of those days, but it seemed they were likely to be overwhelmed anyway. The Argamaro's crew and the remaining men from Herelstrom were being driven back by the superior numbers of seamen and marines led by heavily armed marine soldiers. As Denquinar looked around he saw the *Imrahall* bearing down on them. He could see the huge steel tipped ram as she rose on a wave and was sure they were finished. But then the *Imrahall's* huge bows came around and he saw she was trying to grapple on the opposite side. If she succeeded, it would soon be over, and the *Argamaro* would be captured before the Bernadians even got close enough to help.

Denquinar could see Cherulia on the deck. He fancied he could see the look of satisfaction on his face as he issued his orders and the *Imrahall* shipped her oars to slide alongside the hapless *Argamaro*.

Denquinar cast around desperately for something he could do to change the tide that was running hard against them. His racing mind hit on a hopelessly impossible solution.

He yelled onto the breeze with all the voice he could muster, "Yo Ibinithy, Yo Ho Ho

Nothing happened and the *Imrahall* glided closerer; her captain making slight adjustments with sail and tiller now that he could not maneuver using oars.

Denquinar could see the face of his nemesis clearly now. Cherulia even seemed to have spotted Kiri standing at his post by the signal box as men fought and died all around them. A smile of derision crept across his face as he savored much delayed demise of the former grand admiral.

As he watched Denquirar's expression must have turned to one of amazement as a huge purple head rose twenty cubits out of the water just off the stern of the *Imrahall*.

The great tooth-lined maw opened in a chuckle. "Ho, friend Denquinar. I see you have very kindly brought me a snack - nothing nicer than a grand admiral as a mid-afternoon morsel."

Admiral Cherulia whirled around in horror at the nightmare that peered down at him. Frozen with fear or else transfixed by the stare from the huge eyes he stood rooted to the deck.

The ibinithy's great neck plunged down and the jaws closed. Cherulia was lifted off the deck with only his lower half protruding from the sea monster's mouth. The jaws closed shut and the admiral disappeared down the huge gullet.

Men on the *Imrahall's* poop deck scattered, terrified, and the big Quinquereme slewed off its course.

The ibinithy swam effortlessly up to the side of the *Argamaro*. Denquinar grabbed a stay and stood on the railing to speak with the creature. He knew now from several encounters that the ibinithy enjoyed banter and distained fear.

"Ho, Ibinithy, I hope you will not develop a taste for admiral. I may yet achieve that rank with my new country."

"Fear not Denquinar. Admirals are juicy enough, but the medals do tend to get caught in one's teeth. I see I came just in time. I felt disturbance in the waters and heard the movement of many large ships. 'That will be a battle about to happen' I said to myself and swam underneath to see what was happening. As I put my head above the water to have a closer look, I heard you cry out."

As they were speaking a ballista bolt from a Corriian Quatrareme whirred past the sea monster narrowly missing its target.

The ibibnithy looked around surprised by the audacity. "I will continue to play my part as I can, friend Denquinar" and the ibinithy disappeared under the waves.

The Battle of Lyre raged for the rest of the day. Admiral con Vortez threw his ships into the fray, but they were bigger and slower than the Corriian ships and struggled to bring them to battle.

There were vicious exchanges. Most of all the Corriian ships seemed determined to destroy Admiral Norrens and his men. The ships were all of a similar size and capability except for the magic ballista bolts. There were many times when ships crashed side to side and men surged across the decks and swung across on ropes to engage in bloody fighting. Once it came to hand to hand battle the defectors and the men from the southern end fought desperately and drove back the Corrii every time but with heavy losses.

In one encounter the *Argamaro* battled the Corriian battleship *Vendvora* until late in the afternoon. The sailors on the *Vendvora* had fired grapnels into the *Argamaro's* side planking and winched the two ships together until they were side to side. Heavily armed marines and sailors with an eclectic assortment of evil looking weapons surged over the side of the *Argamaro* to meet a grim group of defenders. Men of both ships battled and hacked at each other in close quarter combat until all were killed or could hardly raise their weapons for another stroke. The two ships then drifted apart and stood off as if in shock, at the horror of the encounter.

The evening brought a standoff. The Corriian ships had maneuvered closer to one another for protection to leeward of their enemies. Many ships had been rammed and sunk. Others had so many losses that further battle was all but impossible with insufficient men to row the ships and barely enough sailors left to work the ships at sail.

At nightfall they could be seen sailing back south with minimal sail.

Denquinar asked Verna to bring the Argamaro into hailing distance of the Margarita so that he could hail con Vortez.

As the wind dropped con Vortez stood by the railing and hailed him. "What now Denquinar! We haven't won yet. What next?"

"Admiral, I think we put up navigation lights and remain together tonight. We have no fight left in us. Then tomorrow we sail for Pinitera to get help for the wounded and determine the progress of the war."

That night a meeting of the captains aboard the *Margarita* decided on their tactics and options. Denquinar and was keen to sail straight to Cair Neren as all the intelligence they had suggested this was the main point of the Corri attack. In the end they decided it was foolhardy to sail south without information and Pinitera was the first port suitable for so large a naval force. There was also a good chance that the capital was still holding out, but no one knew about Cair Neren.

32

Home Fires

An elderly man in a green cloak was led into the map room of the palace in Pinitera. He wore a three-quarter length sword and a leather jerkin. He was unshaved and dusty from a long journey.

He bowed to the king who was alone contemplating his map of the country. The king turned and extended a hand. "Baeri, they found you; I am glad you are here. How goes it with our secret allies?"

"… Perhaps not so secret as they were but we have taken all possible steps to keep your nephew's men from telling the whole country what they know. As you know the driadora have great skill in slipping away silently into the trees and leaving no sign other than a dim memory."

"It is better that as few of our countrymen as possible know of their existence but if we survive this war many things will be different."

"We have to survive it yet, Sire."

"Yes indeed. You will not have heard yet, but your son has returned with his friend and Tom Roper, and they have brought naval forces from Bernadia."

Baeri's tired old face broke into an instant smile. "Have you seen Norri?"

"No but he went south to the southern end by sea to try and relieve your home from occupation by the Corrii. Apparently, they have all had an interesting time and played a much bigger role in the affairs of the world than either of us. He made it to Bernadia and returned with part of their fleet – to help us in our fight. Their naval assets will change our situation and give us an immediate advantage at sea."

"I look forward to seeing him and hearing his story. It is wonderful news that they are alive."

"Do you know anything of the whereabouts of their wives?"

"Yes, Tom and Norri's wives are safe and protected by the driadora deep in the forest. The other girl, Gordy's wife was killed by grimulves."

"How do our secret allies fare; what is their strength?"

"They are struggling as we are. They have had heavy losses to the wyverns and the wulves and they have lost children which is a terrible thing for them. There are very few children born to driadora women even though they generally live longer than our people.

They still have several arborites with reasonable strength, enough to make the Corrii pay if they venture too far into the forest."

"Mmm. As I said, the Bernadians have sent ships and some marine soldiers, but we still have a Corriian army camped around Cair Neren that outnumbers all of our forces many times. Our best hope is to try and disrupt their supply and communications and make them think we are stronger than we are. Your attacks with Tillion and the driadora have helped. We want them to think they are surrounded by enemies on every front.

If your son and Tom succeed even in weakening the hold of the Corrii in the southern end it will be a help a great deal.

Can you get a message quickly to our friends in the forest to help them at all?"

"I can ride south to Tillion's secret camp in the forest and then go south on foot to make contact with 'our friends'. I will see how it is with them, but I am sure they will help in whatever ways they can. They fear the 'tree killers' as they call them. They will also want the southern end rid of the Corrii."

"Go south then, Baeri, but wait and listen to the reports of the navy men so you have the best information to report."

"Yes, your Majesty."

The two ships approached the beach south of the bay at Greyton. They were using oars, and these were muffled. The progress was necessarily slow, and Gordy sat next to Tom and Norri. He fished out a small parcel from the inside of his shirt.

"What have you got there, Gordy?"

"I sneaked out and bought these for Jenny in Bertola. They were a little skeptical about my money but decided that silver was silver."

Norri suddenly felt bad. It had never occurred to him to buy anything for Kirin. "That was well thought of Gordy. I didn't even think of that. What did you get her?"

"These combs made from tortoiseshell and a clip for her cloak made from a seashell. Pretty thing, isn't it?"

Norri looked at the beautiful clip. "I think we had better go back, Tom. We'll be in trouble when Jenny shows off these to our wives."

Gordy smiled now quite proud of his little forethought, "I'll tell the captain to bring her about, shall I?"

Tom gazed at the dark shoreline. "I'm all right. I can plead injury – it's Norri that's in real trouble. He has no excuse. He has been to the other end of the world and was too busy hobnobbing with Bernadian royalty to pick out a nice gift for his wife...."

Norri smiled and thought it would be time to worry about presents when he found her safe. They crept closer to shore. The boats were already being towed astern ready to put ashore the landing party. This was a first reconnoiter. The *Swiftsure* and her sister ship would stand out to sea again and come back tomorrow night and the night after further down the coast to pick them up if they failed to make the first rendezvous.

Tom knew these waters and guided the boats into a little rocky cove well south of Greyton. The two boats ground their keels against the gravel in the shore break and they jumped ashore. The boat crews shoved off immediately and Tom, Norri and Gordy and their party began to climb up the headland under cover of the dense scrub and rocky outcrops. The top of the bluff was wooded and Tom thought this would give them a chance to get well clear of the coast without having to cross any open ground. This proved to be true and the first sign of civilization they came across was only a path used for fishermen's carts and it didn't look like it had been used for a long time.

They crossed this path and struck out uphill. They hoped to be able to circle around through the forest and see what had happened to the town that had been their home. But Tom wanted to check on Greyton first. They came to the small town from the north and looked out at the buildings from the forest. All was in darkness and there was no sign of life at all. They risked leaving the trees for a little and came up closer to the town. There was a vile smell coming from the buildings that they soon saw had been burnt and mostly destroyed.

The small kirk in Greyton was just a shell. The roof was caved in, and the beams were charred and blackened. Amongst the debris; even at this distance bones could be seen - small bones. Tom guessed at the horror of what must have occurred there, and it made him want to retch. The urgency of finding out what had happened to his son and Lettie grew and he began to feel desperate.

"This is a terrible place. Let's get away from here and find out how strong the Corrii are in the Southern End. If they are not many – God help them they will pay for this abomination."

As they walked back up toward the forest, they heard a dog bark. A small dog yapped and growled at them from the doorway of a burnt-out cottage. Gordy took a few steps toward it and bent down, holding out his hand.

Surprisingly the small dog came toward him and sniffed his hand. He was dirty and bedraggled, but he seemed to sense that Gordy was not a threat. Tom urged them to head for cover and the dog followed quietly.

"Finding a friend in this mess is well and good, Gordy as long as he doesn't give us away."

They climbed back to the relative protection of the forest and were only barely under cover when their new-found friend growled and ran for cover under a large fallen trunk. They peered out from among the trees and saw movement on the edge of the forest.

They slipped back into the trees and watched. Two big grey shapes were moving along the edge of the forest with stealth.

Tom hadn't had as much to do with grimulves as Norri and he looked to his friend. "Do we hide or fight?"

Norri whispered back as he shrunk against the trunk of a big tree. "I wish I had a rope, and we could get into one of these trees. I am worried that Gordy's little friend might give us away as well."

"There are seven of us and we have our bows. We should be a match for just two grimulves."

"The danger is, Tom that one gets away and raises the alarm. If it comes to a fight, we have to make sure we kill them both quickly and they are hard to kill."

"We had better hide first; then and see if they pass us by. Do you think they are patrolling or hunting?"

"Hard to tell and I don't want to stumble into them on our way back either."

They went deeper into the forest and found a thicket where they could still see the edge of the trees and kept still. Gordy's little dog turned out to be intelligent enough to read the situation. He followed them and slunk into a cleft of a tree and was silent.

Norri looked at the little patch of hair and the little black snout protruding from the hiding place. "He may be an asset after all. If he can warn us of approaching grimulves he will be well worth his rations."

Tom looked back at the dog and saw a slight elevation of the eyebrow at the mention of rations. "Poor little thing. Looks half starved!"

Then they hunkered down into their hiding place and watched. It seemed to take a long time for the two brutes to get to their part of the forest. When they did, they could tell without looking. There was a fear that the grimulves engendered wherever they went preceded them and lingered after they were gone. Tom found his hand shaking on the bowstring. He also felt an unexpected urge to draw and shoot but guessed this was part of the fear. It would have given away their hiding place immediately. If they had to fight these two monsters, they should gain all the advantage they could. Norri was right. If one got away they would be hunted down.

Tom shrunk back into the shadows and waited. They could hear muttering as the grimulves spoke to one another, if you could call it speaking – sort of a combination of speech and growls.

The two creatures seemed ill at ease and stopped in the lee of the forest for what seemed a long time then loped away down the hill toward the burnt village.

When they dared to breathe again Tom said what they all thought. "Enemies behind and in front now, let's get moving."

They veered into the forest for some distance and then turned northward. When they felt they were safely away from the grimulves they stopped and had a sip of water a morsel of bread and a piece of cheese. Gordy gave the dog a strip of dried, salted meat which Jimmy (Gordy decided he needed a name) devoured eagerly. Gordy also gave him a little water in a pan.

"Jimmy will be useful in the forest. He will scent any grimulves before we ever see or hear them."

A full day's march north brought them to the forest east of the new castle. They cautiously approached the edge of the forest and found that it was much nearer than they expected. They heard the sound of axes against wood before they saw anything as they watched from a darker patch of forest, they could see groups of men shackled and working in teams - cutting down trees.

There were numerous logs lying were they fell. Some were partly stripped of branches, but most seemed to be just lying about wantonly destroyed.

Norri thought that this was the payback to the driadora. The Corrii knew the people who had defeated them at the Battle of Cair Neren had come out of the trees. Now they were hitting back out of pure vindictiveness.

The guards were not too numerous; probably because the prisoners were all chained at the ankles, so they had little trouble circling around and approaching the hill of Beckwood Brae under some cover. What they saw horrified them even though they had been steeling themselves for what they might see.

The hill was covered with tracks and rough wooden compounds. There seemed to be activity everywhere. Groups of people being led about on various tasks walked with heads bowed and broken spirits.

At the top of the hill were tall poles with people strung up by their wrists; dead they thought until they heard a faint moan from one of the sufferers and realized to their horror that it was a woman.

Norri began to move forward but Tom grabbed his arm. We cannot attack a whole garrison by ourselves!"

"But what can we do, Tom. Some of those people they are torturing to death will die. We are too far away to see who they are. They could even be...."

"We need more men. Then we can possibly take the garrison by surprise."

"That will take at least a day. By then these people will be dead. Some of the poor souls look like they are already."

Gordy slipped on his pack. "The best chance is to make the rendez-vous tonight and bring as many of our people as we can to attack the garrison. I will take Framos and Giles and meet with the ships. If you want to try and free the people strung up on the poles. They don't seem to be guarded."

Tom nodded and watched as Gordy and the others set off through the trees with little Jimmy scampering along beside his new master. "Gordy has really taken a shine to that little fellow."

Norri watched them disappearing into the gloom of the forest. "It seems to be mutual."

Tom smiled. "Gordy would no doubt say that he only likes him because he gives him food."

"Speaking of food, we may as well settle down until it is as dark as it is likely to get."

Samuels who was sitting next to Tom has been staring through a gap in the trees. "There is a new moon."

When the night was at its darkest, they got up and moved forward. They moved along the edge of the trees. Everything looked different to Norri because of the mass clearing of the trees. It seemed so insane, as if great trees had been cut down just to keep men occupied. Norri thought wistfully that some of these trees were the very same that had stood when his great, great, great grandfather had won the battle of Beckwood Brae near this very spot.

There was a whistle from a tree above them.

They froze and searched the trees for some sign of persuit. There was a rustling sound in the branches of a nearby orkya tree and a rope dropped to the ground. Norri guessed who it was from the way the man slid down the rope.

He took a couple of steps toward the figure and whispered. "Father! What are you doing here?" I am trying to help whoever I can, while you are away getting a Bernadian army to help us. Where are they by the way?" Then he saw who was standing behind Norri. "Tom! Is that you? What are you doing here? I know someone who will be very, very glad to see you alive and not in enemy hands."

Tom grabbed Baeri's arms. "Lettie and Dillon! Are they safe?"

"Yes, and Kirin, Norri. They are being helped by the driadora. They have built a camp for refuge far on the other side of the forest."

Norri hugged his father. "That is the best news."

They had a very tough time escaping and many have been lost. Gordy is not with you?"

"Yes, he is. He has gone back to make the rendezvous with our ships and bring up the people so we can attempt to free these captives."

"I am afraid that Jenny has been killed by Grimulves; helping Kirin to get Lettie to a safe place."

Norri went pale as he thought of the shock this would be to his friend. "You will have to tell me the details when you have a chance. For now, we were thinking of going to help those poor souls tied to the poles."

"That was also our plan. I have just come south with the driadora because their reports were that the Corrii here were carrying out worse atrocities. Here is someone you know."

Lefgild stepped silently out from behind a tree. "Good to see you, old friend."

Norri and Lefgild embraced. Tom looked amazed. The young man was obviously a seasoned warrior and leader.

Lefgild noticed the amazed expressions of Samuels and Tom. "It has not been possible for us to keep entirely hidden any longer. I have convinced our king that we must fight as we can with your people, but we will remain elusive and will fiercely protect our lands in the future from any that threaten them. For now, the largest threat is the Corrii." He indicated the tracts of fallen trees piled high on the edge of the forest.

"For now, if you wish to make an attempt to save those hanging from the poles, we will cover your rear, and none will pass the edge of the forest."

Norri nodded. "Well, we had better make the attempt then. Come along Tom. Father would you and Samuels try those on the right we will see if we can help those in front. Lefgild, will you have you enough warriors if the guard is raised?"

"Yes, enough for the guards in the hilltop compound. Not sufficient if the whole garrison is aroused. We estimate they have almost a thousand. There seemed to be more originally, but they have marched north to join the attack at Cair Neren. I can say with some pride that most of them did not reach their companions. Were it not for the Gordril and the grimulves not even that many would have survived."

Norri looked out at the lands that were his home. There were fires glowing in dozens of compounds made from the felled trees. "...Not the home fires I had hoped to return to.

Come on Tom lets see what we can do."

They crept on hands and knees across the top of the hill staying behind whatever cover of felled tree trunks and rubble was available. There were no guards to be seen.

The girl that they had heard moan was silent. They felt horrible that she might have died while they waited for nightfall.

They saw that she was tied at the wrists and a rope suspended her wrists from a pulley at the top of the pole. The rope was tied off to a stake. Norri untied the half hitches that secured the rope and paid out some of the bite.

As the rope slowly paid out the girl moaned softly, and Norri quickly paid out more rope and Tom grabbed her legs to take the weight of her body and lay her on the ground.

Norri lifted up her head and wiped away her hair from her face and suppressed a gasp. "Janina!" But there was no response. Norri could see that her lips were dry and cracked. "Tom some water!" Norri held the water bottle to Janina's lips and wet them enough for her to take a sip.

Tom looked around. "Your Father is shaking his head. The person on the far pole must be dead. They can check the others. Let's get Janina back to the cover of the forest."

I'll carry her the first part, if you can take her the rest. Tom lifted Janina over his shoulders and crouched down as he carried her toward the forest. It was a long run with the dead weight of the girl on his shoulders and Norri took her the last part into the forest. When they reached the relative safety of the trees, they lowered her down.

Norri cradled her in his arms again and offered the girl a little more water. She was barely able to move but desperate for some water and was able to lean forward to take a couple of sips.

She looked at the faces of her rescuers. "Norri…"

"Yes, Janina it's me."

"Why did they do this to you?"

"It was Tribune Baubachus. I complained that they were working the little kids to death dragging logs down from the hill. They were exhausted and their hands were bleeding from the ropes. When I said he was a monster he ordered me taken to the poles."

"You are safe now. We will get you safe into the trees."

Lefgild looked down at Janina. "She cannot walk. I have made a stretcher. It'll be a bit rough, but we can carry her further into the forest to a place where we can hide."

Baeri and Samuels came back across the cleared section. Baeri looked at Janina. "How is she?"

"Alive Father. We are taking her deeper into the forest. How are the others?"

"All beyond our help, I'm afraid. One of them was Sanders. Do you remember him?"

"Yes. I never liked him much but didn't wish him this end."

Janina looked toward Norri. "He struck a guard. It was very foolish but very brave."

Baeri looked at her. "Do you think there is a will to resist among the captives?"

"If they think there is a chance, they will end up hanging from a pole until they die, no. If they think they can win I think there is a chance they will turn against Baubachus."

Baeri looked out into the empty night. "The trouble is that now we have rescued you the garrison will be doubly on guard. They will be more than ready when Gordy returns with reinforcements."

33

Stalemate

*G*eneral Groeballas sat in a comfortable room in what had been the bailiff's home at Neren Keys. The wine store had been supplemented by additional stocks from the storehouses by the wharves.

"The campaign depends on supply by sea Cerios, and the Bernadians know it. I am stuck here like a shag on a rock. I can send out troops to forage but crops have been gathered or destroyed for a long way north and the king of this confounded country is holed up in his capital with plenty of grain and food stored up while we run the risk of starving here and the castle is not even taken.

"Baubachus is doing well in the south – using slaves to sow and reap the crops and vegetables. But they are very isolated down there."

"They barely grow enough food for themselves and their slaves. They cannot do much to help us."

"I have a report saying their grain crops are nearly ready and they should be able to send us some extra supplies. I think he is enjoying making life bad for the people who destroyed his interdiction force in the last invasion. He is driving them mercilessly and he says they have actually increased the areas under cultivation by half again. They have potatoes, beans, and cheese stored up already."

"It may help. The navy is contained here in the Neren River with the Bernadians and that renegade Norrens blocking the way north. But we will not have enough ships to evacuate the legions out of here unless they can smash the Bernadian fleet and bring down transports from Orsimater. And if we risk a naval battle and lose, we will be here till we run out of food and the men are too weak to fight. Then even the garrison here in the castle will be a handful. Cheese, eh? It would go nicely with this excellent wine." Groeballas took a sip and swilled it over his educated palate.

"... and we have those confounded raids from the people of the forest who have now shown their hand."

"The worst of that is that we have no real idea how many there are. For all we know we may already be outnumbered."

"The king of Herelstrom will want to relieve the castle here. His brother has been stuck there for a couple of months now and things will be getting tough in there. They will have lots of wounded after our constant attacks and even if they have enough food and water, they will have had it with being cooped up in that place."

"I think you are right, Cerios. I think it will come to a head soon but what will break the stalemate who can tell. Help yourself to some wine, Cerios. And we will write some orders for Baubachus to send some supplies north as soon as possible. I don't care a whit if he flogs the backs off his slaves to produce food and get it up here. We have a war to win, and I cannot do it without food for my men."

Cerios took a sheet of their precious supply of linen paper and began to address the orders. "The battle of Lyre has presented us with many problems."

"It is a good thing that Cherulia was killed; after losing a battle to an equal force and putting me in this spot...."

"Eaten..."

"What?"

"Eaten. The ships that put into the river sent a report." Cerios took up the paper. "They say that a sea monster appeared and ate him."

"... Ate him?"

"Yes; in one bite apparently."

"Are the reports reliable? It isn't just some silly sailors' fable?"

"No. An officer on the *Margarita* saw it and made a report. He sounds like a sensible senior officer."

"Idiot! It's just like Cherulia to go and get himself eaten when we need him to win a battle."

"I don't think he exactly planned it, sir."

"No. I suppose not. This wretched place is against us, Cerios. Even the sea creatures are dining out on our admirals."

"It was an ibinithy apparently."

"I thought the ibinithy was just a legend."

"Cherulia probably did too. It appears you were both wrong, sir."

"More of an issue for him than for me."

"Not any more sir."

"True. Who is now in command of the naval squadron?"

"Third Admiral Verkamah, sir. I have his report already."

"Why does he say he disengaged?"

"He says in his report, that they had lost too many ships sunk by ramming or captured. Apparently the rescued Herelstrom prisoners fought like demons alongside the traitor Norrens' men. It was do or die for all of them, of course.

He says he decided we would need his ships intact much more than an indecisive victory which in his opinion was the best possible outcome. He doesn't say so of course but a complete defeat was a more likely outcome by the sound of it."

"He was right; the loss of all the ships would have been disastrous for the campaign. We would have no escorts for transports or supply ships. I hope for his sake that they take that view in Corrimar. Those fools can't think beyond death and glory charges whether they advance the course of a war or not.

This Vermakah sounds like a good man. Send orders to bring him here for a strategy meeting. I need to know what his squadron is really capable of; not meaningless political speak."

"I'll issue the orders, sir."

Cerios took a last sip of his wine and grabbed a piece of the local cheese as he left.

Groeballas picked up his cup. "Eaten! Amazing; the poor thing will probably get indigestion. ...Always said Cherulia was a bit sour." Baubachus smiled at his own joke and leant back in his chair."

Tribune Baubachus was having his second sip of the local coffee. He was acquiring a taste for it. He would enjoy being ruler of this remote province. There was excellent food, and *he* was in command. Everyone would do anything he said, and there were the women. They would be even more compliant now they had seen the way he dealt with that girl yesterday.

He heard shouts from up on the top compound. It was about the time to roust the workers for more tree felling. Perhaps they had to make an example of another worker.

He put down his coffee and went outside. His own stockade was the largest with a two-story, wooden huts for his men, and a parade ground in the centre. They had made themselves comfortable. There was a group of men around a trivet and pot brewing coffee to have with their bread for breakfast. They were also standing and looking in the direction of the upper stockade and listening to the shouts.

Baubachus wasn't too worried, but it was always better to be sure than sorry. Grab some weapons you men and find out what is the matter up there.

His men grabbed for weapons and unbolted the main gate. Baubachus saw a centurian who had also come to investigate. "Get your men armed, Flotius and send a patrol to the upper compound. It sounds like there is some trouble up there. Even if it is just Soronius and his men *keeping order* it is still good for the slaves to be reminded of who is in charge and that we have the power to ensure that we remain so."

"Yes, Tribune!" The old battle-scarred centurion snapped his fist to his chest in salute and went to the door next to his own to issue the orders. In minutes a line of legionaries was trotting out the gate and heading for the upper compound with shields and lances. They did not take time to put on their full armor. This was unlikely to take long or be much of a problem.

Flotius formed up a larger group to make a real show of force and as soon as they were ready on the parade ground, led them out the gate and up the hill.

Baubachus ordered his other tribune to prepare the rest of the garrison against any contingency and rouse the men in the other compounds.

Gordy saw the legionaries coming up the hill. He gave orders and hid a group of his men behind a wall out of sight. When the soldiers entered the open gate of the upper enclosure and saw the fallen guards and armed slaves they faltered, aghast. Before they could turn back to warn their tribune, they were hit with a hail of arrows at close range. They had no armor to protect them against arrows and all fell where they stood.

By the time Flotius was halfway up the hill the freed slaves had been armed and Gordy had a large force of men ready to overwhelm the garrison.

Flotius wasn't anyone's fool though and guessed from the unexpected silence that all was not right. He approached with great care and soon saw the dead legionaries. Gordy silently kicked himself for not having them removed immediately. Now the Corrii were ready it would get harder from here in.

Gordy ordered the archers to shoot at the legionaries who immediately formed into tight ranks with spearmen in front and bowmen behind and began a steady retreat down the hill to their defendable compound. Gordy and his men followed the legionaries down the hill and shot a good many in the retreat.

Baubachus was now fully aware of the threat and opened the gate of the compound enough to bring the remainder of his men inside.

Gordy's ire burned with a fire that could not be quenched; he quickly set fire to huge balls of woven oil-soaked branches they had prepared in the night.

The balls rolled down the hill setting fires to grass and wooden structures as they went.

Some rolled past the fort but five crashed up against the walls and the timber structure caught fire. It was not long before the fort would be useless. The gates opened and Baubachus' men came streaming out. They formed a knot of soldiers and held their shields up against the hail of arrows the southern enders loosed against them. They retreated toward the old town. Baubachus was looking for defensive options when he saw three Corriian galleys in the river. He heaved a sigh of relief. This meant reinforcements from the north. What excellent timing by Groeballas!

He called for horses and he and Flotius rode down to the river.

By the time he reached the bottom of the hill boats were being pulled up onto the bank and it was then that Baubachus realized his mistake. These ships were full of men from Herelstrom; instead of reinforcements he got arrows and the two officers rode back up the hill as fast as their mounts could carry them.

The men from the Ships were well armed and had a favor to return and the freed slaves that were backing them up were eager to take such revenge on their tormentors that it would become a byword.

Gordy had charged down the hill and led his men into the ranks of legionaries with a fury that even he didn't know he possessed. He cut and hacked the men in front of him until the lines of grim legionaries broke and the Corrii were beaten into small groups, fighting for their lives.

Then instead of the red-hot fury his mood cooled into a disciplined ruthlessness. He ordered the bowmen to shoot into the tight knots of Corriian legionaries to break them up and kill as many as possible without physical blows. Then his men hurled javelins into the groups before charging in to finish off the remaining soldiers. It was clinical and brutal.

Unable to get back to his men and realizing they were beaten, Baubachus rode to the southern stockade where they had some horses, they grazed on the fields to the south of the old town of Egleton. The garrison was already on alert. When the tribune arrived, he saw immediately that there were too many men in this southern garrison to escape in the one ship they had available so he and Flotius reined in their horses and approached casually so as not to make the men alarmed. He had a quiet discussion with the garrison commander and with a handful of men they all rode to the bay at Greyton where the ship rode quietly at anchor. They took boats and rowed out to her. There was an instant flurry of activity as anchor was weighed and the twin sails were hoisted.

Reynolds who was on the poop deck of the Swiftsure saw activity around a small dhow tied up in the bay and gave orders for the Swiftsure to give chase. The smaller ship was quicker however and made better speed out the entrance of the bay. Reynolds was still able to position his ship to windward so they could cut her off if she tried to turn north.

The dhow turned south instead and Tribune Baubachus on her stern could look back at the ship pursuing them and the smoke rising over the town where he has lost - yet another command.

A centurian and two mounted legionaries came out of a forested part of the road near Thornton bearing orders to Baubachus from his commander in the north. Coming toward them up the coast road was a column of spearmen and archers led by a couple of men on horseback. They were clearly men of Herelstrom and the fact that they were marching north toward Thornton could only mean that the southern garrison had fallen, and these were going north to relieve the small village of Thornton as well. They turned and spurred their horses back through the forest road. A couple of the mounted soldiers who the centurian took for officers gave chase and they saw a couple more mounted men who were probably scouts riding along the edge of the forest call out and join the chase.

They drove their horses into a lather until the sound of pursuit died away and they assumed they had escaped. When the centurian could draw breath, he dismounted and led them into the trees. "The south has fallen. We must assume some of the ships that came with the Bernadians have landed and defeated or surrounded our garrisons. We must get news to General Groeballas. We will separate into two groups. One group at least must get through.

I will take Trentorian and ride slower through the forest about fifty paces from the road. You two take the road and go as quickly as you can to the general with news that we have seen soldiers of Herelstrom coming north from the direction of our garrison."

That afternoon the centurian was struck by an arrow from an unseen archer. His companion rode behind a tree to hide but moments later was also hit and fell from his horse, dead.

Late the next day two messengers were ushered into the office of General Groeballas to report that they believed their garrison in the southern end had fallen.

Groeballas examined a map that Cerios had laid out. "They are about a week away if they come north in force."

"We do not know how many they are, Sir. They cannot have brought all that many men by ship this far."

"We can assume they have freed the captives and armed them – probably with weapons taken from our troops who have fallen."

"Perhaps we can assume only a thousand at the most, even with some of the slaves armed. Baubachus was keeping the slaves intention-ally underfed and surely, they cannot be up to a march north to take on our army. They were probably only marching north to re-take this village, (Cerios indicated a spot on the map - on a promontory, north of Newcastle) here."

"You are probably right. But it is one more group of enemies where we had been counting on support and supplies. Food is going to be a bad business unless we can crush the defenders of the castle here at the river mouth and plunder their supplies."

"Perhaps that should be our goal for now. It buys us some time and hurts our enemies."

"Sounds easy! Haven't we been trying to take it ever since we got here?"

"Yes, but maybe there is a useful development on that front." Cerios was scanning a note on a wax tablet from one of his duty officers. "There seems to have been a development. In routine torturing of prisoners, it seems that one has offered a piece of information in return for keeping his skin whole."

"What have they got?"

"There seems to be a secret entrance to Cair Neren Castle from a cave somewhere along the cliffs. Apparently, their king used it to enter the castle in the last campaign."

"It may have been filled in by now. They have renovated the whole castle between the last war and now – surely, they would not have left a secret entrance for a future invader to find?"

"You may be right sir, but it cannot hurt to go and have a look."

"Yes, why not? Arrange some of our sappers to search the cliff to see if there is any cave that looks promising – even if we can dig though...."

34

The Dark Forest

*B*aeri had left three days before with a large group of refugees who wished to get back to Newcastle as quickly as they could. Many had friends or family who had been slaves of the Corrii, and they were eager to return to see their homes and if possible, find their loved ones.

Norri and Tom stayed in the makeshift camp. They were tired after months of travel and wanted to rest and spend time with Kirin and Lettie. The little temporary refugee camp was on the edge of a sparkling stream with water blue and cold as it splashed and gurgled over the stones on its way down out of the mountains.

It was full of hungry trout which Mort had taken to catching for their evening meal. He always got great plaudits when he returned to camp with his catch, and it didn't take Tom and Norri too much convincing to join him in his daily forays. Kirin commented that they were like three boys and smiled at them as they walked off with their fishing poles.

They had comfortable huts – partly built with the help of the driadora and warm fires to sit around at night telling the many stories of all their travels and adventures since they were parted.

Norri was very impressed with the part little Mort had played in their escape. When he walked into the clearing with Baeri four days earlier and Kirin jumped to her feet in excitement, he had noticed the reticent smile on Mort's face and immediately recognized him as the little boy that had been the source of the altercation in the main street of Newcastle; now it seemed like an age ago.

But pleasant as it was in their little camp; drinking in the wonder and excitement of being with Kirin and Lettie again, Tom and Norri began to feel the need to return to Newcastle and join in the efforts to restore the city. There was also the small matter of an occupying army that had to be dealt with.

No-one would have blamed them if they refused to join the forces that must eventually march north to join the fight against the main Corrii force at Cair Neren. They had done much already but both men felt responsibile. Maybe it came from the positions and titles they had received from the king. Maybe it was that because men would follow them, they felt that they must lead; whatever it was, they both got up one morning and felt they must get back.

Both Kirin and Lettie knew this time had to come and agreed to prepare for the journey. It wasn't as if they had many possessions to pack. It was just collecting a bit of food to help them along the way. They hoped to find some food in the forest as they went along. It was three days journey back to Newcastle on the other side of the forest, if they managed to go the straightest way.

That evening when all were asleep Norri climbed a large orkya tree a little way away from their camp. He didn't know why that particular tree – it just seemed to be the right one.

When he reached the uppermost boughs, he saw two familiar faces looking down at him. He clambered up the last couple of branches and sat on a large lateral branch.

"Mother, Lefgild, I somehow thought I would find you two here. Is there any news?"

The arborite leader reached out his hand to clasp that of his friend. "None that we know; the Corriian army has moved little – it remains encamped around the fortress at the Neren River and the forces around your town in the south have all surrendered or been killed."

"Tom and I feel that we should return to our own town and see how things stand with the people there. The rebuilding task will be huge."

"My scouts say that much has been done already. The townsfolk have begun cleaning up. Much more I cannot tell you."

"We already know that many have died during the occupation and the deportation. There may be enough accommodation for any that need it. Tom and I hope to find somewhere to shelter our families anyway."

"When will you leave?"

"As soon as we have gathered some provisions. Kirin and Lettie have smoked some of the trout we have caught, and we can gather some nuts as we go."

Isherri indicated a pile of leaf-wrapped packages on the branch beside her, "I and a couple of warriors have been assigned to guard the camp. Since you are the only people left, we will shadow your progress through the forest. I have collected some provisions that will help you on your journey."

"Thank you, mother. I think the dangers of the grimulves and wyverns have past, but the forest is vast and who knows what lurks in the denser places. I would be glad of your protection. There would only be Tom and I otherwise."

In the morning Kirin woke first in their little shelter of woven branches. Mort was still fast asleep. Kirin woke Norri once she had started the fire and put on some coffee to brew. Luckily Norri had thought to bring a coffee pot and there were plenty of beans to gather this side of the forest.

As soon as she got up, she noticed the parcels of provisions and smiled. They had had such provision before; Kirin thought she knew who was responsible.

With the extra food they decided that they could leave immediately and decided to make a start after breakfast.

They didn't rush. Lettie and Tom had to carry Dillon and Norri was keen to make sure of their direction as much as was possible in the dimness.

They reached the part of the forest where the trees were very large, and it was almost dark on the ground, even at midday. Here iridescent lichen grew on the tree trunks and the effect was eerie and strange.

They plodded on in the hope of getting to places where the trees were smaller and more normal.

Norri heard the call of an owl from above and ahead and knew it was Isherri's signal that she was with them, watching from high in the canopy.

The day waned and the dark forest became blacker. Many strange sounds could be heard from above and they became more on edge, often starting at some sound behind them or stopping to listen to the sound of a creature running in the forest but nothing seemed to come near them.

That night Norri and Tom took watches and stoked the fire with fallen wood. It gave the only light in that dark place.

The dull greyness that was the only sign of the day broke into their camp to find that Tom had fallen asleep on watch. They woke up little

Mort and Dillon and made what breakfast they could. After the meal they packed their food bundles and utensils and resumed their march.

They began to see a thinning of the trees by what they judged to be the afternoon. Now despite the increased light Norri began to feel the strange fear that he had felt the night before. No-one could accuse Norri of being a coward and even he didn't consider that anymore. He took the growing sense of fear to be some internal sense or even some outside force warning him. The feeling nagged at his mind and his fingers felt clammy. Something was not right! Now that he had Kirin back with him and safe, Norri was unwilling to take any risks. He began to search for possible places of safety. Perhaps there was a tree they could all climb, but what kind of threat was it?

He didn't want to alarm the others, but the feeling was growing stronger. He slipped the bow and quiver off his shoulder. Kirin noticed.

There was a growing greyness on the forest floor to their right. So, something was wrong. Norri didn't know what it was, but he strung his bow and Kirin quickly did the same, anxiously following Norri's gaze.

"Kirin, quickly get Mort into that tree. Give him the baby! Mort, take Dillon and climb as high as you can!

They had only moments before a shape appeared out of the trees. The wolf king of Sihon had come to the fornvelt, to the forests near Norri's home. The largest wild Goroth Norri had ever seen emerged from the shadows.

Many other wulves lurked behind in the trees but this wulf seemed fearless. A voice that came from within the wulf. "So here we arr forresterr. You and yourr loved wanes at my merrcy herr in the deep forrest. You have ruined my plans and killed my people for too long. Now the wrath of Lord Groemelian will be visited on you herr with narn to help.

The wulf king is my serrvant and we have carm ar long way seeking thrr ultimate revenge."

Norri and Kirrin drew their bows but as they did twenty more great wulves emerged from the trees.

Kirin yelled at Lettie, "Get into the tree!"

Lettie hesitated and moved closer to Tom.

The wulf king snarled at this and took a couple of paces nearer with his eyes fixed on Lettie. "You carn die quickly or starrv slowly. We do nort mind. We have come a long way to keel you."

Then there was a sound of an arrow in the air. Isherri shot from a low branch and two other driadora warriors did likewise. Two arrows stuck into the hides of a couple of the goroths, and they yelped in surprise.

Then there was the sound of more arrows, many more from deeper in the trees. A couple of the wulves leaped into the air and fell silent. There were more arrows and more of the brutes fell. They came from behind and to their right.

And then a voice that Norri throught he recognized. "Leave the creature and be gone. You have no power here."

Out of the shadows stepped Ibinichari and close behind him stood an Arionite warrior that Norri immediately recognized.

Ibinichari thumped the ground with his auguror's staff. "Be gone, I say! In the name of Almighty God whom you fear above all. Be gone!"

A scream of fury and despair came from the drooling jaw of the wulf king, and it slumped to its knees.

Wengenevy stepped forward and hacked at it with a shining blade. In two blows the creature's head was removed. Any wulves left alive fled into the darkness of the forest.

Norri looked at his two friends and the saviors of his family. "How did you...? How did you know...?"

Wengenevy smiled. "It isn't all that amazing, old friend. Some of my warriors sent a message that a large pack of wulves larger than they had ever seen were hunting in our mountains and moving northward. I had decided to go and track them when Ibinichari came to me and said that he had been warned in a dream that you were in grave danger in the forests of the north. So, he came as well. As you can see his leg is healed since the battle with the Corrii and he set the pace as we followed the pack northward."

Norri embraced both the young warrior and then the young man of God and warmly introduced them to Kirin and Tom and Lettie. Norri could see that Kirin felt proud of him and he smiled.

Norri surveyed the carcasses of the dead goroths. Unlike the jungari-inhabited grimulves they did not give off a foul reek of smoke as they gave up the spirits that inhabited them. These were wild wulves and only their chieftain seemed to be controlled and he by the living lord of the covens.

"Your timing was good. Much longer and we would have been food for the goroths."

The young auguror smiled. "I do not think it was our timing that was good. Don't forget Norri, that it is the great corlion's timing that is so perfect. We are just His servants."

Wengenevy grumbled that Ibinichari had kept up a pace that even challenged his warriors, so he must have had some sense of urgency but the auguror only smiled. It was a new thing for him to outpace the fabled warriors of the Wangadilla.

They marched together to remove themselves from the scene of the goroths slaughter and found a space where some sunlight filtered through the canopy of the forest, to rest and make such a meal as they could. Isherri and her warriors descended from the trees and met the warriors of Arion. They soon found much in common and speculated that some of their stories of their ancient past were the same.

They journeyed through the forest in the afternoon and camped together in parts of the forest that Norri knew. He was able to guide them better and brought them to Beckwood Brae on the following morning.

To his surprise Norri found that his little hut was still there. It has been used for a tools store by the Corrii and was a mess but at least it was intact. They made a camp and Tom went with Norri to find out what was what.

They found that Gordy had set up his command in the old Corrii upper stockade. The meeting with Kirin and Lettie was bitter-sweet. Norri could see that his friend was genuinely pleased at seeing the girls and poignantly aware that there was one girl who was not there. He was very glad to have them back nonetheless and said he would organize food for dinner if only Lettie and Kirin would cook it. They agreed; happy to have the luxury of proper utensils and pots and Tom went to fetch the girls and their guests.

The next morning Tom and Norri went with Gordy to survey the town. They reckoned that keeping Gordy busy was a good thing. They left Kirin and Lettie to make what they could of the rooms in the stockade that Gordy had turned over to them.

They didn't bother about investigating the castle. Even from a distance it was clearly a burnt-out shell. They went up through the town to see how things were going with the returned refugees and free captives.

There was activity everywhere. People were working at the restoration even if the mood was somber. Many had been lost, killed in the invasion or subsequently by the Corrii when they controlled the town.

35

The Battle of Arenstead

General Groeballas scanned the orders on the table in front of him.

From Commander in Chief, Imperial forces.

Re: Your communiqué relating to the desperate state of your supplies for the expeditionary forces in Herelstrom.

Your orders from the highest source are to make redoubled efforts to supply the needs of your troops from the local resources. If you manage to obtain sufficient supplies from the southern holdings and from foraging parties, redouble your efforts to take the fortifications at the Neren River.

Efforts are progressing apace to assemble sufficient naval forces to escort a convoy of supply ships to assist in the supply of the 5th army. The ships are ready in Orsimater to depart.

Groeballas passed the orders back to Tribune Cerios who scanned them for any nuance. The reference to, 'The 5th army' was a little sinister. '…legions under your command' was the usual form. Did it mean that Groeballas was to be replaced as commander of the 5th Army Expeditionary group?

Cerios didn't speak his thoughts out loud. He was sure Groeballas hadn't missed the significance of the words. What would it mean? If his commander was facing the loss of his command and ignominy at best and possible accusations of cowardice with the inevitable consequences if found guilty, what was his own future?

Cerios decided it was better not to think about it and focus on the present. He knew his general and it was now likely that his commander would act decisively.

He was right. Groeballas immediately gave orders for extra rations to be issued to the men from their dwindling supplies and then left his office to consult with his field officers. Cerios knew that a plan had been taking shape in his commander's mind and he was now talking to his officers to see if it would be possible.

Groeballas didn't waste any time. A meeting the next morning with several centurions resulted in men hurrying to make preparations. By the end of that day men had left camp on their appointed tasks and a lightly armed foraging party was marching out with all the equipment they would need to bring back supplies. Flanking the foragers were a much larger than usual force fully armed, and all the foragers were bowmen who still carried their weapons.

Groeballas watched them leave with some pleasure as if satisfied with his idea. Cerios noticed his satisfied expression and enquired about his plans. "General have we not decided that there is little to plunder farther up the valley?"

"Yes, we have, and that there is always the danger that the cavalry will inflict heavy casualties on our foraging parties. We will see…. Have you eaten roasted horse meat Cerios?"

"No General but I hear it is quite acceptable at a pinch. I feel I could eat one on my own at the moment."

"Good."

A driadora warrior ran along the narrowest branches that would take his weight; toward the camp of the horsemen of Herelstrom. He had communicated with them before and was one who had fought with them against the Corrii and destroyed the supplies for the wyverns.

He arrived at the camp to find it almost empty. When he jumped to the ground he searched desperately for the commander. Running up to one of the soldiers he asked where he could find the officers.

The sergeant at arms was called and came running from his tasks of organizing an evening meal for the return of the cavalry. He recognized the driadora warrior and immediately guessed the gravity from the messenger's face.

"What has happened? What is your message, warrior?"

"Sergeant, has commander Tillion left?"

"Yes, a Corrii foraging party has been seen by our scouts and he has gone to intercept them."

"Sergeant, it is a trap. They have many more soldiers and bowmen hidden in a narrow place where the forest approaches the road. If the commander attacks the foraging party, they will be able to surround him with many times his numbers. They have set the ambush well in advance and hidden the ambushers well. Our people almost missed them hidden in the small trees at the edge of the forest."

The sergeant wheeled around and sought for the fastest riders. Unfortunately, those left in camp were not chosen for their speed. He picked the most hopeful and ordered them to gallop after Comander Tillion and try to get a warning to him before it was too late.

The two riders rushed to saddle their mounts and rode out of camp as if the hounds of hell were on their heels. The driadora warrior watched them go but feared they would reach the commander too late. The sergeant saw the worried look.

"Yes warrior, I too fear that they will arrive too late. You have done all you could in getting the message to us. Perhaps we have become too confident and forgotten that we fight a wily and experienced foe. All we can do now is wait and prepare the meals in anticipation of their return. Come, have water and food. Do you drink our coffee?"

The driadora warrior nodded and the sergeant led him to the cooking fires where a fire glowed and a pot simmered on the hot stones of the camp oven. Both their thoughts were for the courageous cavalry men who rode into their enemy's trap.

That evening, by the same fire the seageant sat with his commander who held a good sized cup of brandy for the pain in his leg where an arrow had been removed.

"Can I get one of the cooks to bring you anything to eat sir?"

Tillion took another sip of his brandy and shook his head. "What I cannot understand, sergeant is the strange tactics. They seemed to be trying to kill our horses not us. Our mail and armor provide good protection against arrows, and they would certainly know that, yet the ambush was mainly made up of archers."

"Perhaps that was their plan; not to destroy your force but to kill enough of the horses to limit our effectiveness in harassing and destroying their foraging parties."

"The loss of good cavalry mounts is serious, I'll warrant, but it seems a lot of trouble to go to to slow us down for a week or so while we send for more horses. Once we picked up the men who had their mounts shot under them, we were able to ride right through the Corriian archers and cut many of them down as we went. If it hadn't been for the horns of your messengers, we would have been in desperate straits. Another fifty paces and we would have been right in the middle of the Corrii trap, and I may not have been talking to you now. As it is we lost twentytwo men and forty horses..." Tillion seemed to be making mental calculations.

"That's it! They were not an ambush but a hunting party. They were hunting – horses. Sergeant, get me your fastest riders! I need to send a message to the king!"

The seageant nodded to a soldier nearby who dashed to obey the orders.

"You are thinking that food is so short in the Corriian camp that they have had to resort to this extreme measure: just to get enough meat to feed their men."

"Exactly! And that is a very important piece of information. It explains why they have ceased their attacks on the fortifications at Cair Neren. The men are too weak with lack of food to continue the attacks. It is critical that we get this information to the king. If we can stop any supplies from reaching them, by sea and prevent them from foraging, we can defeat this army without having to fight a battle. Unfortunately, we have inadvertently provided them with food. It is a great loss, they were proud beasts and deserving of a better end. My concern now is that they have some immediate plan once their men are fed and returned to full strength."

In the map room the king of Herelstrom sat beside an untouched cup of wine and studied the table. Admirals Gresham and con Vortez entered.

They bowed at the doorway and entered. Gresham came and stood before the king. He made a pointed glance at the uneaten food.

"Your Majesty should eat. You may need all your strength before this is finished."

"I greatly fear that both food and wine are in short supply at Cair Neren where my cousins are besieged. Have you sent for Admiral Norrens?"

"He is on his way, your Majesty. He and his family are billeted with a family outside the walls. I have sent a runner."

"I want his opinion on some new information that has come to hand. I will explain to all of you when Norrens arrives. For the moment, what capacity do we have to block a naval convoy from Orsimater coming south with supplies for the Corriian army?"

Gresham looked at the map. "It would be almost impossible to prevent them unless we could be sure they would stay close to the coast. Surely any Corriian Admiral worth his salt would stay well out to sea and only approach the coast when he reached the Neren Mouth; especially if he already knew that we could outmatch him with our combined naval forces here in Pinitera. The only chance is to put to sea and deploy our smaller ships to the north in the hope of spotting them."

Admiral Vortez stroked his short beard. "I agree and there would be no point in trying to blockade the entrance to the harbor at Cair Neren. We couldn't maintain enough ships at sea to prevent a serious naval attack; especially if it was supported by the vessels that we know are still in the Neren River estuary."

There was a knock at the door and the guards allowed the former Corriian Admiral entry to the map room.

The king acknowledged Norrens and then turned to the other three naval men. "Some news has come to hand. The Corriian army in the south has just conducted a complicated operation to lure out our cavalry under my cousin's son thinking they were conducting a foraging operation. My nephew survived with most of his men but noted in a dispatch that the Corrii had sent mainly archers to the ambush. Do any of you have any thoughts?"

Con Vortez looked at the dispatch. "I am no soldier, your Majesty but my first guess would be they they are desperate for successful foraging parties and sick of them being harried by your cavalry as I'm sure they have been."

"Yes; Tillion has been harassing them mercilessly on my orders and we have made sure there is no food for them to get their hands on in the vicinity of their encampments so that any foraging parties have a long way to go to find any crops still standing and leave themselves exposed for a long time to harvest those we have left in the ground."

Gresham took the dispatch offered to him by Con Vortez and scanned it. "Your nephew does not say what he thinks the reason is."

No, but he sent me his guess with a trusted messenger in case it was very sensitive information. I am interested to know what you all think.

Admiral Norrens paced the floor as if struggling to remember something. "Groebalas is famous for a campaign on the Island of Moristas where he kept his men alive when storms prevented supply ships getting through. He gained his reputation and the enmity of every cavalry officer in the army. He took their horses and fed them to his men. Perhaps that is what he is doing. Probably the attack was not to destroy your cavalry but to kill their horses to feed his men."

"That is also what Tillion thinks, Admiral. You are of the same mind."

"I would also offer, your Majesty that he would have been unlikely to have taken such extraordinary steps if he didn't have a pressing need. He has been stuck here for a while now and has had no success. I expect he is under pressure to take the objective and quickly and have something positive to report to the emperor. I think you should expect an attack in the next couple of days when his men are restored by the meat they have been eating."

"I think you are right Admiral."

Con Vortez studied the map on the table. "If he is that desperate and his men are weak from lack of supplies, should we not attack them quickly before they have time to grow strong again on the meat from your horses?"

The king frowned. "We cannot bring our army to bear quickly enough. It would take a few days at least; enough time for the Corrii army to eat many a meal of horse stew."

"I see."

"That does not mean that we should not attack, however. If this is the last throw of the dice, General Groeballas will attack the defenders at Cair Neren with all the force and ferocity he has. We cannot leave them unaided."

Admiral Norrens looked at the king. "I think you have summed up his mind, Sire. He will also probably lead the attack himself. He cannot afford it to fail and will probably be in the thick of the fighting."

The king turned to the map again. He measured the distance between the marker which represented his army and the fortress at Cair Neren. "That is a good thought. If we are right, then he may not be looking out for an attack from us while he concentrates on the final attack on Cair Neren."

Norrens looked at the king. "If your Majesty is planning a major attack as well, what can we naval men do?"

"I am glad you asked that, Admiral. My army is not strong enough to match General Groeballas. We need reinforcements; quickly!"

"You are thinking of the soldiers that relieved the southern end. It would take days – even with good winds."

Gresham picked up the dividers. "Four days at a minimum, your Majesty, if we leave tonight."

Con Vortez added the number of ships needed to transport a sizable force from the Southern End. "It will take all our ships. That will leave the gate open. If the Corrii send a convoy to bring the supplies to Groeballas, there will be no ships to stop them."

The king nodded. His mind was made up. "There is nothing else for it. If we lose Cair Neren to Groeballas, they have a foothold in our country and ultimately, we will not hold back the tide. If we can defeat them now, we have a chance that no emperor of the Corrii will risk another invasion for a long time. See here on the map is a small estuary just north of the Neren River. It is usually silted up and useless, but the high seas have broken through the sand bar, and we have been thinking of using it as a way of getting troops behind the Corriian troops who are positioned north of Cair Neren. That would effectively cut them off from the main force and divide the army. It would also enable us to attack Groeballas without warning from his scouts."

Gresham pointed to a spot on the map. "You need to watch out for this reef but on the southern side there is plenty of water. There is a little fishing town here that is now deserted called Arenstead. We can send a fast cutter to the south to warn the people Tom has in the south and have the troops ready to board the larger ships as soon as they reach the estuary at Egleton."

The king looked at the men assembled around the table. He thought himself a good judge of men and judged that they all shared his commitment to doing the utmost to save the kingdom of Herelstrom; all their hopes were tied up with its survival.

"Gentlemen, we are outnumbered and the army that we face is well equipped and exceptionally well trained. We need to ask God for all his help in this endeavor and for good winds for Admiral Norrens. For our part we must do all we can in planning and preparation." The king looked at Norrens. "If it had not been for the part you played in destroying the Wyverns, we would not even be able to consider a counterattack. They made battle with the Corrii impossible."

Con Vortez nodded. "And I am sure no Bernadian force would have been sent if our armies were still beset by the horrid things."

"My last task is to inform you all that I have decided that Admiral Denquinar should command the combined fleet." At this point he looked at Con Vortez. "This is with your agreement, Admiral. He knows the ways of the Corrii navy like no other and was not their commander in chief of navy for no reason. He has also earned the trust and respect of his new country and its king. I believe he has also done great service to your country as well, Admiral."

Con Vortez smiled. "He is respected by every Bernadian captain as the wiliest and most dangerous military mind alive. He is a very good choice, your Majesty."

The king folded the map and reached for its leather case. "Let us be about the work we have set ourselves, gentlemen; God be with you all, allies and new-found friends."

The work of rebuilding the town of Newcastle had been abruptly halted. Everyone who could fight was being organized into centuries and the southern cohort was being equipped as best they could with captured Corrii weapons hastily repainted with the blue and green colours of the southern end. The Arionite warrriors were afraid of the water but agreed to stay and guard the people left behind lest any of the Corrii return.

Tom nudged Norri as they watched Gordy yelling at the militia who were drilling with shields and lances. "This is good it will keep him from thinking too much; and provisioning and planning is keeping his thoughts busy every waking moment."

"Mine too," said Tom yawning.

They worked and drilled for the next two days. Every available boat was marshaled in the river to ferry the men to the ships. They had been told to be ready as soon as the light atop the re-built signal tower at Thornton warned that the ships were coming and be ready at the wharves.

It was raining when the ships came. There was too much mist and rain for the tower at Thornton to be seen even if they had spotted the ships as they came like huge grey phantoms out of the rain and mist.

Tom was called by a runner from the lower fort, and he hastily reached for his bags that contained his armor and weapons as well as a few clothes. He met Norri and Gordy on the wooden verandah outside their rooms in the Corrii-built wooden fort. Kirin came out moments behind Norri wiping her hands wet from washing breakfast dishes.

Norri drew her close to him. "The ships are in the river. There was no warning, I'm sorry, darling. I seem to always be rushing away with no warning or much chance to say goodbye."

"You are already a hero Norri. You have saved our town and the country more than once. Let others have a chance at being heroes as well, please."

Lettie gave Tom a look that said she felt exactly the same and little Dillon held out his arms to his dad, to reinforce the unmade point.

Tom and Norri promised to be back and started out the gate with their bundles. They had had this discussion in the last few days. They were needed to lead and rally the men, but they had both agreed that they would be careful and not seek out danger. Kirin ran and caught up to them. "Gordy you be careful as well. You are a dear friend, and we want you back in one piece as well. Please keep an eye on these two for me."

Gordy smiled. "It's what I do Kirin. My job is looking after Norri, but I must say I am getting sick of always having to watch out for him." He nudged Norri who smiled and reached for one last cuddle with his wife before kissing her and heading down the hill with his bundles and his bow and quiver wrapped in a long unwieldy canvass bundle against the weather.

The girls and little Dillon watched them struggle down the hill with all their equipment. They had to climb up the sides of the ships from the boats in windy weather. They had decided that wearing armor and weapons would make it even more treacherous, so they simply wore their jackets and breeches and sandals. All their weapons and mail could be hoisted up the side with ropes. They reached the bottom of the hill and waved a last time before climbing down the last embankment to the river and the small staging area where the five southern companies were drawn up in their companies. A few stragglers were still arriving but many of the men were there ahead of them. They likewise had bundles and weapons tied up ready to be loaded onto the ships and pre-designated boatmen began to ferry men out to their waiting transport.

Denquinar had sent messages that the ships would fly various colored flags so that each company knew where they were to assemble, and the loading progressed with surprising efficiency. They were all loaded with their equipment stowed by the crews of the warships and the line of ships was led out into the waning light of dusk by the *Argamaro* with the pennant of Admiral Denquinar of His Majesty's navy standing out across the gold and purple cloud-wrack of the western ocean sunset.

Room had been made for Gordy, Norri and Tom in the officer's quarters which occupied the second deck stern cabin of the large warship. There were small glass windows in her ornate stern and the small table and chairs that enabled them to see the lights of the ships astern as each rounded the headland and moved into formation for night sailing. The wind was strong, and all the ships had reduced sail set. Even so they could see from the wake that they were making good time.

In the morning the wind turned southerly. The sails filled with the stiffening breeze and the prows of the great ships plunged into the troughs showering everyone on the decks with spray. They seemed to be making good time, but they were out of sight of land, so it was hard to judge how good. Admiral Denquinar sent constant signals to the ships of the fleet ordering them to close up or alter course. He had to keep his fleet close enough to the coast to reach their objective in the best time while at the same time keeping out of sight of any Corrii observer on land or any ship that dared to put to sea.

Their objective was the Inlet at the village of Arenstead and he wanted to arrive there without their enemy knowing what they were doing. In his cabin he made constant measurements to make sure of his estimates and drove his ships toward the agreed rendezvous. At dusk on the second day out of Newcastle he raised the signal to turn eastward; silently praying that he had got their position right.

The dull outline of the seawall could be seen in the moonlight and as the first ships approached the coast, they saw a small inlet ahead with what appeared to be a small village perched on the hill behind it. There were some lights in some of the cottages. There was no time to find out what these may mean. His job was to get his men ashore, every soldier from Newcastle and every marine they had for the last great battle.

The marines went ashore first. They were lightly armed and fast and met no resistance as they leapt ashore and pulled their boats up onto the gravel of the bay. Their officers deployed them towards the lighted houses and in minutes several handfuls of Corrii officers were surprised and killed before they had time to call for their men or get a warning away.

By the following morning, twelve hundred marines and soldiers of the southern militia with Gordy at their head marched over the crest of the hill and made their presence known. The battle of Arenstead was about to begin.

36

What Seems to Be Must Be

roeballas marched with his frontmost troops among the siege towers that crawled across the field of knee-high grasses with soft cloying turf. His armor with gold trim glinted in the morning sunlight making him easy to spot. One messenger after another came running toward him across the open grasslands with information; everything was coming to a head: The army of Herelstrom had been seen marching south and would come up on his position by mid-morning, a large fleet had been seen off the coast and here he was with his final assault on the fortress of Cair Neren about to begin.

He had deployed a large part of his force under Tribune Cerios to the north to strengthen their northern position and he, himself led the final assault on the castle. Cerios would have enough experienced men to keep the king of Herelstrom occupied until he had taken the castle. It was now or never, and he had more than enough men to do the job. There would be no retreat now. He was an experienced soldier but in this campaign everything had gone wrong. He couldn't take Cair Neren against determined defenders without supplies for his men. Anyone sane would understand that but he also knew that many in power in

Corrimar weren't entirely sane or were driven by motives that made them poor military decision makers. It amounted to the same thing.

The emperor had an irrational determination to conquer the country, probably somehow tied up with the death of his mother. Whatever the cause, he dared not return without some success for the emperor to boast about. The fresh horse meat to supplement their remaining supplies had restored the legionaries to full strength and his men had had a good breakfast. If they took the castle today, all would be well. They would not be able to do it tomorrow. Groeballas raised his sword into the air to signal the attack, centurions around him shouted orders and it began.

General Costina led his twenty-three legions of the Second Bernadian Army into the south of the Corriian Empire while General Degrarius led his much reinforced first army north and east of the lands that belonged to the twin free cities. The two Corriian armies they met fell back before them after a couple of brief skirmishes. The Bernadians were not supposed to have such numbers. It was said that the southern part of their country had been overrun by packs of savage goroths out of the forests of the far south and the first army had been all but destroyed, and yet here it was, and the second Bernadian army as well which was supposed to be only of questionable existence.

Corriian generals sent messengers on the fastest horses to the capital with the news that dozens of legions invaded their realm and asked for orders. Their messages were quite clear: they did not have the numbers to fight such forces; the best that they could hope to do was contain the invading forces.

In the Bernadian Command tent, General Tumarind, Chief of the army met with Degrarius. Outside the centurions shouted and drilled their men most of whom were new recruits in the hope that if they did have to fight, that they could make a proper showing.

Degrarius sipped on a mug of water mixed with the strong wine they kept to prevent the water from making them sick. "I still worry that we will be badly mauled if the Corrii turn and fight us. The legions we are driving north are veterans. It was lucky that when they did engage us, they chose the two legions we have who have some real battle experience and as it is they have lost many of their centurions to train the new legions."

"It is a risk, Degrarius, but we must take risks in war. The plan hasn't changed. We chase them as long as they keep withdrawing. It will give our soldiers confidence and hopefully give their masters in Corrimar something to think about. We just want to let them know we have an army and that we can still challenge them. I want to give Con Vortez and our friends in Herelstrom a chance and prevent any reinforcements being sent to join their legions there. The task is to engage the enemy on every front. If they are busy watching us – they cannot be spared for the assault there. It is the least we can do."

"I cannot disagree, general; you know that, but it will not stop me from drilling the new men and trying to turn them into soldiers."

"By all means drill them, Degrarius, but make it look as though you are preparing for an attack. Our men will think so too, and it will keep them focused. Our enemy is uncertain and doesn't want to take risks. We have given him a bad beating thanks to you and the Arionite warriors. We want to feed his uncertainty."

The defenders on the walls of Cair Neren had developed a small catapult that could fling a pot of oil with a lighted fuse twenty paces with
ease. Although they couldn't stop a siege tower, they could set it alight
and make climbing it a nightmare. These had been developed in pref-
erence to the weapons used in the last war which the Corrii had now
countered with wider carriages for their siege towers and the use of
green wood soaked with water to avoid fire.

Brian ran along the wall encouraging his men. Every bowman was
ready every catapult loaded ready to be lit and fired, men with axes
and pikes were ready below to rush up to the battlements and repel the
attackers.

Down below Groeballas stood urging his men on and the towers lurched
closer to the wall. Two were already burning but their handlers pushed
and pulled them toward the walls anyway. The oil would soon burn out
and they could be climbed with care. Groeballas could see the desperate
defenders firing arrows at his men but each man pulling a rope was protected by a shield man and his archers went bravely ahead of the towers
shooting at any defender who showed themselves on the parapets; it
was costing many of them their lives. His losses were mainly his brave
archers, standing in the open shooting at the parapets.

There was no word from Cerios, so he assumed the Army of
Herelstrom with its king had not engaged with his forces yet or they
were in the thick of battle and Cerios was too occupied to send a

message. The main part of their army was with the Tribune to halt the King if Herelstrom in his tracks and give the legions tasked with the taking of the castle time to complete their work.

Several arrows whizzed past his helmet, and he wondered about the wisdom of wearing his good armor into arrow range of the walls. Perhaps he should have dressed as a regular legionary. It was too late now. Groeballas was aware of another sound over the screams and battle cries of his men. It was the sound of battle horns. Groeballas wondered what it meant. He saw a scout calling to him as the man struggled through the mass of seige-towers and their handlers with their compliments of archers and assault troops.

"What is it soldier?"

"The enemy have landed a force from the sea – more than a whole legion. They are marching this way. Groeballas turned toward the north and briefly saw a host of infantry cresting the hill from the bay with their guidons fluttering above their ranks and their armor flashing in the morning sun. It was the last thing he saw. Moments later an arrow from the wall struck the general in the throat and he fell, choking on his own blood.

Cerios was watching the approach of the king's army. He had deployed his best legions on the right to prevent his army from being outflanked and his front ranks were preparing for a frontal cavalry attack. They had planned and drilled this strategy many times. The general would have time he needed to capture the castle.

He looked back and could see smoke rising from around the castle then Cerios saw them: Troops behind him with blue and green pennants of Herelstrom; marching over the hilltop from the bay of Arenstead and toward the castle. Cerios' trained eye saw that they marched in well-spaced lines of spearmen and archers three abreast with archers in the middle row. And to make matters worse, cavalry was approaching from the east drawing up in line of battle ready to charge the legions attacking the castle. Cerios knew they had lost. With another infantry force and a couple of companies of cavalry coming to their aid the defenders of the castle would hang on. His general would have to disengage and defend against the new attack and there was every chance that a sortie from the castle would leave him outnumbered and attacked on all sides. Cerios had his orders, but they had not been expecting these new forces. He had to withdraw or risk having his own army surrounded and separated from their camp and what supplies they had left. They had to retreat or lose the 5th *army*. He gave his orders and the centurions rushed to carry them out. They too could read the situation. None wanted to be prisoners; locked away until their emperor saw fit to pay their ransom, if he ever did.

The King of Herelstrom immediately ordered his cavalry legions into the field with orders to drive a wedge between the forces attacking the castle and the northern part of the Corriian army. Cerios would be forced to march along the edge of the forest, which he didn't like at all.

Within an hour the Corrii had withdrawn to their camp by the river, skirting well around the new force that was marching to the defense of Cair Neren. With his commander impossible to contact or fallen, Cerios made his plans. He would save the army. His commander would bear the blame and he would probably get a commendation for saving so many legions from possible disaster or starvation surrounded by their enemies. That night he gave orders for every ship to be loaded with as many soldiers as they could take. He might just get all of them on board. He ordered his men to leave everything they could that they would not need to defend the ships in the event of a sea fight and began to embark his troops.

The Thane of Cair Neren met his king by the walls of the castle. They had observed the body of General Groeballas lying in the mire and blood of the fallen below the walls.

"This seems an unlikely victory, your Majesty."

"It is all due to the efforts of our friends from the Southern End, again, and the skill of our sailors."

"Will Admiral Denquinar attack the Corrii ships as they flee up the coast?"

"He may chance it, but they will stay close together and capturing them will be difficult, loaded as they are with soldiers. I will leave naval decisions to him, but my guess is that Denquinar is of the school which believes that there is no benefit in attacking a defeated enemy. A cornered animal will fight most fiercely when brought to bay. There would be significant risk in a sea battle. I think he will choose to see them off and keep his advantage of numbers."

"If there is a best way to win a battle this has to be it. Few lost on either side and an effective stalemate."

"Yes cousin, 'stalemate' is the correct word. Our enemies have been outplayed. The advantage they thought to have with the evil creatures they brought to our shores has been neutralized. Here come our friends and the saviors of our bacon for a second time."

The columns of militia men from the south were approaching the castle. At the head of the column was Gordy. Tom and Norri strode along beside their men who marched as well as they could toward the castle gate.

As Gordy approached the king and the thane reached out hands in greeting. The thane looked at the relief of his people who were hurrying out the open gate of the Cair with Brian and Gillian leading the way. "Well done Sir Gordonae! Your timing was perfect. You brought a sizable force to the right place at just the right time. I see you have brought Tom and Norri as well." Tom and Norri strode up through the knee-high grasses and shook the hands of the king, the Thane and of Brian who came running up to greet them. "All the stories I hear are of breathtaking achievements that have saved more than our small country. I do not even know what honors I can bestow that will be adequate."

Norri spoke next (much to his own surprise). "Your Majesty, there have been many of us playing our parts in this struggle and I cannot help but think that the events of the world are ordered by a greater understanding than any of us possess. We southern enders have been embroiled in this war, but we were dragged into it first and have only done what we needed to do to survive."

"That is graciously spoken from one who has done the most and has won honors from far greater rulers than myself. Come let us go to the castle and hear all the news and some of the stories first-hand. I would hear how the Southern End fares. The south of our kingdom has borne the worst of the depredations of our enemies."

The king turned to Tom. "Warden, have you any ideas yet on what is needed to restore your towns to normality?"

"Some ideas, your Majesty: there will inevitably be shortages of building materials, but we can make everything we need in time. Much of the food that the Corrii garrison was accumulating – we presume to send to General Groeballas." He indicated the slumped form of the general. "For his men is still good and will help feed us while we rebuild houses and other necessary buildings; the Corrii did not destroy everything of course."

Gordy nudged Norri, "Even your salubrious boyhood home still stands, doesn't it Norri?"

Norri smiled. He wondered if the king had any idea how small his home had been. "It has survived fairly well intact, hasn't it Gordy? Some restoration work will be needed on the western wing of course!"

Tom chuckled. "Let's just say the castle was a step up from his boyhood home, your Majesty."

"I think the gatehouse was a step up." Gordy stared at the fallen general. "If this is the end of all soldiers, I don't think I want to be one."

Tom followed his gaze and grimaced at the general in his fine armor and his terrible death. "The castle, however, is a mess and though much of the stone-work is partly intact – it has been burned badly and will need to be re-built."

The king stopped and regarded his fallen foe. "It may be a while before a Corrii expeditionary force attacks us again. We have beaten them off twice and that will make them think carefully about another attack. Hopefully they do not know what a near thing it was. But for the perfect timing of Tom and others it could easily have tuned out very differently."

37

The call of the Little Child

Kirin was very excited to see Norri. He and Tom had prevailed on the king to allow them to go home to see their wives and he could not refuse. Gordy had stayed to take part in the celebrations and to look after the contingent from the Southern End to see to their billeting and make arrangements to their journey home. The king was not ready to risk his entire navy to transport so large a force south. Nobody knew what the Corrii would do, and they still had most of their force ashore in Orsimater. The emperor might even turn them around and attack again hoping to catch Herelstrom off guard; thinking they had won and never expecting a renewed attack.

On the positive, Admiral Con Vortez was in no hurry to return to Bertola. The weather was bad in any event, and he felt sure the emperor would want the naval successes consolidated. They had a wall of wood and sail around Herelstrom, and he was content with that for a time. He and Denquinar were considering another journey south: sending a couple of ships to retrace the route Denquinar had taken in the Swiftsure. As they discussed and planned such a trip, Gordy and the king were discussing what might be done to secure the on-going friendship of the

Arionites and whether some kind of alliance might be forged and even whether a land route to Bernadia was possible.

Back once more in his home, with the girl he loved, Norri walked through the town with Kirin to visit her mother. Cheryl had survived the invasion. She had worked hard in a kitchen making food for the workers; trying to make the limited victuals into food that was at least somewhat appetizing.

Norri was watching as they walked to see how people were getting along. They seemed to be doing better than he had expected with so many of the men away north with the army. The older tradesmen that were left had obviously been hard at work setting the town to rights and farms were producing all kinds of foofstuffs.

The Corrii had also needed to eat, and the areas of food production had been increased to provide for the Corrii garison. Now they were gone there seemed to be food and drink aplenty. What was noticeable was that there were many fewer people. Norri felt very lucky to be alive and have Kirin there beside him. As they had told one another their stories, that seemed more and more amazing. Norri felt a strong sense of the two of them being spared and well…protected.

They arrived at Cheryl's small house at the harbor end of the town, within sight of the ruined castle.

She welcomed them in and immediately put on a kettle for some tea. A fire burned warmly in the stove and the house showed signs of the long neglect having been put right.

"It is so lovely to see you both here and safe. I prayed for this every day since the Corrii came. God has heard me, and I am so happy I could do a dance if my old knees were up to it."

Norri looked across the table at Cheryl. She seemed tired and older than he remembered before the Coming of the Corrii. "How are you? You must have had a terrible time over the last few months."

"Oh, I'm all right. Because I was in the kitchens, we had a bit more access to food than many of the others. We didn't pinch any of the food that was being sent to the workers of course but we weren't above sneaking a bit of the food we were preparing for the Corrii when their quartermasters weren't watching."

Kirin looked at her mother who seemed frailer now than any time she remembered. "You should take it easy now and build yourself up a bit. I am so glad you had your own house here and they had no idea that you were related to Norri. We now know that it was revenge against Norri that was one of the reasons they attacked here."

"I'm fine, Kirin. There are folks that have had it much harder than me and I want to do what I can to help."

"Kirin just wants you to put your feet up when you can; and let yourself recover from the horrible time you have had." Norri noticed a bad burn on Cheryl's arm. Cheryl covered it up again with her sleeve.

"How did you get the burn?"

"It isn't much. I got burnt with a bit of hot oil when one of the Corrii victualers was throwing his weight around in the kitchen. He was worried that his officers would return for their meal, and it would not be ready in time."

Kirin came around to take over making the tea. "Let me have a look at that. I think you need to keep it covered."

"I didn't have a chance to do much for it when it happened, and it seems to be healing up by itself. It just catches a bit when I move my right arm."

"Norri looked around the kitchen and there seemed to be some food." Do you have any money, Cheryl?"

Kirin looked back at him a bit surprised. "Do you have any?"

"Yes, I do actually. Tom and I went to the old Tavern and checked Gorigond's old hiding place for money. I never had a chance to move the money from the Bernadian emperor from there to the Castle and the Corrii never found it, which is amazing considering they ransacked the place. And Tom and I have found a stash of Corriian coins hidden in our quarters. So as things stand, we have plenty of money. I will bring you some so that you can get things for the people you know of who are in need."

"Thank you, Norri. I won't pretend I cannot make use of it."

"I also want you to go to the apothecary and get some ointment for that burn. Did he survive?"

"Yes, and his apprentice as well. The Corrii are not foolish; they sorted people out very quickly and kept those they needed in their various trades: farmers, wainwrights, blacksmiths, coopers and the rest and assigned working parties to go out to work on the required tasks with the farmers and tradespeople. They were producing much more of everything than was needed and seemed to be storing it up: grain, cheese, and all sorts of goods. The cooper couldn't make barrels quickly enough."

Norri tasted the cake that Cheryl had put in front of him. "I can see why they had you in the kitchen."

Cheryl smiled. "Thank you, Norri. I was one of the lucky ones. I think the unluckiest were the young girls; especially the pretty ones."

The smile disappeared from Norri's face. He looked at Kirin and was very glad that she had escaped into the forest, desperate a strategy as that had been, that made him think of Gordy and his pain for his friend's loss.

Kirin saw all these feelings flit across Norri's face in a moment and felt grateful to have him back. She wondered that she knew him so well already.

Gordy didn't have enough time to think about Jenny during the day and he worked until he was exhausted in the evenings so that he didn't have to think about her. This evening he walked through the postern door of the fortress of Cair Neren. He had a meeting with the King and the Thane. He had met with them several times in the last couple of weeks and had communicated more times via messengers.

This night they had a different matter to discuss than his cohort of southern militiamen and all the issues of men getting drunk and disorderly.

Gordy walked across the courtyard and up a narrow flight of stairs to the door of the keep. He was greeted by guards who knew him and instructed him to go to the northern meeting hall.

When he arrived, he saw a small group waiting outside and he was instructed to enter the chamber.

The King turned to greet him. "Thank you for coming, Sir Gordonae. You will have seen the couple outside with Admiral Norrens. We have to meet with them directly and would value your involvement and perhaps your wisdom when we have finished the meeting."

"All my friends call me Gordy, your Majesty. I'll do my best. Who are they?

"They are an interesting pair. They forced their way on board the Argamaro just before Norrens and the naval people defected. Admiral Norrens tells us Bentonius is a former spy master of the Corrii Grand Coven. He forced Norrens to take him and the woman on board or use his knowledge of their plans to betray them."

"He is familiar. He looks very like a character that was hanging about in the Southern End some time back."

The Thane nodded to his cousin. "We think he was the very man. He seems to have been spying on you and somehow got back to Corrimar with critical information that made their attack on your home so successful."

"Who is the woman?"

Taulin Ginroyal stood and went to the small table set out with coffee and cakes. "She is almost as interesting. Coffee Gordy?" The Thane poured his own and a cup for the King.

"Yes please. I haven't had one since breakfast. What do you know of her?"

"Norrens says he only knew about her before she came on board his ship. She is a high priestess of the grand coven; formerly a confidant of the late empress and we understand an intimate acquaintance of the present emperor."

"Why would she defect and why take such huge risks?"

The thane passed Gordy a cup of coffee. "Our questions exactly. We hope to find out more at this meeting."

The king noticed that Gordy was trying to remember something. "What is it? Do you have anything else to add before we bring them in?"

"It's just that about the time this Bentonius fellow disappeared, the driadora told Norri that they had the guards who watch the entrance to the underground river, poisoned!"

"And a small boat was missing; never recovered. There is no way to be sure that it was Benton, but it seems a good chance that that was his way back to Corrimar. He must have had information that would not allow for the slower journey north and passage on a trading ship."

The King stroked his beard. "There were very few of these anyway; just the occasional trader from the neutral free cities in the west."

"We can bet some of the information was that our friend Norri had returned home as a hero after his escape from their dungeons."

"We seem to have underestimated the trouble that Norri caused them. It obviously had much deeper implications than we realize."

"Probably deeper than even Norri realizes. The Ibinithy said he could feel the power of the word Norri spoke in Corriamar reverberating through the seas."

The king drank his last sip of coffee. "Let's get them in here and see what we can find out. Be on your wits, gentlemen. We don't want to give away more information than we get until we are sure these people are on our side. We have a clever man here. He is resourceful and well used to power and how to obtain it."

The king nodded to his attendant and Admiral Norrens was invited into the room with Bentonius and Ingwit.

The king noticed right away that Ingwit was very nervous and pensive, but Bentonius was harder to read. Ingwit curtseyed and politely declined the proffered coffee. Bentonius accepted some from the attendant.

Admiral Norrens accepted the cake that was offered by the royal servant. He took a bite with relish only to realize that it was probably his duty to break the uncomfortable silence that followed the introductions.

"Your Majesty, I thought it would be valuable for you and the thane to meet these two *sailing comrades* of mine. From what you know already, you will realize that they have much knowledge of the workings of the covens and the way they interact with the emperor. I am guessing they may be a useful resource for you in assessing the movements of our enemies."

The king looked at the two sternly. There was no place here for being gentle. These two were powerful former enemies. "My lady, perhaps you can answer the question we were discussing before you entered. You obviously had a position of some power in the grand coven and from what we hear, the ear of the emperor himself. Why would you choose to defect and give up all that position and influence?"

A hint of a tear came into the young woman's eye. She thought back through the thoughts that accompanied the realizations that she had built up an emotional armor against the years of abuse until she had no feelings and compassion left and that all that armor had been pierced by a tiny girl - in her care until she was sent to the priests of Baal Giborachir to be sacrificed to their god. All this passed through her mind in an instant. Ingwit looked at the king and saw something she had never seen before. He had seen the tear. And he had compassion!

Ingwit could almost feel Bentonius' tension beside her without even looking at him. She decided in that moment that there was no point in changing everything – unless she did. She decided to tell this King the truth and hang the consequences.

"Would your Majesty mind if I started a long way back?"

"Not at all, my lady, please have some refreshment if you wish, and sit with us on these chairs. Tell us your story."

Ingwit turned to the attendant. "May I just have a little water if you please." Her mouth felt incredibly dry, all of a sudden.

As Ingwit told her story, she kept her focus on the two rulers before her and did not look at Bentonius. She knew somehow that he would disapprove of her baring her soul to these rulers.

As she told her story she noticed a strange look of recognition come across the face of the thane. She stopped and looked at him enquiringly.

Taulin Ginroyal paused for a moment and then spoke slowly. "Ingwit, I know what you speak of is the truth. A long time ago I had a dream. It recurred over three nights. It was of a little child, cold and alone in the dark, crying. She seemed to be dressed as one of the children that you have described. At the time I thought that it was some part of an abomination of our enemies. I now realize that it was, and that we ourselves would be drawn into the net of this evil. It sounds to me, Ingwit that the cry of the little child has been heard. You were one who heard her cry."

Some time after the meeting, Gordy was still sitting with the king and Taulin. The servant had cleared away the coffee and cakes and they sat talking quietly into the evening.

"Your Majesty, I think I should take the men from the southern end home. Some have been away for many months now."

"They have done gallant service to their country, and thanks to some perfect timing, many have lived to return to their families. I am sad that many have no families to return to, Gordy, as your King I also understand that your loss is among the greatest."

"I have been selfish really, your Majesty. Keeping busy here has kept me from thinking about Jenny but many of the men have families to return to and it is my responsibility to take them back."

"Very well, then. We cannot keep men mobilized forever and if the Corrii are still a threat, we cannot know where they will strike."

The Thane who had been deep in thought spoke, "Thanks to Norri and Gordy the Southern End has become an anathema to our enemies. They struck there, last time and may do again. You must keep your militia trained and ready, Gordy!"

"I will do my best, my Lord. It will be hard once they all settle back into normal life."

"Just remind them what happened last time."

"I'll try my best."

The king nodded. "We will do all we can to help. We will send our troops south to conduct exercises to keep up their skills as well."

As Norri and Kirin climbed up the hill toward the Corrii Stockade that was their current home, they could see Lettie working in a garden patch that was behind their old home. The cottage that they had lent to Norri and Kirin still stood but it had been used as a storage-shed by the Corrii and needed a lot more work to make it habitable. They turned to their left and followed the path that led over to where Lettie worked. As they got closer, they saw that Mort was helping and that together they had finished weeding a large bed of vegetables that the Corrii had planted – probably for the officers' own table.

Lettie got up and wiped the dirt and sweat from her face. She spotted Dillon escaping among the red cabbages and caught him by his braces. "How is your Mum, Kirin?"

"She seems fine, maybe a little the worse for the last few months but well enough. You have done a wonderful job with these vegetables!"

"That's good about your Mum. This garden was planted by the Corrii. Many of the vegies are ready to pick: potatoes, cabbages, turnips, beans; we need to make some soup, I think Kirin. Do we have any barley?"

"We bought some bread in the town. Soup would go nicely with it. There are lots of hungry mouths to feed up at the stockade. Everyone has been working really hard."

There was the sound of a horn. All three of them looked down the hill and saw a long line of men appear on the northern road. At the head of the column was a militia man carrying the standard of the southern militia. They couldn't see clearly from the distance, but it looked like Gordy at the head of the column.

Norri looked for a while with his hand shading his eyes. "I think it will be a good idea to make some soup girls – we seem to have guests."

The stockade was full to bursting with all the returned militiamen. Those who still had homes and families went home with them. The rest bunked down in the old Corrii Upper stockade or went to stay with friends.

Kirin was very busy with her soup this evening. It was a week since the men returned and she had the main responsibility for the food. There were plenty of helpers but many hungry soldiers.

Tom was sitting by the gate to catch the evening breeze. He had a pannikin of barley and lentil soup and a hunk of bread. Beside him sat

Gordy who seemed distant. Tom kept silent to make space for his friend to speak if he wished. He knew he must have been feeling incredibly lonely. After a long silence Gordy put down his pannikin.

"Tom, I have found someone to talk to who seems to understand how I feel."

"I'm pleased. Do I know this person?"

"No. Would you like to meet my friend?"

"Yes, I would. When? Now?"

"Tomorrow afternoon if you like. We need to take a short ride."

They continued to chat. Tom turned the conversation to Bernadia and the many strange things they had seen in their travels. They finished their soup and went back for more. Kirin was standing by a huge caldron of the barley soup, her sleeves rolled up and a lock of recalcitrant hair in her eyes.

"Can I get you some more Gordy? Tom always wants more." She smiled at Tom.

Tom pretended to be offended. "What can I say, Kirin? I've missed your excellent barley soup."

"There are more crisp loaves over there. I'm going to have some soup myself." Kirin took a piece of bread and a bowl of soup and went to find Norri.

As Tom and Gordy ambled back to their spot at the gate, Tom wondered about Gordy's friend. He wondered if he had made friends with another soldier on the road back south. If both had suffered loss it might be a good thing. Tom was very conscious that Jenny had died defending his wife and son and that their presence must be a constant reminder.

He sat and again turned the conversation to the wonders of distant lands.

The next afternoon they saddled their horses and Gordy led them south to Greyton. He dismounted by Tom's old boatshed, and they tethered the horses.

"Now I am intrigued," said Tom once they had stowed the saddles in the boatshed. "I take it we have to sail somewhere to see this friend of yours."

"Yep."

"Allright, be mysterious." Tom untied his little cutter from the wharf and jumped on board.

Gordy hauled up the sail and tied it off before settling in the back of the cutter with the tiller. They passed the northern entrance of the bay and met the more serious ocean swell. The little cutter bounced and crashed over the waves, and they were soon wet from the spray. The wind had picked up a little and Tom looked to seaward, becoming a little concerned about the weather.

Gordy was sailing north and didn't seem perturbed. Tom was used to rough weather and decided to relax and trust his own skill to get them back if the wind got up.

"I suppose we are heading to Thornton." Tom commented as Gordy made no attempt to turn into the estuary of the Erne River.

"Not particularly," was Gordy's cryptic comment. "Oh, there you are."

Tom turned to see who Gordy was speaking to and almost fell overboard in shock.

A huge purple and green head protruded from the water only a boat-length off the bow.

"Hello friend. Who have you brought to join our party?"

Tom was speechless; to say nothing of terrified.

"Hello Ibi, this is my friend, Tom. He wanted to meet the new friend I told him about. Tom, this is Ibi. Master Ibinithy, to be strictly correct."

"Well met Tom, you can call me Ibi. I am no longer master of anything. My only home is the sea; and that is too great for anyone to master. If you are Gordy's friend, you may count yourself my friend as well. I am sorry if my appearance is a bit of a shock. I am not quite myself these days."

"What were you when you were yourself?" gasped out Tom.

"Well, not much then either, for that matter. Gordy says he thinks I am a much better person now than I was then. I rather fear that he is completely right. I am not a man, yet I am a better man than I was when I was a man; if that makes sense."

Tom was beginning to get over his shock. "How often do you two talk?"

Gordy was enjoying Tom's amazement. "Most afternoons."

"When Gordy asked if he could borrow my boat for a bit of fishing, I believed him."

Gordy laughed. "I have located a big one."

The Ibinithy seemed surprised by the idea of Gordy fishing. "Would you like some?"

Gordy was intrigued. "Well, I really just came out to chat. Are they hard to catch?"

"No! Easy! I will get you some to take home." The ibinithy seemed genuinely pleased to be asked.

Tom was not so much thinking about fish but about his friend. "What do you two talk about?"

Gordy looked particularly bereft in the rear of the launch, bouncing about on the waves and wet with spray. "We talk about the ones we loved that we have lost."

The huge green and purple head nodded. "My loss was my own fault. There was a girl who loved me – or could have loved me if I had not been to obsessed with power to notice that she was there. Now, in my abject loneliness, I ache over what might have been."

Tom had a picture of the two sad souls: Gordy and the Ibinithy; out on the ocean sharing the sadness of their loss and becoming even more desperate. He sought for the right words. "Doesn't that only make you even sadder: sharing your sadness like that?"

Gordy shook his head. "No. It seems to help a little actually."

The huge purple and green head nodded slowly, its eyes like huge, inscrutable pools.

After a time, it spoke again. "Of course, we don't only speak of lost loves. We also speak of greater things. Gordy has told me of the time when he saw the Lord of the Mari. He appeared as the great corlion: the Lord of the men of Arion. We think that perhaps He is the master of the Mari that we have seen over the seas of Helerstrom, taking the form of great sea-eagles. It is a radical and a dangerous thought that Gordy has had."

The Ibinithy paused and waited for Gordy to say what he thought. Gordy paused. "This seems like an idea that is so strange and dangerous that one can only talk about it here, out at sea where there is no one else to hear. Norri has an idea that seems outrageous and yet so obviously and perfectly true that God is our Father. Ibi said that when Norri called out 'Father' in the prison hold in Corriamar, that he called out to his father Baeri: the broken prisoner; and to his Father - his God at the same time."

The Ibinithy nodded. "The echo of that sound reverberated through the ground and through the seas and I heard its sound – afar off and at the same time growing stronger as the power of the words broke the power of the Coven Masters – one of whom I once was but am no more."

Gordy had a strange expression on his face, an expression of joy amid his suffering and loss. "Tom, we think that the Father has a SON and that I met him with Norri and the young auguror of Arion in the mountains, before the great battle."

Tom seemed shocked; shocked as one who has suddenly confronted a new and staggering truth. "If this is the truth and the Father has a Son, then the Son is…"

Gordy nodded but also hesitated to speak the word.

The Ibinithy laughed its strange chortling laugh. "If we are to be heretics we may as well be well-fed heretics. Would you like those fish?"

That evening Gordy was the hero. He looked on with pleasure as the people of the southern end tucked into huge steaks of tuna and sword-fish, grilled over coals, served with lime pieces, and utterly delicious.

38

Ceilidh

*E*veryone was talking about the coming night. Several structures that the Corrii had built had been demolished with extraordinary enthusiasm and some of the wood taken to the green outside the village and piled up to make a huge bonfire.

A pit had been dug and several beef cattle had been turning on a spit for most for the day. Musical instruments that had been forgotten for many a day, were brought out for the Celidh.

Lanterns were hung from tree branches around the green and everyone wore their brightest cloths. It promised to be a fine night. It was their way of putting the sadness and loss behind them and starting life again.

Martin the new innkeeper and his staff came down to the celebration with trays of hot dripping pudding, fresh and hot from the ovens. They were a traditional accompaniment to the beef, and everybody cheered and rushed to fill their plates with beef and pudding and hot boiled potatoes, buttered beans and sprouts.

When vast quantities of food had been consumed by all, the ale flowed, and then came the dancing. The musicians put aside their tankards and began to play with a will; and the people danced as if none of the horrors of the past year had happened.

Tom and Lettie were cheered as they entered the dance and they spun and twirled in the traditional folk dances that they had learned as children. When Lettie came off the dancing green and took Dillon from Kirin, her friend nodded in the direction of the dancers. "Look at that! Janina has lured Gordy out onto the green." Tom turned and smiled. "It will do them both good to get wild for a bit and forget about everything they have been through. It is very good to see Janina has recovered enough to dance like that." They watched and cheered as Gordy took Janina's hands and swung her around vigorously in mock annoyance for dragging him into the dance.

The warriors of Arion who had their camp on the edge of the forest had joined the celebration at Norri's insistence and performed some of their own tribal dances to the great accolade of the southern enders some of whom tried to join in the dances with great enthusiasm.

The evening wore on and fire burned lower. Horses appeared at the top of the hill by the tavern. A group of latecomers were walking down the hill. As soon as they came into the light Tom called, "Brian, Gillian, My Lord" for Taulin Ginroyal, the Thane of Cair Neren and his daughters has come to the celebration. There was much joy at the meeting and more dancing and more ale. The bonfire was built up again and the celebration continued long into the night.

Norri noticed a beautiful young woman with blond hair on the fringe of the celebration. She had two dark haired children with her. Norri sidled over to the Thane and asked about her.

"Her name is Ingwit, Forester. She and Benton defected and came to our country with the two small children you see, on board the Argamaro with Tom. She came to me several nights ago, quite upset. Benton has disappeared."

"Dissapeared?"

"She can find nobody who knows where he has gone. The only thing is…"

"What, my Lord?"

"I did a bit of investigating myself and a ship left the day before, a merchantman of the free cities in the East. I wonder if he has gone back to the East."

"If he has gone back to his old masters, will they receive him?"

"That is the thought that is in my mind as well. I do not know the answer. I think that man may be destined to be mistrusted by everyone - not a life I would choose."

Norri looked at Ingwit. She was sitting with the warriors of Arion. The two small children had been drawn to them and were now playing happily with some of the warriors. "That will leave the girl Ingwit all alone."

"Indeed. I brought her and the children here. I wondered if you would take them in. They have nobody at Neren Keys and the Southern End is smaller and perhaps more welcoming. She also knows Tom, of course."

"We will certainly make her welcome. Kirin and Lettie are good at that."

"That is what I hoped." The Thane pointed to the two children and the warriors. "I wonder if those two would be better here or whether they could possibly find their way home."

"I will speak to Wengenevy and see what he thinks before we say anything in front of the children. If the children go home, it may be hard on the girl."

"Yes. She will need to find friends and a life somehow."

"I may be biased, my Lord, but I think this is a good place to find a life."

"Yes, perhaps I should come and live here."

HELPFUL NAMES & KEY CHARACTERS:

General Groeballas: Commander of the Invading Corrii force

Tribune Cerios: his lietenant

Bentonius Velonia: master spy and secret lover of Ingwit. Discovers all the secrets of the new castle at egleton and comes with general Groeballas

Captain Baubacus – young Corrian officer of dog soldiers, who saved the remnant at the first battle of Egleton and is now joining the general for the new assault with Bentonius

Reynolds: From Beckwood Brae - Captain of the Swiftsure

Captain Henderson: Captain of the Suresafe

Captain Gresham: Captain of the Repulse

Grand Master Groemelian: Master of the Corriian Grand Coven

Master Velulf of Ba-al Giborochir: Master priest the dragon men with their Wyverns

Legrarff leader of the priests of Ba-al Gibrochir

Prince Anabund: Crown Prince of Bernadia - the brother of Omari

Prince Conamund: Anabund's younger brother

Wengenevy: son of the chief of the Wangadilla tribe

Eliachar: auguror of the Wangadilla

Admiral Gustass Norrens: Commander of the squadron attacking Herelstrom

Norrens' wife and daughter: Ghezia and Chloe

Kristina wife of Former Corriian Grand Admiral Denquinar

Post captain Verna: flag captain on the Argamaro

Second Lieutenant Cornelli: Of the Argamaro

Third Lieutenant Plenny: of the Argamaro

Vertori Captain: of the *Vorsero*

Grand Admiral Cherulia: Commander of the Corriiam Navy

Cherulia's battleships: *Orcharhite, Vendvora* and *Catavern*

Flagship – Flagship *Imrahall*, also *Ilchorne*

Third Admiral Verkamah: Cherulia's second in command

Bernadian Officers

General Bregarad: Comander of the Bernadian northern army

Tribune (Later General) Degrarius: of the northern army

Von Etchens: Grand Admiral of the Emperor's fleet.

General Tumarind: Chief of the army

General Costina: commander of the second army.

Tribune Fortinez: commander of the relief force attacking Newcastle

Con Vortez: Admiral of the Bertola squadron.

Priests of Bernadia: Corscerrus, Wingerentus, High Priest Vernus and
    old Tiresius

Bardleamun: priest in Margaritta River

Driadora: Quen Illuin's maids: Summerwind, Rilly, Jemma

The Story Continues:

MAGI
The Chronicles of the Corriian Wars
BOOK THREE - Redemption

It has been years since the last Corriian invasion. Everything seems stable and happy, but it is not as it seems.

Bentonius, the spy who defected has returned to his old masters and convinced them with a plan to get ultimate revenge against all the leaders and heroes of past wars.

While the deadly plot takes shape, the world is ravaged by a plague that is spreading through all the nations.

Norri with the help of the local apothecary finds a cure, a tea made from a small shrub that grows on the verge of the forest. He wishes to help the people of Bernadia who they hear are suffering terribly, but much has changed in the world in a generation.

Also perplexing, is a strange prophecy, and a call Norri receives from a heavenly messenger, a Mari, that draws him and his Driadora friend, Lefgild into another long journey, seeking the meaning of the words on a bark-paper scroll.

They journey to an unexpected destination, to be witnesses of an event that will change them all in many ways.